THE LAMA'S LOVER
AND OTHER STORIES

THE LAMA'S LOVER AND OTHER STORIES

TEN SHORT STORIES FROM AROUND THE WORLD

ULI SCHMETZER

TIZULI

TIZULI

PUBLISHER: Tizuli Publishing
EMAIL: ulischmetzer@gmail.com
WEBSITE: www.uli-schmetzer.com

The characters in this novel are invented.
Any similarities to living persons are purely coincidental.

CATALOGUING-IN-PUBLICATION DATA

AUTHOR: Schmetzer, Uli, 1940–

TITLE: The lama's lover and other stories : ten short stories from around the world / Uli Schmetzer ; editor, Jayaram Nughalli .

ISBN: 9780980637564 (pbk.)

SUBJECTS: Short stories.

DEWEY NO: A823.4

EDITOR: Jayaram Nughalli
DESIGN AND PRINT MANAGEMENT: Reno Design | www.renodesign.com.au | R32005
DESIGNER AND PHOTOGRAPHS: © Graham Rendoth
AUTHOR PORTRAIT AND LAMA PHOTOGRAPH: © Tiziana Turatello
PRINTING: CreateSpace

For Annette

CONTENTS

TO BEGIN

Fantasy is always stimulated by reality. No story is the pure figment of someone's imagination. The protagonists in this collection of ten short stories are often a composite of many people I met during my travels on assignments around the world.

I am grateful to all of them.

I also owe thanks to Jayaram for his gentle editing, my designer Graham Rendoth for his creative input, Margaret Gee for her constant encouragement and my wife Tiziana for her support and photographic contributions.

Uli Schmetzer

ONE

Ballot Box Ballad

El Tiburon approached the bench gingerly. He walked the way a peasant moves through the poultry pen, afraid to trot on a wayward chick.

"Name?" The official asked sharply, using the harsh let's-have-no-nonsense-here tone that never fails to intimidate the illiterate and the poor.

"Jose Cabezavaca, Senor," El Tiburon replied, politely.

The official ran a quill down the list and stabbed a name: "Ah!" he cried, "Here it is." He ticked the name off and a second official passed the peasant a blue ballot paper and a ball-point pen.

El Tiburon carefully laid his faded straw sombrero on the bench before he studied the ballot paper. The stern, steel-eyed face of El Candidato was easy to recognize: It was framed in the red, green and white colors of the national flag. Below El Candidato's photo was the face of a man wearing horn-rimmed spectacles perched on the tip of a long nose. This had to be him. The soft-spoken informant in the market had been explicit. Besides, no one else was on the ballot paper.

El Tiburon wiped his writing hand on the side of his trousers, planted his left thumb on the face of the Long-Nosed One and ran his right index finger slowly along the dotted line to the square. He was about to make his mark when Don Miguel, standing beside the bench, clutched his wrist:

"Not there, you fool," Don Miguel hissed. "The other square."

For a moment El Tiburon hesitated, then he straightened up to face

Don Miguel. Behind him the people of Mitzipotla stood in silence. The men, bare-headed, ran the rims of their sombreros through calloused hands as if the rims were worry-beads. The women wrapped themselves deeper into their black rebozos. All stood with heads bowed but all squinted covertly at the official bench below the Ahuehuete tree.

El Tiburon pushed back his shoulders and lifted his head a little higher. He felt a lump in his throat and cleared it with a loud rasp: "Don Miguel," he said: "I'll vote for the man with the long nose." He glanced at the Haciendero just long enough to note the momentary expression of surprise, quickly followed by the flush of rising anger.

"Like hell you will!" Don Miguel snapped, taking a menacing step forward and staring down at the bareheaded Indio: "You'll vote for the Government as you've always done."

His voice was harsh, loud. He was accustomed to give orders and be obeyed.

El Tiburon rubbed the side of his trousers with one hand. The other was holding the pen, awkwardly, like a tool never used. He could feel the eyes of the people stabbing his back and mechanically squared his shoulders.

"No offense, Don Miguel," he said: "But we've decided to vote for the man from the opposition. All of us." He made a feeble sweep with his right hand to include the quiet throng behind.

"Just put your cross in the top square, dummy. Never mind what you decided. And get on with it," Don Miguel snapped.

El Tiburon's toes dug at the sandy soil. He had heard Don Miguel's harsh voice all his life, the way his father and grandfather must have heard the voices of the other Don Miguels in the past. The voice was law. He shifted his weight from one foot to the other and swallowed. But his mouth remained dry, his legs heavy and his fingers itched for the soothing rim of the sombrero on the bench. He only hoped that furtive little man in the Market Square had known his facts.

"Don Miguel, I have the right, the right to choose my candidate," he blurted, staring at the Haciendero's belt: "It says so in article forty-nine clause fourteen. That's what it says."

He did not see the quick exchange between the men from the Electoral Board and Don Miguel, nor the bright flush of anger on the Hacienda owner's face. But their silence told him his information had been correct.

Behind him the wall of voters, backs and heads bent like wheat stalks in a breeze, stood silent. Yet he sensed their agitation between his shoulder blades. Images and sounds tumbled through his mind: The Old Man's lowered head, Don Miguel's haughty laugh, one boot on a sack of maize, smoke curling from a cigar. Mother on her knees, imploring; Anna's tears and the brutal roar of young Don Alfonso; a duck waddling and the sharp crack of a rifle; a leather boot; a kicked-over water bucket, merciless heat, parched lips and sprinklers gushing on the Patron's land; a boy's heart bursting over a blood-stained duck; line after line of lowered heads and bent backs, sombrero rims nervously running through calloused hands – and Anna's swollen belly.

The ballpoint pen was hot in his hand as he pressed his mark into the square next to the face of the Long-Nosed One. He looked up and longer than he had ever dared held the blazing eyes of Don Miguel. Then he snatched his sombrero from the bench, grateful for the comforting rim in his fingers, turned to the line of bent heads and black rebosos and announced: "We vote for the opposition – all of us."

And they did. One by one, all the men and women of Mitzipotla over the age of twenty-one scrawled their coarse crosses on the blue voting slips next to the picture of the Long-Nosed One. Done, they snatched a quick peep at Don Miguel's flushed face and walked away, heads bent just a trifle less, backs just a few degrees straighter, all just a little taller.

When it was all over the officials sealed the ballot box and fastened it to the roof rack of Don Miguel's jeep.

The officials climbed into the jeep and Don Miguel drove them away, the sealed ballot box bouncing drunkenly on the roof. The whole village jogged alongside the jeep in a tacit farewell, not to the officials or to Don Miguel, but to the box – their box, ballot box number 1039.

* * *

After lunch at the Casa Grande of the Hacienda de San Carlos, the three men from the Electoral Board, the Government Party scrutineer and Don Miguel leaned back and grinned at each other. Then Don Miguel picked up Ballot Box Number 1039 and sat it on his lap. He slid the sealed lid with a letter opener, delved inside and handed the sixty-eight voting slips in bundles to the scrutineer who tossed them into the fireplace and lit them with a match.

The senior official from the Electoral Board took sixty-eight new voting slips from his briefcase and the five men quickly filled them out using the Electoral List to obtain the names of the voters. Don Miguel closed the lid and taped it down. The men toasted each other with tequila, told a few stale jokes and finally embraced. Then the four visitors drove away in the Governmental station-wagon with Ballot Box Number 1039 securely squeezed between the two men in the back seat.

Two days later the three municipal policemen from Teototlan, dressed in their faded blue uniforms and shouldering their ancient Thirty-Threes, marched El Tiburon off to jail.

And that's how it begins.

—

TWO

Black & White

{ S O M E W H E R E   O N   T H E   H O R N   O F   A F R I C A }

THE GOOD GUYS

The Captain of the Spy Ship lounged on the open deck of the bridge in a swivel chair bolted to the floor. The chair was custom-made, the kind of periscope contraption in which Hollywood directors ride above the scene and shout: 'Action!' The leather was of the finest chamois. The head rest was button adjustable; buttons also controlled the angle of the lean-to. The Captain doted on his chair. Woe to the officer who forgot to slip the tarpaulin cape over the chamois at the first plop of rain or the swish of bow spray.

The Captain swiveled, away from the hack standing in front of him with his notebook poised. Now the Captain faced the deck below.

"Faster! Faster!" he shouted down at the men. The chief gunny looked up. "Put your back into it, you mother fuckers!" the chief gunny barked at the platoon of squatting Marines disassembling and reassembling their assault rifles. Under the scorching Gulf sun the Marines sweltered. Their bare torsos trickled like defrosted beer cans.

The Captain wore a black baseball cap with the ship's name emblazoned in gold letters. He swiveled back to face the hack: "We've got to keep them busy, keep them on edge," he explained. "These guys are fight'n men, trained to kill. Sitt'n out here in the Gulf waiting to kick ass is like keeping a pack of pit bulls caged. Them guys are mean sons of bitches! We train them that way."

The hack dutifully wrote this down in his notebook.

"No, no, son, don't quote me on this," the Captain interrupted. "Just say: 'These guys are fighting men, the best in the world and they're ready for action any time.' OK? Got it?"

The hack scratched out what he'd written and substituted it with the 'official' quote.

The Captain leaned back. The chair obediently reclined. "The job we are doing out here is the diamond tip of our national security and the security of all our allies. It's the silent war, son; the war that doesn't make headlines. It's the war against terrorism at its goddamn roots. This is a sophisticated search and destroy mission. The gadgets on this ship are unequalled anywhere in the world.

"Now you can quote me on that, son.

"What? Do we locate them? You bet your ass we locate those mother-fuckers. And you bet we send them to their goddamn paradise with all the virgins waiting for them. Quick as hell we do, yes Siree! We blew away three of the mothers last week. The sons of bitches were motoring along a dirt road in Yemen. Zapped the fuckers good. Wasn't anything left to ID, judging by the bird's view.

"No, no, son, that's not for publication, that's off the record – just to answer your question. What you can say is this: We do locate terrorists and we pass on the information to the proper authorities. OK? Got it?"

"Now between you and me – and put down your pen – we know these sons of bitches are out to get us, so we better get them first. Makes sense, doesn't it?

"You ask me about collateral damage?

"Shit, son, this is war and in war, God forgive us, the innocent die with the guilty. And that's a fact. We didn't start this war, they did. They killed our innocent, so I don't feel so bad if some of their innocents get it – and don't you dare quote me on that or I'll have your ass over a Texan barbecue."

The Captain swiveled back to observe the Marines on the deck below.

"We keep these guys around to board suspect vessels. Believe me, son, these Marines can kick ass.

"What? You're asking me how we know who to hit?

"Son, look around you, you are standing on a floating intelligence fortress. We pick up the images from the high-altitude birds; we get them from the low altitude drones; we get reports from our allies and, son, we can eavesdrop on any conversation on any landline any mobile in this region – and that includes listening to the chatter of any president. And that's a fact, son.

"Now don't you quote me on us eavesdropping on presidents. That's classified. Besides the suckers might stop yapping … and son, before you go, remember you're embedded and if you bust the rules we'll kick your ass from here to kingdom come and neither you nor your paper will ever get access again – anywhere".

"Have we made mistakes?"

"Now son: Who hasn't made mistakes? As I said: We regret civilian casualties but we realize they are unavoidable and usually due to human error. The missiles don't make mistakes, son, it's those damn informants on the ground that do … we suspect sometimes they want to get rid of their own personal enemies and may be, and I mean just may be, tell us to zap them … and that's not for quoting either, got it?"

The hack nodded.

The Captain swiveled to face the cockpit of the bridge.

"Isaac! Take him down to the ops room. But make sure they turn off the sensitive stuff on the monitors before he gets in. Are we clear?

"Yes sir!" Isaac snapped.

"By the way, son," the Captain called after them: "How was the chopper ride out?"

"A bit bumpy," the hack replied.

The Captain chuckled: "When you get back to base with the landlubbers there's a great movie in the mess hall tonight. Go and watch it. And have a nice day, son."

* * *

THE BAD GUYS

The Mullah sat crossed-legged on the mat. A morsel of saffron-spiced stew had snared in his wispy white beard. Like everyone else around the floor he ate with three fingers, squeezing meat between slabs of folded bread. He gulped a mouthful of water from his glass, wiped the back of one hand across his beard, burped deeply, once – a sign of well-being – and explained: "All we teach is based on the Koran. We need no other textbooks. All we need, all we have, is written in the Koran …

"… Do have another piece of goat-meat. It's tender. It's a kitten."

The hack put aside his notebook and squeezed a chunk of meat into a slab of bread. The meat slipped out and slithered along the floor. The hack quickly retrieved it and stuffed it into his mouth. Then he shoved the bread after it. He intended to appreciate their hospitality, a hospitality so sacrosanct he believed he would be able to ask any question without recriminations.

"The madrasa is the cradle of pure Islam." The Mullah continued, masticating: "All great fighters of Islam came through the madrasa. Sheikh Omar was one of my students. He was eight years old when he came to the madrasa. Now Sheikh Omar is the leader of the Taliban. And Allah loves him."

"What was he like," the hack asked, wiping his soiled fingers along his jeans so he could pick up his pen and notebook.

"He was a good student. He was always ready to fight, always ready to be a martyr. Like all our students. He lost one eye in the war against the Russian infidels but he sees more with the good one eye then others see with six eyes. He has learned the Koran well. We have taught him well. We are the messengers of the will of Allah."

The bearded men around the floor nodded. Outside the room of their religious school, below low archways, students ambled by casting curious glances at the Mullah, ferocious glances at the hack.

"Our students learn the Koran by rote, from the age of eight until fourteen. Then we interpret the Koran for them, the true meaning of the word, the true messages. We teach them who are the enemies of Islam; those who want to destroy our faith, our culture; those who will rape our women and steal our land. But, really, we are no more than the interpreters of the will of Allah."

The Mullah smiled. He looked at the translator who had accompanied the hack. The translator was an educated young man dressed in a white shirt, slacks and jacket. The Mullah wore a white robe and fine leather shoes. The translator and the Mullah came from the same clan. That was why the Mullah had agreed to see the hack.

"What do your students do for entertainment?" the hack asked.

The Mullah glared: "Entertainment? The Koran is our entertainment. All you people think about is entertainment. My students read the Koran. No music, no television, no listening to radio. These are the evils that have made your civilization weak. The Koran makes us strong. It is all we need."

"We would call this brainwashing," the hack interrupted.

"Ah!" the Mullah cried, throwing his piece of meat on the floor in disgust: "If Moslems study the Koran it is brainwashing. But if Jews study their Book they are pious. If Moslems want to be martyrs they are fanatics. But if Jews and other religions defend their faith by force you call it piety. Why do you always see us as fanatics and your people as the faithful?"

The hack quickly said: "A good point," something he always said when he wanted to mollify and compliment the other.

"One of the reasons western people think you are fanatics," the hack explained with the most ingratiating smile he could muster: "Is because you keep saying you will wipe out Americans and Jews. We don't say: 'We're going to wipe out Moslems!'"

"You just do it!" the Mullah snapped.

The hack thought it was perhaps time to change the subject: "Really though, don't your students miss social intercourse, contact with women, for example?"

The Mullah's eyes narrowed. "Unmarried Moslems do not have contact with women. It's impure. The women have their part of the house, the men theirs. No woman comes into the men's part of the house. So how can my students miss women when they never see them?"

"Hmm!" the hack mused: "Do your students still believe in a paradise where seventy-two virgins wait to service martyrs. Do they?"

"Only if you die in battle," the Mullah hissed, glaring at the hack. The

Mullah was no fool. He knew the hack was being facetious. "That's how it is written in the Koran," he added.

"I went past the Mosque today," the hack said: "What were all those young men doing at the bottom of the stairway leading to an upper road? There must have been a hundred of them milling around."

The Mullah looked at the translator. The translator looked down at his crotch. Through the side of his mouth the translator whispered: "I'll explain to you later. Change the subject."

The hack obeyed: "Why are there so few older students at your madrasa today?"

The Mullah put down his glass of water: "Because I give them time off when there is a jihad. There is a jihad now. The older students go and fight in the jihad. The ones not fortunate enough to become martyrs return to continue their studies. This is the way of true Islam ...

... My friend, you have not eaten well, please eat some more."

Once outside the madrasa the hack turned to the translator: "So what gives with all these young men at the bottom of the stairs?"

The translator sighed. He was tired of the hack's probing into his faith, asking delicate questions, like why did he not have a girlfriend at his age. He had already explained how difficult it was to be married. For the last four years he had been engaged to a young woman chosen by his parents. He was working hard to obtain the dowry and build a house. But he had never seen the woman. His sister sometimes told him what the woman looked like, how white her skin was, how full her bosom, how lush her lips. He would ask his sister to tell him over and over details of what this future wife of his looked like. Then he would go to his room and abuse himself.

The translator had explained among devout Moslems it was a custom along the border villages that the husband did not see his bride until their wedding night, when both had retired to the bridal chamber at the back of the house. There, after reciting romantic poetry to her and praising her beauty – a beauty he had not yet seen under the swathe of garments and the burqa – he would finally be allowed to peel the headdress back. Only then would he see what she looked like. Of course, some men dispersed with such romantic niceties and hurled themselves at their bride, mounting her bull-like, stifling her shrieks of terror and pain with a sweaty palm pressed over her mouth.

The hack was stubborn: "But what was this mob of young boys doing below the stairway?" he insisted. The translator sighed: "Ah, my friend," he said: "These poor boys are waiting for women to walk up the stairs."

The hack was amazed. He pointed out all the women were veiled and wore billowing black robes that covered everything, including their ages and their shoes.

"But my friend," the translator said: "When the woman goes up the stairs her robe lifts a little and you can see her bare ankles."

—

THREE

The Lama's Lover

An icy wind whistled down from the high Himalayas, so stiff the premature peach blossoms shivered on their twigs wishing they hadn't stuck their necks out so early. The stray dogs, of which the kingdom has in abundance, snuggled in doorways, curled into ringlets; peoples' necks vanished into high collars or wrap-around sashes. The river reflected the milky color of the sky as it rushed over polished boulders and pebbles towards the Ganges and Brahmaputra; a man loaded dried dung packed into sacks onto a mule's back, periodically slapping both hands against his thighs and a schoolboy hurried along, fists buried in the folds of his gho.

Shaun wrote these details into his notebook as a prelude to his investigative story about a kingdom whose monarch had made 'happiness and harmony' the official policy. The slogan had elevated his reign in the West to the fabled status of the Shangri-La, the mystical Himalayan nook explorers had tried to locate for centuries. Later Shaun would re-read these notes and admit, ruefully, he too had been initially beguiled by the myth until he discovered happiness and harmony had only become the camouflage to preserve the status quo of an absolute monarchy and the accompanying privileges of its aristocracy. Happiness was an empty slogan without justice and equality. But the king had been wise in many ways. His policy was now the subject of international seminars. He had opened the door to the outside world. Conscious of a free world that frowned on monarchic tyranny, he had decreed – against the will of his people or so it was said – the first 'democratic' election for a parliament. Though at home the king enjoyed near divine status he was admired abroad as an enlightened ruler.

On the day Shaun wrote these observations into his notebook he had spotted the monk squatting on the pavement, a figure immobile, apparently insensitive to the cold, ramrod straight, watery blue eyes fixed on an invisible distant target. Shaun wrote that he wondered whether this monk was a holy man, a madman, a Hindu Sadhu or a Buddhist lama. For a moment he thought the man was dead, until he saw thin trails of condensation drift from lips hidden by the wild tufts of a white beard. Shaun was mesmerized right from the start. And that was his undoing.

Of course, in the weeks to come he must have wished he had looked the other way, or taken another route. Had he done so he would have avoided the initial obsession, the infatuation – and finally the threat to his own life.

But none of us can escape fate, a fate often attracted by our weaknesses. And we all have a weakness, an Achilles heel, a vulnerable spot, a gift deposited by nature in our genes. Shaun's weakness was his curiosity. Though curiosity has been the most important stimulus for human progress it can also be a scourge, itching like a rash. The cure is an ointment some call illumination. Shaun had always been curious though rarely illuminated.

His first news editor once said, rather bluntly and not quite fairly: "Shaun you may not be the brightest of my cadets but you certainly are the most determined." Shaun loathed this news editor, not for what he said but for his conservative mindset which drove the man like a bulldozer. This news editor taught and judged by the book, a burly, melon-headed individual who applied past wisdoms to current practices and believed, like a trade union apparatchik, that seniority is the only route to promotion. He indoctrinated his cadet journalists with a basic recipe he considered essential to any news item before it could see print, a holy trinity he called the three 'Ws' - Where, When and Why. Once these fundamental ingredients had been resolved, so he preached, the rest of the story was no more than spicing. The yarn virtually cooked itself.

Shaun often told his friends it took almost a lifetime to realize 'where' and 'when' are easily satisfied but it is the 'why' that remains so elusive, simply because any story has too many 'whys'. You may find out why we went to war was wrong because we only examined one why. And if you are embedded in a war with one side you are unlikely to see or understand the other why. You may work for a media organization whose why is the policy that the country's patriotic and humane duty is to liberate other countries, if necessary by bombing their infrastructure and killing their people. Or you may work for a boss who believes (or pretends to believe) that politicians are 'basically' honest and that democratic governments desire the good of all the people and not just the good of the privileged few (who finance their election campaigns and ladle funds into their party's pork barrel).

One way or other Shaun believed any intelligent human being must come to the conclusion 'why' is as difficult to come by as is truth. What is one man's 'why' may be another man's lie.

So why, he wrote, did this holy man squat on a crossroad in a spot where everyone was bound to see him? What was his purpose in being so visible in a kingdom where modesty is a virtue, a kingdom in which neither protests or strikes ever existed – or were tolerated – where harmony and happiness is the official policy decreed by the monarch who has supreme authority?

The moment Shaun spotted the figure, cross-legged on the pavement, a begging bowl in his lap, an ethereal smile on his face, his curiosity could not be satisfied with the evasive explanation by his guide that the monk was begging for his daily keep. Monks in the kingdom did not beg for food on the streets. The government paid every one of the six thousand monks in the country a monthly stipend. Besides, Buddhists bring food at least once a week to their local temple. This supply ends up feeding the monks and enhancing the donors' karma.

So why sit there begging? More baffling still, he was a Khenpo, an abbot, so Shaun's guide whispered almost in awe, an abbot made even more venerable by a white beard and straggly white hair partly tugged under a gaily-colored Tibetan beanie. This beggar-monk simply did not fit into the local scene of an orderly, regimented society classified into social strata by the color of a man's lambskin boots and the sash slung over his shoulder. The beggar-monk even wore his own strange garb, a long blue smock tied with a thick rope, an unusual get-up in a kingdom where it is compulsory for women to wear the ankle-length Kira to work, to school, to any government office or public function while the men must wear the knee-length Gho and the sash. This sash is wound across the shoulder in such an intricate manner that with a snap of the wrist it can be converted from a decorative role to a defensive weapon whirled like a gladiator's fishnet against sword, knife or even pistol attack. Then there was this: Only the king wears orange but the beggar Khenpo sat on an orange-colored mat. Yet no one protested or admonished him for sitting on the king's private color.

Judging from his notes, Shaun had continued to ply a native acquaintance with questions about this beggar abbot. He was assured the man was a local who had become a trifle barmy with age. Shaun was not satisfied with this explanation. He felt senility or mental instability is the common excuse these days for the foibles of all elderly people who, once liberated from kowtowing to bosses, from being shackled to mortgages, job-dependence and the cost of education for their children, have tossed away conformism and the fear of being fired but now express their thoughts freely – and are then often classified as 'demented'.

During the following days Shaun kept pestering his friends for more information, aware an aura of secrecy surrounded the abbot like an invisible halo. For those who knew Shaun this stubborn perseverance was the main reason for his astonishing success in hunting down stories others had already abandoned as impossible. As usual he did find a link. One young man, more frank than the rest, let slip the monk had been a famous Khenpo (abbot) in charge of the most prestigious monastery in the kingdom. But before this young man could elaborate, his companions cast him dagger-looks. He fell silent, even morose as if he knew he would be punished for his indiscretion. Further coaxing on Shaun's part was met with the standard reply: 'We don't know' ... or 'he's just an old man gone a little crazy.'

"So why don't the authorities simply remove him, put him in an institution or a home for handicapped elderly people?" Shaun asked.

"Oh, our king would not like that," was the instant reply.

The mystery only stimulated his curiosity and he swore not to leave the country without lifting the veil on the fate of a Khenpo begging on the sidewalk when he should be venerated by his compatriots, a people who believe a monk, more so an abbot, turns holier and closer to Nirvana with age.

* * *

Shaun's second opportunity came during the Tshechu, the spring festival when the thangka, an ancient image of the Buddha, is taken out of its protective metal casing in the Dzong, the local temple-fortress. The monks carry the thangka, still in its case, down to the temple hall in a candle-lit procession. The parade looks like a phalanx of black-clad pallbearers shouldering a huge coffin – the long metal case with its precious treasure still furled inside. The highlight, the unfurling, occurs at dawn as the first rays of the sun edge a yellow ribbon along the horizon or, if it is cloudy, as the first grey light washes the blackness out of the night.

During this auspicious moment the pilgrims stand shoulder to shoulder, mesmerized as the thangka slowly unfurls, cascading from the top of the huge wall on the festival hall down to the pavement. Buddhists come from all over the kingdom and from abroad to receive the coveted blessing of the image. In the growing morning light they line up to witness the unfolding, a view that is said to send electric flashes through participants or cause moments of exquisite pleasure to worshippers. Viewing the unfurling of the thangka is supposed to propel the beholder to a more propitious reincarnation.

The ceremony is charged with hollow Gregorian-like chants and the ritual dances of the black-robed monks mixed with the almost tactile faith of a people who still believe they are about to take a significant step towards a better personal future.

Shaun was touched by this collective adoration though his own belief in religion was tempered early in life and then virtually extinguished by the hypocrisy of the pious and the falsehood of their leaders. His favorite subject at school was history and he soon discovered every religion has been misused for political, personal or imperial purposes and has been a convenient tool to foster 'Hatred of the Other'. History is scarred by wars fought under religious tutelage, wars in which those about to die had been promised eternal life in paradisiacal luxury. Glorious life in the next world or spoils in this are at the root of wars and the fake carrot of peace and justice is dangled as a bait to expunge the atrocities committed often in the name of a deity. The original messages of prophets such as Jesus, Mohamed, Buddha or Confucius were rapidly adulterated and adjusted to serve worldly ambitions. Many of the world's great rascals sit in the front pews of churches, kneel in the first row of mosques and prostrate themselves before altars. Faked religious fervor is common among political scoundrels whose piety convinces the gullible of their righteousness. If the devil really exists, Shaun wrote, he surely has slipped into the souls of those who sent out men – and now also women – to kill fabricated enemies with the pretext of doing God's work.

Shaun saw the Khenpo sitting not far from the wooden cantilever bridge, a bridge financed by a German charity organization and which everyone has to cross to and from the Tschechu. He sat on the orange mat, legs tucked under him. He was knitting a piece of woolen cloth that resembled a glove. The beggar's bowl, made of metal, sat crookedly in his lap. Bundles of paper money spilled over its rim. The pious, returning from the Tschechu in a compassionate mood made generous offerings with reverential bows and clasped hands. The Khenpo accepted their donations without any expression of gratitude. He simply kept knitting, his bushy brows furrowed in concentration; the hands, sheathed in cut-up gloves with the final joint of the fingers exposed, trembled at times.

"Why are you begging?" Shaun asked bluntly, standing in front of the abbot, determined to have an answer.

But the abbot kept on knitting, granting Shaun not even a squint of recognition. But this time Shaun intended to make him talk. He was alone. No guide to stop him.

"Why don't you answer me?"

In his notebook Shaun wrote that people began to stare at him, a foreigner, not with interest but disapproval. He guessed one did not address a Khenpo without being introduced first and after requesting permission to speak to such Holiness. The kingdom had precise formulas and traditions, its people nurtured from childhood to respect hierarchy.

"Don't you have a pension, like other monks and abbots?"

The Khenpo kept knitting.

"Why are you the only beggar monk in the kingdom?"

For a moment Shaun thought a smile had played around the man's lips but it quickly disappeared in the tufts of white around the mouth. He kept knitting.

"You must not disturb his Holiness!"

The man was short and stubby. His bowlegs reminded Shaun of Mongolians who spend a lifetime in the saddle and in the process develop legs like incomplete 'Os'. Or maybe they are born that way. The man's dark brown and light beige colored gho was exquisitely woven. The red stripe on his boots identified him as a village elder. He bowed slightly now as he took Shaun's arm, gently but with determination, and guided him away from the squatting abbot.

"What is it you want to know?" he asked.

"He doesn't answer, does he? Does he speak English?"

"Yes he speaks English. He is an educated man. But he does not speak. He has taken a vow."

"A vow of silence?"

"Yes. He will not speak until the king is dead."

"And why is that?"

The man with the bowlegs looked at Shaun and sighed: "I cannot say," he muttered.

"Why can you not say? Is it a secret?"

The man looked down at his feet: "Our king would not like it."

Still he must have felt pity for Shaun after seeing the look of disappointment on his face because he leaned closer, confidentially as if he was about to impart a deep secret, and whispered: "He was married."

"The monk?"

"Oh yes, monks in our country can get married."

"How is that?"

"We have two types of monks, the celibate monks and the married monks. Married monks, known as gomchen are not complete monks and belong to the Nyingma sect while the full monks are part of the Drukpa Kargyue sect, the official religion. But the gomchen are still monks. We do not defrock them, like your Catholic Church does. They belong to another caste, that of married monks. They no longer live in monasteries but in normal village houses and become what you might call civil servant monks or social worker monks. The villagers seek their advice and they arbitrate in disputes, pacify neighbors or bickering couples, write letters and read letters to the illiterate, offer medical advice or apply herbal cures to the sick and wounded. The villagers pay them in goods. The government gives them a monthly salary."

"So the beggar monk is married?"

"He was."

"Divorced or a widower?"

For a moment the man hesitated, weighing up how to answer or perhaps whether to answer at all. He may have been confused since divorce did not exist in the kingdom, simply because marriage in the western sense did not exist. People moved in with one another if they were attracted and split up when they were no longer in love. It was a simple solution. No lawyers were required. In case of a conflict over property a gomchen was consulted. Usually the female, if she had children, received the lion's share of any property.

"She left him," the man finally said.

"Why?"

He shook his head, conveying nothing.

"Did you ever talk to him," Shaun urged: "I mean before he took a vow of silence?"

"Yes. When they were still living together I asked him why he gave up everything for a woman."

"What did he say?"

Again the man weighed up whether to answer. Again he decided in Shaun's favor, though Shaun realized he was running out of patience, balancing politeness against expediency.

"He told me a parable."

"And what was that parable?" Shaun said, possibly with more urgency in his voice than he had intended, for the village elder smiled for the first time.

"You are a very curious foreigner," he said. "But this is what the

Khenpo told me: Two monks were hiking to their monastery when they arrived at a fast-flowing river. A young woman stood by the river bank and when she saw the monks she approached them with a distressed expression on her face. 'Dear holy men', she said. 'I have to cross this river but I cannot swim and although the river is shallow I am too short to ford it. Can you carry me across?'

"One of the monks picked up the woman and carried her across the river. He put her down on the other side and the two monks walked on. Then one monk said to the other: 'How could you pick up that woman and carry her in your arms when you know we are not permitted to touch a woman? You have broken your vows. You have touched a woman. You are no longer pure.'

"The second monk said: 'I put the woman down on the other side of the river. But you still carry her.'"

For a while Shaun and the bow-legged man walked without speaking. The town buzzed with festive crowds, all dressed in the compulsory ghos and kias and gathered in groups or families; people chatted, laughed and strolled along the stalls at the festival market, eyeing the goods on display, fingering blue jeans and brand-label T-shirts, still a novelty worn only privately in the evenings. Finally, Shaun could not contain himself: "Was the abbot the one who carried the woman?"

The man with the bowlegs cocked his head to one side, perhaps amazed by Shaun's naivety: "Have you noted," he said, "it is always the stickler for laws and regulations who breaks the rules he so shrilly defends. Their fanatical defense of the forbidden hides their own weakness."

"Ah," Shaun said: "So the abbot was that monk, the one who could not put the woman down in his mind. Did he marry her?"

"No," the man with the bowlegs replied. "He had carried another woman in his heart for a long time. She was the village beauty and he had fought for years to overcome the temptation of the flesh. In the end the flesh won. He went to live with her."

"Was there a ceremony?"

Again the indulgent smile of Shaun's companion: "We do not have weddings in the kingdom. We say a couple is married when the two live together. Either of them may have children already but that is accepted by both partners. Couples stay together until one of the partners moves out or lives with someone else. There are no weddings and there are no divorces and there is no stigma for children who move from one family to another because all of them were born in love. In the kingdom a man can have as many wives as he can afford but a woman can have only one man at a time."

He chuckled and went on: "Until recently we had no birth certificates either because no one knew their real age. We never ask someone 'how old are you?' because the person could not tell you. But once the kingdom opened up to the outside world many of us applied for passports to see this outside world. But passports need birth certificates. Those who wished to travel went to the authorities for such certificates or at least a date to put in the passport. Since no one knew when they were born and our mothers had only vague ideas, the clerks decided to have everyone born on January 1 with their age more or less according to their looks."

The man with the bowlegs suddenly burst into laughter: "You know my mother believed I was born in 1960 but the man at the passport office put me down as born in 1965."

As fascinating as such information was, Shaun was not about to deviate from his interest in the Khenpo. "Did the village beauty leave the monk?"

"Yes," the man with the bowlegs said.

"And she left to live with another man?"

"She did."

"So why did the Khenpo take a vow of silence until the king dies?"

The man stood still, suddenly. An awkward silence remained between them. Then the man looked straight at Shaun: "Our king would not like us to talk about this."

With that he executed a quick bow signaling farewell and turned so deftly and unexpectedly into a side street he was hurrying away before Shaun had time to ask his name or how to contact him. He neither turned nor replied when Shaun shouted after him. Obviously he did not want to see him again. Shaun's curiosity had taken politeness beyond the limit of tolerance.

* * *

Sometimes, fortune smiles on people or in Shaun's profession someone has to be in the right place at the right time. Shaun wrote that he did not give up on the Khenpo but he did become despondent, even skeptical that he could ever coax the full story out of a people apparently sworn to a kind of omerta that would have made the Cosa Nostra proud.

Fortunately human nature has many faces. One of them is the face of the whistleblower who gives away secrets inadvertently or who does it with the premeditated intention to rectify perceived wrongs or rebut official lies. The monk who waited for Shaun and his guide at the gates of the Dragon Nest monastery belonged to the first category, the ingenious one. Shaun realized quickly the monk was deliriously happy to talk to someone, having been cloistered for two years into one of the tiny cells at the monastery. Such enclosed meditation is the first step on the long ladder to a lama's illumination.

Everyone in the Kingdom sooner or later and at least once in their lifetime climbs to the Dragon's Nest to be offered the most powerful of all blessings. Shaun and his guide had climbed through dense forest on winding tracks for three hours to an altitude of four thousand meters. Up stone steps hewn into rock, the climb went on and on until, finally, a breach in the canopy of trees opened and the white monastery-temple complex appeared as if it had been glued by magic onto a sheer rock face. This astonishing feat of construction happened four hundred years ago. It must have taken thousands of men to move the stones and timber from the valley below to the dizzying height on the rock. Many workers had plunged to their deaths during construction, their fears lulled by the priestly pledge of innumerable merits gained by being part of the sacred chore and perishing for it.

During their ascent, every now and then a father carrying his newborn baby passed them at a trot, bowing and smiling, as he rushed the newborn to be blessed at the monastery. He would then run down the mountain again, in time to work the afternoon shift in the fields. At four thousand meter altitude the breath of these proud fathers was hardly more labored than someone hurrying along at sea level. The babies piggybacked, bobbing along swathed in shawls, eyes wide open or shut in fitful sleep. Children had to be blessed at the Dragon's Nest the sooner the better to ward off evil, illnesses and the demons always ready to snatch newborns. Then there were the elderly, women and men, shriveled with age, barely able to walk, dragging their emaciated bodies hour after hour up the steep track. These pilgrims clung to rope and iron railings on the more perilous parts but were determined to receive a redeeming blessing before their time was up. And there was the odd foreigner, perhaps a seasoned mountaineer accompanied by a local guide, eager to make the climb and descend within a certain time frame. For such foreigners, it was a race for the record, a feat to boast of: "I made it up and down the Dragon's Nest in two hours and fifty-two minutes." These were people who left their garbage and oxygen tanks on Mount Everest and other iconic Himalayan mountains. For them the mountains were only challenges to be conquered. Their exploits would be recorded in texts and photos in coffee-table volumes with poetic superlatives describing the splendor of the mountains. The majesty of the mountains is merely a dressing for their own egocentricity, just as the natives' deification of the mountains is no more than a quaint local custom to them. Such mountaineers speak badly of the kingdom for banning them from climbing the sacred virgin summit, a seven thousand-three hundred meter high giant venerated as a living being.

Before the last steep ascent to the monastery, a near vertical climb on steps carved into the cliff, the pilgrims have to cross a hanging bridge across a seemingly bottomless gorge. Once across begins the last climb to the Nest, if the visitor can sneak by a huge vicious dog, a kind of Tibetan Cerberus. This shaggy beast tends to single out certain pilgrims by barking and snapping at them ferociously while utterly ignoring others. The dog is nearly as famous as the monastery because he seems to decide who may and who may not make the final climb to the monastery and its three temples. For those singled out by the beast it must be soul-shattering to be turned back on the last stage of the arduous ascent. Fortunately the hound selects only a few, though no one can explain on what criteria. He pounced past Shaun on paddle-sized paws to attack an elderly Chinese who shrilly berated the animal as it faced him, barking thunder, with fangs bared. In the end the hapless Chinese wheeled and hurried back the way he had come. Only then, placated, did the beast withdraw, slowly ambling into a narrow opening in the cliff-face where it disappeared.

On top of the last stairway, Shaun paused yet again to recover his breath and ease a crazy head spin, a nasty characteristic of high altitudes. It was then that the young, rosy-cheeked monk attached himself, perhaps eager to practice his English. Right from the start he appeared uninhibited in offering information. In fact for the next half hour he was so forthcoming Shaun was certain he would have talked frankly even about homosexuality among monks had he asked him. The subject of gay practices among monks has puzzled many though it is never discussed in the kingdom where gay men simply don't exist according to the official version, a denial probably borrowed from their Chinese neighbors who argued in Maoist days that homosexuality was a disease and was eradicated in the era of the Great Helmsman. In the kingdom this kind of argument is difficult to believe since monks are taken from their families at the age of six, kept exclusively in male company, passing through elementary and secondary school at board-in monasteries without being able to touch a female until they reach university level at the age of twenty-one. Then a monk can decide whether to continue a celibate life in exclusive male company or join the ranks of civilian monks who may live and interact with women. Those who opt to remain celibate enter cloistered meditation for two years before they reach the first stage of enlightenment.

As soon as Shaun realized he had come across a well of information, he was determined to steer conversation towards the case of the begging Khenpo. His opportunity came when he entered the second temple and the garrulous monk explained in great detail the significance of the statues of the various Buddhas around the altar – the Buddha of Medicine, of Health, of Longevity, of the Beggar Bowl and of Compassion – and then pointed to an ancient thangka on the wall showing a lama being dragged along by a tiger he held on a leash.

This is when Shaun saw his chance.

"The face of the Lama on this thangka reminds me so much of the Khenpo, you know the one begging on the pavement in the city," he said: "The two really resemble one another, don't you think? You do know who I am referring to?"

"Oh yes," the monk replied, without the slightest hesitation: "His Holiness was the abbot of the Dragon Nest when I was still a young student here. But he fell in love with a village woman and chose to become a gomchen. He became famous for his herbal cures, especially for colds and coughs."

"Did you know the woman?"

"No. On that sad day I only saw her from the distance. But those who did see her close up said she had the skin of milk, the eyes of black coal, hair down to her rump and the high cheek bones of the aristocracy. People said one glance from her and men melted like butter lamps. It was said she had a constant gaggle of moonstruck men wander in the vicinity of her parents' home. Her father who was a simple peasant often shooed the over-eager suitors away by swinging a hoe at them."

"So how did the abbot conquer her? Was he a man of means?"

"Our abbot was a handsome man. He was wise and educated and had the knowledge of nature given to him by his shaman father. It is said he used Shaman magic to bind the woman to him. It is even said he sent her a potion made from the roots of certain shrubs and this made her fall in love with him."

All this was manna for Shaun's curiosity.

"Did he leave one day, did he just walk away?"

The monk nodded and for a few moments he said nothing perhaps visualizing the scene when his beloved abbot shed his title, his monastery and his reputation to follow the call of the flesh.

"Oh yes," he said finally: "It was a sad day. It was raining when we saw her sitting under the gate at the entrance of the monastery down there," he said pointing to the distant gate posts. "We could see the wet hair pasted on her face; a shawl was wrapped round her shoulders; she was gazing up at the monastery hour after hour and in the end the news reached even the young acolytes and the cloistered lamas … one by one everyone drifted to the balustrades and windows to stare at her. That's why we all saw what happened. We caught our breath when the abbot slowly walked down the stairs towards the gate. He carried nothing, his hands were crossed in the sleeves of his gho; we thought he was going to ask the woman why she was sitting at the gate in the rain. That's what we thought. By now even the last of the monks had come to the windows and to the balustrades. When the abbot reached the gate he stood next to the woman and stared down at her. Her head was tilted back and she was staring back at him; this is the way they remained for a long time; I don't think they spoke, just looked at each other as if frozen in time. Then he made a gesture asking her to get up. We thought he was asking her to leave. Instead he took her hand in his. Every one of us gasped. He had touched a woman. By touching her in front of all the monks he was resigning as abbot, he was surrendering his status as an enlightened lama and he was joining the other monks – those who can never obtain full enlightenment."

When the monk paused Shaun urged him on: "And they just walked away?"

"Oh yes," he said, sighing at the memory: "The last we saw of them before they vanished into the forest they were still holding hands. I believe both lived happily together for a few years before she left him."

"Do you know why she left him?"

The monk lowered his head. "The new students only reported she had left him. It is common practice in the kingdom. Men leave women and women leave men. Everyone accepts that. Since there is no formal marriage, each partner follows their karma. If they have children the children are looked after by both the new and the old family."

"Did they have children?"

"I don't know. You see once the Khenpo left we no longer spoke about him. We were not to speak about him, ever again. I picked up the news that she had left him from a new student. He was scolded by a senior lama for gossiping about someone who no longer belonged to us."

"Did you hear any other 'gossip'?"

"I don't think our king would like that," the monk said and then pointed to a wooden statue on the right side of the altar, the torso of a smoke-blackened Buddha, still smiling and with blue-painted hair. The Buddha's singed torso was a sign the temple, like so many temples in the kingdom, had burned down when a butter-lamp spilled fire, igniting the wooden structures. Burned down temples were always rebuilt as exact duplicates of the original. Artisans, many of them monks, were schooled in the ancient craft of building without nails, of using the same kind of mortar, woodwork and frescoes as their predecessors hundreds of years ago. Evil tongues claimed that in times of poverty local artisans deliberately burned down old temples to have jobs and a government stipend while they rebuilt them. Miraculously the statues of the Buddha were always salvaged. Allowing a Buddha to burn would have brought ill fortune for generations.

"Notice this statue of the Rimpoche?" the monk said: "It is dedicated to silence and in our Buddhist belief no one must speak ill of others."

Once again Shaun's curiosity had run into a dead end.

Obviously he had reached the bottom of the monk's knowledge on the fate of the Khenpo or, worse, the monk had realized he had been prattling. Whatever the reason, Shaun wrote in his notes, the well had run dry. Other methods had to be applied. Shaun allowed the monk to complete his guided tour and then offered a generous donation to the monastery, a donation expected of visitors and justified by the expense of maintenance. Before he parted he donned his most ingratiating smile and asked: "You come from the River Village, don't you?"

"Yes," the monk said.

"You still have family there?"

"Oh yes, my brother lives in the village, right next to the ruins of the old dzong. He runs a grocery store. It is the same village where the Khenpo lived with his lady."

The young monk smiled unaware he had just given Shaun the next important morsel of the story.

* * *

The village named River Grove nestled above the confluence of two streams. Silt washed down from the high mountains and deposited in river beds was swept across the land in spring when rivers spill over with melted snow. This annual ritual repeated itself over thousands of years and ensured the land remained richly fertile. The village itself was two rows of huts lined up on both sides of a high ridge with a dirt track running down the middle. This track followed the contours of the land and served as a thoroughfare for mule-drawn carts, motorcycles, bicycles, pedestrians and the odd truck carting logs towards the big cities in the south. The wealth of the land was contrasted by the poverty of the village. The wooden huts were semi-detached like Siamese twins. This was to save the cost of constructing one more wall. Inside were simple dirt floor rooms, dark and dinghy, serving as habitation, stable, store and in some cases as shops selling cucumbers, radish, salad, grain, cheap sweets and a few utensils such as batteries and basic agrarian tools, hoes, spades and rakes. The customers stood outside a window and were served from inside. Shaun immediately noticed the women were tall, slim and fiery-eyed. Not one of them was obese. Women queued at a pipe to fetch water from a tap trickling all day. Yet down below, half a mile away, the twin-rivers gushed millions of gallons of water all year round. No local or national authority had built a pipeline to supply water if not to every village house at least to a few more water hydrants.

The monk's brother was named Wangdi. He owned the largest of the grocery stores. A broad-shouldered man with a smooth face and narrow hips, he told Shaun all villagers worked for the manager of the land along the river banks, the land owned by a member of the royal family. The manager's house, a summer villa, was occupied at times by this royal personage. The villa stood apart from the village on a high rise overlooking the paddocks and the fields tilled and harvested year after year by the villagers. The walls of the two-storey villa were elaborately decorated with painted flowers and ferns, though the windows were grilled with iron bars and the two entrances were narrow and easily barricaded. This gave the construction the aspect of a mini-fortress, a reminder of the days when Tibetan armies led by Tibetan monks broke into the kingdom to ransack and subjugate its people to a more rigid Tibetan Buddhism. In spite of the small size of the kingdom, its population fiercely fought off the Tibetans using temple-fortresses called Dzongs and privately reinforced homes as refuges and defenses. The kingdom refused to accept Tibet's sovereignty or renounce its own brand of Buddhism, a faith heavily spiced with shamanic animism.

Like his brother the monk, Wangdi was garrulous. He said most of the fertile land in the kingdom belonged to the royals and the aristocrat who paid the peasants to work it for them. He said he had known the Khenpo's woman. Her name was Yuden. Everyone in the village had known her. She was one of them. Besides one could not miss her, people elbowed each other when she passed. She was that beautiful. She walked like a queen, which was surprising, as she was born and brought up in the village, having only attended elementary school. Her startling looks made her stand out; her eyes set fire to men's heart and singed their souls; her hair was so black the night was jealous; her breasts so high they stood out like pears. And she walked with the light step of a deer, her kira swishing from side to side.

Shaun could tell Wangdi too had fantasized to possess this beauty. Oh yes, Wangdi added, everyone knew everything there was to know about her, who she talked to, who she had rejected – until that fateful day. After that the villagers had to be content with rumors.

Yuden had lived with her parents in the fifth last house at the forest end of River Gorge. When Yuden and the Khenpo arrived from Dragon's Nest they set up house in a deserted home whose owner was only too happy to cede the useless building and a bit of land around it to such an exalted personage.

As soon as he had made contact with Wangdi, Shaun decided to seek out Yuden's parents. But he was told both had left the village mysteriously soon after she disappeared. His inquiries turned up more bizarre details: the man who had offered the Abbot and Yuden his deserted house had also vanished without a trace.

Wangdi lowered his head when Shaun suggested something sinister might have happened to the missing people. And where was Yuden? Wangdi shrugged his shoulders. "I am sure she is well, better off than you and me," he said. This puzzled Shaun even more.

Determined to pursue the story, Shaun asked Wangdi to take him to the house where the couple had lived. It turned out to be a simple one- floor wooden structure already derelict through neglect. The house was located on the forest end of the village, a short walk uphill from the nearest neighbor, almost certainly a deliberate choice to be separated from a society curious and invasive. When the couple moved in, the house had already been abandoned for some time following the death of its owner. Most people shunned a house in which an occupant had passed away. Those who had shared such a house with the dead person moved out and built a new house, as far away as possible. The abandoned buildings quickly deteriorated; decorations painted on their wooden walls faded; roofs were ripped off by storms; the structure, open to rain, sun and wind, crumbled. In his notebook Shaun wrote that he noticed a few withered chilies still dangled from the eaves.

The house made of mud and wood was deserted. The roof, its shingles held down by white river stones, had gaping holes and the red rhododendron bush in the back garden looked as if it was already a ghost. A few ragged prayer flags, their red, white and yellow colors faded, fluttered on poles. No one would dare even salvage wood or tiles from these haunted places. In fact, as Shaun could later verify, the kingdom was pockmarked with derelict ghost houses, deserted by an ancient belief that evil and mischievous demons haunted the abode of the departed. The advent of Buddhism failed to eliminate such superstition. The lamas preached against such folklore but the common people's belief in demons, spirits and the presence of Death Himself in the house of a deceased person persisted.

"Don't whistle now," Wangdi said anxiously.

"Why not?"

"Whistling calls the spirits," he whispered.

"So how can we placate the spirits if I want to go inside?" Shaun asked half joking, half feeling queasy as he always did when confronted by the supernatural.

"I'm not coming," Wangdi said emphatically: "But if you go in you might sprinkle a few drops from your water bottle as an offering. The ghosts are always thirsty and they are content with tiny portions."

In the end Shaun decided not to go inside. Why upset the spirits, he wrote into his notebook while to Wangdi he explained: "No need to see what's inside. It'll have been cleared out by the neighbors."

Wangdi was startled: "No one would touch anything. The inside will be the way they left it."

Shaun's curiosity was pricked. He wanted to see how these two had lived. He was about to enter the house when Wangdi shouted: "If you see any holy books don't step over them. Go around them or you will die."

"God, what other taboos are there?" Shaun asked. "The place is probably haunted and full of spiders and snakes. Let's go back to the guesthouse."

On the way back Shaun told Wangdi he was sure the Khenpo could not have shared these superstitions. Whatever the reason, Wangdi said, the abbot did not explain his choice to anyone nor did anyone ask him. Yuden seemed to have moved into the haunted house without protest; convinced perhaps that the Khenpo's spiritual powers exceeded those of any evil spirit or Death Himself. The villagers could only guffaw at the couple's daring. Some whispered the word 'sacrilege' and predicted a sticky end for the two.

* * *

No doubt it takes patience, intelligence and endless compassion to overcome the obstacles faced by a man and woman from different social environments. The bar is raised further when one of the two is a scholar, the other barely literate. Shaun drew that conclusion quickly though no one in the village was particularly forthcoming when he brought the subject around to the lifestyle of the Khenpo and the local beauty. He spent two days talking to villagers using the monk's brother both as interpreter and introducer. He sought out those who might be able to shed light on the strange relationship. Everyone appeared to agree the couple, at least initially, appeared happy and in love. As for Yuden's reputation, apparently she had rejected all offers of marriage or concubinage. Not one person indicated she might have enjoyed a romantic liaison before she took it into her head to go with the Abbot.

Shaun's task was painstaking. No one wanted to talk, that was obvious, yet out of politeness, everyone did add a small piece to the puzzle until, eventually, a viable picture emerged. Yuden's parents had mysteriously disappeared one day, soon after she disappeared herself. And neither her father nor mother had ever prattled about their daughter, their only child. In fact one woman suggested the daughter had turned out so perfect in looks she must have exhausted all the procreative powers of her parents.

During his time in the village Shaun lived at a rickety house, guest of a taciturn old woman, the only one to offer accommodation. He ate her strange broth made of vegetables and thickened with oats. He slept on a mattress with so many dents and hollows he was curled up like a question mark.

Shaun managed to piece together, more or less, the saga of the abdicated abbot and the local beauty. Initially it seemed the two lived in harmony, keeping away from others, visibly in love, so the neighbors agreed. At least no one heard them argue, which in any village is unusual. But after a few months the villagers perceived a difference: The Khenpo appeared preoccupied, Yuden nervous, even irritated. When she met other villagers she answered their questions with short snappy phrases like 'mind your own business!' or 'how should I know?' Soon the villagers, including her own parents, shunned her. In a rural society where a woman soon gets pregnant, the villagers had no doubt her gruffness was due to the absence of any such development. The consensus was that either Yuden was barren or the Khenpo was. One way or the other it was a serious matter in a country where even casual relationships are crowned by the birth of a child. Of course there were those who said the ghosts of the dead were to blame for the couple's infertility. Equally inexplicable was a serious omission: The Khenpo had not suspended the customary four wooden penises from the four corners of his house. The penises were to covet fertility, protect against evil spirits and ward off the kind of idle gossip now making its rounds.

Shaun's suggestion that the couple might have desired to have no children was considered outrageous. Children were always wanted. Children were the divine result of the pleasure of copulation.

No one in the village was surprised when Yuden set out on a pilgrimage to Lama Kuenly's temple, two day's walk and half a day's bus ride away. The Khenpo accompanied her but, as custom demanded, went only as far as Thornbush hamlet on the edge of the forest. Yuden had to cross the maize fields along a meandering track flanked by small irrigation channels and then ford the river on her own, taking off her sandals and lifting her skirt right up to her thighs to wade across. She then climbed the steep incline to the top of the hill where the temple stood. The clay track was so slippery after rain many had fallen and hurt themselves before arriving at the lama's altar.

The temple was a surprisingly simple construction given the fame and veneration of a lama who put his personal stamp on the kingdom's hybrid religion. The structure had none of the grandeur of other monasteries. Its appearance resembled a large farm house. This would probably have pleased the Lama who shunned any show of ostentation and pretension. Even the Stupa in which he was buried next to his temple was so simple it could have contained a well-to-do peasant. Next to his tomb a smaller Stupa contained the remains of his pet dog.

The legends and myths surrounding this 14th century Lama were more appropriate for a Himalayan Bacchus than a holy man. But his legacy, a mélange of Buddhist devotion and Shamanic magic, still cohabits today in the souls of the people of the kingdom. The Lama loved women, wine and good food in that order. He not only performed miracles, such as resurrecting dead animals or creating new species, but was a notorious serial lover. He seduced virgins, single or married women without distinction or consideration for their social status. To him a royal lady was just as welcome as a lowly peasant girl. If a handsome wench on the road caught the fancy of this itinerant lama, who was always accompanied by his dog, he would lift her skirts right there and then – at least so the legend goes. And the lady would marvel later on why she had allowed it. Lama Kuenly had no respect for the rigidity and pomposity of religion, admonishing his own Buddhist brethren for their arrogance, stupidity and aloofness. Nor did he have respect for etiquette or the normal rules of society. Endowed with a glib tongue, useful to argue his case, he was known to bed the wife of his host if she caught his eye. His reputation as a miracle maker and potent lover spread and the number of women seeking him out grew. He had a narcissistic obsession with his treasured private part. The veneration of his penis survived the centuries, perpetuated in graphic larger than life-sized specimen painted on house walls mainly in rural areas and mostly in full eruption to covet fortune and fertility.

At the entrance to the temple a monk would have received Yuden, bowing respectfully as befits the consort of a former abbot. Keeping his distance so as not to contaminate himself he conducted her to the interior where the chief monk would eventually attend to her, once she had concluded her mumbled petition, deposited a bundle of money in the metal receptacle conveniently placed in the lap of the Buddha's statue and once she had lit the obligatory butter lamps.

Often a woman had to wait, sometimes for hours, while the monks attended and processed other petitioners, some praying for a child, others offering gratitude, usually in cash, for the birth of their child. Then there were those who came to select an auspicious name for their newborn or about to be born offspring. A monk would hold out to them a thick folder with dozens of thin wooden tablets. On each tablet was written a name. The woman would draw one of these tablets and give the name written on it to her child. Since most names in the kingdom could be attached to either a son or a daughter the choice was final.

Some women did not have to wait. Somehow the monks always knew the status of a visitor. For those obviously of superior means or from the aristocracy, there was no waiting. They were ushered into the inner sanctum immediately, unlike the humble peasant women who awaited their turn, sometimes in the temple garden, seated on rough wooden benches.

Yuden was instantly ushered inside to perform the usual ritual of obeisance before the image of the Buddha, an image which had an uncanny likeness to the defunct lama. In contrast to other famous lamas, perpetuated as reincarnations over centuries, no one had dared to search for a reincarnation of the Kuenly, perhaps convinced his amorous feats could not be duplicated. So his temple was run by a chief monk rather than a reincarnation.

Having knelt and bowed in the four directions Yuden approached the chief monk with some trepidation, aware the magic of the dead Lama was about to descend upon her. In the penumbra of the temple she could hardly see the monk's face or the swift move of his hand which emerged from the folds of his smock with the erect penis she knew she had to clutch in order to be impregnated with the dead Lama's magic powers. It was sculptured of the finest pine wood and lacquered with bee wax which made it feel slightly sticky to the hand.

Trembling with anticipation Yuden clasped her fingers around one end while the chief monk held on to the stem. She felt, like other women, an electric current flash through her body. Woman and monk held the opposite ends of the piece of wood for nearly a minute, enough time for the woman to be aroused. At that point the monk withdrew the tool, mumbled a last incantation and vanished through a curtain.

The villagers soon discovered the Lama's magic stick had not produced the desired result. This precipitated a heated argument as to why Yuden had not made a second pilgrimage to the temple. There were those who argued she had accepted her fate as a childless woman. Others whispered the Abbot had prohibited further experiments, conscious of the dark forces that often take advantage of people's religious credulity to satisfy their own evil desires. Yuden's neighbors did not blame her for this failure as a woman. Instead, so Shaun felt, even though no one said it outright, the villagers blamed the Abbot. After all Yuden was one of them. And no village woman in living memory had failed in her duty as a breeder. With her startling beauty and her ample hips how could she not be a perfect child-bearer?

One can always make a case for a logical conclusion, no matter how illogical. People do it all the time.

When Shaun suggested, in a circumspect way, the childless situation must be the reason she had left the Abbot, the villagers, those he prodded with such a possibility, were outraged. Their denials came with the vehemence of people who know the real reason but are either sworn to secrecy, fear retribution or keep silent as an act of faith. For Shaun their silence gave the affair an even greater sense of mystery because the 'why' was within his grasp yet remained as remote as ever. Why had she left a man who, by all accounts, was a good and caring husband? The question became an obsession as well as a challenge to his journalistic pride. He had to find out.

So he stayed on, another day, and another until even the flirtatious daughter of his hostess lost interest and transferred her coquetry to an Indian truck-driver whose vehicle had broken down, leaving him stuck in the village until spare parts arrived.

But just as he was about to give up and leave, noticing people now avoided him in the street, an old man took pity on him. Shaun had managed to involve the old-timer in a conversation (grateful someone finally spoke to him). Suddenly the old man pointed to the mansion on the hill and muttered: "Ask the lords up there. They own all of us and take what takes their fancy."

When Shaun asked the old-timer what he meant the man pretended he had become deaf.

Until that moment the thought that the solution to the riddle might be found up in the mansion had occurred to Shaun only vaguely. Going up there meant an approach to a member of the royal family, a tricky procedure since approaching royals required recommendations at high level. In fact royal power in the kingdom reminded Shaun at times of Europe's feudal history rather than life in the 21st century. There was a second problem. Shaun suffered the inhibitions of people born into lower social rank or, like him, born into a worker's family. He became either timid or forced himself to appear overbearing, excessively confident, with a touch of impertinence when confronted with high-born individuals. His boisterous front usually collapsed when the subject retaliated with an acid remark or ignored him altogether, as if he were not worth the effort of attention. Over the years Shaun had failed to find a comfortable way to interact with such people or deal with them in the casual and amiable way that came naturally to him with ordinary people. He felt far more at home among workers, peasants and trades people who generally became his main sources of information.

For an hour he contemplated the pros and cons of climbing the hill. Eventually he had to admit there was no choice if he really wanted to solve the riddle of an abbot begging on the pavements of the capital after his woman had left him. The villagers could not or would not help him further in his inquiries. He had run into a stone wall, perhaps of silence, perhaps of fear. At times he felt people knew but had been hypnotized, mesmerized or terrified into silence.

So he set out on the walk uphill.

* * *

The mansion had neither fences nor walls, unnecessary for summer villas in a kingdom where social barriers are not material but mental. On the outside, these large rural houses looked quite humble which convinced the population the royals lived modestly. But of late critics had pointed out that most of the kingdom's fertile land, principally along the rivers, was owned by their majesties and the princes and princesses of the royal families and their in-laws. Until recently such royal prerogative was accepted as divine right in the era of absolute monarchy when citizens were brought up to believe and accept what their fathers and grandfathers had accepted. But since the opening to the outside world, people had begun to ask questions: Why was any land worth cultivating or coveted as site for five star hotels and resorts always owned by the royals or their closest allies who leased the country's finest scenic spots to foreign corporations for development?

Such questions sink root. During the campaign to elect the kingdom's first democratic parliament a party which named itself 'The Workers Party' was instantly banned from participating in the general election with the official excuse "The party does not have sufficiently educated people among its candidates." A government official told Shaun the pre-election rules specified only candidates with a university degree could contest the election. It seemed 'The Workers Party' had plucked most of its candidates from the ranks of ordinary people. Few 'workers' in the kingdom can afford higher education or, unlike the aristocracy, can send their children to America, Australia, or England, for a degree, or at least a certificate of competence. In this way the kingdom, in spite of its new facade of democracy, remained solidly in the hands of those who most benefited from its wealth. Members of the 'lower classes' who voiced their discontent in pamphlets or letters sent to the media or who had found political enlightenment in books, in neo-socialism and in cyberspace, tended to lose their jobs or were bundled together with unwanted immigrants under the ever-ready label: 'Terrorists.' This term was useful to preserve the status quo and to justify excesses or official injustices. Dissent has often been converted into 'terror' in the vocabulary of the world's most powerful nations. Smaller ones too have learned. In this small insignificant Himalayan kingdom 'terrorism' became a convenient scare-recipe to neutralize opposition once the old communist bogeyman had lost its stigma by embracing capitalism with ardent gusto.

The figure greeting Shaun in the garden of the mansion was visibly tipsy. He was tall and thin with a face that would have been handsome but for the small craters left by smallpox. By the color of his felt boots he was of royal blood. His gho was of the finest material but disheveled. It fluttered on his gaunt frame like a flag in distress. Since it was still an hour to midday Shaun wondered if the man was an alcoholic or simply depressed.

"What can I do for you?" the figure slurred, maintaining his balance and a sense of dignity by leaning casually against the trunk of a pale-barked birch tree.

"Excuse the intrusion," Shaun replied politely: "But I am a researcher and wondered if I could have a few minutes of your time to acquaint myself with the customs of your country."

The figure leaned harder against the trunk, visibly content for this steadying anchor: "Do come in and have a drink with me," he said, giving the tree a shove to send himself off in the direction of the mansion. For a moment Shaun contemplated whether to offer his host a steadying arm but decided this would be a gesture of excessive familiarity. He need not have worried. The man managed to reach the porch and immediately sank into an upholstered deck chair gesturing to Shaun to take a seat in a similar chair opposite. Without further introductions or questions the man shouted something which Shaun imagined was an order for drinks. The assumption proved correct. Then, maybe as an after-thought the owner of the mansion turned to his guest and asked: "Arra or cognac?"

Shaun hesitated. He had no intention to have a drink so early in the day but realized, from experience, alcohol does loosen the tongue. "I'll have some Arra," he said, wondering whether he would be given Arra from the bottle for workers, from that of the master of the house or from the one reserved for VIPs. Since he was no expert on Arra the glasses a servant carried in on a silver tray (as if he had waited with them in the wings) might have been firewater or ethylated spirit for all he knew.

"Prost!" his host shouted.

"Ah, you studied in Germany?"

"Heidelberg," was the reply.

"A beautiful city – like a stage scene from the Student-Prince, no?"

The man nodded, then made a futile effort to lean forward only to collapse into a welcoming back rest: "I am Prince Zenghe Zhi Tsumphu. What can I do you for?" he said, chuckling at this common inversion of the traditional English phrase.

"My name is Shaun O'Hara, I am a tourist. But I am also researching the traditions and habits of the people of the Himalayas."

"How do you like our Arra?"

"It's powerful and I suspect it has a late kick. Does it?"

"Hahaha," the Prince chortled: "Late kick is good. Like a man who wenches all his life and then, just when he thinks he has become old, satiated and immune to the kind of love eternalized by your Victorian poets, he finds a late kick. Right?"

Shaun's ears pricked up. "Has this happened around here?" he said, attempting to sound casual.

"So it has. We had a venerable abbot who fell in love with a village beauty and left his lama status, his reputation and his students to follow the path of infatuation."

"And they lived happily ever after?" Shaun added quickly.

"Not quite, Mister O'Hara. Not quite. Enter the late kick."

"You mean they broke up?"

The Prince was staring into his glass where the Arra had almost vanished. For a moment he considered whether to ask for a refill or wait until his guest had emptied his glass. Finally the desire for more Arra triumphed. "Come on," he shouted: "You are not drinking Mister O'Hara. Down the hatch my friend, as they say in your country, no?"

Obediently Shaun drained his glass. Instantly his head began to spin. But he saw his bravado had pleased the Prince immensely, judging by the happy smile on his face. Drinkers instantly discover a sense of rapport and brotherhood with other drinkers. The Prince barked another order to the invisible servant and as if by magic – surely prepared in advance – two more full glasses appeared. Shaun was aware he would have to match this professional Arra drinker glass by glass if he wished to reach the bottom of the mystery.

"And so the abbot and the local beauty broke up?" Shaun prompted.

"Oh yes. And it was a guest of mine who caused it," the Prince said, staring into his glass. "But do tell me: How did you end up in this remote part of the kingdom. Tourists never come here. It's off the tourist track. There is nothing to see here except dirt, stones and water."

Shaun had to think quickly and creatively: "There is, you know," he said. "I have a hobby. I study the condition of the soil when two rivers converge. It's fascinating, you know."

"What's fascinating?"

"The metamorphose, you know. Soil is influenced by silt washed down from the mountains. If the snow melts faster along one of the rivers silt from that river is deposited before silt from the other river is swept on top. This then changes the nature of the topsoil and influences whatever is sowed." Shaun was sweating and he wasn't sure whether it was the Arra or the home-spun tale he was spinning the Prince.

"I see," said the Prince, though obviously he didn't.

"Amazing this story of the abbot and the local beauty" Shaun smartly took up the subject again: "And she left him? How did this happen, I mean she leaving him?"

"Love in our country hits you like a bolt of lightning," the Prince said. "It never comes in small doses, like in your countries. It strikes you and possesses you, totally. It ruins everything else, your dignity, your position, your logic, your family ties, a man or a woman's responsibilities. It's a curse. You become a slave to him – to her – until the thirst is quenched … and that reminds me, another Arra?"

"Why not, in for-for one in for-for all," Shaun replied and knew he had slurred his words.

His host grinned and shouted another order. Before the new drink arrived Shaun hastily drained his glass. The Arra burned as it ran down his gullet and he knew the thoughts in his head would soon feel like a knitting ball unraveling. He might even collapse. Arra was reported to have that effect. He remembered the incident when his driver braked sharply on a country road to allow a young girl to drag her obviously drunken grandmother off the road. The girl had the woman by the shoulders and inched her laboriously out of the path of their 4x4 jeep. When Shaun asked his driver, who knew the two people involved, why he didn't give the girl a hand the man shrugged his shoulders … "She would be embarrassed", he said: "If I do nothing she can pretend the old woman is simply feeling ill.'

Shaun wondered if he could now pretend to feel ill. But then he would not hear what he wanted to know. He summoned his brain for one more assault on the Prince's knowledge.

"So your guest fell in love with the village girl?"

"Struck down as if felled by an axe – saw her, wanted her and ordered me to pursue and bring her. What am I a pimp? I, a Prince of royal blood! But all that did not matter. His blood was stronger and he wanted her. Why did she have to walk down that track to the well just as we rode by,

I ask you? And why did she have to turn and stare at him with those eyes, their color plucked from the summer sky, I ask you?"

Through the fog the Arra was thickening in his head Shaun realized he was about to crack the mystery. If he could just focus a little longer; the Prince was ready to talk, he wanted to talk, wanted to get the story off his chest, a story that had annoyed him for so long because he had played the role of the procurer, a role beneath his dignity. He could tell it to this foreigner who was rapidly sinking into a drunken stupor and would not remember a word that was said or at least he would not be able to say with certainty what was said and what it all meant.

"Did you, did you, I mean, did you get the girl for him, I mean your guest?"

The Prince took a hearty sip from his glass. "Hmm!" he grunted, staring at Shaun, perhaps to gauge how drunk this foreigner really was. Shaun did his best to appear uninterested. He shook his head as if fighting off the effects of the Arra.

He was fortunate. The Prince was eager to talk.

"What annoyed me initially was how come I had missed such a gem myself for so long. And she had lived right under my nose. But now she was out of my reach. He wanted her."

"Who wanted her?"

"My cousin, Mister O'Hara, my cousin wanted her. And I had to be the pimp. I had to approach this village peasant and ask her, kindly and persuasively, to come up to the mansion because the great lord himself wanted to see her. Me, a Prince, acting like a common procurer when all he had to do was order her to come! But he didn't want that. He wanted her to come of her own accord, with an invitation from his chief pimp who had to invite the lady as if she was to attend the royal ball. Oh, he knew she would fall for him, not because of his title but he was a handsome brute. Oh yes, he knew that. He and she had exchanged glances at the well and those glances sealed their fate. And believe me, exactly as I had expected, the moment she arrived at the house, my cousin ordered his driver to bring around the car and alert the escort. I don't remember them exchanging a single word before they drove away. I don't even recall that he asked her if she wanted to come. He simply took it for granted, as if no one could resist a preordained destiny, preordained by whom? Of course, by him? No, no, we never saw her again, nor did that abbot, poor sod!"

It took Shaun a few moments before he could formalize in words what he wanted to know. Finally he stuttered: "Is, is your cousin also a, a Prince?"

The answer came back, bark-like: "No! He is the king!"

* * *

Shaun woke up with the aroma of freshly cut grass in his nostrils. The smell was so pungent and so pleasant he closed his eyes again and thought of his youth when he sprawled in the meadows as the mowed grass dried in the sun on the farm of his aunt. This was the same intoxicating aroma of his youth. He had no idea how long he had been asleep in this field below the mansion or when he had left the porch. Vaguely he remembered being led by someone, perhaps the servant, while his stomach churned and his head spun. Had he vomited? Was this the reason the Prince had ordered the servant to escort him away from the house? Shaun hoped he had not disgraced himself on the porch. Gradually, as the fog in his head lifted, he began to recall the final moments before he blacked out. He had tenaciously concentrated, until the last moment, on what the Prince was spouting in a voice harsh with suppressed anger, a voice giving full vent to emotions buried so long. The words came tumbling out in short, staccato sentences and Shaun was aware the Prince had not talked about this matter, probably never. He could not have talked about it. The case was top state secret.

The gradual realization of what he had heard made Shaun sit up with a jolt. Damn, by the combination of Arra and being a foreigner he had become privy to what must be highly classified information. This was sensitive, even dangerous if the Prince discovered he was not a casual tourist who had bungled onto his property but a foreigner who had been asking precise questions about the abbot and Yuden. Once he emerged from his alcoholic delirium the Prince would realize he had compromised not only the king, whose infatuation with Yuden must have become an un-substantiated rumor though talking about it would probably be considered taboo since it concerned the virtually divine personality of the monarch. But if the story was made public it could have fatal consequences. It could precipitate a coup against the king by one of the more powerful princes waiting for just such an opportunity. The facts, if made public, were sure to discredit the royal family, particularly the royal couple. It was such a sleazy yarn, safe as long as it was maintained in private or as rumor but dangerous to the succession if it ever became public.

Though his head buzzed, Shaun knew he had to make a quick getaway for his own good. Once the Prince reasoned again with a clear head and not the resentment of someone who had been used like a servant by his royal cousin, he would send one of his confidants to make inquiries in the village about this Mister O'Hara. Then the cat would be out of the bag. Gathering himself off the grass groggily, Shaun began to stagger down the hill towards the village. All the way he hoped the inquisitor, surely dispatched from the mansion, had not already made inquiries among the mud and wood houses. The man only had to talk to one or two people to realize the foreigner had been nosey.

This time however Shaun's luck deserted him.

He had reached the flat part of the track and then a fork, one path running down to the river the other up to the mansion. He had started to jog towards the guesthouse where he had left his belongings when he spied the horseman. The rider was galloping across the fields towards the mansion. The sight was like a stab in Shaun's stomach. So the Prince had recovered much faster from their binge drinking, not surprising, after all the man was a hardened Arra drinker, Shaun a mere novice.

Shaun began to run. Once the result of the horseman's inquiries reached the ears of the Prince, Shaun's future would be grim. In this part of the world foreigners often vanished without a trace, particularly individuals whose curiosity had far exceeded their prudence. Searches by host countries, on request from the victim's embassy, proved nearly always futile. The excuses were always the same: Remote inaccessible region; natives still hostile; possibly lost trekking in an unpopulated area. From experience Shaun knew that in many countries the cost of making someone disappear was minimal. Servants and retainers were utterly loyal to their masters and would not think twice if ordered to eliminate someone who could hurt their lord. Shaun recalled the case of the goat being consumed by a group of Buddhist monks who were not supposed to kill any living being. When he teased them 'who among you faithful Buddhists killed this poor beast' there was a moment of silence and then one of the young monks protested: "We didn't kill it. We left it on a cliff and it fell off and killed itself."

What the Prince had told him Shaun had not fully digested until now. And the realization of his knowledge suddenly gave him goose-pimples.

He ran into his room at the guesthouse and quickly stuffed his few items of clothing, his cosmetic bag, two books, two notebooks, his computer and a digital camera into his rucksack. The mistress of the house eyed him suspiciously: Was this sticky-nose foreigner attempting an unpaid getaway?

Shaun pulled out his wallet: "How much?" he asked pulling out notes. "I'll have to add it all up," the old hag muttered. Impatient Shaun pressed about twice the amount he owed into the woman's hand. "OK?" he asked. The woman looked at the money and nodded.

"Is there anyone driving to the capital now?"

"The Indian is leaving," she said. "He's repaired his truck. If you hurry you might catch him …"

Shaun was already out the door before she had time to complain that the Indian, so she had discovered, had been given a salty discount by her daughter and now she feared the stupid girl had allowed herself to be seduced by the 'darkie' who, being a truck driver, was sure to be a carrier of AIDS from sleeping with prostitutes. And her stupid daughter knew nothing about condoms which you were supposed to wear just as the billboards advised at the tshechu festivals. Shaun heard only a part of this lament as he grabbed his rucksack and dashed out.

* * *

The truck was a FIAT made under license in India. It was one of those sturdy indestructible monsters that ply the Himalayas. Nearly all manufactured goods in the kingdom, especially vehicles and machinery, came from India. Even the main roads were maintained and asphalted by Indian workers who lived in roadside shacks inside numbered workers' camps. Dotted along the Chinese border at strategic points and off limits to ordinary mortals were Indian military camps, barracks and checkpoints, part of a presence of twenty thousand Indian troops. Officially the presence of these forces was accepted with gratitude by the kingdom as a safeguard against a China that might one day annex the kingdom to its Tibetan territory, just as it had annexed Tibet in 1959. After all four centuries earlier the kingdom had been a part of Tibet and modern China still considers Formosa, Hong Kong, the Spratly Islands, parts of Vietnam and the Himalayan mini-states as part of what Beijing's school maps define as 'Greater China.'

The people of the kingdom, as invaded people do anywhere in the world, resented the presence of foreign troops on its soil, resented the Indian truck drivers it accused of bringing AIDS into the kingdom, resented the Indian merchants who could open shops all over the kingdom and resented the concession to Indians to travel as they pleased in the kingdom. The resentment began at schools where predominantly Indian teachers with antiquated education methods still drummed knowledge and discipline into 'dumb' students and demanded learning by rote. In general Indians, shackled to caste superiority, looked down on the people of the kingdom. Being obedient to the orders of their king and his council the people buried their grudges in their hearts.

* * *

The truck driver was a skinny little man with a leathery brown face and fiery black pupils with red veins in the eye-white. He was happy to give Shaun a lift but could not understand Shaun's hurry.

"We are having no speed to leave," he said. "We are having plenty of time. What is it you are having to run to?"

"Got to catch a plane, mate," Shaun explained: "And I'm afraid I'll be late. Tell you what: If you can get me to the capital in time I'll give you a hundred US dollars. How is that?"

The Indian shook his head and Shaun knew by now this did not mean 'no' but 'OK, done!'

The truck, loaded with rice from the north, began to roll. But Shaun's nerves only settled down after they had been a good hour's drive from the village. Without a telephone, the Prince would have to take matters into his own hands. Shaun had not seen any vehicle at the mansion and a horseman would never catch them or lay a trap. For the moment he was safe. Relaxed, he fell into the old habit of interrogating anyone he came across. Shaun sucked up information like a sponge.

The driver said his name was JayAr, just like the villain in the Dallas TV series. He seemed to be terribly proud to have such an auspicious name and when Shaun pointed out JayAr was a nasty, egocentric type always out to shaft others for his own benefit the driver violently disagreed.

"That fellow JayAr he is having the right idea: In our world only tough man having good time. Weak always stay poor waiting better luck next life. Right?"

"So you are tough like the real JayAr and you are having a good time. Did you have a good time in the village with that young girl at the guesthouse?"

For a moment the driver looked startled, surprised may be by the familiarity of the question. Then he burst into laughter that sounded like a man suffering from serial hiccups.

"Sahib, who tell you this? The mother? This girl is having seen many Indian film, now is trying to be like Indian actress – rolling eyes like this, rolling hips like this, making man hot. But when man is hot she runs. Very silly girl but good fun to pass time, no? She thinks first I am Nepali. Not wanting to speak to me until I tell her I am real Indian, not bloody Nepali refugee. You know about Nepali, they are now calling them Southerners. Terrible story. We are having thousands of them in India as refugees …"

"What's the story?" Shaun asked.

JayAr was very much on the side of his Hindu Nepalese brothers and sisters who, so he felt, had been forced to leave the kingdom thanks to an orchestrated campaign of terror by the kingdom, a campaign he admitted may have been sparked off by the Nepalese militants who burned government offices in the south. These attacks were instantly converted by the official media into an "insurrection by southern terrorists influenced by militant foreign groups." In reality the attacks were only the work of a couple of hotheads influenced by militant foreign ideologies.

"In chasing these people over the border, Sahib, this country is having all the rich land the Nepalese left. You understand?"

"Yes, but officials tell me they paid for the land the Nepalese left."

"But why paying when people having run away from fear?"

Shaun was not sufficiently versed in the subject to argue further. Both sides, it appeared, had valid arguments. No doubt the Nepalese allowed themselves to be influenced by a group of militants who advocated an independent state in the south and the kingdom may have over-reacted to the threat of a breakaway state or might have deliberately used this as an excuse to trim the bourgeoning Nepalese population and repossess much of its territory bought or tilled by the Nepalese.

Feeling more and more at ease as the distance between the village and the truck grew, Shaun decided to find out what JayAr knew about the villagers and perhaps the fate of the local beauty.

The driver was surprised when Shaun broached the subject. He said: "A very sad end, Sahib."

Shaun's ears suddenly burned as they always did when he was about to break into unknown territory or, more accurately, when he felt at edge of a revelation leading to a scoop.

"What, what bad news, JayAr, what do you know?"

"No one is having chance to escape fate. It is written in your destiny. Right?"

"You're a fatalist JayAr. Now tell me what you heard?"

"I drive trucks all my life, Sahib. I driving Calcutta to kingdom many years. So when beautiful young woman run down in Calcutta police tell me."

"How was the woman killed?" Shaun was so eager he bent over the driver who brushed him aside yelling: "Hey, Sahib, I not seeing road."

"Sorry. But how was she killed?"

"Accident, Sahib. Car running down. Car running away; poor beautiful woman bleeding on road. Not dead, only bad cut. Big car, police say. Black four-wheel drive."

"Did they ever find the driver of the runaway car?"

"No, Sahib."

"Was the story on the radio, on TV?"

"I hearing nothing until police tell me."

"Did the police tell anyone else?"

"Police saying woman had no husband, no family, living alone nice apartment good part Calcutta."

"You remember the dead woman's name?"

"Police not telling, may be not knowing."

At this point the truck had begun the long winding climb to the top of the mountain pass and the driver was concentrating on negotiating the bends. This gave Shaun time to write his notes.

* * *

The slow climb to the top of the pass was tortuous but it allowed Shaun to recall details of the Prince's soliloquy. What he could gather from the man's ravings and obvious guilt and self-flagellation the king had become increasingly infatuated with his beautiful concubine as often happens to men in their dotage. He virtually ignored the Queen, mother of the heir to the throne. The Queen was obviously alarmed the absolute ruler might procreate a child with his new paramour and with an old man's folly he could name this child his successor, leaving her son out of the royal succession and her own influence and that of her friends and allies dramatically reduced.

"What would such a woman not do to keep her status in the order of things," the Prince had asked. "And she had her own admirers and her own followers, all keen to see her son succeed the king. For all of them their own future was tied to the current succession. And what would such people not do to ensure their own nest remained feathered and safe?"

As Shaun wrote, he remembered clearly a phrase that had come through his alcoholic haze: "The assassin was a bungler – or maybe he hesitated when he saw so much beauty. Anyway she got away and the king took her abroad so she'd be safe. But the king knew they would not rest until Yuden was dead and the succession was safe. I think there was another attempt to kill her while she was abroad. I guess she survived that too. As the result the king was desperate. I am certain he has made a deal with the Queen: He would abdicate in favor of her son in return Yuden would be safe."

The heavy truck labored up the steep road, around hairpin bends, advancing barely at walking pace, slow enough for Shaun to scribble his conclusions in his notebook without the usual shaking on a badly paved road. He always made notes on paper after interviews or when he had an idea, a flash, a bright analysis or just a turn of phrase that caught his fancy. Ideas are like puffs of wind, once blown by, they are gone. He preferred handwritten notes to his laptop. He would write the story on the laptop but consult the notes. It was an old habit. At the end of his notes he had always added a few thoughts: Had the king really made a deal with the Queen to save Yuden? Was his love greater than the attachment to his crown? Or had the Queen's faction simply gained the upper hand in the kingdom?

* * *

Shaun's notes end there. Two weeks later his editor received the news the body of his correspondent had been located not far from where the driver of the truck was also found. All his documents were retrieved in a rucksack found near the body. The police had meticulously gathered all Shaun's belonging and had handed them over to the embassy. A few days later the embassy reported, unfortunately and in spite of its inquiries following the message from the editor, no laptop was found among the wreckage. Perhaps the laptop, still a coveted item in the kingdom, had been picked up by someone and kept. All Shaun's personal possessions would be sent to the paper by diplomatic pouch within the next days. In the meantime the embassy would like to know what to do with the remains. The embassy also reported that Shaun's government guide and a few local acquaintances had no idea what he was doing in the remote area where the accident occurred.

* * *

Nearly a year later a Swedish tourist trekking through the area where the truck had plunged into the ravine found Shaun's notebook with the explicit description of his investigation into the abbot's solo protest against the king. The notebook was wedged between two tree branches in such a fortuitous position rain and snow had barely smudged it.

But the abbot and Yuden's story was never published because no one could prove its veracity.

In the market square the abbot continued his silent sit-in for some weeks after Shaun's accident. Then one day he was gone and never seen again.

A few months later the king abdicated and handed the crown to his son.

—

FOUR

A Maoist Odyssey

The Home for Old Foreigners was down a narrow *hutong* in the backwaters of Harbin. In my days Harbin, known as 'The Ice City', was famous for ice sculptures and the rusted onion domes of Russian orthodox churches. Once a bustling Russian-Czarist city, Harbin was a Babylon in the early 20th century when a census found fifty-three nationalities in the city spoke forty five different languages. When I visited the city for the first time in the early 1990s only thirty Russians were officially registered, all of them elderly and destitute.

The Home for Old Foreigners was not far from where two sewage pipes converged into a covered canal. The pipes, ochre-colored like the sewage, were a proud symbol of China's modernization. Tacked to the duct was a memorial plaque. It said:

THIS CONDUIT WAS HARBIN'S FIRST
SANITARY SEWAGE SYSTEM
INAUGURATED BY PREMIER LI PENG IN 1988.

During my visit to Harbin locals told me the night-soil collectors a few months ago had dynamited the new sewage conduit. The result of the explosion was apparently quite awful: The waste of tens of thousands of citizens seeped down the *hutongs* like lava slobbering downhill after a volcanic eruption. The stink leaked into basements and settled in cellars. And since water was in constant shortage a total cleanup was impossible. For weeks the waste caused an almighty stink offending not only the noses of ordinary people but those of city officials too. The stink was so great it reached Beijing. Consequently several Harbin cadres were demoted.

No doubt the night-soil collectors were enraged when they lost their livelihood to the sewage canals with their enclosed conduit pipes. For centuries generations of night-soil collectors arrived before dawn to empty lidded toilet pots left outside homes. The pots were emptied into wooden barrels wheeled on carts or strapped on the collectors' backs. Night-soil collecting had always been an honorable and profitable profession passed from father to son. The trade provided employment and fertilizers for market gardens. The profession had become a guild with licenses passed down from one generation to the next. Millions of night-soil collectors existed in China before the modern sewage pipes laid in the late 1980s and early 90s began to make their task redundant. At the same time chemical fertilizers were rapidly replacing biological fertilizers. Still, local government officials continued to sell 'night-soil' for profit (tapping into sewage pipes) to those who still believed human waste made vegetables grow faster and tastier.

After the explosion the official media – and there was no other source of information then – made no mention of the sabotage. Keeping quiet about disasters served two purposes: It avoided public anger or criticism of the government and prevented other disgruntled citizens from turning into copy-cats. In the old days, until the 1980s, earthquakes, floods, mine explosions and any kind of rural riot in which hundreds or thousands might have been killed, could be kept quiet, forever or at least for years until such calamities surfaced as 'rumors.' The official media warned constantly that 'rumors' were spread by traitors and counter-revolutionaries and would be seriously punished. This meant for real serious rumors a bullet in the nape of the neck with the bill for the bullet sent to the family. Rumor-mongers, right-wing deviants and capitalist roaders had to be instantly denounced so they could be punished. Failure to report them to the nearest official made the listener as guilty as the perpetuator of the rumor.

I had no chance to officially confirm the 'rumors.' The Waiban who deals with foreign newsmen donned his most official stony face, lifted his chin several degrees, pursed his lips as if about to swallow something bitter and without blinking an eyelid informed me I was talking nonsense. Like all Waibans, the Harbin one also warned me not to believe the lies spread by counter-revolutionaries who, he said, forever and unsuccessfully attempted to embarrass and belittle the achievements of the Peoples Republic.

"As a guest of our nation we expect you to give no credit to these rumor-mongers, these counter-revolutionaries," the Waiban said looking straight through me from behind his desk.

I could not help but score a point of my own, a tiny band aid for the official lies I had to repeat and the many good stories I could not write because none of them were worth being expelled from China for.

So I leaned forward eagerly: "Are there many counter-revolutionaries in Harbin?" I asked opening my notebook and poising my pen which I knew made Waibans terribly nervous since they are not supposed to be quoted on delicate issues. That privilege is reserved for higher officials, if one could pin them down. But my silly little gibe always worked. The signs were there. The lips trembled; a finger nervously tapped, once, twice on the desk top as the mind, programmed like a computer, searched the software of the grey cells for the right, the official answer.

The reply was always similar, extracted from the list of quotes Waibins learn by heart before they are foisted onto the public: "Criminal elements exist in every society, especially in your capitalist societies. In China we have almost eradicated such elements."

"Eradicated?" I asked: "Do you shoot them?"

He looked at me sternly: "You have been in China long enough to know we re-educate our people … now is there anything else I can help you with?"

Of course I could not write the story without official confirmation and without being branded 'a rumor-monger.'

I have no idea if the Home for Old Foreigners still exists today or if that narrow *hutong* has become a boulevard or part of a commercial mall. Old *hutongs* vanished in modernizing China as fast as did the night-soil collectors. Where once quaint village homes stood built around a central courtyard, a new commercial enterprise, a skyscraper or a sprawling shopping mall has sprung up. I guess, most likely, the last residents of the Home were cremated some time ago. Back in the early 1990s, when I last visited, only seven old foreigners were still resident.

One of them was Amelia.

Like the rest she was officially 'stateless' though she was the only Caucasian there and spoke flawless English. The other six 'inmates' were Eurasians or Asians washed up in China, some as driftwood, others as leftovers from Maoist campaigns or exiles from countries persecuting communists. Amelia spent her days waiting for death. Like the rest of the 'guests' she watched Chinese television or stared at the three trees inside the ten foot high steel bars enclosing the Home. The trees, scraggy things, had been planted on a patch of land five times the size of a tablecloth. On our first meeting, she told me some of the residents had become tired of waiting and had given the Old Reaper a helping hand. But Amelia could not contemplate such a vile deed. A good Christian, she considered suicide a cardinal sin. "We are not like the Buddhists and Shinto-ists," she complained with barely concealed envy: "They can top themselves."

There was little I or anyone else could do for Amelia, except listen to the stories of how she had survived seventy years of turmoil in China. As a teenager, so she claimed, she had held a US passport but Maoist soldiers had burned it. After my story was published, the Immigration Department in Washington denied she was a US citizen. An anonymous spokesperson said if she had possessed a US passport it must have been an illegal one. Given the burlesque and lawless circumstances in Shanghai in the 1930s, possessing an illegal passport was utterly plausible. Informed of the US decision by telephone, Amelia said even if the Americans had verified her citizenship she would never go to such "a miserable country where they see spies, communists and terrorists under every table. I prefer to die here where God surely has no more trials in store for me."

All Amelia's tales of her youth began and ended in Shanghai. The city is all she remembered of her period as a free person. Everything later was vague in terms of geography and location. Once she snapped at me: "When you are dragged across the country in closed railway wagons or on the back of trucks the question 'where are we going?' is usually answered with a rifle butt."

Shanghai in the 1920s and 30s was often called 'Asia's Babylon' for its multi-ethnic population or 'Asia's Paris' for its wild nightlife, its brothels, dance halls, luxury hotels and department stores. These were the golden years of a free city, a receptacle for all and everyone who had neither a visa nor ID papers but needed somewhere to land. No documents were required to gain access to a city partially run by the French, the British and the criminal empire of a Chinese godfather. Art Deco was the rage. Skyscrapers abounded. The commercial hub was along Nanking Road with mega-stores like the Wing On and Sincere. There one could purchase products from anywhere in the world. At night the Paramount Ballroom, the Grand Theater and the Cathay Hotel were the in places in the pursuit of pleasure. Thousands of nightclubs, bars and dance halls mushroomed in what was then considered the world's third largest city. Shaggy Mongolian ponies were imported for the Shanghai Jockey Club situated in the middle of town where punters not only went to bet but to be seen. Big-Eared Du presided over a Chinese empire of brothels, gambling dens and drug distribution. Opium was in abundance and in a final indignity to law and order Big-Eared Du was appointed head of the anti-drug Opium Suppression Bureau. He was the head of a Chinese Mafia of three thousand gangsters who virtually ran the city outside the small international enclaves. Needless to say the city became a must-destination for every kind of cosmopolitan adventurer, fun-seeker, crook, con-man, spy, Bacchanalian or Libertine and, of course, a refuge for anyone who had fallen foul of the law elsewhere. Into this international melting pot dropped twenty thousand Russian aristocrats in the 1920s escaping from communist firing squads.

One of them was Amelia's mother, an aristocrat.

Singled out by Marxist credo as the exploiter class sucking the blood of the proletariat, this landed and urban gentry would have shared the fate of the Czar and his family had they been caught. With their jewels, gold and useless Czarist bonds sown into their clothing or stowed into the private niches of their anatomy, these desperate blue-bloods headed for the only place willing to accept them without a visa or a passport – Shanghai. By the time Amelia was in her mid teens the Russians had run out of hawking their baubles and bonds. By that time no one in Shanghai was foolish enough to lend them money against lands and villas that were expected revert to their owners once the communists had been overthrown. By then only fools believed the communists were a temporary evil. After all the credo had already spread into China where a young firebrand called Mao-Tsetung was inciting the not-so-rich, the idealists and the peasantry to rebel against the feudal landlord class, the mandarins, courtiers and royals who had flourished even after Sun Yat-Sen's Republic disenfranchised the Peacock Throne. By the time Amelia went shopping on her own as a young woman, the prettiest of the Russian ladies had ended up as dance hall hostesses, courtesans and hookers, the handsomest of the men as bodyguards, drivers or escorts for rich elderly ladies.

By the mid and late 1930s the second wave of refugees arrived, thirty thousand German Jews escaping the anti-Semitic frenzy and ethnic cleansing of Hitler's Nazis. They also brought with them what they had salvaged. But unlike the Russians, who seemed useless and unsuited to any commercial enterprise, the German Jews quickly adapted to Shanghai's free-for-all commerce and flourished for a short period before the invading Japanese army dispossessed them once again.

Amelia's eyes would fill with tears when she recalled strolls along the Bund under a pink parasol, white silk gloves, the latest fashion bonnet and a dress from Paris while her father's black Studebaker crawled along the curbside driven by Boris, a Russian count now employed by her father as chauffeur. Her eyes fogged when she recalled being led onto the dance hall floors by gallant and handsome English or French Marines on colonial service in Shanghai. But Amelia remained vague about what her father exactly did in wild Shanghai, except to say he was 'an entrepreneur,' he was American and he had met her mother, an aristocrat, in Shanghai. She believed the two had married in 1920, before she was born but had separated after she was born. Her father had wanted to take her back with him to America.

"But mother kept me with her out of sheer spite," Amelia would say, visibly rueful at having missed out on a normal life in the fabled US of A. Her mother never produced any kind of document or photo about the marriage, though as a good Russian-Orthodox lady she insisted the wedding had been a sumptuous affair attended by lots of foreign friends with fountains of champagne and a 'negro' jazz band from Harlem to entertain the guests. In those days few couples in Shanghai appeared to be seriously married, except the Chinese taipans who wed the daughters of other taipans to merge their small bamboo empires into one larger bamboo empire. It seems unlikely Amelia's playboy father had serious intentions with a pretty aristocrat who was so devoted to her faith she knelt and prayed before climbing into bed. Perhaps to pacify her Christian conscience, Amelia's father went through a mock ceremony, a common scam in those days to seduce excessively pious young ladies or hoodwink their parents. He probably also procured, in the same fraudulent way, American passports for his 'wife' and their little daughter. But when it was time to leave, as soon as the Japanese marched into China, Amelia's father took with him his new paramour, a far younger woman, and left his previous romantic arrangement to the mercy of the empire of the Rising Sun.

Amelia always defended her father, blaming her mother's bitterness at being dumped for another woman for their subsequent ordeal. She insisted, too often perhaps, that her father adored her and was distraught when she could not accompany him back home, though it seems the father made no effort to find her during the next tumultuous decades.

While the rest of the world heaped horror tales on the Imperial Japanese Army for its criminal wartime conduct Amelia had nothing but praise for the diligence, the precision and the orderly conduct of the Japanese once they had taken over Shanghai as part of their conquest of China. Unlike Nanking where the imperial troops were given free rein to kill, rape and loot, exterminating as many as 200,000 Chinese civilians and disarmed soldiers, the takeover of Shanghai was a meek affair. In fact, until Pearl Harbor the Japanese had shown every courtesy to the residents of the international enclave in Shanghai, an area they considered neutral territory. But as soon as the bombs fell on the hapless American base in Hawaii, Japanese troops moved into the enclave and interned British, French and American citizens. The honeymoon was over.

Not so for Amelia.

Yori Hamakashi was a young graduate of Tokyo's Agricultural College. He was one of the imperial pioneers, a member of an order of young agronomists dispatched to conquered Asian colonies to impose Japanese style cultivation of crops. Their main task was to feed the Imperial Forces. Yori was to supervise production and apply Japanese methods. Before he was sent to the countryside outside Shanghai, Yori spent two weeks in the city. As fortune or misfortune would have it he attended one of the Saturday night dances in the international enclave and was moonstruck by the slim, pale-skinned young lady sitting with her mother on one of the tables. The girl, tall, with finely chiseled features, narrow hips and the dainty feet that can enrapture Japanese men, seemed extremely popular with the French and British Marines who virtually elbowed each other out of the way to ask for a dance. Taking advantage of a dispute between competing Marines halfway through the evening, Yori mustered enough courage to ask the young lady for a dance. He was a handsome devil, Amelia would recall, and spoke reasonably good English. "Besides I liked the Japanese. There was something efficient and serious about them. They made me feel safe."

A few weeks later, when Pearl Harbor had changed the lifestyle of Shanghai's foreign community Yori appeared at the internment camp inside the enclave. Politely he requested both Amelia and her mother to have lunch with him the next day. Amelia readily agreed, although her mother was concerned. She did not want her daughter to compromise herself with an Asian. But in the end she admitted: After all this Japanese was still a member of an Asian super-race, unlike those Chinese wretches who eyed her daughter now and then – from a distance. Only the lowest of European women cavorted with the Chinese. Even the Japanese shared the Europeans' repugnance for the 'yellow race.' In fact the men from Tokyo considered the conquered Chinese a subhuman species. The Imperial Army had not removed the British signs on the entrances of public parks in Shanghai which read: "No dogs or Chinese." The signs were utterly justifiable, because – so racists argued in those days – both dogs and Chinese defecated in public.

Yori was not in love with Amelia. He was far too Japanese to consider a long term liaison with a non-Japanese. But he pretended he was. An ambitious young man who had hitched his future to the agrarian prospects of Japan's Asian empire, he saw in his relationship with a pretty European girl a status symbol that would arouse the envy – and surely admiration – of other Japanese. In short it would make him stand out. And this is what Yori coveted most, though he had no intention to win glory in battle. He viewed warfare as a lottery, a Russian roulette during which one could pull the trigger so many times until eventually the bullet would exit the barrel and pass through one's temple. No, he often told Amelia, real glory was to be won among men who pulled the strings behind the scenes of military campaigns. He preferred to be a string-puller, not a target.

Amelia was flattered by the attention of this confident young Japanese who escorted her to the officers' club to which he had access as a senior administrator. He wooed her with presents at dinner or dance outings, chocolates, tins of Russian caviar and once even a German cuckoo clock. Within a week Amelia had fallen under the spell of the charming young man. So when he suggested she and her mother accompany him to his rural posting as his guests, she did not hesitate. She would escape the confinement of the internment camp and could already see herself as the lady of the manor, in charge of flocks of Chinese coolies ready to do her bidding.

The transfer from the modest quarters in the British enclave to the rural estate of a dispossessed landlord was smooth and swift. Amelia and her mother were given an entire wing at the villa. Yori was considerate and chivalrous. Most of the time he was absent on inspection tours of the vast rural estate he administered. He came to the villa only on the occasions of official visits by senior Japanese officials when his presence was required and useful to further his ambitions. Amazingly, Yori demanded no intimacy from Amelia in private though when in public he made everyone believe the two were lovers. Like most teenagers, Amelia lived in this Japanese fairytale in which Yori was Prince Charming – though with black not blonde hair – courting and protecting his Princess and future wife. Neither she nor her mother had doubts the couple would be married, have children and live happily ever after – into old age. Mother fully approved and supported Yori's behavior, labeling him a perfect and honorable Japanese gentleman, so correct he would not even kiss Amelia before their wedding night – a night when all the veils on the mystery of love would be removed, so mother promised.

"All we needed was a gilded coach and four horses to complete the idyll we had created at the villa. We spent the days doing sweet nothing. Mother was delirious with joy. She kept saying it was just like the years of her own youth. She adored Yori. So did I. We worshipped the floor he walked on. In retrospect though, I am sure he had plenty of Chinese mistresses on the estate, one reason why he was always absent."

In those days the outside world with its savage warfare was on another planet for the two women. News from this alien region did not perturb their idyll though in the real world, western allies and Kuomintang nationalists were steadily chipping away at Japanese supremacy in China and the Pacific. Chiang-Kai-shek's Nationalists and Mao's communist fighters inflicted setback after setback on the Japanese occupation forces in China and the time was approaching when the Chinese would be able to take full revenge for the massacres and indignities suffered at the hands of the arrogant invaders.

If Amelia and her mother remained ignorant of these developments, Yori did not. He had no intention to be captured, tortured and executed by spiteful Chinese. While the lower ranks and honor-bound Japanese officers fought on bravely, ignorant or unwilling to admit the war was already lost, senior civilian officials understood the dream and the bonanza were over and made personal preparations to parachute out of the war zones. Like in a financial crisis when the rich nearly always salvage their investments because impending disaster is leaked to them, so in war the hierarchy, both the upper crust military and the civilian sector, ensures its own safety. After all someone with know-how has to lead the country after defeat. Even the allies accepted this wisdom when they allowed compromised German and Japanese officials to resume positions of power in post-war governments.

Yori had cultivated not only crops but sufficient contacts among senior officials during his two years in China. He was constantly kept abreast of military developments. On the day he sent a messenger to the women in the villa informing them he had been called to Tokyo for consultations, they did not imagine for a minute their beloved Yori had decided it was time to repatriate and jettison his two white show girls. The two, the chaperoning mother and the dazzling daughter, had served his image in China well but certainly would not help his image at home.

Yori returned to Tokyo, married the short-legged daughter of a *saké* merchant and was dispatched to Hiroshima as chief rations inspector.

There the atom bomb impaled him in a bright phosphorescent flash against a warehouse wall.

Back in Canton, the Chinese landlord of the estate soon returned at the head of a Kuomintang army unit. He found two Long-Nose women installed in his best rooms, mistresses of the hated Japanese who had run his property.

That's when Amelia's ordeal began. From the day of the landlord's return to the day I met her, life had become a long downhill slalom – with only death waiting at the finish line.

The landlord was known to his underlings as 'Big Fist Chou' because he had a habit of boxing the ears of his peasant serfs with a closed fist. He brought back with him his two official wives and two concubines. All were installed in the villa according to rank. From the beginning the four women conspired against the two white women, afraid their master might take a liking to them, especially the younger skinny one who wore those see-through dresses and had snow-white skin, a contrast to the peasant girls. All four of Big Fist's women urged him to throw the Big Noses to the Kuomintang troops for sport. But Big Fist was no fool: He was certain the Kuomintang administration, supported and armed by the Big Nose nations, would frown on such an insult to its allies. He had a better idea. He would make them work the vegetable garden and have them live in the gardener's old cottage. This way he could argue he had been kind to the two destitute foreign women who claimed to be Americans and who said they had been kidnapped by the Japanese from the international enclave.

For the first time in her life Amelia and her mother had to do menial work. Initially the two women refused. "We went on strike," Amelia recalled. "We told the bastard we would not lift a finger. We were not coolies. He simply shrugged his shoulders and said he could not afford to feed two women who did not work. We could leave whenever we wanted. Well, that sure scared us. Where would we go? The enclave had been closed by the Japanese and we had no one who would put us up. So we stayed and worked. And we worked hard. It was a huge garden and the supervisor came every day to give us orders. If we didn't carry out his orders there would be no rice that evening."

The gardening job lasted almost two years – and ruined their hands.

* * *

The morning fog had cut visibility to a few meters, the reason why no one saw the mob stomping across the tea groves and the apple orchard towards the villa. Only when the cry went up, "Come out Big Fist Chou … come out of your den and bring those whores with you," did Amelia and her mother realize something monumental was about to happen. In fact what was happening all over the country would change the history of China and, eventually, tilt the balance of global power.

Big Fist was no coward. Unlike his neighbors who meekly surrendered to the mob of peasants, Big Fist came out on the porch cradling a hunting rifle with two revolvers stuck in the purple sash that held together his billowing mandarin's gown.

"Who among you bloody dogs wants to die today. Let him come forward and I'll happily dispatch him to his ancestors," Big Fist shouted.

The mob fell back and began muttering. They were armed with hayforks and picks, poor weapons against a rifle and two revolvers. A few of the more brazen advanced a few steps but stopped when Big Fist raised his rifle and pointed the barrel at them.

"The land now belongs to the peasants who work it," a tall man called Chi yelled.

"Who says so?" Big Fist challenged.

"Our Great Chairman Mao," Chi shouted back.

"And my Great Chairman Chiang-kai-shek says go back to work or we will shoot the lot of you and sell your women as concubines and your sons as coolies. Now take your pigtails and hike back to work. Get!" Big Fist yelled, waving his rifle in an arc from side to side.

But Chi was not intimidated: "We have come to take over the land on the orders of Mao and the Peoples Liberation Army."

"Try!" Big Fist shouted: "Come right up and fetch your bullet or get the hell back to your huts, you damn vermin. We didn't take the land back from the Japanese to hand it over to a bunch of illiterate louts like you."

The mob mumbled and muttered among themselves. The man named Chi waved them forward, taking the lead himself as the rest reluctantly edged closer in his wake, not yet convinced, though taking courage from the basic Chinese belief that safety is in numbers and in any crowd one has a good chance not to be among eventual victims. This concept was applied to mass attacks in war, which made the Chinese such a terrifying enemy in the Korean conflict.

Perhaps Big Fist might have had a chance to ward off the advancing peasantry had he fired over their heads or given them another warning. Who knows?

But such considerations were apparently not in his nature. He looked down on the lower classes and, like most mandarins, despised the peasantry as no more than pack animals good enough to be coolies. His arrogance became his undoing. He fired. He was an excellent shot, a ruthless hunter, a man who had killed tigers and served up their penises – the most coveted aphrodisiac among wealthy Chinese men – to senior officials as a gift. For such a man the tall frame of Chi was an easy target. As the Maoist peasant leader crumpled, clutching his chest with one hand waving the mob to go forward with the other, the peasants surged on, shouting, enraged by the shooting. Big Fist emptied his rifle into the crowd killing or wounding until his ammunition ran out. Then he pulled out his pistols. He managed to trigger off two shots before the mob was on top of him, beating, kicking and spitting on the man who had been ruler over life and death for most of their lives. Barely conscious, bleeding, but still cursing and spitting bloody saliva at those holding him, Big Fist was dragged to an elm tree and strung up by the same rope the peasants used to drag ox-carts when no animals were available. In a final act of fury and revenge for their friends shot dead, two men pulled off the mandarin's robes and underwear and one of the men hacked off Big Fist's private part with a sickle and held it above his head while the rest of the mob cheered.

No one ever came to investigate the incident. Settling old accounts with the landed gentry occurred all over China in those days as part of Mao's first national campaign: The 1947-52 'Land Reform' during which property was confiscated from the landlord class and redistributed among the peasants. Even before the Maoists declared victory and established the People's Republic of China, an estimated one to two million landlords perished as the peasants took revenge on the high and mighty. Every day somewhere in China zealous Maoists urged peasant mobs not just to overthrow the local landlord-mandarins but to exterminate 'the blood-suckers of the proletariat.'

The Maoist ideal to invert the class struggle – when the peasants became the masters and the masters the serfs – rapidly deteriorated into a wholesale bloodbath.

Amelia soon discovered the Maoists were confused about what to do with their foreign captives. The later term 'foreign dogs' was not yet colloquial and many of the mob had never seen a 'Big Nose' and gawked at the women the way people who have never been to a zoo gawk at giraffes. Several of the more fanatical peasants were hostile and called on others to teach 'the foreign devils' a lesson. In the end Big Fist's own peasants defused the clamor of hard-line Maoist cadres for a 'struggle session' – the new Maoist name for popular tribunals during which the accused could be tortured and beaten – 'struggled against' – to make them confess to whatever the tribunal committee accused them of. Several of Big Fist's peasants gave evidence the two women were kept virtual prisoners by the mandarin and had to work for their keep. Since there was no evidence the two had become Big Fist's concubines, mother and daughter were spared the shame imposed on the four women, two wives and two concubines, who had their long hair cut to the roots, leaving them bald. The four were then placed before an impromptu struggle session committee and, in front of the assembled peasants, made to recant their debauched former life. The two wives, as members of the mandarin class, were sentenced to be shot together with Big Fist's two teenage sons. The two concubines, who had been given to the mandarin in lieu of a debt by their fathers, were ordered back to their village. Amelia remembered how the two wives threw themselves at the feet of the committee members and begged, not for their own lives, but for the lives of their children. The fate of the boys however was sealed when two peasants came forward and informed the committee (pointing accusing fingers at the two youngsters standing with bowed heads) how they had been bull-whipped by the young masters only for spilling water from a bucket.

"We only heard the shots, we didn't see how it was done," Amelia said: "But everyone else went to see the show. I must admit the two sons were little horrors though that wasn't their fault. It was the way they were brought up. They saw the peasants not as people but worse than animals. Their father's motto was: 'Treat them harshly to make them obedient'."

Once their curiosity had slackened the peasants forgot the 'foreign devils' and began to argue over the distribution of Big Fist's land. The novice Maoist cadres, more skilled in guerrilla warfare and political slogans, were soon in deep water on agrarian matters. It took all their persuasion coupled with threats of reprisals to keep the competing claimants from fighting one another. Good land was scarce and mainly located near the river. Bad land was plentiful, higher up. The peasants shrieked and yelled, shoving each other, bellowing their justifications for priority treatment. Suddenly neighbors who had grown up in close comradeship were ready to kill each other over a *mu* of land. Every peasant demanded a parcel of good land when only the day before no one had owned any land or even saw the prospect of owning any.

The conflict went on for weeks before the distribution was finally settled, never amiably but eventually with the help of an armed platoon of the People's Liberation Army and the drawing of lots. All that time and for months to come, Amelia and her mother kept quietly tending the vegetable garden, swapping its produce for rice and at times a skeletal chicken tough as leather. The peasants were far too busy making the best of their allotted plots to take any interest in the vegetable garden, which, to the surprise of both women, the Maoist cadres had not included in the partition of the estate.

Those months of working the garden would be the last free period for both mother and daughter. In future they would sigh at the fond memory of being in the open air tending cabbages, tomatoes, potatoes, onions, garlic, cucumbers and leaches. Those garden days happened at the beginning of the convulsive Maoist metamorphosis of China from a feudal society run by warlords into a nation shackled to rigid communist ideology. In this new China power was transferred from the mandarin-landlord class to the peasant class, at least on paper. In reality the peasants, once their private plots had been turned into cooperatives, were just as badly off as they had been during the landlord days though on paper they had the right to form committees and voice criticism. But even those concessions did not last long.

The greatest horror was yet to come – tens of millions killed, starved or tortured to death during periodic bouts of Party paranoia when one purge after another was launched to weed out the enemies of the revolution, the deviants from Maoist dogma, mainly intellectuals, diehard capitalists and feisty individuals who challenged the omnipotence of the party, its secretive politburo deliberations and the diktat of chairman Mao.

* * *

The electricity at the Old People's Home for Foreigners had failed, as it often did. The attendant, a crusty middle aged woman wearing a chef's white hat and a blue apron, carried in a lit candle, mumbling something under her breath, surely neither flattering to Amelia nor myself.

"Without your presence we would be sitting in the dark now," Amelia whispered, pushing the candle from the rim of the coffee table where the attendant had dumped it towards the middle. "It's not that they're trying to punish us. It's the whole town. Whenever the power load runs low they turn the lights off for a couple of hours and we usually sit in the dark, just as we did in the camps."

Surely it was the candle light that made her remember the night she met commissar Chu Dao, the cadre in charge of re-education and increasing production at the anonymous location where the army truck had unloaded the two foreign women and fifteen other unfortunates, all sentenced to hard labor by a People's Tribunal in Shanghai. The truck had traveled all day and all night, allowing the convicts to relieve themselves only twice – and then in full view of the cackling guards, squatting on their haunches to see if these female foreign devils were made the same way as Chinese women.

The Peoples Tribunals had been given a twenty per cent conviction quota by the Party's Central Committee in order to implement Mao's first political campaign following his proclamation of the People's Republic of China from the gates of Tiananmen Square. The campaign was called: "Suppress Counterrevolutionaries."

Among the Central Committee's directive was a clause ordering all cadres throughout the country to submit foreigners to the nearest People's Tribunal for judgment. The directive excluded Soviet citizens with the proper identification and laissez fair stamp of the People's Republic. Such a person was to be treated with courtesy and allowed to proceed. In those days the relationship with the Soviet Union was still fraternal. Moscow generously supplied material, technology and advisers to the fledgling communist nation.

In Shanghai the People's Tribunal held court in the concert hall of the Cathay Hotel. Those accused of being counterrevolutionaries were called, heard and judged with the speed of an assembly line. Over two days the Tribunal sentenced more than one thousand people to hard labor for terms ranging between ten and twenty-five years. Another five hundred and ten were to be executed and only fifty-seven were released on 'recommendations' by high ranking members of the party who vouched for their loyalty.

Amelia's mother made two basic mistakes when the two women were marched in and stood before the panel, four men and two women, all seated on leather-covered grandfather-chairs expropriated from a mandarin's villa. The chairs were lined up in a semi-circle on a podium. The accused stood below, flanked on each side by a soldier in PLA uniform. The two 'foreigners' were to be judged together. Amelia's mother told the Tribunal right away – before she was even asked – that she and Amelia were American citizen and therefore demanded to be released and repatriated immediately. When the Tribunal chairman, a thin mask-like figure, asked why she had been living with a Japanese official at a Chinese villa she haughtily replied: "We were the guests of the Japanese who treated us well, far better than your people."

These were not bright remarks at a time when Chinese soldiers were being mowed down in their thousands by US troops in Korea and the news of Japanese massacres and human experiments in China had been generously exploited by the Maoist propaganda machine.

The Tribunal sentenced the two women to twenty-five years of forced labor. Both were officially labeled "Class One Counterrevolutionaries."

By the time the two women had learned how to make brushes from pig's bristles at the labor camp, an estimated ten million Chinese had been struggled to death or executed during the Campaign to Suppress Counter Revolutionaries. The campaign quickly deteriorated into a settling of local grievances and inter-family and village feuds. The newly empowered Maoists were so zealous in prosecuting class enemies the Great Helmsman had to issue a personal order reducing the execution rate. The quota hardly curbed the enthusiasm of Maoist cadres in villages and towns in their hunt for those who had wronged or dominated them in pre-Maoist days. These unfortunates were accused in public of having betrayed the revolution by speaking against its aims, of spying for the West, of hoarding 'common' goods like grain or hiding ill-gained gold. Charges were easily drummed up in those days to be rid of a rival, to settle old scores, acquire the wealth of others or simply show senior provincial cadres one's diligence and efficiency in the hope of a promotion up the chain of command which meant, even in puritanical Maoist China, more power, more privileges. If the execution quota had been filled there were always the labour camps, officially referred to as 're-education' camps. In those days politically appointed judges and committees had often no education. Some at county level were illiterate or drew their guidelines from Mao's little Red Book which everyone had to read or have someone read to them.

Lu was the one bright memory Amelia had of those camp years. He was the only man who seemed genuinely interested in helping her find the key to what was happening in China instead of trying to push her on to one of the straw bales in the storage shed. These quick romps had no serious consequences since everyone knew abortions were free, even for foreigners. But Amelia could not even imagine giving herself to one of those skinny runts from a race of people she detested. An attractive woman with a finely carved face, she made a popular target for the camp's lovers. Many of them chided her for allowing the sun to burnish her fine white skin in a country where the whiteness of a woman's skin is more precious than her figure or her face. Right from the start, Amelia learned to kick, bite and scream if one of these suitors became overheated in his advances.

"After a while most gave up. I guess they thought I was prudish. Sometimes I told them I was sick with an infectious disease. That really scares men. The worst offenders were the cadres. They didn't give up quickly and you had to be diplomatic to steer them away from the scent because they had the power to make your life miserable. One nasty fellow made me sleep in the men's dorm a whole week after I rejected his proposals. I thought the dorm would be a nightmare but the men were rather sweet once the word got around I had given the guy the cold shoulder. I think they appreciated this. Anyway I wasn't molested, not once. Another fellow, an older cadre, kept asking me into his office for political discussions that always turned into a groping game until one day I screamed so hard the camp secretary came running and the cadre got into big trouble for behaving 'in a manner irreconcilable with communism'. But that was not the end of it: For the next few weeks my ration of rice gruel and a ladle-full of cooked cabbage were cut from two to one helping per day. The cadres might ball each other out in public to show their impartiality and loyalty to the principles of the party but behind the scenes they stick together like glue and paper. None of them were lilywhite, except Lu. I guess he was the archetype of the legendary upright communist, the way the lot of them were supposed to be."

The way Amelia portrayed him Lu, truly believed in a better world, in fairness, justice and class struggle. He was an orphan and had tried to join the Peoples Liberation Army as a fourteen year old but was sent instead to a party school for young communists. He graduated with top marks four years later and was posted to the labour camp to see if he could improve the yield of barley and boost the production of brushes and buttons, the three camp industries. The Party was constantly attempting to increase production, even in areas where the government portion of the harvest was already so high the population was reduced to eating grass, roots and wild herbs. Lu was appalled by what he considered an unfair burden on camp workers. Although the party had classified them as criminals, the young cadre pointed out to his colleagues the courts had sent them to the camps not to be punished but to be re-educated. The camps were not supposed to be prisons but intended to convert the inmates into good communists. Such precise interpretations of party directives made the young man unpopular among his older colleagues.

In his spare time, Lu apparently felt it his duty to indoctrinate the younger of the two foreign women in the glorious ambitions of Marxism, a doctrine he considered an overdue protest against the injustices developed and institutionalized by the capitalist system and the enslavement of the working class. His logic was fascinating, even for Amelia, a visceral opponent of the Maoist doctrine which she blamed for her predicament. But the way Lu saw it 'the revolution' would produce a new type of human being, honest, fair and fraternal in all his dealings with other human beings. It would also produce a government whose main task was the welfare of its citizen, the equality of all social classes and the extinction of any type of exploitation of one class by another. The rich would have to share their wealth with the poor and poverty would be eradicated within a decade. The inevitable result of the new ideology was the creation of the 'New Man,' a new kind of homo-sapiens that would take human evolution to a higher level. Maoism, according to Lu, was the stepping stone to an illuminated humanity, ushering in an era without wars in which disputes would be amiably settled in a Council of the Wise just as it was being done now in the Politburo of China's Communist Party. In order to re-educate those who resisted this shining new path, the Council of the Wise had to create camps where the recalcitrant must be reprogrammed through both political education and hard labour, the first beneficial to their spiritual conformity with the new society the second to the physical welfare of that society.

"You must understand," Lu said. "Our party's duty is to organize and educate the people. Those who remain reactionaries or counter-revolutionaries must be re-educated to understand the benefits of party policy. We must eradicate the enemy within, show our enemies the errors of their ways and if they continue to resist we must treat them as traitors. Mao says 'if you don't hit the reactionaries they won't fall. It is like sweeping the floor: Where the broom does not reach the dust will not vanish by itself.' This is a wise saying and means we must sweep the human dirt from even the furthest nook in our house."

Lu was fond of giving the Chairman's sayings his own interpretation and Amelia was a spellbound listener as he opened her eyes to the bright lights of the future of mankind. Lu was fond of such Maoist phrases as: "The enemy will not perish by himself. Neither the Chinese reactionaries nor the aggressive forces of the US imperialism will step down from the stage of history of their own accord ..." And when Amelia pointed out the United States was a champion of freedom and had defeated the nasty Germans, Lu held up his hands as if he was about to bless her: "The United States is not strong, it is a paper tiger. In appearance countries like the United States are terrifying but they are not so powerful. From a long term point of view it is not the reactionaries but the people who are really powerful. The paper tigers are divorced from the people. Was not Hitler overthrown, was not the Tsar of Russia and the emperor of China and Japan?"

"But it was the US that did it," Amelia had interrupted.

"You mean it was US imperialism that did it," Lu replied, his cheeks glowing with the fervour of conviction, so Amelia remembered: "US imperialism will be overthrown even though it has the atom bomb. The US capitalist groups have achieved a global monopoly by advancing their capitalist policies with deadly aggression and war. But the day will come when they are hanged by the people of the whole world. And that same fate awaits the accomplices of the United States ..."

"Who says this?" Amelia asked.

"Chairman Mao. And he is never wrong."

Like hundreds of millions of people across the world, Amelia became if not enraptured, at least curious about the lofty ideals of communism. Whether these were Maoist or Marxist in their interpretation was ir-relevant. The basic ideals were the same. She was unaware the promises and rhetorical fervour of people like Lu reflected indoctrination and party brainwashing which began at a young age. Sometimes Amelia felt as if Lu had opened a window into a world she had not understood and obviously misinterpreted; a window into an ideology she had dismissed as destructive. Lu made sense. Why should some people have all the rights and others be treated like slaves? Why should the industrialists wallow in luxury while their workers earned wages insufficient to clothe and feed themselves? Why should powerful nations impose their will on weaker ones, and why was justice always on the side of the rich and powerful? If Maoism could eliminate these injustices it would take humanity to a new level of existence. Lu was right. Lu was already the New Man and he led by personal example. Although a senior cadre, he shared the same dormitories as the workers. He ate the same food, dressed in the same blue Mao suits, wore clop-clop sandals and used the same toilet facilities, shunning those set aside for the cadres.

"Until Lu opened my eyes and my heart, I had never taken any interest in politics, pondered the injustices among human beings or reflected why nearly all the Chinese were so bitter and so poor. In hindsight I was not different from the rest of the foreigners in this Old People's Home who also believed at the beginning and then, gradually I guess, became disillusioned and aware we had been conned by the lofty ideals of a communist doctrine borrowed from the writings of Engels, Marx, Lenin and the champion preacher of them all, Chairman Mao. These people had no intention to live by the rules they taught. Years later when I finally got hold of Mao's Little Red Book in English I realized Lu's arguments were almost verbatim from Mao's famous sayings. He rarely added anything of his own. Perhaps he felt that by adding his own thoughts to Mao's, he would be committing sacrilege. In those early years he was as naïve as all the other believers, those millions who were convinced that the world could be a better place if only it adopted the right principles and laws, the ones proposed by communism."

Though fascinated, Amelia was never a convert. She only 'flirted' with communism. That flirt was conditioned by her falling in love not so much with Lu's credo but with the man, his ardent delivery, his disarming honesty and his passion to reform the world. This powerful man, at least in the camp which was her world, had taken an interest in her. The initial spiritual magnetism eventually turned into a physical attraction so strong she was ready to discard all her prejudices and principles for that man, for his race, for his country, for what he was and what he stood for.

No doubt her attachment was strongly influenced by years of isolation. Apart from her mother she had no one to talk to. She would have been an easy prey to anyone as articulate and passionate as Lu, most of all someone who showed a sincere interest in her. After five years in the arid desert of the camp, Lu was like a bubbling spring of fresh water. In addition the young man was handsome, skinny may be, but handsome. And unlike other cadres, he was never rude or overbearing, never shouted at anyone but painstakingly explained the error of their ways. He tried to explain and justify why other cadres had punished them. Lu was a living example of the kind of forthright, honest person communism was supposed to produce. If more cadres had been Lu-like, Amelia might have embraced Maoism more readily and more sincerely. But she always suspected, without ever telling him, that he was an exception. She could never quite reconcile a doctrine preaching social equality, with the guardians of this doctrine lording it over the rest and behaving as if they had been anointed as a superior social class.

One day, when the winds from Mongolia had whipped up the loess from the Yellow River into swirling clouds of sand, Amelia hovered behind a sack of rice a prehistoric Soviet Amo-F-15 truck had unceremoniously dumped on the apron of the main thoroughfare. The truck, a relic from the 1920s, was part of the Soviet Aid to its new ally, the People's Republic of China. Its spluttering engine was unable to negotiate the steep rise to the kitchen hall so the driver always dumped supplies on the road below.

The cook, lazy as he was, had ordered Amelia to lug the sack into the kitchen which was attached to the brush factory where she worked. As she struggled upwards with the heavy sack the yellow loess fall-out began to cover her like sugar-coating on a cake, except the loess was ochre-yellow, not white. She had wrapped her headscarf over her nose but tiny particles still managed to drift into her nostrils and into her eyes. She felt miserable, weak and about to weep with the frustration of life's futility, a life that had nothing else but work and suffering to offer. Besides, she had not seen Lu for more then a week. He had been sent away to some committee meeting in a nearby town. He wouldn't even tell her which town though he had previously told her the camp was in the province of Sichuan. Had the wind and the loess not been so strong she would have cried right then. But she was sure no tear would squeeze its way out of her eyes. Then, as if the wind had grown arms, a reassuring hand fell on her shoulder. Next Lu's eyes were smiling at her from above his own scarf stretched tightly over his mouth and nose. That's when they embraced for the first time. He hugged her hard, close to him in the sand storm. She nuzzled happily against his chest. The embrace, with both covered in swirling loess, went on and on for hours, she believed, though in reality, so she admitted now, it lasted probably less than half a minute. Then Lu gently peeled back her arms, picked up the sack of rice and piggybacked it into the kitchen. She walked behind. "It's too heavy for her," he told the cook whose mouth was wide open with astonishment. Cadres did not carry inmates' loads for them.

That was the beginning of the physical part of their romance.

* * *

The candle on the table had burned down to a stump and the darkness hid her face and her feelings. Then, as if talking to herself Amelia launched into the story of their love, a period in her life unique for the magic of a time never to repeat itself. These days and months were engraved in her heart as if they had been chiselled in stone, a time when the mystery of love was unveiled, not the impish adulation for a Japanese official or the girlish infatuation with a handsome Marine. No, the soul of love, the essence from which poetry is brewed, when two human universes meet, mate and memorize forever the delicious joy of togetherness. For once life made sense as it had never done before and never would again.

"We saw each other all the time. He made all kinds of excuses to come over to my work bench where I weaved the pig bristles into brush. So no one would get suspicious, he always spun some yarn about communist doctrine. He often quoted Maoisms in a loud voice so everyone could hear and believe he was talking to all of them when I knew he really only came to be near me. He would say things like: 'If you want to know the taste of a pear, you must change the pear by eating it.' He then explained this meant if you wanted to know the aims and methods of a revolution the only way was to participate in the revolution. He'd come up with other little gems like: 'Politics is war without bloodshed while war is politics with bloodshed … or 'war can only be abolished through war. In order to get rid of the gun it is necessary to take up the gun.'

"But my fellow workers were not fooled. They knew he came to see me. All at once I was a star. I mean I was treated like a star by the others. I had become a cadre's favourite and therefore had moved up a few rungs on the miserable ladder of camp society. I might be able to get favours, an extra apple or pear which I might share, maybe an extra bowl of rice – or two. There was no more teasing, no one dared. And no one had the courage to push me onto a bale of straw, not even the cadres. Believe me it felt great and it felt safe. Nothing is as comforting as power, is it? And you bet I enjoyed it. When you are condemned to a daily routine that never changes, day in day out, year after year, when your future hangs on the whim of a semi-literate oaf, you become delirious when there is a measure of stability, when a shielding hand hovers over you. Believe me if someone had told me Lu was a god I would have prayed to him.

"Sometimes I would take a stroll in the evening and suddenly out of the dark he would join me. We never kissed you know. The Chinese didn't like kissing. They think it's a waste of time. Foreplay didn't exist, not in those days anyway. The Chinese men want to go straight to the core of things. It's got to be quick and furtive. This is the result of the cramped conditions in their homes where two and three generations live together. Any kind of sexual contact has to be furtive and quick, so the others won't notice or at least won't get excited. Lu explained this to me one day … after we had made love for the first time. You have to understand in spite of the men in my life I was still a virgin. No one had broken me in.

"Where did it happen? Of course on a bale of straw in the warehouse, where else? We could have gone for a walk but the ground was dirty everywhere. Hardly a tuft of grass was left. The cadres had fed every blade that grew to their rabbits, the ones they kept for their own table …"

She pauses and the night wraps her memories and makes speech easier, softer. Her words drift through the dark almost in a whisper, almost as if time had not passed, perhaps the same delicate way Lu guided her to the straw and laid her down, spreading his blue worker's jacket to make a makeshift bed. He rolled down her faded and threadbare trousers, the ones she wore day after day for the last three years and peeled back the thin panties the only piece of another life she was able to keep and clean regularly. He unbuttoned the front of his trousers, loosened his belt and allowed his own trousers to fall down to his knees. 'He was so gentle with me. I closed my eyes because I was scared. He rubbed his palms along my thighs and across my belly and then he slowly lowered himself. It was a little painful that first time. But within a week we met every second day in the store room after work and we became so obvious my fellow inmates used to giggle when I walked by. Some of the other cadres came to my work bench, stood there and facetiously smirked down at me. But they wouldn't say anything or do anything. Much later I discovered they had their own little crimes to hide. I knew I was safe and Lu didn't seem to worry. He knew too much about the others to fear they would rat on him. We were so happy. We used to sleep on the straw. Lu had managed to get an old horse blanket. It smelled but it was warm and the nights at the camp could be freezing cold. It was a miracle I didn't get pregnant, you know. Not many of us did get pregnant in the camp, and I can tell you there was a lot of sex going on there. I mean it was the only sport. There was no radio, no TV, no books, nothing. At least when making love you felt you were not yet dead. But our bodies were so weak, I guess, they refused to conceive."

In time Lu began to confide in Amelia. As they snuggled below the horse blanket, he would run his finger through her black hair and talk about the committee meetings, the directives from the capital and the problems of a transformation shaking up all of China. He would talk as if they were a married couple and sometimes he would even ask: "What do you think?"

One day he asked what she thought about the struggle sessions, especially now that they had been stepped up during the Three Anti-Campaigns and subsequent Five Anti-Campaigns both launched to root out opposition and suspected capitalists and black marketeers. When she cautiously offered a meek 'I don't know about these things,' he sniggered. She was shocked when he hissed: "Millions have been struggled to death … and the Sufan Campaign targeted nearly a million intellectuals and reactionaries in our military. Many of them were executed." Amelia was shocked but could only whisper: 'Oh no!' Lu sniggered again: "Oh it gets worse. They are no longer satisfied with eradicating the bad human elements in our society, now they are targeting nature. They call it the Four Pests Campaign and the whole country has been ordered to kill rats, flies, mosquitoes and sparrows. Why? According to our scientists these four – and not our own bad planning – are responsible for our shortages in food. How do you like that?"

Amelia was flabbergasted. Not by the scope of the campaigns or the number of alleged victims but by Lu's tone, as if he were casting aspersion on these campaigns and their authors. For the past weeks she had noticed a difference in his language when he talked about politics and the party. The passion had evaporated, the light gone from his eyes. More and more he seemed to be questioning rather than supporting new party directives, reflecting negatively on old ones, even debating the party itself. One day he asked her: "You are a Christian but what would you do if you found that the promise to go to heaven if you follow the Christian credo is a rotten lie and the only people who went to heaven are the twelve apostles who invented and disseminated the credo in the first place?"

She was too stunned to reply but he was determined to have an answer. "Well," he said "let's assume you are hundred per cent sure that's the way it is. What would you do?"

Amelia said she could not look into his eyes when she replied: 'I would stop being a Christian."

He was not satisfied: "And what about the other believers, you would just let them go on believing?"

"No", she said: "I would denounce the faith." He clapped his hands: "Bravo! You're now a true revolutionary, re-education has not been in vain."

He made love to her then, more gently then he had ever made love before. When they fell back on the horse blanket, exhausted he sighed: "My poor, poor Amelia, what will happen to you?"

She had no idea at the time what he meant.

Two days later Amelia and the rest of the factory workers were ordered early in the morning to move out into the fields. Each was told to carry their metal eating plate and their metal spoon. The cadres formed the inmates into groups and allotted each group a different position in nearby fields. Then everyone was ordered to beat their plates without stopping in order to scare away the birds and prevent them from landing on the crops. The pot-beating was to go on day and night in shifts to make sure no bird could land. In fact all over China a billion people were ordered to beat plates, kettles and anything that made a noise to keep birds from landing. The scientific argument behind this mass mobilisation was that if the birds could not land and eat, they would die. In this way China's food supply would increase by one third, so the anonymous Maoist scientists contended. Loyally people on the day shift beat their plates for a week from sunrise to sunset. The night shift beat their plates from sunset to sunrise. As always the party's daily radio transmission proclaimed –in the screeching voice of the female news reader – the Four Pests Campaign had been a complete success and as a result food rations would soon be augmented.

But Amelia said she saw birds flying merrily a few days later.

About the same time, the loudspeakers on the factory floors announced another party campaign: the Great Leap Forward. Its aim was to convert agrarian and subsistence China into an industrialized nation by increasing steel production to surpass that of Britain. This was to be achieved by creating backyard furnaces in every village and hamlet to produce steel. All private farming was banned. Peasants were to collect wood to stoke the furnaces. All work in the fields was to be reduced.

The candle was now almost down to its last bit of wax. Amelia leaned across the table. "I don't have to tell you the results of that little campaign, do I? The steel furnaces were an absolute failure. The bad quality steel produced was unusable. Entire forests, orchards and bushes were cut down to fire those cursed furnaces. Food production dropped drastically and within a year people starved. I heard from one of the visitors in the Home an estimated forty-five million Chinese had starved to death thanks to Mao's folly which we called secretly The Great Leap Backwards. I have never suffered so much as during those years of the Great Leap. We were hunting rats and mice for food at the camp. We scavenged the fields and the river and no one gave a damn about work, everyone was only interested in finding something to eat to stay alive. More than half of our camp population died of starvation or diseases associated with malnutrition. Only the cadres seemed to be doing well, obtaining supplies from god knows where … women offered them any favour for food. One of my dormitory companions confessed later she allowed a fat cadre to sodomize her with a broom handle to get a bowl of uncooked rice which she believed saved her life. I guess most of the prisoners, if they had the energy, would have done anything just to catch a few crumbs from the table of the cadres. Often the male inmates took away what the women had earned. It was an awful time and everyone tried to survive just any way possible. I survived because Lu shared what he had. But Mother did not make it. She was weak and had lost her appetite. She simply would not eat anything. She said her stomach rebelled and had locked up. All my entreaties failed. Lu even managed to get her some rabbit stew but she said she was sure it was rat stew and refused to eat it. One morning I tried to shake her awake but she didn't move. She had died in her sleep. We buried her in the field behind the factory. I tried to put a cross on her grave but the Senior Cadre ripped it away. No religion or symbols of religion were allowed in Maoist China. The only veneration permitted was the veneration of the Chairman. His portrait and his busts were everywhere.

"I think it was during the third year of the Great Leap when one day Lu vanished for two weeks – which meant I nearly died without his extra ration. When he returned he took me to the warehouse and told me he had gone back to the town to see an uncle who had brought him up after his parents had died. Uncle Wu was a good, honest man who helped everyone in need. He had inherited a fine courtyard house which often served as shelter for people in trouble. The town had appointed him party secretary and he represented them in regional committees. Lu was looking forward to seeing Uncle Wu who he considered his father. But when he arrived in town people he knew did their best to avoid him and the gate to Uncle Wu's home was locked, which it never was. When he called out, a gruff gatekeeper told him Uncle Wu no longer lived in the house which was now occupied by the provincial party chief. He finally heard the story from a neighbour who ushered him into his home as if he was scared to be seen with Lu. The Maoists had accused Uncle Wu of being a capitalist roader and secretly in touch with imperialist foreign agents. They said Uncle Wu had accumulated a fortune through corruption. He was charged with theft from the people. He was 'struggled' during a people's tribunal presided by cadres from out of town. No one spoke up on his behalf. The villagers were too scared to compromise themselves. So Uncle Wu was sentenced to death and executed in public in the village square. Like all those condemned to death he had his eyes bandaged and was made to kneel down. A soldier armed with a pistol came up behind him and shot him in the neck. Usually the cost of the executioner's bullet was billed to the family but since Uncle Wu's wife had died and he had no children, the town committee was ordered to pay, a symbolic gesture to extend a feeling of guilt to people close to the condemned person.

"When he told me about Uncle Wu's sad end, Lu was shaking with emotion. 'There are grave errors and injustices committed in the name of Chairman Mao,' he told me. Lu said he had come across examples of these injustices. At village and regional committee meetings where he was present local peasants had to bring the committee members food, two meals a day and breakfast while the peasants only managed to eat one meagre meal a day. And at night the peasant girls had to dance for the committee members who got drunk and molested them. Many of the girls had to sleep with committee members and even wash and scrub them in bath tubs. Lu said he was considered a wimp by other committee members when he did not participate in such debauchery.

"But what shocked him just as much was the callous and evil nature of many of the cadres. He said during one re-education class a visiting provincial cadre asked a peasant girl 'What would you say if you had the fortune to meet Chairman Mao?' He grinned at the girl and put one hand on her shoulder as if to encourage her to be frank. The girl thought for a moment and then replied: 'I'd tell him that I eat cabbage and rice gruel once every day and the cadres eat rabbit stew twice every day. So where is his equality of the social classes?'

"No one spoke and the cadre simply pretended he had not heard. But next day the girl had disappeared from the camp.

"When Lu told me that story I thought the girl was either stupid or ignorant, probably the latter. A few days later Lu asked me what I thought of Chairman Mao's new Hundred Flowers campaign exhorting everyone to freely express how they felt about the revolution and what they thought could be improved. Well, I told him it was best not to say anything because if you criticised something in China nowadays they might not punish you today but they remember and punish you tomorrow. Best keep your mouth shut or tell them what they want to hear, even if it is the biggest lie.

"Lu burst out laughing. He said 'you are like everyone else who believes this is a trick by the party to lure counter-revolutionaries out of hiding, to expose those who have never said or done anything against the revolution but hate it and work against it in secret. My fellow cadres feel this is a scam to expose counter-revolutionaries. I was also sceptical until today when we were officially told the Chairman was most upset so few people had the courage to express their honest opinion about the party and the way we wanted to see China grow. He virtually told everyone the revolution could never succeed unless we, its teachers, openly exposed its errors and faults.

Mao ordered every cadre to write their opinion. He said those who did not offer their opinion would be punished or demoted.

"So what are you going to do?" I asked.

"He put his arms behind his head and stared at the rafters for a moment, then he said: 'I am going to write down what I feel is wrong with the way the party works.'

"His words sent a cold shiver through my body for I had learned by then you did not survive in Mao's China for long if you complained or criticized the party or its chairman. And Lu was a senior cadre who was supposed to be loyal and defend Mao's ideas whether he liked them or not. But over recent weeks, when we talked about directives and purges, I had noticed he was no longer the enthusiastic young man I had first met. Now he complained: 'We have only inverted the class struggle. Now the peasants are the bosses and the mandarins are the peasants. But the peasants don't know how to run things and the mandarins don't know how to do manual work. The result is the country is deteriorating every day and more and more people are starving and dying.'

"So your great idol, Mao, made an error in judgment," I told him. "He has become just like the tyrant emperor Qin Shi Huangdi who built the Great Wall two thousand years ago to ward off barbarian invaders. He was so scared he had an army of terracotta soldiers protect his mausoleum. Mao is no better."

"He stared at me then and for the first time I was afraid he was about to hit me. But he controlled himself. 'Mao is not like the Qin emperor,' he hissed: 'Mao is being betrayed by the party, by the cadres who are not telling him his Great Leap Forward has turned into a huge disaster. This is why we need to express our opinions.'

"So what are you going to do?" I asked him.

"I am going to follow orders and express my opinion. I am going to post a Dazibao on the camp wall."

"You must not," I told him. "You can speak about it because if you get into trouble you can always claim you didn't say it or it was taken unfairly out of context. But if you have something written down you can't deny it, can you?"

He laughed again and then wrapped his arms around me and cried:

'You've had too much of the wrong education in this camp. We are teaching you the wrong ideals because without debate, without criticism, without an exchange of opinions there is no progress, there is no better world because all power remains with the privileged. We communists have changed nothing since the days of the Emperor unless we allow criticism. Isn't that so?'

"I was still worried so I asked: 'Do you really think Mao is allowing you now to speak out – without punishing you as a counter-revolutionary?'

"… I will never forget how he looked at me, how gently his hand stroked my cheek and how passionate his voice was when he replied: 'If it is a trap, if we cannot rectify our movement, if I am going to be punished for telling the truth then, my love, I do not want to live because what I fought for and what so many died for, is nothing more than a wicked, wicked lie.'

There was silence in the room. Then suddenly the electric bulbs came alive and in their unexpected light I could see tears trickling down Amelia's face. Embarrassed the light had exposed her emotions she quickly brushed them away. "It was the last time I saw him," she said as if to explain.

"What happened?" I asked.

"Oh, he posted his Dazibao alright. I saw it on the wall and will never forget the text as long as I live. Comrades, it said, we have given blood, sweat, toil and precious lives to end the oppression of our people and change a system in which the privileged class lived off the fat of the land while the rest starved. But nothing has changed. We have only exchanged one privileged class for another. In the old days when the local warlord came to town the town elders offered their daughters for his pleasure. Today party secretary Qing comes to town and husbands and fathers tell each other 'hide your women, chairman Qing is coming'. Everyone has always been told Chairman Mao leads a hard and simple life. Even in Yan'an the party cadres ate two meals a day while the army lived on grass and roots. Now they have isolated our dear Chairman in the Forbidden City where he lives unaware of what is happening in the rest of China. He does not know while he is eating as many meals a day as he can stomach the rest of the country is dying of hunger. He is surrounded by dancing girls and sleeps with virgins to preserve his youth and vigour. Outside, his cadres execute people who speak their mind. Our cadres sent to labour camps entire families, then occupied their homes. If you don't like someone you can simply denounce him as a revisionist or a counter-revolutionary. Comrades, is this a rational society? Has the class struggle changed anything? If the party does not change course we will be worse than the imperialists."

Amelia sobbed.

"The Dazibao was on the wall for less then twenty-four hours. Then it was torn down. I was told Lu was taken away by four PLA soldiers and rumour had it he was executed as a foreign spy who had consorted with a known imperialist-American agent in the camp – me. After the rumour no one had the courage to talk to me. Even the cadres gave me a wide berth. I had been officially stamped a foreign spy. I did not even have my mother anymore for company. Branded a foreign spy I was worse than poison to everyone."

* * *

After that evening in Harbin I did not see Amelia for another six months. During that time I was on assignment all over South East Asia, especially Cambodia where the United Nations spent almost three billion dollars to bring democracy to a country savaged by the Maoist-inspired madness of Pol Pot and his Khmer Rouge who believed that the best way to implement social justice was to physically exterminate all intellectuals, many of them identified as people wearing spectacles.

In spite of the expensive internationally-funded 'pro-democracy mission', the status quo in Cambodia did not change. The people who had bandied the red flag of the Khmer Rouge now flew the 'democratic flag' of the United Nations and were promptly elected because they still wielded the power of the gun. The result: Cambodians who had been in power prior to the UN intervention remained in power. A political opposition was created but it soon collaborated with those in power. Now and then, this opposition voiced criticism to placate protests by western 'lefties' calling the UN campaign a waste of money. Cynics would say all that Cambodia got from the international peace-keeping force was venereal disease, pornography and paedophilia.

I had completely forgotten Amelia, not unusual in our trade where one day's story, though it might ignite compassion, is quickly superseded by the next day's which in turn does not survive long because another arrives. It reminds me of kangaroo mothers who have one Joey in their pouch while the next, mere worm-sized, is already waiting for the pouch to be vacated. Production in journalism is constant, news is fickle and quickly forgotten and editors are constantly whipped into action by profit-minded executives representing greedy corporate shareholders. In turn, editors whip their correspondents to produce new fodder to feed the just as greedy audiences waiting for their next fix of sensationalism. Old stories or follow-ups do not make scintillating reading. Still it was an editor – perhaps touched by the tale of a woman who had lived through Mao's hell – who told me one day: "By the way, the immigration department says they have no record of your Amelia being a US citizen. So Washington can do nothing. The poor woman is just another stateless person. I am sorry."

"Do you want me to do another story on her?"

"No, no, no!" the editor protested. Then reverting to laconic media logic he added: "We'd look stupid telling our readers that after your tear-jerking story the woman is not an American. Worse than that: She might have lied about other parts of your story which makes us and you look even more silly and gullible. We'll let it go away."

"But if readers start asking …?"

"So far no one has. People forget. People never ask. But if someone does ask we'll have to tell them she turned out to be a liar. That'll keep them quiet."

Poor Amelia! I felt guilty. By her own confession she had no burning desire to go to America, a country which she believed, from her point of view, was playing global cop and sticking its nose into too many affairs with the excuse of safeguarding national security. I didn't have the heart to tell Amelia she had been turned down by the stiff shirts in Washington who saw no reason why a derelict old lady with a weird past in China should be cared for. Besides she had never asked me to bat on her behalf nor had expressed any interest in being repatriated to the country she claimed to be her homeland.

But I did have a bad conscience.

So when the Chinese government announced a trade conference would be held in Harbin, I immediately told my editors it had to be covered. As usual they assented, unable to gauge from afar whether the meeting was of any substance. I knew the conference was hardly news worthy but my intention was to see Amelia again.

She had previously left off the story at the Great Famine. During that catastrophe Mao was almost replaced by outraged senior party members who blamed him for the death of millions. He was criticised by some of his closest associates, even ridiculed for his heinously stupid brainwave to convert pig-iron into steel in backyard furnaces. Afraid of being replaced by more pragmatic party luminaries, among them Deng Xiaoping, Mao and his most fanatical followers (headed by his radical fourth wife Jiang Qing) launched the Cultural Revolution, activating the country's youth to persecute his critics. Those who had planned to replace him were executed, committed suicide or died accidentally. Others, such as Deng, were sent away. In the end, the Cultural Revolution proved almost as costly in human lives and far more destructive than the Great Leap Forward. But it saved Mao and eliminated or silenced his critics. From then on until he died the Great Helmsman remained beyond reproach.

Amelia came out of her room and we shook hands. Nothing was said about Washington or her future. Before I had time to inquire about her health she said she was happy to have lived long enough to see printed in the Peoples' Daily, Deng Xiaoping's latest slogan: 'To get rich is glorious.'

"Finally the Maoists have understood the truth," she said: "You can't eat words. People want what other people have. America and the West were labelled capitalists and capitalist meant they were bad elements, they were the enemy, they were like the feudal lords before Mao saved everyone. But people no longer believe what the government tells them. They see in films and on TV how the enemy lives; they see the gadgets, the motor cars and the spacious modern-furnished homes. Now they want the same luxuries enjoyed by those running dog imperialists. In the end the communist party also discovered people work much harder for refrigerators, motorbikes, motor cars and cell phones than they do for an ideology. The result is what I never expected: Capitalism has triumphed in China though the government describes it as 'Socialism with Chinese Characteristics.' Mark my words, without Mao's chains the Chinese will be unstoppable as capitalists."

I was amazed. From her secluded Spartan room in the Old Peoples Home, Amelia had correctly interpreted China's current mood and its inevitable march towards economic world dominance. She realized China's phenomenal growth rate, unprecedented in human history, had to be maintained if the Party intended to survive in power. I agreed with her assessment but was more interested in her experience during the Cultural Revolution. She in turn was fascinated by the phenomenal changes occurring in China. Gradually I steered the conversation towards those years in the 1960s only to discover Amelia had no idea at that time there was a campaign named the Cultural Revolution or that the mobs of youths ransacking and running through the country were known as Red Guards.

All Amelia saw one icy February morning was a gang of young people dressed in Mao suits and waving big-character posters. The posters bore a portrait of a benevolent Mao in the centre of a radiant sun. The mob surged through the brush factory barking slogans into the faces of the shocked worker-inmates: 'Remove all revisionist running dogs.' Only later would she learn these youths were known as Red Guards and had been sent out by Mao to re-educate society and eradicate his enemies. At the time however she thought they were just another bunch of over-enthusiastic teenagers ventilating their political exuberance. After all it was not the first time young people had invaded the re-education camp to harass and harangue the inmates with lectures on the superiority of Mao Tse-tung Thought. In the past however these zealots had never been as boisterous and as aggressive.

"Once they had shouted themselves hoarse, the Guards inspected the labels on the machines moving between benches, rudely pushing workers aside. If a foreign label was sighted a screech went up, the machine was wrenched from the bench and smashed on the concrete floor. Mao's China had no room for foreign gadgets, Mao's China was self-sufficient. Other Guards armed with sledgehammers then set about converting these dia-bolical foreign contraptions into twisted metal, especially those machines that had been screwed down. Whatever could be burned the Guards then set on fire together with the small Taoist temple at the rear of the factory which had survived as a storeroom. As the temple burned, the mob waved fists at the fire shouting: 'Smash! Smash the old to build the new. Smash the Four Olds: Old culture, old ideas, old customs, old habits!'

"When there was nothing more to smash or burn, the leader of the Guards, a lanky fierce-eyed fellow the others called Wu-Chang, ordered his gang to ransack the dormitories in search of forbidden literature. In those days that meant any pamphlet, magazine, book or poster praising purged party leaders or any foreign publication."

Amelia chuckled as she recalled that while the Guards smashed foreign-made machines Wu-Chang stood on an empty upturned crate of crackers imported from Canada as food relief. He would refer to the inmates as "you counter-revolutionary scum" and howled with glee when his minions returned from the dormitories with armfuls of banned literature. "Burn it, burn it" he shouted and soon a flaming bonfire was lit at the entrance to the factory, fed constantly by the arrival of Guards triumphantly carrying more evidence of mind-corrupting literature.

"Oh I knew right away," Amelia sighed. "It could only get worse after that."

And it did.

"The first person singled out was an old man who had been a senior provincial official. They said he had protested against the crop quota each province and county had to deliver to the State. He argued the quota left the peasants without enough food to survive. He must have been a party bigshot once because the camp cadres had been unusually respectful when dealing with him. But the Red Guards had no such inhibitions: They singled him out and stuck a dunce's cap on his head. His hands were tied behind his back, nearly wrenching his arms out of their sockets. Then the old man was marched around the factory while the Guards whipped him with bamboo canes and kicked him for good measure. Every now and then Wu-Chang on his cracker box yelled: 'Recant! Recant!' But the old man remained stubbornly silent. What the Guards wanted from him was to say he was sorry that he had questioned Mao's wisdom and had refused to obey his directives. But the old man didn't say a word. He kept looking at his feet. So he was kicked and beaten again but he didn't make a sound. This enraged the Guards even more. Worse, the old man kept falling over. Wu-Chang ordered the rest of us to clap and berate the old man, waving our fists at him. We were even supposed to spit on him. You would never believe this, would you, there we were, already condemned and suffering as prisoners but everyone followed Wu-Chang's orders, everyone screamed and spat at the old man, pretending to hate him in order to save their own hides. I didn't shout and I didn't spit but everyone around me did. It was disgusting to see what people will do to save their silly little life. The old man was falling over more often and the Guards were whipping him more savagely, ordering him to get up, kicking and beating him until he collapsed and no kick could get him up. I figured he was dead or nearly dead. They immediately lost interest, just left him there on the factory floor and turned to other victims.

"One of the new victims was a young woman. She was quite pretty and since she had only recently arrived she was not as skinny and emaciated as the rest of us. Three of the Guards grabbed her by her braids and pushed her into the Secretary's office, closed the door and drew down the window blinds.

"The rest of us 'bourgeois running dogs' were told to stand and remain in the kowtow position and repeat 'we apologize, we apologize, we apologize … on and on. Three male inmates had their hair shaved off with a pair of scissors. It was done so badly and cruelly the men bled a lot, which only made the Guards laugh. Others had paint splattered into their faces.

"Then it was my turn. What got me into trouble was Moby Dick. A girl Guard, she could not have been more then twelve years old, had found the book under my cod in the dormitory. Screeching like a crow she was holding it above her head, a trophy. In her shrill voice she yelled a foreign devil was in the camp.

"Who owns this book?" Wu-Chang demanded. Half a dozen people immediately pointed at me. I guess, by denouncing me as the book owner they hoped to avoid to be classified collaborators and avoid their own torture.

"To be honest I never found out how Lu had managed to get hold of the Moby Dick book in English. He gave it to me one day without explanations. I must have read it a hundred times over the years. It was the only English book I had during those camp years, my only companion after they took away Lu and after Mother had died.

"Moby Dick was to be my undoing.

"'Come forward Big Nose!' Wu-Chang shouted and I was immediately pushed by other inmates towards the soapbox of crackers.

"'Are you a Big Nose bourgeois foreigner?' he asked.

"I had to smile. Obviously he was not quite sure I was not a native or a member of a local minority. Dressed in the grey Mao suit and grubby as I was, with my hair cropped short, I probably looked just like another Chinese.

"'Can you read this book?' he asked. I kept silent.

"'She's not talking. She wants to rebel. Good. Strip her and we'll soon see what she has to show us.'

"I don't know if you can imagine what it feels like to be stripped by the hands of strangers tearing away at you, their eyes filled with hatred, their bodies pressed against you as they tear away all your dignity right down to the panties you have only washed the night before. You are aware your fellow inmates, people you have known for years, can see you naked, see you humiliated. Mercifully most of the inmates looked at their feet, not at me. I think I could happily have died at that moment. But the Guards had other fun in store."

I never discovered what other 'fun' the Guards had in store for Amelia. All of a sudden she fell into a state of catalepsies, her face a frozen mask, expressionless, eyes dull, far away as if she was seeing something no one else could see. I felt too intimidated to urge her back from wherever her memory had travelled.

We sat in the small lounge as the night slowly dimmed the day. It must have been a good ten minutes before she looked at me, surprised, amazed I was still there.

"Maoism had its positive sides, you know," she began after her long lapse: "No one could ever be sure about the next day. Uncertainty hung over everyone's fate, from Mao's closest allies to the lowliest peasant. There was Deng Xiaoping running the country as Mao's number two one day and the next day he was paraded around in a dunce's cap with people spitting and punching him. One day you would be sending people to re-education camps and the next day they would be sending you to the re-education camp.

"That's how it worked.

"You know only a few months later some of the same Guards who terrorized us arrived as new inmates. Apparently Mao had decided enough was enough, the Guards had become a government of their own, their power unlimited and uncurbed. China was in chaos. So Mao launched a new campaign – the 'Down to the Countryside Movement.' He ordered the Red Guards to work and learn from the peasants in the rural areas. He ordered PLA soldiers to enforce his orders. So from one day to the next these young zealots were sent into the fields as manual labourers. Most of them were students who had never done a day's manual work. Did they suffer! And we made them suffer until their hands bled, their stomachs turned because they were not used to the miserable rations; their lungs burned because they could not keep up the pace. By then our factory had been closed, all the machines had been wrecked and we were split up and sent out to work in the fields. The new directive was that China had to produce more food. All inmates of the re-education and hard labour camps together with the Red Guards from the Down to the Countryside Movement were to be used as agrarian help.

"One day I was weeding in a rice field right next to one of the young men who had been sent to the countryside. He kept looking away each time I tried to catch a glimpse of him. But I caught him when he carried the weeds we had torn from the rice field to the dung heap. It was Wu-Chang, the guy who had ordered me to be stripped naked and to crawl along the floor like a worm. He must have recognized me too because he kept looking away. After the day's work I made sure I stood next to him in the meal queue. 'What does it feel like to be the victim?' I asked. He pretended he had not heard, so I repeated it. He turned around and snapped: 'We are not victims. We are volunteers to help bring in the harvest.'

"'Wu-Chang,' I said: 'If you are volunteers why are you treated like us running dog reactionaries. Why are you queuing up for your ration with me? You're being punished for what you did, you little scum.'

"I could tell he was scared, the way he looked around. I guess he thought we'd take revenge for the humiliation he had inflicted on us. 'Please don't tell anyone,' he said. 'These were terrible days and I am ashamed of what we did. Believe me.'

"Sure, I could have told the others and we would have made his life miserable. May be he would have deserved it. But it's a strange thing when you are in the same boat, eating the same ration, falling down half dead with fatigue at night, scraping for a little extra food. The last thing in your thought is revenge. All you want is to live and find something to eat. I do not believe anyone did anything to those Red Guards who had been sent to join us. We often talked to them. Stripped of their power, they could reflect on what they had done and I can tell you some of them did feel ashamed.

"Wu-Chang and I would nod to each other when we happened to meet. But one evening, it was a balmy night and everyone was sitting outside enjoying the starry night sky when Wu-Chang came and sat next to me. 'Thank you for not telling them,' he said. When I did not reply he was silent for a while, then suddenly he said: 'I often wonder how it happened, how it ran away with us. We were not bad people. I knew everyone. We came from the same campus and I would say no one was really a bad person. We did what we were told to do. We denounced people we were told to denounce. We shouted slogans against them in front of their homes. And when they came out we started a struggle session just as we were told. It was just shouting in the beginning. Then, someone refused to recant and one of us pushed them. And then he pushed harder. Others joined in the pushing and soon we were hitting that man. The public who were ordered to attend these sessions cheered us because, I think, they all wanted to show how loyal to Mao they were, because they were afraid to be next. So on the following struggle session we started right away with pushing and hitting and the crowds cheered and clapped us. We thought: everyone is on our side, we are doing the right thing. So we armed ourselves with canes and wc began to strip the traitors and after we stripped them we beat them. And people cheered even louder and that made us even more confident we were doing the right thing. Then someone died during a struggle session but the crowd cheered us all the same. So now we were not just accusers we were also executioners. And we thought that was meant to be so because everyone cheered us, everyone was polite, everyone was scared and that made us feel very important and untouchable. We could do anything we wanted. People would always cheer us. The whole thing was like opium. My cousin told me you start with a very small dose but gradually you have to increase the dose to get your high. In the end you might take an overdose in order to get up there. That's how it was with us. We became meaner and more diligent every day. But people always cheered us, whatever we did. And they gave us food and drinks, and sometimes even offered us their wives and daughters. Fear is a terrible thing. People will do anything to escape it. They'll do anything to live. You know, not one person ever confronted us or told us we were doing wrong. That means we were doing right, doesn't it?'

"What Wu-Chang told me was chilling. Was it really that easy to become a monster?

"After a while he went on, obviously intent on clearing his conscience.

"'The worst was our headmistress. Someone accused her of being a capitalist roader and they raided her home and found books in English and French. We took her out to the town square for a struggle session. She had always been a fair woman, stern but fair. None of us disliked her at school. As usual we asked her to repent. She said: 'What you want me to repent?' 'We want you to admit you hate Mao Tse-tung Thought, we want you to admit it!'

"'She looked at us and then she said: 'I love you all as if you were my sons and daughters! It is not your fault you are being misused.'

"'That was it. We were furious. We didn't want to be loved by this old crow and in front of all those people who expected us to be tough and uncompromising. And she said we were being used. 'In China,' I told her, shouting so everyone could hear: 'The only love is for Chairman Mao. You are a bourgeois reactionary.' She looked at me and then she said: 'You poor, poor deluded boy. Mao is not you father, he is not your mother, he is not your teacher. Mao is using you ...'

"'After that we beat her to death. And everyone cheered.'"

I did not see Amelia again. She continued to live in the Old People's Home to which she was sent after Deng Xiaoping became Chairman and 'corrected' many of the Maoist purges, allowing the victims of the persecutions to return home. Amelia was swept up during the clearing of the camps in the late seventies and since no one knew what to do with this emaciated foreign lady she was transferred with other stateless old foreigners to the Home for Foreigners in icy and remote Harbin. When she and I parted at our last meeting she accompanied me to the door. "Being a pawn in someone's political game is a terrible curse," she said: "We were all pawns in those days and I never want to be a pawn again."

Many years later I sat in the lounge of a hotel in Peshawar leafing though an old American magazine while waiting to interview a local mullah, when I came across a story written in the exuberant style of young journalists trying hard to extract extra pathos. The gist of the yarn was that an American Senator had gained universal praise – and lots of votes for his re-election campaign – after rescuing from China and bringing to the US an American citizen lost during the turbulent Maoist and post-Maoist era. The story, full of praise for the patriotic energy of the Senator, had virtually nothing to say about Amelia's half a century long ordeal in China but was full of detailed praise for and quotes from the Senator and the generous souls now helping the poor woman to 're-adjust' to American life.

Like all of us, Amelia was still a pawn in someone else's political game.

—

FILIPINO TRILOGY

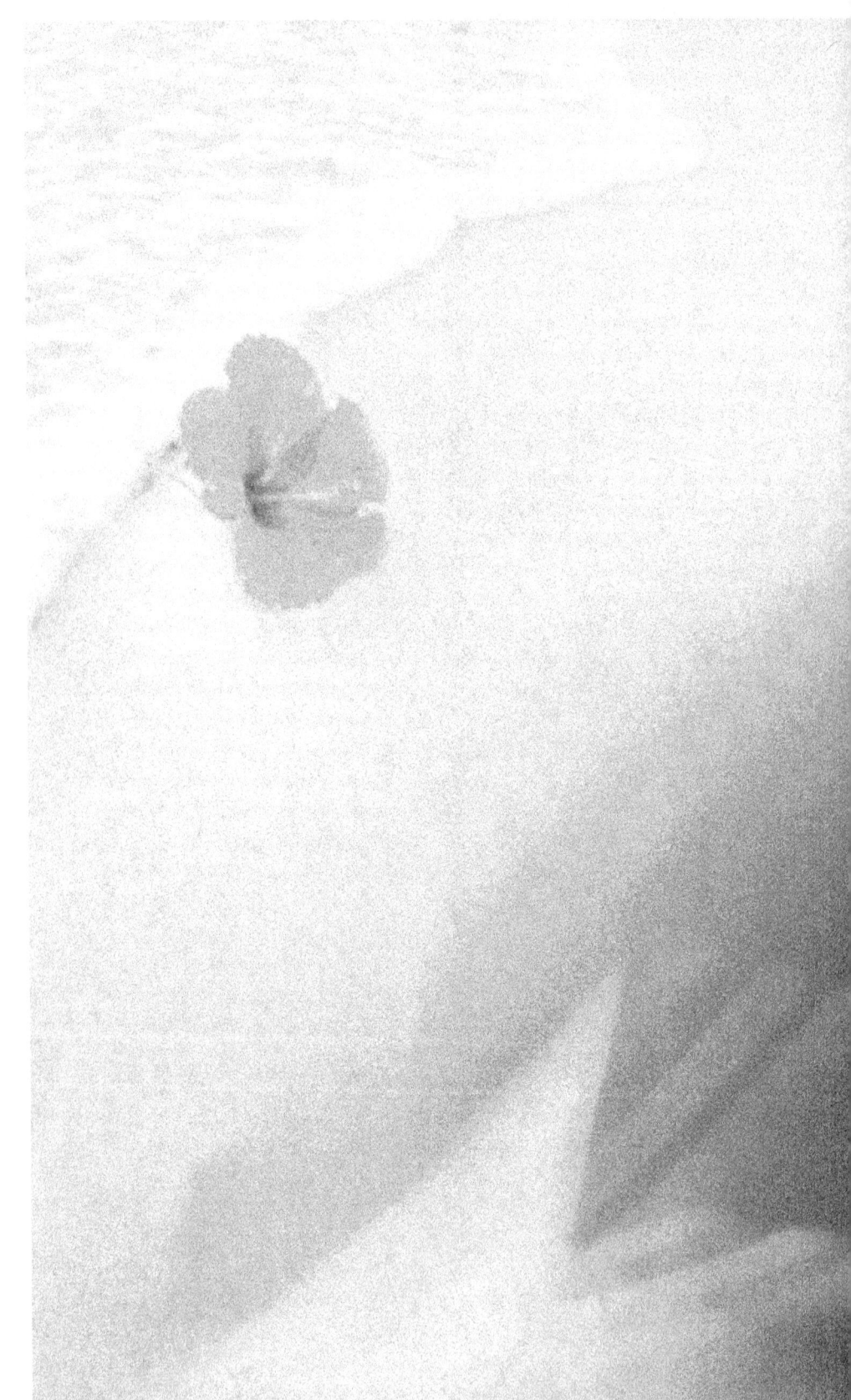

FIVE

Myra

Myra Acosta's body was found floating off Greentree Beach at six o'clock in the morning by Jon-Jon. He was a lanky kid with rickety legs and a mouth always open in astonishment at the world around him. The locals cruelly dubbed the boy 'The Halfwit' but treated him with the kind of tolerance and condescension people who consider themselves normal reserve for the non-normal, in short those not like them. As was his habit Jon-Jon had fossicked through the shallows for mussels which he then sold at ten pesos a kilo to Mrs Celestia. She, in turn, offered them at 30 pesos a kilo to customers in her mini-market. Such commercial deals are common in all impoverished countries where the exploitation of misery raises the wily and the crooked up the poverty ladder.

When Jon-Jon stumbled on the body he ordered it gruffly: "Get up!" and when the body refused to rise he yelled louder: "Get up! Get up! Its daylight! Get up … Get up you lazy pig!" But the body remained immobile. So he took hold of Myra Acosta's limp left arm and dragged her into a sitting position. But the corpse refused to remain upright. The raised torso simply rolled back into its supine position. Enraged, Jon-Jon kicked it, viciously and repeatedly, the way his father kicked him if he slept in.

It was a good ten minutes before anyone took notice of Jon-Jon's exhortations for the body to rise. That was not unusual. The people of

Port Perry had become accustomed to the solitary shrieks and monologues emanating from the throat of the disturbed son of a canoe fisherman. Myra's body would have remained in the shallows for most of the day had not old Tom Tatabunga, nursing a buzzing headache after too much fermented coconut juice the night before, yelled at the boy to shut up. But Jon-Jon kept shrieking and Tom, who had a terrible temper, more so after a heavy drinking bout, came out of his hut, staggering a little but determined to clip the 'halfwit' behind the ear. He stopped short when he saw the body. His raised fist slowly dropped until it hung loosely by his side, his fingers opening and shutting nervously. For a while he stared silently at the grim sight, not quite sure whether he was seeing reality or having one of his boozy spells. Since the image would not go away he decided it must be real and so he began to yell at no one in particular but to all and everyone within earshot: "Call the Barangay Captain! Call the Barangay Captain …"

No one in Port Perry had need of a post mortem to determine Myra Acosta had died as the result of a bolo (machete) blow that almost severed her head and must have left a pool of blood on the sand before the high tide washed it away. What the villagers saw was a pallid, sapped version of the shapely body that was once Myra Acosta, proprietress of the PalmaAlta resort, mother of three children, the closest Port Perry had ever come to a femme fatale and a business tycoon. Her feminine charms and silver tongue sold to gullible foreigners dreams of hammock life among coconut trees on the shores of a gently lapping South China Sea. Her product was tailored for both young and old, all those romantics of the white race in search of a tropical paradise which only exists in novels and the fantasies of travel writers who have never lived in the tropics but allowed their imagination to run amok, penning lusty lyrics of palm trees gently swaying in the breeze while dusky maidens clad in lap-laps and skimpy bras administer exotic cocktails. Myriad scribes have passed through the sultry, humid tropics on the run, like an occasional gust of wind. Their fleeting, preconceived impressions are reinforced by swanky five-star beach resorts built to perpetuate the idea of a tropical paradise peopled by legendary beauties and beaus. These resorts are no more than air-conditioned artificial atolls fenced or walled off from surrounding poverty in which emaciated natives and naked toddlers live short lives in sapping humidity.

Motherhood had left Myra as shapely as it does the majority of Filipinas who tend to give birth with baffling ease. After delivery their bodies simply snap back to vixen shape. Myra's wavy black hair, high cheekbones, burning dark eyes and quivering strawberry lips fitted perfectly into the peddled visions of promiscuity under the hot sun. Her looks and her coquetry were proof the ardently imagined and so frequently promised did exist. Blinded by this vision the foreign dreamers readily embraced the commercial joint ventures, spiced with amorous extras Myra so casually dangled under their noses.

The dead woman's dress had shimmied above her knees and the villagers saw she wore no underwear. This was not unusual in a tropical corner of the world where sex is like a snack, guided by appetite and opportunity. Copulation is so constant and so enthusiastic in less then half a century the population has tripled. Of course the Catholic Church has a prominent part in this demographic explosion. Its ban on any kind of birth control or birth control instructions is largely accepted in what is possibly the world's most devout catholic nation – at least the poor segment of the populace. The rich are not as pious as the poor because they are not dependent on sons and daughters to see them safely through old age in the absence of decent pensions and a social safety net. The rich have no aversion to preventive measures to limit the number of off-springs, legitimate or not, who might turn into financial burdens like demands for alimony by dumped mistresses. Like the Church the Upper Class encourages the poor to breed. The more poor there are the more souls for the Church and the more bodies for the rich to exploit and the merchants to sell to.

When someone noted Myra's dress had been ripped at the hem and at the bodice the locals had no doubt she had been raped, the charge of rape being commonly applied by the public to any unseemly sexual activity. Mrs Celestia was the one who noticed Myra's wallet was missing, the one she always carried on a metal chain around her neck. Instantly popular consensus, as good as a post mortem in these parts, diagnosed that Myra had been raped, robbed and then brutally hacked to death. Only toothless Boy Bongo expressed his opinion, loud enough for people to hear, that Myra's end had been long in coming and was utterly predictable.

"I always knew she would end up this way," Boy declared. Though no one voiced disagreement no one had the courage to say he was right. Only old men with one foot in the grave can afford to upset the spirits of the dead.

The problem was now what to do with the corpse.

Myra had no relatives in the village and no close friends. Well, no one who liked her enough to pay for her funeral. Someone suggested a telephone call on the recently installed mobile network to her ex-husband in Sweden. But no one was willing to foot the expense of such a call even before the question came up what number had to be dialed. People were still debating the phone call when Darwin, the boatman from Parrot Island, pointed out their debate was useless because the cell-phone system was down again. As usual the diesel for the generator at the relay station had run out and the company had sent no money to the guard on duty so he could buy more. Someone in the telecommunications company was sitting on the funds, investing them in short term interest and leaving entire villages without communications for weeks while the interest matured. But people did not complain. So the practice continued.

With the Swedish ex-husband out of the fry the next suggestion was the church.

Port Perry had no catholic priest or parish. The Church had run short of priests once the Vatican had decided to crack the whip on priests breaking celibacy by seducing little boys and girls or cohabiting with adults. In Port Perry Catholicism had quietly surrendered its dominance to a schismatic populist sect called Iglesia ni Cristo. Its simple church, a long nave with a cross over the entrance, was the only temple in town. Unfortunately, so someone pointed out, Myra had not been a member of Iglesia ni Cristo because she was vehemently opposed to handing over tithes from her earnings to the church elders, having neither faith in their honesty nor their commercial skills. So the corpse could not be dumped at the expense of Iglesia ni Cristo.

As always when the people of Port Perry ran into a dilemma the problem was taken to the Barangay Captain who had been informed of the presence of the corpse but had decided to keep away from the grisly sight so that he could argue later he had not seen the body. This way he could never be called as a witness and could later plead ignorance. The Barangay Captain is a kind of mayor elected every four years. Teofilo Arias was an impressive man, barrel-chested and build like a little bull. He managed to have himself also elected to six regional committees, each one a source of income. He was a man of instant action with a nose for an opportunity and the conviction he was always right. No one ever contradicted him

Arias called in his factotum, Ernesto, and told him what he wanted done, though the order was to come from Ernesto and not the Barangay Captain. Ernesto was to tell Jon-Jon and two other slow witted young men to dig a hole in Myra's garden and bury the body there. First he said they should borrow a wheel-barrow to cart the body to Myra's resort. After finding two shovels and a pick-axe in Myra's tool shed the three boys set to work watched silently by a crowd of villagers standing back far enough to be able to see but not to be co-opted for help. Once the hole was deep enough, two boys picked up Myra, one taking the legs, the other the shoulders, and held her over the hole. On the command of 'one, two, threeee ...' the boys allowed the corpse to plop into the hole. One of them used a shovel to hammer down the legs which had become stuck. Then the boys shoveled dirt over the mutilated corpse. An old lady fashioned a cross with two bamboo sticks and stuck it on the little mount of dirt. No more was said about the murder, at least in public, lest the authorities got to hear of it.

No citizen of Port Perry was prepared to spend the gasoline on a boat trip across the bay to Saint Jeremy where a part time policeman was supposed to look after the entire archipelago of islands. What could he do? The government had not even given him a boat to visit his island domain. He would insist the boat that brought the news must take him back to the site of the murder and later back to St Jeremy. This meant four trips across the bay, at least an outlay of 400 pesos in gasoline, equivalent to a week's wages and a day in lost and unpaid time. So everyone agreed, without saying so, it was best – and cheapest – to do nothing.

That evening Bing Gonzales, Myra's young caretaker and rumored to have been her last joy-boy, approached the Barangay Captain and complained Myra had not paid him for the last three months. In lieu of payment, however, he was willing to take the generator at PalmaAlta, the one the English tourist had sent out a few months ago, who knows, perhaps for services Myra rendered, so Bing suggested, grinning lewdly.

The Barangay Captain let the quip go. But he was no fool. He realized the generator was worth ten times the amount of money owed to Bing in back wages, if the claim was true, which was unlikely since Bing was not the kind to wait three months to be paid for his services.

"So you are owed six thousand pesos and the generator is worth fifty thousand pesos. Now how do we work this one out, Bing?"

Bing protested, of course. He was on a special wage because he had a special relationship to Myra. And the Barangay Captain must know what he was talking about.

"Bah!" the Barangay Captain huffed: "Myra has never paid for 'special relations'. It was always she who was paid for special relations, so don't give me that caribou shit."

"I got to be paid. It's only fair," Bing whined. But a lot of wind had gone out of his sails and his confidence had ebbed away like the tide on Green Point leaving nothing but a man stripped of his pretense and ready to negotiate any deal.

"Where will you sell the generator?" the Barangay Captain asked.

Bing saw the opening and dived for it: "I know this fellow at Puerto who is willing to give me thirty thousand for the generator," he said, looking expectantly at the man who stood between him and his windfall.

"Hmmm!" the Barangay Captain mused, stroking his chin then rubbing his hands together. He knew this fellow was even now trying to put one over him. But he let it go and said: "Don't sell the generator for less then forty thousand. Understood? You give me half and you keep half. So now you owe me twenty thousand pesos. Once I get the money I give you a piece of paper saying you were given the generator in lieu of wages. If I don't get the money I'll inform the police you stole the generator. Are we agreed?"

Bing made a last futile attempt to raise his percentage of the sale, arguing it was he who would be doing all the work, the transporting and the selling and it was he who was owed back wages. But the Barangay Captain only laughed and finally cut him off: "Take it or leave it. You are getting a damn good deal and you know it. So don't piss me off."

Nothing was secret in Port Perry. Everyone was watching everyone else and if conclusive evidence was missing, creativity substituted. Feuding families gave each other a wide berth in public but in private busily demeaned each other with vile stories. Envy was rampant. So when Bing had the generator loaded on a jeepney headed for Puerto next morning everyone knew he was taking the generator in lieu of back wages, just like everyone realized the generator was worth twenty times as much as Bing could possible be owed in back wages, even if Myra had not paid him since the day he started to work for her, over a year ago.

People catch on quickly.

The first to arrive, while the jeepney driver tied the generator to the roof, was Mrs Celestia who owned the grocery mini-market on Manila Street. She told the small crowd, all gawking at the generator now perched on top of the jeepney like a gigantic icebox, that Myra had left a large debt in groceries. To collect this debt in goods Mrs Celestino had brought her two store factotums. She also knew exactly where to look for her money. Within ten minutes the factotums had carried off Myra's scuba diving equipment, stored in a concrete hut built right on the spot where the Bermuda grass of Myra's resort met the sand of the beach.

Most people in Port Perry knew the equipment, the latest of its type in underwater sport, had belonged to two young Austrian tourists. Myra had convinced them her resort was the ideal place to start a scuba-diving school which they could run during the main season between Christmas and the end of February. The two Austrians, young men from the backwaters of the Steyermark, were delighted with the idea of spending two months a year in a tropical paradise teaching scuba diving to pretty tourist ladies and maybe some dusky local maidens. Their enthusiasm was fueled by Myra's offer to give them, free of charge, one of the resort cottages and include the scuba diving as a service in her brochures, two page pamphlets praising the delights of her resort. She clinched the deal after she had a concrete shelter built to house the scuba diving equipment, a safe storage while the two young men, both plumbers, were back in Austria. At a little ceremony, made more festive by a bottle of bubbly, Myra handed the two young men the key to the concrete shelter. "No one will touch your equipment when you're not here," she said, raising her glass.

Yet every time the two young men wanted to discuss percentages Myra waved them away: "Let's see how the business goes and then we will talk about percentages."

The young Austrians loved Myra – in more than one way.

A week after the shelter had been completed two inspectors arrived from the Department of Land and Environment. An anonymous tip-off had alerted the Department that Myra's shelter containing the expensive scuba equipment had been built too close to the beach in violation of regulations. The two inspectors confirmed that and declared it was now confiscated by the Department.

When the two horrified Austrians pledged to remove the shelter immediately, the inspectors pointed out this was not possible since the shelter must remain as evidence in the case the Department intended to file against Myra and the two men. The inspectors explained that Myra was the owner of the property and thus liable while the young men were the owners of the equipment and thus equally liable. The two Austrians begged the inspectors to let them take their equipment out of the shelter before the construction was taped with a red ribbon and a sign 'off limits'. This was not possible either, the inspectors pointed out, since all the contents of the shelter now came under the jurisdiction of the Department and must remain both as evidence and a guarantee in case the two owners absconded prior to paying a fine, if they were lucky, imprisonment if they were not. There would have to be a court case to determine the verdict. Unfortunately, as always in the Philippines, the case could take a few months before it came up in court, perhaps even a year. But this was a very serious matter.

The Austrians had learned that court cases proceeded at a snail's pace in the Philippines and could drag on for years, even decades. Decisions in the lower courts were immediately challenged and appealed to a higher court. All the way up the judicial ladder palms had to be greased and decisions tended to favor those who paid most. Lawyers had to be paid monthly retainers and cases were 'postponed' dozens of times. Each postponement earned the court – and its judges – hefty fees.

The young Austrians packed their bags, hired a jeepney and had themselves driven to Puerto in time to catch the afternoon flight to Manila and from there the late flight to Frankfurt with a connection to Vienna. Their escape was galvanized by common gossip about Filipino jails, places rumored capable to grind inmates into babbling baboons – unless one had the funds to convert them into homes away from home and the wardens into willing servants.

The two were still on the road to Puerto when Myra wined and dined the two inspectors and suitably greased their palms at the end of a boozy afternoon. She sent them off each furnished with three bottles of Red Label, part of her monthly consignment from a 'friendly' customs official.

When the Austrians phoned two days later from the Steyermark, Myra promised everything would be fine. She would let them know once she had resolved the case. Nothing to worry about, she knew how to handle these matters. She had connections. Leave it all in her capable hands. Meanwhile everyone in Port Perry knew once the Austrians had left the red tape on the abusive shed was immediately removed. From now on any PalmaAlta guest willing to spend US$25 was welcome to the scuba-diving equipment for the day. As for the Austrians: They never returned. A few weeks later when they telephoned again, Myra told them the case had gone badly. She had been fined one thousand dollars and the two foreigners would be arrested if they ever came back to the Philippines. As for the equipment, well, that had been confiscated by the State. Oh yes, she was appealing the verdict, but to hire lawyers and bribe officials she would need money. If they wished to go ahead with the appeal they would have to send her a thousand dollars. She would put in the rest. Oh yes, she told the two, the appeal had a good chance of success. In fact her lawyer was certain the verdict could be overturned by the Regional Court. All she needed was their money.

The two young men from Steyermark, by now smart enough to realize their joint venture had become a bottomless hole, gave up and never heard from Myra again.

A day after Myra's murder, Mrs Celestia made out a cheque to the Barangay Captain for an undisclosed sum. In return she was given a certificate from the municipality. The piece of paper stated she had taken possession of some diving equipment from the estate of the deceased Myra Acosta in lieu of an outstanding grocery bill.

Of course it did not end there.

Over the next few days, the residents of Port Perry discovered Myra had left a long list of debts. Suddenly everyone who was anyone in Port Perry had a bill to collect. In no time PalmaAlta was stripped of its more visible assets, kitchen utensils, a stove, a refrigerator, cutlery and plates before the creditors moved on to the light fixtures, the decorations, the windows, the trellises, the electric wiring, the furnishings and finally the toilet bowls in the five cottages. Some kid even collected the toilet rolls and a guy named Socrates dug up the garden, not for the shrubs planted there, but the treasure Myra had supposedly buried. When he struck human bones he crossed himself and gave up. That's how the rumor started Myra had robbed and then buried some of her foreign guests, lovers and investors, in the garden. Wasn't it justice she should be buried there herself?

On the third day after the murder, Bobot the master carpenter from Puerto, arrived, worried he might have come too late. He had driven the 142 kms on dirt roads as fast as the old truck would go once he heard Myra was dead and people were ransacking her resort. He came with four of his assistants. He took one look at PalmaAlta and sighed with relief: The creditors had not worked their way down to the wood yet, thank God. And so he and his men began to dismantle the dining and playrooms, both built with expensive hardwood that could no longer be logged under a new federal government ordinance. The floor boards alone were worth a fortune.

Bobot could never understand why Myra's old partner, an American, had forked out seven thousand dollars just for hardwood when he could have built the entire structure with a fraction of that amount in softwood. The hardwood would last a lifetime but the American had only a ten year partnership lease on PalmaAlta. You had to hand it to Myra. She had a way with these moon-struck idiots. First she seduced the American, dragging him up to the eagle's nest, the room built high into the roof of the main resort cottage where she slept. Then she had coyly agreed, for the sake of love and her weakness as a woman, to sell him a partnership that must have cost him many times more then he would ever extract from it. Bobot had been hired by the American to restructure and refurbish the entire resort. How did she do it? She was nearly forty, no longer a spring chicken and had fierce competition from all those ravenous young girls looking for a foreigner to marry. If marriage was impossible, because the foreigner was already married back in his foreign country, a girl was satisfied to become his mistress, as long as she was offered a monthly retainer during the time her beau was back with his family in his native country. Of course, as soon as such a mistress managed to have a child with the foreigner the monthly remittance had to be increased. Unless a man was wealthy the expense of two families, one in his native country one in the Philippines, kept him working all year.

By the time the renovations had been completed the American had tired of Myra and was casting his eyes around for a younger version among the dusky Port Perry maidens. And that was when Myra struck. Young girls were terribly promiscuous and more interested in money then love. The American, with a visible penchant for minors, was easy prey. The girl he persuaded played coy for a while and then succumbed to his entreaties and his promises of a pair of jeans and a new T-shirt. She struggled a little and pretended she was scared to lose her innocence, an innocence usually broken even before puberty by someone in the family or from among the neighbors. She even bit him, not too deep, and then she succumbed.

When Myra found out the American had strayed again she found the girl, who was fourteen, and persuaded here to accuse the American of rape. Since the girl was still a minor the American had committed a crime and could be punished with the death penalty under a recently passed law. The intention of this harsh law had been to reduce the prevalence of incest and rape, much of it stimulated by the vicious films spiced with atrocious acts of violence against women. These films had become a trademark of the national cinema in a country where many rural families, often illiterate or backward, really believed what they saw on screen was real. Only the uninitiated were surprised when the country's swashbuckling actor hero, Josef Estrada, better known as ERAP, was overwhelmingly elected President as soon as he decided to take up national politics. Most of his supporters, the great mass of the poor, really believed he would distribute the wealth of the crooked rich to the poor just as he had done on the silver screen. The distinction between fantasy and reality had not yet sunk in.

Needless to say the American was made aware of the severity of the punishment and the fact that foreigners are rarely given the benefit of the doubt in Filipino courts. He escaped as fast as he could reach the airport in Puerto and flew home. And there was little chance he would return to claim his share of the joint venture. His name was now on the blacklist.

The rape victim, so Bobot knew for a fact, received only 5,000 pesos, two months' wages, for making the charge. But she didn't see a single peso of that. An uncle pocketed the lot. When the girl asked for a couple of hundred pesos to buy a cheap cell phone all she received was a smack in the mouth.

As for Myra, she got her resort back, all of it, renovated and restructured. That had been her master stroke.

But Myra was not a woman to rest on her laurels. Within a month she had an Englishman in her bed and on the verge of buying the now vacated partnership in PalmaAlta – even though the American's contract was still valid, at least on paper. But the Englishman must have had second thoughts, or someone tipped him off, because once back in Manchester with his family he sent Myra the giant generator but not a signed joint venture agreement. This was only a temporary setback for Myra. Within a few weeks she had a young German in tow and was seeing her lawyers to draw up another partnership agreement. This time she was going to build a hotel on the resort – with the young German's inheritance.

Her brutal death stymied the plan.

PalmaAlta survived Myra for a fortnight. By the end of those two weeks only the low concrete walls of the cottages stood, like ruins from a bygone era. Even the thatched palm-leaf roof had been ripped off by a late debt collector. The last items carted away were the sewage pipes. Someone even dug up and rolled up the Bermuda grass and sold it to the Alaskan pilot building a villa on Long White Beach. In no time tufts of sturdy beach grass had grown over the resort.

Throughout this cannibalization of PalmaAlta, the Barangay Captain had left his accountant and the girl's assistant at the resort, seated under a tree in two deck chairs they had requisitioned. The duet worked around the clock in shifts to register every item removed from the premises, its value and the name of the person who carried it off. They then sent out the bills.

Just before Independence Day the Barangay Captain drove into Port Perry in his new four-wheel drive Safari SUV.

—

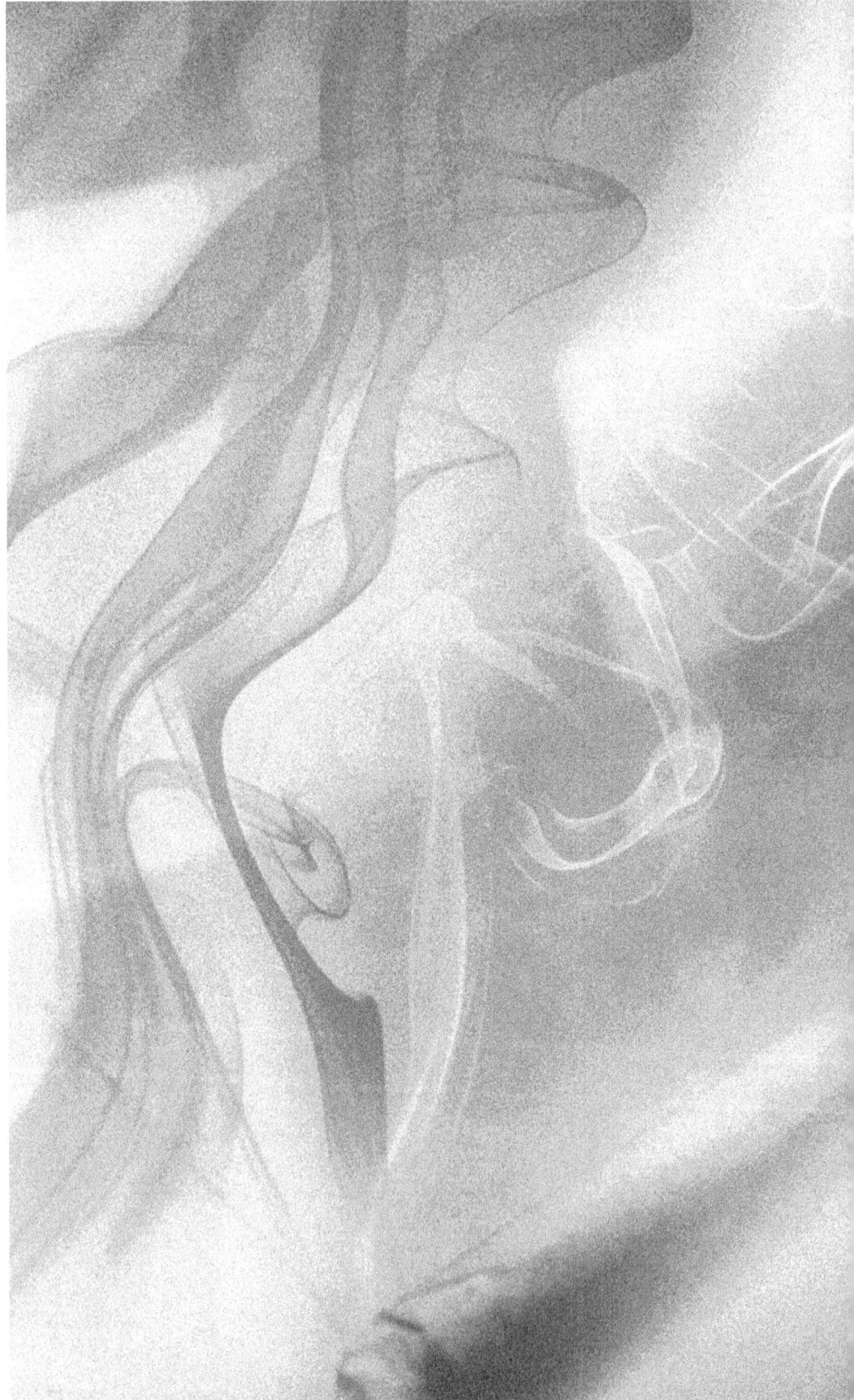

SIX

Evelyn

Two days after Danding's funeral, Governor Morphin Madraga set out after breakfast to hunt communists. The urge to 'bring in a couple of scalps,' as he used to say, came upon him periodically and usually followed reports of the sightings of fighters from the communist Peoples Freedom Army (PFA). Lately there had also been reports that hooded "terrorists" had infiltrated from the Islamic regions in the South. The report of separatists dubbed terrorists on his territory gave Madraga the moral and legal right to hunt two types of prey.

The Governor had never been too selective as to who he gunned down as long as they were bipeds and could be classified 'enemies.' He would bring back the bodies, slung over the bonnet of the Humvee like stags or wild boar. He never shot more then two. None of the corpses had their weapons with them. The rifles, so the Governor's minions explained, had already been confiscated and 'neutralised' which meant they had been destroyed. No one ever asked the Governor how he had destroyed the captured arms and why he couldn't bring them in, together with the corpses. Of course, evil tongues claimed the corpses had never carried arms and the Governor had fired a warning shot at them as they peacefully strolled on back roads or toiled in the fields. The victims had then run for cover pursued by the Humvee. Eventually the Governor would fire the fatal shot or shots.

But this was only whispered gossip among close friends. No one had ever come forward with proof or found a witness willing to denounce these extrajudicial killings, if they were such.

Each time he left the governor's mansion at Puerto Rey Governor Madraga stood inside the gun turret on the roof of his Humvee, like a soldier on parade. On the streets people stopped to stare at this military figure in the turret, dressed in battle fatigues and tipping his temple with a right index finger to acknowledge his intimidated audience. The Governor, puffing on a Cuban cigar stuck in one corner of his mouth, leant against the armour plate reinforcing the rear of the turret while his left hand held the grip of an M240g/b mounted machine gun. The Humvee, a US military version, was outfitted with armoured doors, bullet-resistant glass, a ballistic windshield, rear armour and floor plates to protect the occupants against explosions. All of this was elite US military equipment. The Governor's personal bodyguard, Bobot, was at the wheel of the Humvee. Behind him sat two other security guards, both armed with US Army issue Armalite AR-15 rifles, each with a 25-round magazine. Stuck in a holster on his belt the Governor carried a Beretta M9 pistol with a 15-round clip.

On that particular morning Madraga was particularly anxious to impress two American correspondents and a radio talk-show host who had come to interview a Governor notoriously successful as a guerrilla hunter.

No one was surprised therefore when the Governor returned with two bodies draped over the bonnet of the Humvee. Both had been shot through the chest, or as cynics would have it, shot through the back as they ran, the dum-dum bullets exiting through the chest leaving ugly gaping holes and blood-drenched bodies.

While his American colleagues gaped at the bodies, Akile Ortiga walked up to take a closer look. No expert in matters of gunshots, he was uncertain whether the holes clearly visible in the backs of the corpses were exit or entry wounds. When he tried to roll over one of the bodies the Governor shouted: "Don't touch them. They might be booby-trapped."

"Give us a break," Akile replied: "They'd have blown up when you lifted them onto the bonnet, wouldn't they?"

"There could be a timer on them," replied the Governor who was never short of an answer.

"What are they, Moslems or PFA?"

"PFA" the Governor said with the kind of authority that tolerates no contradiction.

"And they were armed?" Akile went on.

"Kalashnikovs. Made in China. New models I can tell you."

"Pity we couldn't take a look at those Kalashnikovs," Akile said turning to his American colleagues. "The police might have determined the origin and the sellers, don't you think?" he asked, turning towards the Governor.

"These Kalashnikovs are weapons of mass destruction and need to be immediately neutralized. That's what we do. We don't want them to fall into the wrong hands while they are kept at the police station. I've ordered all captured weapons to be destroyed immediately when found."

Akile cocked his head to one side. "Governor," he said, "does that mean you don't trust your cops? Are you afraid the cops might sell the weapons, to the highest bidder?"

Madraga chomped down on his cigar and squinted through his left eye, a habit whenever he scoured his brain for an answer to a tricky question. He took the cigar out of his mouth and spat a petal of lose tobacco which landed a foot from Akile's right sandal.

"I'm glad you brought this up," the Governor began. "I've been requesting the government for years to provide us with funds to build a safe, secure police station where we could deposit captured weapons and prisoners without fear of someone breaking in and liberating both weapons and inmates. But the government ignores my requests. So we have to destroy the weapons ..."

"And the prisoners," Akile added, sotto voce, though everyone heard it.

The Governor ignored the aside.

"So everyone has to take your word these men were armed, right?"

The Governor squinted at Akile. "Are you calling me a liar, Mister Voice?"

"No, I'm only stating a fact, Governor."

"I have three witnesses with me all the time. My guys can collaborate what happened and I am also the elected governor of this province. My word is my bond with the people. Is that enough for you? Now if you've finished gawking at these poor misguided idiots, or what's left of them, you might want to come in and have a drink. Terrorist-hunting is thirsty work, my friends."

But Akile was not finished. He intended to sow some doubt into the minds of these American correspondents. The only unpunished criticism the local tyrants tolerated in the Republic was the one that came from the American media.

"Governor," Akile said: "I've heard rumours some of these so-called terrorists were ordinary peasants provided with arms by your men and told these arms were to defend themselves and their families against communist and Moslem terrorists. What do you say?"

For the second time the Governor took the cigar out of his mouth. His face went red. Those who knew him braced against a violent outburst. He had a notoriously short fuse. But Governor Madraga could also control himself when necessary, particularly in the presence of a foreign media that could make him or break him in the eyes of an America which treated the Republic as a surrogate colony, stationing air and naval bases on its territory. The two American correspondents gawked at the Governor, partly baffled by the accusation, at the same time tasting the stench of a dirty story, something that would sell newspapers.

"My dear American friends," Madraga began, bowing slightly to the American female correspondent, "the Communists are sons of bitches who invent lies and propaganda every day. And this is a good example. Are they saying I give the peasants weapons so I can shoot them later? My own people? The people who voted for me, who keep my Province running? Am I a maniac? Do I look like a maniac? Come on, Akile, you know better then to repeat these puerile Commie slanders. You're an intelligent man, how can you ask me a question like that? You know the Reds are desperate. We've nearly eliminated them in this province so they're grabbing at straws to undermine my administration. You should hear what else they say about me: That I beat and torture my wife, my wife, the mother of my children? And that I brand my body guards with hot irons if they look at my wife … and so on and so on. Is this really worth wasting our breath on, trash like that? Is it? Now let's go and have that drink."

Akile could have pressed the matter further but Danding's funeral had left its mark.

* * *

On the day his best friend was buried, the hibiscus was in full bloom, its flowers a garland of red and yellow petals. Across the cemetery wall, fringed by bougainvillea, clouds of black-winged butterflies gambolled drunkenly. No one knew where the butterflies came from or where they were headed. Some locals speculated they must have crossed the Sea or danced up from the Moslem South, wave after wave of black pilgrims returning, like the turtles on White Beach, to their place of birth to deposit the embryos for the next generation.

Maybe they were lost souls, Akile thought, bound for a mysterious destination. Possibly neither the butterflies nor his dead friend had any idea where both were headed, where it all ended. Still he felt a morbid satisfaction in this coming of the butterflies and their passing over Danding's simple black coffin, swathed in Myral crowns and bouquets, strapped down in the back of a hearse that had seen better days but was apparently the best the city could offer 'The Voice'. Akile curled his lips in a cynical smirk: It was obvious any kind of governmental mourning would have been considered excessive for the funeral of a man who had nothing but venom for the city fathers and their regional and federal masters. Thank heaven for the bouquets. There was something honest, sweet and straight from the heart to the bunches of wildflowers, ribboned with cheap cloth or the hibiscus and bougainvillea petals tossed handfuls into the open hearse by people visibly grieving for the man who had spoken every day on radio what they did not have the courage to say out loud, at least not in public. The spontaneous offerings covered the coffin like confetti. To Akile's delight, the shower of popular love smothered many of the Myral wreaths, tyre-sized ornate monsters trailing silk banners big as flags to accommodate the embossed black letters offering condolences from the Mayor, the Governor, the police chief, the Municipal Council – and even one from the President.

Everyone among the suspects had made sure their wreaths were prominently displayed to avert suspicion of involvement, of being branded – by vox populi – the guiding hand behind the bullets that ripped into

Danding's chest while he stood watching the shapely figure of fifteen year old Adelita Barok disco-dancing at Aquinaldo Square, admired by a crowd so thick and so mesmerized by her erotic contortions no one noticed the killer who pulled the trigger three times, certain the shots would be drowned by the infernal din of the massive loudspeaker system or would be mistaken for the occasional backfiring of badly tuned tricycle engines.

The three bullets had not been sufficient to wipe out Danding's life in an instant, not before he managed to whisper something into the ear of the young woman, a passing nurse, who had bent over him to offer first aid, believing he had fainted, when any aid was already too late. Akile was determined to find that woman, a certain Amelia Potong who worked at DocD's psychiatric clinic but had not shown up for work ever since the shooting. Nor had she been seen at the boarding house on Mayflower Street where she bunked with two other nurses. At least four people had witnessed Danding whisper something in her ear before he died, so they told reporters who covered the assassination. The media believed Danding's whispered message was now the key to the murder. His supporters were convinced that with his last breath he had named the hand that armed the killer. But no one could find the recipient of this vital clue. She had vanished into thin air. Perhaps the 'black hand' that armed the killer had already taken care of her or she was smart enough to realize her life now hung on a thin thread and had run away, hiding among relatives or friends in the remote and unexplored parts of the Republic. It was so easy to vanish in this country.

While the assistants of the mortician, four men dressed in frayed black suits, lowered the coffin into a gaping hole the toothless cemetery custodian had dug that very morning, Akile wondered who among the senders of these ostentatious wreath tributes had also sent the killer.

* * *

A day after the funeral, Akile decided the time had come to take up the causes of his dead friend. He wrote a letter to Amnesty International on the pink notepad paper he had inherited from his late mother. In the letter Akile offered some of the sentiments he had shared with Danding, like the belief the Republic had become the best example of how neo-liberalism, no longer tied to social laws and brakes on its activities, had sucked the lifeblood and decency from a country that once prided itself on its Christian faith and sense of justice. He complained that religious sects and a fundamentalist Catholic Church had channelled the passion of ordinary people into pious rituals rather than a rebellion against blatant injustices and official crimes. He compared the Republic to its mentor, the United States, which also had been a beacon of hope for humanity before it fell into the hands of unscrupulous profit-obsessed corporations who had presidents and legislators elected on the power of their campaign contributions and their control or ownership of the media. Akile asked Amnesty International to denounce the murder of dissidents and journalists in the Republic, people who had criticised the government or exposed the crimes of local governors.

Akile gave a second letter to Boy Perez, the only person he could trust because the young man was simple and incapable of harbouring mercenary or ambitious thoughts. He told Boy to make sure the letter reached his wife should something happen to him. Boy looked at Akile with his dark, fathomless eyes chewing over the order before he asked: "What could happen to you?" Akile placed his arm on the young man's shoulder: "Nothing," he said: "It's only a precaution." Boy sighed and then his face lit up as if a weight had lifted off his shoulders, together with Akile's friendly arm.

In the letter to his wife, Akile gave a detailed report of two bank accounts and the location of a bundle of government bonds. He had bought the bonds four years ago, prior to joining the race for governor as an independent candidate funded by environmentalists and citizens, all hoping against hope for an end to the Mafia-like dominance of political caciques and family clans. Akile knew his candidacy was no serious challenge to the oligarchs who rotated leading roles on the electoral merry-go-round. The clans did not fear his performance at the polls but his acid tongue which had always supplemented Danding's, now silenced. Rather than waste the campaign funds on expensive placards bearing his photo or on flyers distributed throughout the province Akile felt he had the right to use the donations more wisely.

Since he was taking a major risk to his life, it was only fair his family should have something to tie them over if the worst happened. After all, at every election throughout the Republic, a fair number of those standing in opposition to the entrenched political forces were shot dead or met mysterious accidents. So he bought the government bonds. To hide the absence of the funds de-routed for personal use he had the bright idea to campaign as a pauper. For his campaign rallies he dressed simply in a T-shirt, jeans and sandals. He banned balloons and other decorative election gimmicks, among them mini-skirted dancing girls and the handout of presents. To give his campaign a 'green' spin (since the 'greenies' had been his major contributors to the bonds) he wrote his slogans on discarded plastic bags with black felt pens. Finally he re-activated his parent's ancient and rusted jeep to serve as his campaign wagon. He did not even bother to give the rust-bucket a coat of fresh paint except the slogan in green on both sides of the chassis:

AKILE ORTIGA FOR GOVERNOR

From the roof of the jeep he had addressed the people of Puerto Rey and the surroundings towns. In his white barong he had talked in short bursts in the common man's native dialect spiced with the idiosyncrasies of a language rarely used in its colourful original form by the upper crust of the Republic, which spoke American-English just as their grandfathers had spoken Spanish, in both cases the language of the colonial masters. Akile addressed his audiences while standing corralled inside a wooden platform with railings, a platform precariously balanced and fastened by ropes to the cabin top of the jeep. Whenever carried away by his oratory, the platform began to slither perilously, now in this and now in that direction like a high-rise building swaying during an earthquake. But on such occasions, Akile was immune to all external phenomena. Once he gave vent to his oratorical indignation he became a man in a cocoon, oblivious to surrounding phenomena. He was like someone dreading water unawares he is dreading in the shallows. His most loyal supporters would rush forward to clutch the ropes with one hand, steadying the platform with the other. So engrossed was he in his fiery denunciations of evil, spiced with invectives against the ruling nomenclatura, their corruption, their misappropriation of public funds destined for hospitals and schools, their illegal levies and arrogant manners, the excesses of their spoiled children, the inequality of laws and a justice system for sale to the highest bidder, he and his platform might have been slithering into the vortex of the Madre Volcano unaware and still gesticulating with both arms, shaking accusing index fingers in the direction of the Municipal Hall and the Governor's Palace as the vortex swallowed him up.

Yet Akile was also a realist who harboured no unrealistic expectations. He knew he had zero chance of being elected even though thousands and thousands attended his rallies and listened, enraptured by his rhetoric about the inadequacies of the justice system, the corrupt education and health care systems, the greed of doctors and teachers who extorted money from the poorest of the poor and pocketed most of the allotted budget; how officials hawked the region's natural resources to foreign bidders with no profit for ordinary people; how logging had depleted the only rain forest, felling hundred year old hardwood trees until not one was left, at which point the king of loggers suddenly converted to environmentalism and gained positive publicity by restocking the forest with cheap and fast growing softwood trees. The scheme was touted to the public as an environmental success story. A gullible or corrupt media applauded enthusiastically while environmental agencies praised the logger king when only months earlier they had vilified him.

Akile was aware his candidacy had only nuisance value because it allowed him to express in public what most people, even the poor and uneducated, either knew or suspected. Under the freedom of speech prerogative during election campaigns, he could expose the evil of a governing system that vaunted itself as a democracy but was in fact an oligarchy subdivided into provincial fiefdoms run by families, their retainers and militias, the latter thugs grandly labelled 'security guards'. During election campaigns he could name those who had deprived the people of their constitutional rights to free education and adequate health care. He talked of federal budgets that found their way into politicians' pockets or the pork barrels of political parties, immensely enjoying the animated faces of his audience, their wild clapping and the constant nodding of their heads. Everyone was on his side – until the moment their ballots were cast.

The reality was this: He simply could not match the blatant handouts of money and goods, the pledges for projects he knew would never be delivered, the promises of jobs and constructions not even on blueprint yet, the universities, high schools and hospitals that would never be built, the pledge to asphalt or cement roads that would remain dust tracks, the water pipes and electricity cables no one ever received. People, the poor gullible public, fell for such promises coupled with campaign parties where candidates offered roasted pigs to the populace, plastic bowls and buckets for the housewives, cheap Barbie dolls and toy tanks to the children and bottles of cheap plonk to the men. Common folk fell for these empty gestures just as readily as children fall for the story of Santa Claus and his sack of presents at every Christmas.

He knew the campaign machinery of his opponents was well greased, the messages well peddled and if everything failed the thugs and stooges could deliver entire towns and villages, making sure people – if necessary by knocking heads and rubbing out a few trouble makers – voted for the right candidate, their candidate. In this way clans had clung to power for decades. Generations of voters had never known anyone but the same names at the head of local or federal government. The clans alternated governorships and mayor-ships between husbands and wives, sons and daughters, nieces and nephews, sons-in-law, daughters-in-law. In this way the law which allowed only two terms was easily circumvented and the façade of democracy maintained for the outside world.

Akile realized he was hated by those he denounced as thieves and hypocrites. He knew he might not survive for long if he kept up his verbal tirades. Already the number of assassinated critics of the elected democratic system stood at one hundred and forty-seven and the number kept going up in spite of the irate denunciations by foreign media backed by a plethora of toothless human rights organizations pocketing funds in return for useless sanctimonious rhetoric. He did not have to wait long before he received the first death threats, inside envelopes delivered by mail with letters cut from newspapers and pasted into ridiculous messages such as 'STOP.' Soon these messages became more menacing: 'WATCH YOUR BACK' until one day a dum-dum bullet was sent to his radio station inside a parcel tied with a ribbon in the colours of the Republic. Then, always in the mail, came a photo of his home with two of his children playing outside. In panic and by night he dispatched his family to a friend in a far away province of the Republic. Two days later a rock crashed through the front window of his home. Wrapped around it was a piece of paper with the message: 'LAST WARNING.'

By then, however, he was too involved, too involved in soaking up the adoration of those who saw him as the torchbearer of a better tomorrow. In reality only simpletons believed Akile had a real chance of becoming governor. Some who followed his bandwagon were leftovers or discards from other electoral camps who joined for the free ride, wisely keeping their own mouth shut, letting Akile take the heat, and, if it came to that, the bullet. Of course the bulk of his supporters were bona fide believers, idealists with a steadfast faith in miracles and the goodness and courage of the common man. These people visualised Akile as the Messiah leading the faithful to the promised land of true freedom and true democracy – though everyone had different opinions what constituted true freedom or true democracy.

Akile was an intelligent man, aware he had been inescapably dragged into ever deeper waters by a populist current he could no longer control or escape. Deep down in his heart he knew he could not turn back and there was no safe beach waiting for him, nor the miracle of a passing bam-boat or a fisherman paddling his dug-out. Neither did he want to seek protection from the church. He was not religious and could never accept that the God humans invented could permit the injustices and barbarities of the creatures he had made in his own image. He loathed a religion which had subjugated the poor by promising them riches in the Afterlife, channelling their passions into a faith that made sure nothing changed in daily life and no one rebelled against the evil earthly system.

Oh yes, more then once Akile had been approached by the devil in the unctuous person of one of those third rate lawyers, favourite messengers of men in power. When he rudely rejected the thick envelope the lawyer had tried to squeeze into the pocket of his denim jacket, clumsily probing for an opening before Akile brushed his hand away, the man came back a few days later with the question: "How would you like to head a new modern veterinary hospital? The government feels you are just the right man for it."

Akile knew no such hospital would ever be built and the offer was a carrot to throw in his lot with the status quo. As a reward for dropping out of the race and keeping his mouth shut he would be offered an official post, some obscure tenure as 'assistant forest inspector,' or 'sub-director of public health', tasks he would never have to perform. Still there would be an office occupied by a dried up secretary, a former mistress of someone with a name, now shunted off to a state of semi-retirement rather than a pension she could not live on. She would be manning a telephone and one or two empty filing cabinets, one of the hundreds of thousands of petty bureaucrats parked uselessly in public offices to swell the voting pool and provide employment for loyal past services during political campaigns or in bed – or both. Often dubbed parasites by the public, these minions were left to supplement their lean government stipends by soliciting bribes – cash in the city, food in the rural areas – for the smallest favour or the procurement of the myriads of bureaucratic documents any citizen required in order to set in motion any task, from connecting electricity to selling cucumber on the street corner to legally burying their grandmother. Each year more of these required documents and fees were invented to allow the inflating bureaucracy to fatten itself on kickbacks and at the same time fill government coffers depleted by the growing greed of the elected politicos.

If he accepted the bait he would be granted a decent monthly stipend and become, in time and if he proved his loyalty, eligible for a more senior official post. Akile had rejected the baits.

In the election four years ago he had polled five per cent of the ballots cast, more than he had expected.

The governor's 'palace' was a pretentious affair, the floors paved with Carrara marble, the brass-knobbed wooden furniture as kitschy as could be expected from a man who had gained his culture and education in swanky schools and colleges in Las Vegas and California, hobnobbing with other international scions of the rich clans who dominated and still dominate the Third World and the liberated colonies of the fallen or faded European empires. The three media personalities sank into easy-chairs so deep it would be a struggle to rise under the influence or make a quick getaway, so Akile thought.

As he sipped his gin and tonic, only half listening to the exploits of the governor and his boasts of achievements in the province, he remembered

Danding's description of a similar visit and the outrage Danding sparked when he went on the air and referred to the Governor's manhunts, making it clear the victims were not always, or maybe never, what the Governor claimed. The transmission caused enough public anger to prompt the President to make a tepid pledge that the administration would look into the allegations. Danding knew Madraga's political clout in delivering votes was far too big for any presidential sanction. So two days later he went on the air again and told the story of how Evelyn Madraga had taken him aside during a drinking session; how she had rolled back the long sleeves on her dress to reveal deep burn marks which she claimed were made by her husband with a lit cigar during fits of jealousy. In his talk show Danding had pointed out that the governor's wife had no recourse to the law because the Republic had no laws to protect battered wives against brutal husbands. He had called on the President, herself a woman, to push legislation to protect battered wives. The answer from the presidential palace had been that if a woman was maltreated she could go to the police.

In his next talk show Danding said the police would probably laugh at a wife's complaint or make fun of her, even worse, try to take advantage of her. He had indicated that men like Governor Madraga had the police in their pockets, that men like Madraga could kill and claim those they killed were terrorists, they could torture their wives and claim they burned their arms while ironing – and everyone would have to believe such men because they were above the law. Madraga's own mother had been a victim of male chauvinism. She had been a successful actress before she married the governor's father, a small landowner with a penchant for gardening, who immediately banned her from participating in any further cinematic ventures. For the rest of her life he kept her – just like his coveted geraniums and rare orchids – hidden from public view. She died, emaciated and pale, not unlike the way his orchards and flowers had died when dementia made him forget to water them.

Danding had raged against a system in which those in power were untouchable, a country in which the rich and the powerful could kill and get away with it, could torture and malign without fear of the law ever catching up with them. He told his listeners the entire government system was corrupt, from the president down to the smallest official in some municipal office.

A week later Danding was dead.

Governor Madraga's wife Evelyn had been a teenage beauty queen and a budding film star when the Governor decided to make her his own. He was fifteen years older and had just been elected Mayor of Puerto Rey, a post he virtually inherited from his father who was Mayor for four terms, two of them nominally, with his wife as the official Mayor even though everyone knew her husband was in charge since the wife was never seen in public and her signatures were surely forged. The young Madraga had already made a name for himself outside Puerto Rey with his exploits as a lover, a wild carouser and a young man caring little about law and order, conscious his father and the family's political connections would quash any official complaint or illicit folly. His best mate and roust companion was the son of a former President. The two youths spent days trawling the capital for fresh female flesh. Popular rumour had it they often forced girls into their cars. These unfortunate victims, most of them teenagers, some no more than twelve years old, vanished behind the smoked windows of the limousine where the seats folded back into instant beds. No case was ever filed in court against such abductions and statutory rapes. The relatives of these mishandled girls usually settled the case out of court with pacifying pay-offs or hand-outs. The Governor, now in his late forties, was still proud and boasted about his hell-raising days which ended, at least so the story went, when he set his eyes on Evelyn Maldonado the day she won the Republic's Miss Teenage beauty contest. He swore to his buddy that he would marry her.

Following the wedding, life ran rapidly downhill for the beautiful Evelyn.

As usual Governor Madraga gave his media guests a tour of his sumptuous palace, built around a portico of Dorian columns on a hill above the city, a hill from which the Governor could look down on the city while the people of the city had to look up to him. It was not the first time Akile had accompanied foreign journalists to the palace, the only way the Governor would speak to him. So he lingered behind. Passing along one of the corridors he jumped when suddenly confronted by Evelyn

Madraga, who not only stood in front of him but whispered in a panicky voice: "Please help me. He keeps torturing me." Taken aback, he could not find words. Evelyn was pale and shaking. Without any makeup she was still stunningly beautiful though her face was drawn like someone who has been in pain for a long time.

"Look what he did to me," she hissed, dropping the straps of her dress, wheeling so he could see her bare back and the bright triangular red mark left by the perfect imprint of a hot clothing iron. "He says I cuckold him which is not true. He's fired shots at our driver because he carried a shopping bag for me into the house. Then he sacked the poor man after punching him in the face and accusing him of trying to seduce me. He's gone mad. Please help me. I've to get out of here but he keeps me like a prisoner. He sends two bodyguards out with me wherever I go. And he says if I leave him I'll never see our two children again."

She held out her arms: "Look at the bruises, he drags me across the floor and kicks me. He is getting worse."

"Why do you think he's is doing this?" a shocked Akile asked, lamely.

Evelyn leaned forward until her face was close to Akile's nose: "He has become impotent. Now he thinks I must be doing it with someone else. He took Bobby the bodyguard into the basement a week ago and thrashed him with a leather strap. He burned him with hot branding irons because he was convinced Bobby was having an affair with me. Please, you must help me."

"What you want me to do?" Akile asked.

"Tell the President. She's a woman. Tell her to send someone to rescue me."

"Why don't you write a letter to the President with a copy to the newspapers? Surely you can post them somewhere."

"I cannot. He has his men watching every one of my moves. He's even bribed the servants to give him full reports of what I'm doing and who I see, who I talk to and what I say on the telephone. I think he is monitoring all my calls."

She bent forward again until Akile could smell the coffee on her breath: "He's abusing me," she hissed, "sexually if you know what I mean. He uses things on me, you know. I got to get away. Help me."

"Why don't you write a letter now and slip it to me before I leave. I'll make sure it gets to the right people. And I can also read it on my talk show. I don't think the President will move if you appeal only to her. She's more interested in votes then in justice and she's not going to jeopardise a whole province for the sake of a battered wife. You need public outrage."

"What you want me to write?"

"What you told me. Alright?"

She nodded and vanished just as mysteriously as she had appeared.

Akile walked briskly to catch up with the rest of the delegation. When he did, the Governor paused in his explanation of a painting he had acquired. He claimed it was a lost Picasso. He spoke over his shoulder without looking at Akile: "Did you say hallo to my wife. You know she used to listen to your radio shows. But she listens no more. Poor thing, she's a bit confused these days. She's under psychiatric treatment, you know. She talks a lot of nonsense and I'm rather worried. We might have to send her away for a cure for a while. We'll see."

Giving his attention again to the painting, Madraga went on with his explanation of how he had obtained the unknown Picasso from an art dealer in Paris. The painting, he pointed out, resembled an abstract monolithic image that could be interpreted, with some imagination, as a male sexual organ in full eruption.

Evelyn Madraga came into the Reception Hall as the Governor said goodbye to his three guests. She was tall and regal and carried a small wicker basket. The Governor, visibly taken aback by her entrance, quickly introduced her: "This is my beautiful wife, the joy of my life," he said walking towards Evelyn.

But she walked right past him towards Akile who felt his heart beating rapidly with anxiety. What was she going to do now? Maybe the Governor was right and she was a little mad. Obviously she had told the story of being mistreated to quite a few people.

Evelyn was smiling in the way she smiled as a hostess during the Governor's receptions. "I'm a great fan of your talk shows," she began, standing in front of him: "So I want you to have this little cake I baked this morning as a gesture of my admiration for your courage in saying to the people what needs to be said."

With that she offered him the little wicker basket. "It's a plum cake, you know, from plums we grow in our own garden."

"Thank you, that's very kind of you," Akile said, taking the basket, fully aware that inside would be a letter. He began to sweat, hoping the Governor would not order his guards to examine the contents of the wicker basket. He obviously did not trust his wife and he seemed to be as stunned as Akile by the present. But would he risk a scandal in front of the two American correspondents?

"That's very sweet of you, my darling," the Governor said. "But you mustn't spoil our friend Akile. He can be quite naughty. But we must be indulgent for he has just lost a very good friend, a man we all admired. Now we hope and pray nothing like that will happen to our friend Akile, don't we?"

With that the governor turned briskly back to his guests and cried: "Thank you, lady and gentleman, for your kind visit. And do come back any time you want. My doors are always open because we have nothing to hide here. Do we darling?" he added, turning to Evelyn who had not taken her eyes off Akile, as if she was pleading with him. Evelyn did not reply.

"My wife is not feeling well these days," the Governor explained with a sigh and a suitably crestfallen expression. "Good bye, my friends."

As the taxi moved away from the Palace, with Akile clutching the wicker basket, the Governor shouted from the stairwell: "Now you be careful, Akile. It's a dangerous job you're doing."

A chill ran down Akile's back. The warning could not be more blatant.

Before he delivered the letter, Akile intended to consult DocD, the only man he could trust for a fair assessment whether Evelyn Madraga was sane or suffering from hallucinations, some kind of mental disorder or a type of childish paranoia in which the husband becomes the monster he probably is but not to the extent the imagination of the sick person creates. In reality, if Akile were honest with himself, he would have had to admit he did not want to stick his neck out for a cause most people would classify as a domestic dispute best kept at an arm's length. Danding had become involved and look where he had ended up. But Danding had always shown more courage. He had taken on the hospital and the crooked health system, the greed of the medical profession and the chronic hand-out system of mayors and governors. Danding had cojones. But what use were cojones to him now? In the end Danding became just another statistic: The 147th media person assassinated over the past decade by killers paid as little as a mechanic's monthly wage to pull the trigger. Did he, Akile, really aspire to be number 148?

Dr Dagoberto Alvares had a small cabin at the back of the Puerto Rey Provincial Hospital. The cabin, divided into two parts housed his reception and consulting room. The reception had only two seats for patients waiting to see him. The rest had to stand outside under an acorn tree. DocD, as everyone referred to him, had a reputation for bucking the system. He often denounced his fellow medics for their refusal to offer services unless they were paid first. He claimed the hospital was 'a filthy rat-hole unfit even as a pigsty.' He did not simply hint on such issues but bluntly told anyone willing to listen that funding for the health service ended in the pockets of politicians and local officials. The Hospital superintendent and the hospital committee (as well as most of his colleagues) loathed DocD. For years they had tried to have him kicked out of the hospital, banned as a psychiatrist and rubbed off the medical register. But DocD was cunning. He associated himself with foreign aid agencies, Good Samaritan organisations like the Alliance of Christian Churches. Their generous donations to his practice made it easy to offer services without insisting on payments.

His fame as an honest doctor who medicated without demanding fees made him not only popular in the Republic where he was considered a saint by the poor but famous abroad. He became virtually untouchable after the World Health Organization (WHO) named him as one of their outstanding practitioners of the year and paid his fare and accommodation to attend a seminar in Geneva. The WHO label was DocD's insurance against being gunned down in the street by someone riding pillion on a motorbike. And he could no longer be kicked out of the hospital or stricken from the register without undesirable international reaction and world-wide attention. In a last desperate slap the Hospital Superintendent argued there was no space for DocD's psychiatric clinic. But DocD foiled even that attempt to have him evicted. He took over the hospital's backyard cabin, a storage room for discarded items. The cabin now wore the bold sign above an entrance without a door:

PUERTO REY PSYCHIATRIC CLINIC
PSYCHIATRIST: DOCTOR DAGOBERTO ALVARES
(and in smaller letters)

NAMED 'WHO' OUTSTANDING MEDIC OF THE YEAR.

SUPPORTED BY THE ALLIANCE OF CHRISTIAN CHURCHES.

NO APPOINTMENTS NECESSARY. FEES PAID AFTER CONSULTATION.

DocD had tried to make the cabin as friendly as possible by applying a fresh coat of paint. One of his patients, a graffiti artist, had sprayed happy clown faces along the walls. DocD's enemies would say the faces appeared to be borrowed from patients in a mental asylum. But Akile had always liked the graffiti. There was something healthy about their grimaces as there was something healthy and abstract about people deemed insane. Such people were simply different. But their difference made others uneasy. So the others had them certified.

The nurse at the reception, behind a desk requisitioned from a schoolroom, informed Akile that DocD's presence had been urgently requested by a surgeon at the hospital who could not handle a difficult patient. "He must be over at surgery," she said.

So Akile wandered through the hospital in search of the psychiatrist. As always the hospital depressed him.

In the wards the beds stood narrowly next to each other, all made of plywood, de facto wooden stretchers with legs. The families or relatives had to provide mattresses or covers from home or leave the sick resting on bare plywood. The hospital claimed it had no linen, mattresses or covers – except, of course, for those who paid. Relatives nursed the sick and remained in attendance around the clock to alert the staff if the patient suffered a crisis, became agitated or lapsed into a coma. Nurses, immaculate in white uniforms, wandered through the corridors bearing that aloof air of superior beings looking after inferior creatures. The head nurse sipped coffee all day in her office when she did not supervise the hospital pharmacy which her daughter ran. The entire hospital was covered by an aura of indifference and abject poverty. Akile often thought the abattoir felt more hospitable, the smell was certainly no worse. He could understand why anyone in Puerto with money had themselves flown to the capital's prestigious Medical Center the moment a health problem emerged.

In a way the hospital was like a big bazaar where medics negotiated prices for operations with patients' families and every medical implement and necessity was on sale. Family members shopped among doctors for the lowest price, usually offered by the least qualified or the fourth year medical student. Men and women with brooms were constantly passing along the corridors sweeping up discarded tissues, plastic bottles, soiled bandages and any other garbage tossed away by patients or medical staff. These sweepers worked off debts for a medical intervention they had not been able to fully pay. They were commonly known as 'debt-sweepers.'

A permanent stink of rotting flesh, puss-infested wounds, ointments, human excrement and flatulence wafted through the wards. Cots stood in crowded corridors along the walls, some even in the toilet. In this place, Akile knew, poor people died without ever seeing a doctor or faded away because their relatives could not afford the medicines required and the hospital would not make them available without being paid first. Patients died because they were not operated in time, because their relatives could not be found or because doctors refused to intervene unless someone coughed up cash. Even then, when the price was agreed and the money handed over, the relatives had to rush to the hospital pharmacy to buy the catheter and cotton wool, the ointments, bandages, the thread to close the wound and anything else the doctor required. All of these purchases later remained with the hospital and were recycled through the pharmacy as new products.

As Akile approached the surgery he stood aside to make way for a man rushing by with a young girl in his arms. The child was moaning in pain. The man stopped a doctor coming the other way down the corridor and begged him to examine his daughter. The doctor gruffly felt the girl's tummy and diagnosed on the spot that she had appendicitis. He said the girl required an operation at once.

"Can you do it?" the father asked. "Yes," said the doctor "but it will cost you five hundred dollars."

"I don't have that kind of money," the father pleaded.

"Find it, get it from someone," the doctor said.

Akile knew what would come next. The father would rush off to the governor's palace or to the Mayor's office to beg for a hand-out known officially as 'emergency funds'. He would stand in line with the rest of the petitioners waiting for the great man to arrive. In the meantime an official henchman would question the waiting throng one by one. He would note down their names, their occupation and their address or home town. Then he would scribble a recommendation next to the name. Eventually, sometimes after hours, sometimes after days, the exalted personage would show up and see a few of the petitioners, offering them financial help but making sure they understood the favour required, eventually, repayment not in cash but in another favour. No petitioner was ever turned away. Their turn to see the exalted personage would simply never come and after being ignored for days or weeks the ignored did not come back. Turning away petitioners would make them lose face and alienate them.

In the corridor the doctor shrugged his shoulder and started to walk away.

"You can ask someone else if they do it cheaper," he shouted over his shoulder at the distressed father.

"Please, please," the man pleaded: "You've got to help her."

The doctor kept walking.

"If this girl dies," Akile called after him "I'll personally hold you responsible."

The doctor turned and frowned. "How many of these cases do you think come in here every day," he snapped: "If we operated on all of them without being paid I'd be a poor man and the hospital could close down."

"Listen," Akile shouted: "There are emergencies and non-emergencies and you said yourself this girl had to be operated at once. So do it!" Akile's indignation was rising. He suddenly felt, as he did often during his talk shows, the onus was on him to try and make a wrong right. He could become obsessed on such occasions.

The doctor stared at him head whipping up and down, lips pursed.

"Who the hell are you to tell me what to do?"

Akile was not intimidated.

"I am the Voice," he snapped. "And if this girl dies I'll make sure you are rubbed off the medical register, I swear."

"So you are that rabble rousing radio showman," the doctor said: "The guy who criticizes anyone with authority. A real know all. Now listen to me Mister Voice. This girl is in no danger of dying. She has an inflammation of the appendix which will probably go away in a couple of hours. It happens all the time."

"Are you saying she doesn't need an operation?"

"Not right now."

"So why did you tell the father she needed one right away."

The doctor gave Akile an indulgent smile, the kind doctors offer other mortals to indicate their superiority in dealing with life and death. "I was preparing him, just in case," he said.

"Ah, I understand, you want him to have the money ready, in case she does need an operation, right?"

"Yes."

Akile took a step towards the doctor, a thin man with a thick black wart on his right cheek.

"And if this man raises the 500 dollars you will operate on her anyway, whether she needs an operation or not. Isn't that right? After all who can check if she had acute appendicitis or not, right?"

The doctor looked at Akile with an air of mock compassion.

"My dear man," he said: "You are allowing your imagination to run away. If this girl doesn't need an operation why would I go to all the trouble to whip out her appendix?"

"For the money."

"Dear me, I can do twenty operations today if I want to – and on people who are in need. Why would I do one on someone who has no need?"

"Because the twenty in need have not come up with the cash yet, dear doctor, but this one has."

"You are sick, Mister Voice. If you broadcast this kind of slander, I will sue you."

"Sue away. Maybe then we'll be able to shed some light on the crooked ways of the medical profession in this part of the world …"

"Now you are being insulting," the doctor said: "I'll have to call security to have you removed from the premises ..."

Akile was about to say something when he was interrupted by a booming voice from down the corridor: "What's going on here ... is that you Akile?"

DocD was tall with the face of an inquisitive schoolboy and a slight stoop that gave him an aura of academia. He was carrying a bundle of the geological charts of the region. He had taken up geology ever since the first foreign mining companies made deals to exploit the island's mineral resources, among them oil and gas.

"I am sure you didn't come to see this third rate butcher," DocD added, waving his charts at the nonplussed fellow medic who was about to open his mouth but thought it better to walk away shrugging his shoulders as if to say who wants to argue with these two idiots.

"Don't forget to look after this girl," Akile shouted at the vanishing figure in white.

"So what brings you to me? You are not suffering from anything mental, apart from the usual paranoia expressed in spasms of indignation prevalent in your profession." DocD chuckled.

On his next radio show Akile made no mention of the letter. Nor did he send a copy to the President or the Ministers for Social Justice. He kept the letter in the locked drawer of his desk and tried to put it out of his mind, though at times his conscience nagged him and he found it impossible to banish the memory of the burn mark on Mrs Madraga's back which, so he admitted to himself, could hardly have been self-inflicted. But over the next weeks the memories and pangs of conscience came more seldom. When they did he would quickly rationalize them away with DocD's impromptu diagnosis that Mrs Madraga was the victim of a common ailment among women married to famous and powerful men. She suffered from chronic neglect. To alleviate her ailment she sought attention in different ways; one of them was accusing the husband of mistreating her. This would draw sympathy for her and punish the spouse for ignoring her needs and withdrawing his affection.

DocD found Mrs Madraga's case was worse because she knew her husband had at least one or more mistresses. The Governor made no secret of his ravenous taste for young flesh openly flaunting his conquests in his wife's face during wild parties at the palace with his buddies and women of dubious reputation. Mrs Madraga could not digest her new role as a sidelined, discarded wife, left to rear two children and appear at official functions with her husband. Since the Republic did not allow divorce, a ban imposed by the powerful Catholic Church, men continued to be married even though they spent more time with their mistresses. The legally married wives were expected to adjust to these conditions in a society dominated by male chauvinism and a Church stubbornly safeguarding the sanctity of marriage, a potent whip, just like sin, of its spiritual powers over the flock. In general the status quo suited the men: They enjoyed it both ways, the wife chained to the children and the marriage – and no right to alimony if she ran away – and the freedom to womanize because the marriage had broken down. Men openly took their mistresses to parties and outings while wives had to be secretive and scared if they indulged in romantic extra-marital liaisons. Marriage was a good deal for men, lousy for women.

DocD's reasoning, presented in his usual 'no-argument' style, had convinced Akile. Still his conscience sometimes pricked him because his intelligence told him DocD was not the ultimate oracle of psychiatry, in fact DocD had a fairly rudimentary education and his fame far exceeded his academic achievements. But one always grasps at straws in order to avoid making painful – and dangerous – decisions. Why did the silly woman marry the Governor anyway? She must have known he was a notorious skirt chaser and had a violent temper. He had never been any good. But most women are attracted to power and money, like flies to honey or moth to the light. They always think they can change the man once he is wedded. And the Governor was filthy rich: His family's bus company had a monopoly in the Republic and their rural estates were among the largest in the nation.

Over the next few weeks Akile did his best to erase Evelyn Madraga from his thoughts – until the day she appeared on national television seated demurely next to her husband, holding his hand or rather having her hand held by his. She told the interviewer in a calm and measured voice, staring straight ahead into the camera, that she had made certain allegations against him and she would like to say here and now these allegations were not true. She had been under considerable mental and nervous stress and now agreed with her husband that she must seek treatment in a rehabilitation centre. She regretted having embarrassed her husband whose public image had been damaged by her allegations. She now wished to recant these allegations and tell the public her husband was a good man and people should vote for him next month when he was standing for another term as governor.

Mrs Madraga poured out her confession in a steady monotone as if she had rehearsed the text many times. All through her monologue her husband firmly held her hand and stared at her each time she appeared on the verge of pausing or faltering. One could tell he knew the text so well he would have prompted her had she lost the thread.

Initially Akile congratulated himself for having been prudent in keeping the letter in his drawer. But something at the end of the interview caught his attention and raised his suspicions again. Almost as an after-thought Evelyn Madraga said: "I am doing this for the good and the safety of my two children. My husband has promised to look after them while I am incapacitated and recovering from the treatment."

At that point a frown had swept the Governor's face like a passing shadow. He had looked at his wife sternly as if this part of the confession had not been included in the rehearsed version. But Governor Madraga quickly caught himself and re-donned the mask of a fixed public smile.

Akile bit his lip. Obviously Mrs Madraga had made a deal. This meant the contents of her letter must be true, why else would the Governor go to all this length to humiliate her in public and present himself as the victimised husband of a mentally unstable wife?

Worse, even if Akile decided to go public with the letter now no one would believe its contents. Who would give credibility to physical and mental torture, threats to harm the children, fits of jealously or that he dragged young girls into the Palace and staged rowdy parties with his pals or that he screamed at the sixty year old gardener: "You've been trying to screw my wife" and tortured and fired the twenty year old assistant chef after accusing him of sneaking into his wife's bedroom to watch her undress.

The contents of the long handwritten note, a note she must have prepared long before Akile and the Americans arrived at the Palace, was short and graphic. But the skeletal sparseness of the incidents she described stimulated the imagination just as a button undone can conjure up visions of much more than a glimpse.

Akile suddenly had no doubt Evelyn Madraga had been tortured and beaten just as she claimed in the letter he found inside the wicker basket. The Governor had subjected his wife to horrendous mistreatments and Danding had been justified in denouncing it all along. And he had died for it. But now she had publicly recanted on television what her husband had done to her. Did this mean Danding had died in vain? Certainly the letter was useless now since she had labelled herself a woman with a mental problem. And people would now say Danding was a gullible fool for believing what she had told him in an ante-room of the Palace. He had paid with his life for his gullibility.

Worse, Akile thought, anything Evelyn Madraga said or wrote in the past would be considered now as no more than the ravings of a mentally disturbed person.

Of course, many people would be sceptical and some would realize her TV appearance was a put up job she was made to perform for the sake of the governor's re-election. But the great mass of people and the paid-off media would pity the Governor – and vote for him.

Akile shuddered at the thought of what she had to suffer before she agreed to denounce herself in public. And why had she done so weeks after the letter? Had she waited all this time for the president or someone to act after receiving her letter, a letter which he had not delivered? Or had her husband subjected her to another torture session and she had confessed to the letter? The Governor must have known the letter had not been handed over – yet. So he made sure, even if it was delivered later on, its contents would be neutralized by her confession of mental instability. This had been a fiendish ploy to silence her forever because no one, in future, would take any of her claims seriously.

He sat with his hands clasped over his face and silently cursed himself and DocD. And he knew there was no way he could remedy the situation or extinguish his cowardice. God, she must have listened to his program every night, waiting, waiting for him to expose her case. In the end she must have realized he would not do it, the man they called the Voice had lost his voice in her case. What a let-down it must have been. And what was this diabolic deal the Governor had made about the 'security' of his own children? Had he threatened to harm the children if she did not recant? He was a monster and would stoop to anything to have his way. And she must have known her confession not only exonerated her husband but placed herself at his mercy for the rest of her life.

News is fickle and quickly forgotten. Yesterday's news is tomorrow's fish-wrap. After the usual headlines the confession quickly dropped from the front page to the inside page. After three days it was out of the papers and the radio shows. No media outlet asked why Danding's killer was never found, nor was the nurse who listened to Danding's last words.

But the headlines prominently announced Governor Madraga's re-election with a large majority, mainly collected on a sympathy vote after his mentally disturbed wife Evelyn jumped to her death from the twenty-second floor of an apartment building where she was kept under surveillance for treatment of her illness.

Evelyn Madraga's suicide did have an effect. Though no one had the courage to blame the governor, a law was tabled in the legislature to create a shelter for 'battered wives' and several women legislators jointly proposed an addition to the penal code making violence against spouses a crime.

Two days after Mrs Madraga's 'suicide' Akile Origa resigned as 'The Voice,' a job he had shared with his buddy, the assassinated Danding. He disappeared and it was rumoured he was dedicating himself to the cultivation of a piece of land his grandmother had left him. He eventually made the news again as the author of a novel. The main character in the novel was a battered wife who took her own life as the only way out of her ordeal.

The book was called *Lidia's Letter*.

—

SEVEN

Sheila

The Fat Fellow had been browsing along shop windows when the two girls hit on him. Both were young. One was dressed in faded jeans and a cheap blue blouse, the other in beige denim shorts and a beige denim jacket. Theirs was the kind of clothing the poor buy from rag-trade street vendors. One of the girls was good-looking, in a skinny sort of way. The other was so plain the Fat Fellow described her in a phone call to friends the same day: 'You wouldn't notice her, mates, unless she stepped on your toes.'

It was the good-looker who had sidled up to him and, out of the corner of her mouth, hissed:

"You like a massage?"

The question was so unexpected in a crowded shopping mall he glanced about him startled to see if someone had heard or if people had stopped in their tracks. But everyone kept on walking. He took a closer look at her then: An elfin face flushed by a smile to make your heart melt. She cocked her head to one side in a coquette sort of way and looked up at him, blinking: "Well?" she said.

Stone a bat she wasn't joking.

The Fat Fellow was flabbergasted. Girls did not proposition men, not back home in Goolagonga, back of Cairns. He remained mute, shell-shocked, even after she had poked a finger in his ribs and promised in a fake seductive voice: "You'll have the time of your life."

And when he still made no reply she added, with a sweeping gesture to include her companion: "We'll both work you over good, you'll love it, Mister." The Fat Fellow had then turned his attention on the plain one. He noticed she had a good pair of pins sticking from Daisy-Mae denim shorts, the kind of legs that could make you forget how plain the rest of her was.

"What's your name then?" the good-looker said, slinging a friendly arm around the Fat Fellow's waist in a sort of 'we're already pals' way. The arm barely managed to cover his back. He was a six-footer of blubber, she was five foot nothing.

"What's your name, love?" she insisted.

"Bruce," he said, lamely.

"Where you from, Bruce?"

"Australia," he said.

"Oh, I love Australia. I have a cousin who lives there."

"Oh yeah," he said: "Where?"

She frowned: "Can't remember. Somewhere where they have kangaroos … you on holiday or business?"

"Holiday," he said.

"Which hotel you in?"

"The Daffodil," he said.

"We can walk there," she said.

So it was true. Young girls actually approached you. His mates had not been peddling fibs, inventing erotic tales to make him feel better about Shirley walking out and taking up with that short-legged, potato-nosed mechanic from Innisfail, a fella' half his size. His mates had promised the place was the Mecca for mending broken hearts, for getting yourself laid, for making your wet dreams come true. And it wasn't hard on your wallet either. In this place, they said, it didn't matter if you were fat, bald, old or ugly – the local sheilas still went for you. These brownies just loved white men, so they had said, any white man, any size, any look, any age, as long as it was white. Mate, they said, for them catching a white man is like winning the lottery. The place was paradise for single and for married men, they said, as long as you didn't bring your wife with you. And the place was crawling with Aussies, they said, mainly men over fifty, looking for a bit on the side or looking for a permanent mate. There were bars just for Aussies and the bar sheilas had learned to speak Oz lingo, like: 'G'day, mate. How's it hang'n today?' and: 'S'truth, cobber, she'll be right.'

"So how much is this massage going to set me back?"

"What you mean?" she asked, feigning innocence.

"How much?"

He was still unsure exactly what this massage was about. The two were so young. It couldn't be what he half suspected. No, the two didn't look like hookers, but then what did hookers look like these days, if you left out the mini-skirted curbside image perpetuated by Hollywood. One only had to read the scandal sheets to discover how many wholesome young sheilas married old buggers but bristled if anyone defined them as gold-digging hookers setting themselves up for life with an old fellow who they figured would soon croak and leave them the loot. Certainly those two who had approached him looked poor, dirt poor. Probably couldn't find a job at a normal massage parlor so they went freelancing.

It was best to get things straight, right away.

"How much do you want?"

The girl looked down on the tiled floor of the mall, as if he had embarrassed her. For a moment he felt uneasy: Maybe the two were simply looking for company and a meal. People in this country were so visibly in need one could count their ribs and the days of grime on their skins because they could not afford to buy water to wash. He was just about to say: "Sorry" when she muttered: "One thousand for her, one thousand for me. You'll have the time of your life, Bruce. I promise. We'll do you good."

"Dollars?" he asked.

"Yeah if you want, you can pay in dollars," she said, smirking at her own crack.

"Right-o," he said: "You'd like that. Wouldn't ya?"

He felt better now. The deal was in the open. He was the customer not the petitioner. And the customer is always right. That was the first rule they taught him when he had started working for the supermarket.

"So what's your name then?" he asked giving his voice the master to servant tone he thought was required to assert his role as the customer.

"Sheila!" she said and frowned when he burst into a kind of horsy laugh that rippled up his throat from a prominent Adam's apple.

"What's so funny?"

"Oh, mate," he said, still cackling: "All women in Australia are known as sheilas. Who gave you that bloody name?"

Sheila didn't tell him she no longer cared about her name. Men had called her Dumb-Bell, Blow-Babe, Recycle-Anne, my Little Brown Fucking Machine and Fanny Galore. She couldn't care less as long as they paid and didn't beat her up as part of the bargain. She knew her mother had given her the name because the handsome blonde fellow who promised her a life of ease 'Down Under' had called her 'My Sheila.' But the blonde fellow took off one day promising to return within a month. He was never heard of again. At the time Sheila's mother was four months pregnant and beginning to show. When there was no sign of Blondie coming back and once the baby was born Sheila's mother took up with Vincent the bus driver down the road, the one who could afford a concrete base for his shack in their shanty-town. He was already married and had four kids, one after the other, like a row of little organ pipes. But he gave Sheila's mother a bit of money now and then, when he had it and when she put out for him.

"It's just a name my Mum gave me. Don't know why she called me that," Sheila lied, looking at the Fat Fellow with eyes 'so innocent,' he would later tell his mates over the phone: 'You could have washed your sins in them and come out clean.'

"You do this for a living?"

"Oh no," she said, her expression horrified at such a suggestion: "We're good girls. But we lost our jobs and we need to pay the rent. And we think you're a handsome man, so strong and big, and maybe you like our company for a while." While Sheila talked, she stroked his back with one hand and smiled up at him, the way a miniature poodle looks up at his master hoping for a biscuit. "We can give you a number one massage. We are very good. And we need the money, Bruce."

The Fat Fellow was still confused.

"But you's don't need two for one massage. So why should I pay both. One sheila is good enough."

She lowered her head the way it was done in the movies when a girl played coy with a fellow: "But you are so big. And we are so small," she said, eyes rolling: "One of us is not strong enough to give you a good time, Bruce."

That made sense to the Fat Fellow. After all he was over a hundred and ten kilos with a beer belly the size of an oil drum and two thousand pesos was barely fifty bucks, just about a decent feed Down Under these days.

"Alright," he said: "Let's go then."

The two girls skipped with joy. Then each grabbed one of his hands and that's the way they walked out of the shopping mall. People barely cast a glance at them. People were used to see bald, potbellied old foreigners towed around by cute young things from the shanty-towns. No one gawked when an elderly Caucasian or Japanese (often unsteady with age or booze) was shepherded to a restaurant in the mall by a girl half a century younger but pretending she was madly in love with the old geezer. You had to admire these girls. They made sure the old boy was seated properly, had his cutlery ready, his meat cut if necessary and was being pecked periodically on the cheek or kissed on lips, shriveled and flabby like an octogenarian's scrotum. Never mind if the old geezer put his hands between her legs now and then in a kind of proprietary manner rather than to satiate a sudden burst of lust. Or if that doddery Japanese, with the two last wisps of hair sticking from a pear-shaped skull, literally drooled over a girl in braids and dressed in school uniform.

Of course any local girl with pride – a pride she could afford because her parents made a decent living – would rather be dead than be seen holding hands with an old foreigner, fat or thin.

* * *

The file in the Prefecture marked 'The Republic v. Sheila Gomez' contained a fair amount of investigation, prompted by the Australian consulate and the family of the Australian victim. The investigation found Sheila had been physically weak from the day she was born, perhaps even while she was still in the womb, a fact that would work in her defense, although, so the prosecution pointed out, a girl did not require a great deal of strength for what had been done. Her mother (deceased), an odd-job woman who whored now and then on the side to make ends meet, had barely enough to buy a handful of rice and some powdered milk to supplement the lactating of her baby. In the end both money and teats ran dry, round about the same time. So Sheila was farmed out to distant relatives. Since she wasn't their child the couple fed her just enough to keep her alive. She was ten when her mother turned up one day and took her back, leaving a thousand pesos and a used cell-phone as reward for having looked after her daughter. The couple screeched that Sheila had cost them a fortune in food and clothing but her mother told them: "Take it or I'll leave her!" The couple took the money and the phone and cursed Sheila and her mother all the way to the bus stop. But when Sheila did her own screeching, unwilling to be taken away by that strange woman who claimed she was her mother, her foster mother smacked her. And when Sheila screamed even louder she smacked her even harder and for good measure Sheila's real mother joined in. That's how Sheila learned to keep her mouth shut and do what she was told.

By the time her mother reclaimed her it was too late to build her up. So she remained thin and rickety, badly nourished all through her formative years. But she had the face of an angel and that face acted like a magnet for all kinds of men, worse of all to Vincent, her mother's long-time lover. He could not keep his hands off her as soon as her mother brought her home. By the time she was eleven he had introduced her to the full gamut of sexual games while her mother pretended it wasn't happening, already visualizing a more lucrative future thanks to her daughter's good looks. Besides, mother always allowed Vincent to have his way, afraid to lose him if she made a fuss.

From such foul beginnings it did not take long before she was offered money by her first Johnny. Her innocent looks, her luminous round eyes, her light skin and crinkly black hair made her an instant success when she took up soliciting – first on the side and after work – and then permanently once she realized, so she told friends, she was expected to give it away free to the bosses at the shoe factory. Her fortune was she didn't look like a whore, she looked more like someone's lost little daughter.

The police investigation and the interrogations yielded evidence that pedophiles had paid her mother top money when Sheila was only eleven years old. The mother would paint the girl's lips red and rouge her cheeks to make her look older. Together they would stroll through Paradise Plaza, smiling at the old foreigners who haunt the place in search of young carnal pleasure. Mother would do the negotiating, always warning the fellow there could be no rough stuff, no penetration and he could keep Sheila only for an hour in the bedroom while she waited outside. Sometimes the men would try to squeeze it in, but Sheila was too small and it hurt, so she yelled and the men stopped, afraid of the mother outside. Some of the men smelled so bad she vomited. But in time her nostrils and taste buds became immune to the stench. When she was older and more confident she asked the men to wash first.

Later on, after she had run away from her mother and taken up with the first pimp, she became a coveted commodity among the pimp fraternity. Her pimp took eighty per cent of her earnings, sometimes all, and often lent her to another pimp or pawned her to a competitor if he was short of money or in need of clearing a drug debt. At seventeen she ran away from the pimps and went to the City Center to work on her own, stalking foreigners in the big shopping malls where only the odd security guard had to be paid off, now and then. Sometimes she worked in twosomes because it was more social and safer too.

The records showed over the years she had developed a pathological hatred for all foreigners. She would tell anyone that she preferred the natives though they paid a third of what the foreigners were charged. The natives always laughed and joked and played up when they did it. Sex was fun and doing it was natural and you didn't have to use broom sticks or dildos or have a golden shower to make it more stimulating. She had definitely developed a loathing for foreigners. For a lousy five hundred to a thousand, peanuts for them, they always tried to squeeze a little extra out of the deal, a second-helping or something kinky so they could boast they had a bargain and they had done this or that abomination free of charge. She would often tell friends these rich foreigners behaved the same way with shopkeepers and souvenir and bric-a-brac vendors. Foreigners bargained and squabbled over a couple of lousy pesos with salespeople who made just enough to buy a couple of bananas for a meal. For those foreigners a bit extra was a mere drop in the ocean. But they bargained as if their life depended on it to fetch the lowest possible price. For foreigners bargaining was a game, their wits against those of the vendors, a game they knew they could always win because the other party had to back down in order to survive. The court record showed Sheila admitted spitting into one foreign lady's face. The lady, so she told her friends, had walked in a cloud of perfume and dressed like a movie star. But she squawked like a fishmonger demanding a discount for a wooden statuette that cost a lousy eighty pesos and took a man a day to make. The record showed she had constantly complained the foreigners she had known were mean, fat, old and ugly. They had beer-bellies, blotched skins and smelled of stale sweat. They treated her like a toy they had rented for a couple of hours and made her do things, not just in bed but little things like 'go and fetch me a towel in the bathroom' or 'go down the shop and get me two aspirins and a packet of Marlboro.' Foreigners rarely took a shower even when she asked them nicely. She had become chronically nauseated by their smell. She was poor but she took a shower each time she walked into a hotel room. Showering was a luxury. In the shack where she lived with two other girls the three had one bucket of water a day and that was for drinking and for cooking too. And that bucket cost a lot of money.

(A note was attached to the file, apparently for the benefit of the Australian legal adviser. The note said water had become an expensive commodity in the shanty towns ever since the urban water supply system had been sold to private enterprises which paid the government a fee. The government argued it could not be blamed for the exorbitant cost of water since the private companies' always defended their greed with the excuse of 'rising costs.')

* * *

The Hotel Daffodil was already notorious among expatriates for its colorful history. During the years of the Vietnam War and the US bases at Clark and Subic Bay, it had been a favorite hang-out for G.I.s and their local girlfriends during weekend R&Rs. But the hotel lost its main clientele when the war ended and many of the bases were downsized. Then in a shock decision for the Americans, the Philippine legislature had voted against renewing the leases on the two bases. Both were dismantled. By the late 1990s the hotel enjoyed a revival thanks to the peaceful return of the Japanese who exploited the cheap labor market and the loss of handouts and kickbacks when the Americans left. All of a sudden the Hotel Daffodil was booked out by elderly Japanese men who came on organized package tours. These tours included a girl companion for the duration of their stay. The packages fell into two categories: The "De-Luxe" tour offered a girl who spoke Japanese because she had been to Japan as a maid, an entertainer – or worse. The "Standard" tour provided a young girl who did not speak Japanese and sat there at breakfast, lunch and dinner mute. But she had been trained to arrange the cutlery, cut the meat, fetch more coffee and do the talking to the waiters while her master sat ramrod straight, Buddha-like, being fussed over – exactly what he had paid for and what he had envisaged in his fantasies.

The nineties were the golden days of Japanese tourism. The men from Nippon took up the slack the GIs had left. The birth rate in Japan had declined rapidly because Japanese women refused to marry and become servants of their salary-men spouses who would drink themselves stupid in obligatory after-work parties and then come home on the last Metro expecting a meal on the table and the wife ready to service them. The shortage of women willing to marry was particularly acute in rural areas. Any reasonably attractive female headed for the cities to escape the drudgery of male domination and the back-breaking work in the fields. Traders in human flesh exploited the shortage in women willing to wed. Japanese peasants needed wives – and workers. And the rapidly exploding Asian population had a surplus of eligible women, many of them already married but ready to pretend they were single so they could earn money for their families.

In small towns and on the outskirts of cities Mayors and local entre-preneurs organized bridal shows for tour groups of Japanese men seeking a Filipina bride. The shows were mostly held at the municipal halls and as many as one hundred girls would offer their physical assets on stage for prospective Japanese buyers in the audience. The girls paraded in dress and swimsuit, like the Miss World and Miss Universe contestants on TV. Each girl had a number glued on her thigh and the prospective buyer, or husband-to-be, would tell his tour guide he would like to meet the number that caught his eye. If two or more contenders were interested in marrying the same girl, she was asked to make the choice. If the viewing of the ware was successful and the buyer was satisfied he made an offer, a gesture known as 'a donation' to the girl's parents and another 'donation' to the town fathers for arranging the show. But there was no free sampling of the goods prior to the wedding vows. The 'bride' was treated like a lilywhite virgin, untouchable until the wedding night which followed a mass wedding ceremony officiated at the municipal hall by the Mayor. He also issued the couple a civil wedding certificate. All the brides wore long white dresses, white veils and pretended to be as innocent as on the day they were born. The Bridal Agencies on both sides made a killing from every bridegroom and so did the municipalities. The groom also had to pay for the wedding dress – and the honeymoon.

The boom in the bridal trade lasted a few years. Then the sad stories of how these brides became beasts of burden in rural areas in Japan, Korea and Australia, treated badly by husbands, in-laws and locals, triggered an official ban on such municipal match-making activities. But the trade continued, though more discreetly and out of the public eye. In later years, after the ban on municipality-hosted mass weddings, the secretly matched couples often held their weddings at the Hotel Daffodil. One day a billboard in the foyer announced in bold gold letters:

14.00: WEDDING
Miss Recycle Contreras
and
Mister Horni Hamamoto

By the new century South Korean package tours, just like Korean investments in the Philippines, had taken over the Hotel Daffodil from the Japanese – and with it the bridal trade. The Japanese, caught in an economic backspin at home, were now seldom seen. The change in nationalities changed the tone of the hotel. While the Japanese had generally behaved with refined and gentile manners in public the Koreans were boorish and loud. And that is how they treated their girl escorts.

* * *

Bruce was one of a handful of white foreigners who had taken up residence at the Daffodil, not because he liked the place but because his mate, Harry the Horse, had been a guest there years ago, during the days of the American servicemen. Harry insisted there was no better place in all of Asia then the Daffodil: 'You'll have no hassle bringing in girls and no hassle finding them because the place is right in the middle of the red light zone and the shopping malls where the bar girls and factory girls hang out on their days off, looking for company to make an extra buck. Got it?"

Bruce had taken the Superior Room though he didn't know it differed from the Standard Room only by the charge of an extra 300 pesos. In the elevator up to the fourth floor he finally asked the plain girl for her name.

"Anne," she said.

"She's Number One leg massage," Sheila said.

The details of what went on that first day in the foreigner's hotel room remained vague because Anne seemed visibly reluctant to offer details and the court was indulgent enough, allowing her to sketch the activities in broad general terms. Excerpts from the court transcript provided a glimpse into the sleazy ways of the sex trade as it is still practiced today, especially in the capitals which have become receptacles for rural girls seeking their fortune in the big smoke.

"So what did you do once you were in the room," the State prosecutor asked Anne in the witness box.

"We asked permission to have a shower."

"And that was OK with him?

"Yes, he said: 'Go and get yourself wet'."

After the sniggering in the court room faded the prosecutor continued: "What was he doing?"

"He was spread out on the bed and Sheila asked him: Why don't you take a shower too?' But he said: 'No, thanks, I took one yesterday."

(The record showed the judge then shouted: "Silence in the court," to stop further sniggering in the public gallery.)

"Was he on the bed naked or dressed?"

"He was dressed."

"So what happened then?"

"We came out of the bathroom ..."

"... Wrapped in towels?"

"No, sir, naked."

"How did he react?"

"He just stared. His mouth was open. But he didn't say nothing."

"So? Did you give him a massage or not."

"Yes."

"Dressed?

"No sir. Sheila told him to take it off. He asked if we could help him. We did."

"And then you gave him a massage?"

"Yes, sir."

"Both of you?"

"Yes, sir."

"How did you do that?"

"We kissed him, sir."

"Together?"

"No, sir, one each end."

"You call that a massage?"

"Yes Sir, it's a full body massage."

And he behaved well?"

"Yes, sir, he just lay there and made noises."

"What sort of noises?"

"I don't know, sir … like pigs make when they eat."

"So it was all very normal. There was no violence? He didn't ask you to perform any unnatural acts or anything like that. He was nice to you?"

"Yes sir. He was alright. But he smelled terribly, and he sweated a lot and Sheila wanted to vomit."

"So he paid you the amount you asked for, no complaint, no haggling, hmmm?"

"He paid."

"Did he say anything?

"He told Sheila to come back next day at eight o'clock in the evening. He wanted to take her to dinner and then back to the room."

"Did she agree?"

"She asked him if he wanted her to sleep over. He said maybe."

"You then left, I presume. Did Sheila say anything once you were outside?"

"She was angry."

"Why?"

"Because … because he did not take a shower, because he stank, because he sweated and made strange noises. He made her stomach turn.

You know what I mean?"

"You mean she vomited?"

"Yes, sir."

"Did she make any threats or indicate she would do what she did later?"

"Well, she said one day she'd get even with those pigs. But Sir, she was always saying that, we all were saying things like that. It didn't mean anything."

The court then adjourned for lunch.

* * *

The media feasted on the story, lapping up the gory details with the diligence of sparrows rutting in a bread basket. Writers performed verbal acrobatics to hide the unsavory parts with cryptic phrases or words that did not offer the proper label but left no doubt about the injured part. The story developed into one of those soap operas that mesmerize the public. Only this one was real.

In people's minds a good story must have a villain. In this case it was Bruce, the rich foreigner who took advantage of the poor native girl. Sheila, on the other hand, was elevated to the role of heroine. In the minds of common people, she had struck a blow against a humiliation to which they had all been subjected. Hers was a protest against living in subservience, of being colonized by one or the other of the world powers or dominated and exploited by one or the other of the regional economic tigers. Of course the narrators of the tale, the journalists, carefully avoided such allegorical escapades since their editors and owners were clearly conscious that a large portion of the country's revenue was derived from tourism. Any drama detrimental to the contrived image of the country as a tourist paradise could result in billions of dollars in lost income. No one had forgotten the bunch of foreigners kidnapped from a resort by a gang of Moslem bandits. For three years international tourism had virtually come to a standstill before it revived, gradually. The media's reporting generally remains loyal to the status quo which basically means safeguarding the System.

In the competitive race to extract and sell the last kernel of pathos from any popular story, the *Manila Tribune* sent its brightest reporter, one Rommel Betancor, to interview the aunt who had close contacts with

Sheila following her mother's death. Rommel was a thickset fellow with horn-rimmed glasses that hid his blinking left eyelid. His parents named him Rommel after the German field marshal who had fought the British and the Americans, both nations vilified by the Betancors as imperialist exploiters of the masses. Impoverished or politicized natives often gave their children the names of military or political heroes such as Eisenhower, Macarthur, Patton, Nelson, Napoleon, Bismarck, even Stalin or Lenin. Their hope, in countries still attached to spirits and native folklore, was that these names would rub off and ensure fame and fortune for their offspring, a fortune the kids would, of course, share with their parents.

Rommel had never been to Smokey Mountain, though he had heard about the place, the towering trash heap on the edge of the city. On its slopes lived thirty thousand people, jammed into lean-to huts built of corrugated iron, asbestos sheets and cardboard boxes. Thousands more came from nearby suburbs daily to scavenge through the waste as it was trucked in. Now and then the monsoon rains would wash a cluster of shacks down the mountain with inevitable loss of life or provoke a landslide that buried entire families in their shacks. These huts and shacks were stuck precariously on top of two million tons of waste, a mountain of trash rising above the plain through forty years of garbage dumping. The scavengers sifted through the waste in search of bottles, plastic material, iron, tins, wood, old utensils that could be repaired, rags, old clothing, any item that could be sold to recycle merchants down below. Each time a garbage truck arrived, hundreds of people, emerging from the layers of waste and shanties, rushed towards this new source of potential revenue, hotfooting over layers of consolidated waste, still so spongy the runners seemed to be bouncing across a trampoline. Each scavenger dragged along two or three empty or half empty Hessian or plastic sacks to hold their pickings, mainly plastic or glass bottles, metal and tin. In the mad rush to gain a frontline position and the first choice at the new treasure being dumped, people fell over each other and sometimes fought one another.

The smell on Smokey Mountain was a combination of putrefying carcasses, decomposing vegetables and the gases produced by this combustion. Now and then the fumes would burst into flames. The gases, simmering below the surface, produced spiraling plumes of smoke, veil-thin, all around the mountain as if someone in the entrails of the gigantic trash heap was permanently boiling water or smoking cigarettes. Sometimes this smoke flared into fires that ignited nearby shacks and roasted its inhabitants, who, like any other people attached to their possessions, were reluctant to run away in time and desert them. Sometimes the mountain moved, especially after the torrential monsoon rains, causing landslides that buried hundreds.

In this perilous wasteland everyone dreams of finding a treasure that would set them up for life. Perhaps a tin filled with hundred dollar notes, a satchel stuffed with silver cutlery, a carton filled with precious jewelry or just gold tossed into the garbage by accident. The hope of such a discovery, just like the bait of a lottery win, keeps everyone's spirits up. At night in makeshift bars – shanty huts decorated with liquor ads where men and women drink fermented coconut juice until their eyes turn red, their tongues turn thick and they collapse into noisy sleep – the talk is always about rumors that someone, somewhere, stumbled onto a bar of gold buried in the trash. Inevitably the story is told of how one resident, years ago, displayed a small golden hammer he had found. But the true treasure, the one that would make someone a millionaire, was still buried somewhere waiting to be found.

Rommel had to cover his nose with a handkerchief. His eyes watered all the same. He also felt nauseated and faint. The grubby urchin who had offered to conduct him to Aunt Mammy held out his hand for the reward as soon as they arrived at her shack. The boy had dashed away as soon as he held the money in his hand. The aunt, allegedly related to Sheila, was a lean lady of indistinguishable age. Her hands were blackened and she wore a soot-stained smog. She asked him in. But Rommel made it clear he preferred to remain outside in what he sarcastically called 'the fresh air.' He sat down on a bench made of a board propped on two sawed halves of another board. He lowered himself gingerly, convinced he was sure to pick up some bug or worse, a life-threatening virus. Aunt Mammy became loquacious the instant he offered her two hundred pesos as 'a donation' towards her livelihood. The media knows money pries open the mouths of the poor. Strangely enough the poor, once paid, always feel compelled to tell the truth and all they know.

The story Rommel wrote later cast light on Sheila's perverse childhood days on Smokey Mountain and endeared her even more to the have-nots who always show more compassion for distraught fellow human beings while the middle and upper classes make politically correct noises but in reality despise the poor because, so they argue, the poor are poor because they are lazy, spendthrift, drunks, gamblers and to top it all 'the poor breed like guinea pigs'.

In the one thousand word piece he wrote (a limit imposed by his editor) Rommel speculated Sheila's best years had been spent with her foster parents before she was ten, in spite of the frugal food rations on which she was reared. The moment her mother took back custody she was sent out to work as a scavenger. The girl was physically so frail even the younger children beat her in the rush to the dump trucks. She trailed so far behind she became frustrated and gave up chasing the trucks altogether. She knew there was nothing worth picking once the fastest scavengers had bagged the best morsels. Day after day she came home with empty sacks or material her incensed mother called 'the garbage of garbage.' Her mother's yelling and the belting by Vincent had no effect on her productivity. In the end and after a few weeks of scolding, biffs and kicks, the couple came to the obvious conclusion that Sheila would never be capable of pulling her weight in the trash trade. That was when her mother took her to the shopping mall, though only after Vincent had demonstrated to the little girl what those pedophiles expected of her.

"It sounds awful to you," Rommel quoted the aunt as saying: "But up here we have to earn our keep, one way or the other, more so if you're a woman. A woman has a value, something she can hawk, at least while she is young, if you get my drift?"

The rest of the story was slashed from the print-out copy by the editor who ran a black felt pen through the offensive prose because he complained 'the stuff is far too sordid for public consumption.' The editor ignored Rommel's argument that canceling his piquant prose catered to fake bourgeois sensitivity and the hypocrisy of an oligarchy which knew this kind of horror existed but pretended it did not. Besides why should editors have the privilege of deciding what the public should know and not know? Wasn't it more productive to rub the public's nose in the sordid misery of their fellow humans? In his opinion more should be published about the cases of female overseas workers in the Middle East and Japan who ended up as sex slaves or as toy girls in foreign households, chased by their male patrons, taunted and tormented by jealous wives and kept in virtual isolation for years to ensure they completed their contracts, in spite of the ill treatment. Rommel argued that if these stories were constantly exposed, not as the occasional oddity but as routine, it would save tens of thousands of other poor Asian girls from sharing similar fates. It would also alert international opinion and organizations to the horrors of enslaved and exploited domestic labor.

His editor Tungsten Arroyo was the scion of one of the country's wealthy families. He listened to his young reporter, stone-faced. In the end he leaned back in his easy-chair and squinted through both eyes at the heavy-set young man standing in front of his glass-plated office desk, a desk made of solid oak-wood. "What do you want?" he finally snapped: "Ruin the country's main revenue, the export of labor? Ruin nine million families who depend on the remittances of our overseas workers. Who the hell do you think you are, you half-baked socialist throwback? Now get the hell out of my office and just hope I forget all this nonsense you just spouted. And try to lose some weight. You're beginning to look like the Michelin man."

But Rommel had his day.

In court he collaborated readily with the defense to tell the censored version of his truncated epic. He did this with some relish, not at all convinced he was ruining the country's main revenue and taking away the livelihood of millions. Besides he was aware that rival newspapers, possibly less squeamish than his own, might print his story, now key evidence in Sheila's defense. And if they did not print the story it would surely find its way onto the Internet. One way or the other people would know.

The court was hushed when Rommel began the tale Aunt Mammy had offered. "She did so without prompting, Your Honors," Rommel told the three judges, ensuring the suspicion of coaxing (a common and valid charge against media hacks) would not cast a shadow over his scoop.

"So what happened?" one of the three judges asked, impatiently.

"Your Honor, when Sheila was twelve years old her mother auctioned her virginity to the highest bidder ..."

"Alright, tell us more about this auction?" the judge said, leaning across the bench, unable to hide his lascivious interest in the matter.

Rommel was anxious to narrate what he had extracted from Aunt Mammy but in the end he could not contain his literary bend to embellish the account with his own interpretation and descriptive details as well as his profound admiration for Filipino women who made up the majority of the nine million overseas Filipino workers. These women were often exploited, abused and treated like slaves by their employers in the Middle East and Asia but suffered these indignities and crimes against humanity in silence so their monthly remittances could continue to feed their families and educate their children back home.

"Women are the backbone of this nation," he told the court: "Without their daily sacrifices abroad and at home this country would be a basket case. Abroad they live under stairwells or locked into rooms, their passports are often confiscated; they are exposed to the sexual urges of their employers and the wrath of the employers' wives; these women work eighteen hours a day so they can send back money to their families and their husbands, husbands who often squander these earnings in girlie bars and gambling dens ... we should build monuments to these women..."

"Alright, alright! The Chief Judge interrupted: "We know you are a great admirer of Filipino women ... we all are ..."

When the sniggering in court had ceased the Chief Judge added: "You better tell us now what all this has to do with the case."

"Your Honors," Rommel said: "What I am trying to say is that only on rare occasions do we hear of an incident when a woman is accused of retaliating to abuse – and that is amazing since there are probably seven million Filipino women active in domestic and nursing service around the world and probably more than that in the sex industry at home. Yes, we've had the odd case when a domestic worker stabbed her employer after she had been regularly and brutally abused. But these are amazingly rare cases given the prevalence of abuse and the vast number of overseas female workers and foreign tourists taking advantage of women. Why do more Filipino women not snap like Sheila did? I think it is a credit to the resilience, the patience and the good nature of our women. But we should not be surprised that now and then someone like Sheila does strike back …"

"We get your point," the Chief Judge said: "But can you get on with the auction …?"

The auction, Rommel said, took place on a vacant lot behind the Municipal Hall, a lot, so he had ascertained himself later, littered with car wrecks and rusty metal, cartons and garbage tossed into the bulrushes. An old mattress, stained, had served Vincent as a podium. Mother's partner had acted as auctioneer. Before the bidding started Sheila had protested at having to stand on an upturned crate in a red mini-skirt, schoolgirl socks and a blouse so thin you could see her barely developed breasts. Her mother told her to 'shut up.' Aunt Mammy said the girl had no idea this was an auction and she was the item on offer. Her obvious confusion (so Rommel interpreted for the benefit of the court) heightened the lust of the bidders who pay for innocence, whether real or faked does not matter.

There were five bidders according to Aunt Mammy, "all fine gentlemen – people of means," she had said. Three of the bidders were Chinese, two of them tough foot soldiers obviously acting on behalf of their elderly taipan, not willing to show his face during the auction but apparently present back in the shadows, perhaps trembling with anticipation at the prospect of the competition – so Rommel told the court. It was obvious to everyone the taipan was present since the two thugs turned around each time the price went up, waiting for a signal from the dark. The invisible participant could have used a mobile phone but attended personally to enjoy the perverse pleasure of the bidding which for gamblers can be just as orgasmic as winning – so Rommel said. The third Chinese was highly visible. He was a small elderly merchant from Chinatown who apparently had no qualms about going public. The remaining two bidders were 'sharks,' private flesh merchants anxious to buy the girl so they could resell her privately to an interested party for a fat profit. Aunt Mammy said the 'sharks' had made independent bids for the girl prior to the auction but Vincent turned them down. He was convinced that at an auction he could fetch a much higher price. As always the bids were in US dollars.

Like all natives Sheila's family was aware the competition to break in the little elfin-faced girl would be mainly among or on behalf of rich elderly Chinese who still believe in their ancestral credo that deflowering a virgin extends a man's longevity. The Japanese have a similar belief, apparently inherited with their Chinese ancestry. Yet rarely did any Japanese attend such a public spectacle. They shied away from exposure and preferred private deals.

But if Sheila's family expected a lucrative windfall they were quickly disappointed. The Chinese set limits on such transactions to ensure the price of breaking in young girls is not inflated by greed or by the unrealistic dreams of natives who go through life seeing fortunes just around the next corner. The Chinese method about such purchases is similar to their dealing with kidnap gangs who snatch the wives, daughters or sons of rich Chinese for ransom, a chronic malaise in countries where the wealthy Chinese minority is considered the easiest target to shake down because they rarely go to the police. In a tacit agreement the Chinese community sets a scale on ransom payments. The highest ransom is paid for the snatch of a young woman or wife. Payment is made quickly, without much haggling, to avoid the woman being returned as 'damaged goods' which would mean loss of face for the husband or father. But woe to those families who pay more than the specified amount agreed by the council of elders. The community will not only shun such a family but undermine their credit rating and if possible their commercial activities. The argument is this: If a higher ransom amount is paid in one case the kidnap gangs will expect to receive the same amount for future hostages. There have been occasions when the community asked the family that paid an excess ransom amount to reimburse the difference to those families who subsequently had members kidnapped and were forced to pay higher ransoms.

Convinced he was about to make a fortune, Vincent started the bidding at one thousand dollars. Had he made inquiries he would have found out the price for a native virgin among the Chinese oscillated between two hundred dollars and three hundred and fifty dollars depending on the girl's looks and her age.

Needless to say no bidder reacted to the one thousand dollar opening price. In fact one of the two 'sharks' laughed loudly and called out to Vincent: "It's not Christmas yet!" This induced the amateur auctioneer to launch into a litany advertising the indescribable pleasures awaiting the successful bidder. The continued apathy that followed his colorful marketing of Sheila's 'untouched body' was finally broken by one of the sharks who blurted: "I'll take her for a hundred dollars."

Forgetting his role as impartial auctioneer Vincent yelled: "For that price I'll screw her myself."

"One twenty!" the second shark yelled.

"One twenty-five!" the first one topped.

"One-thirty"

"One thirty-five."

"Two hundred" the lone Chinese merchant offered.

At that point the two Chinese heavies looked over their shoulders. Then, apparently given the nod from the dark, one shouted: "Two-twenty."

"Two-twenty-five" the first shark yelled.

"Two-fifty," the Chinese merchant replied.

During a pause in the bidding Aunt Mammy said the two thugs consulted with the person in the shadows. Then one of the thugs ambled over casually to the two 'sharks' and whispered first into one's man ear, then into the other man's. Instantly and with unusual hurry the two 'sharks' walked away. The Chinese merchant immediately followed, even though no one had whispered into his ear. It seemed from somewhere in the dark a Big Boss had let them all know this prey was his.

"Two hundred and fifty-five," one of the thugs shouted, advancing on Vincent who had followed the events with visible trepidations but was not so stupid as to protest. In fact he humbly accepted the cash one of the thugs counted into his palm.

Sold for two hundred and fifty-five dollars, Sheila was taken away by the two foot soldiers who simply took one arm each and propelled her off with them. Once she realized this time mother was not coming with her she began to yell. But mother, standing next to Vincent, gruffly told her to shut up and do what she was told.

* * *

The media reporting about the auction endeared Sheila even more to the public. But the story also infuriated the nomenclatura and political hierarchy which, like in any country with sins to hide, is always at pains to sweep under the carpet the unsavory parts of native civilization. It also upset the Chinese community which owns the majority of the country's wealth as Chinese minorities do all over South East Asia. And since the upper class and the affluent Chinese set their own convenient rules and standards for the rest of the country they quickly activate damage control systems to ensure any 'incident' does not harm the country's image excessively or diminish the wells of wealth – in this case the booming and highly lucrative tourist and sex industry.

Politics and media work in symbiosis because the media barons are also members of the upper class hierarchy and belong to the few dozen families that traditionally provide the presidents, ministers and members of parliament of the Philippines. So the word went out to the media moguls to give the story another slant in tune with the obvious verdict – yet to be pronounced.

Rommel, still basking in the limelight of his scoop as told in court, was called in to the office of his boss, Tungsten Arroyo. The editor told him bluntly and without preambles he was fired for going public with the auction story, an office secret. In doing what he had done in court, ventilating a sordid story, he had damaged the image of the paper and the nation.

Staring at him from behind his oak-wood desk with undisguised hatred, Arroyo tried to control his fury by balling his hands into fists. Not fifteen minutes ago he had been dressed down by his uncle, the Minister of Information, who told him he could forget running the family media empire. How could the family trust a man whose judgment was so bad he hired a young reporter who acutely embarrassed the country with his communist ideas. To minister Boy Arroyo, anyone spouting about social justice and defending the disgraceful sub-human wretches of the lower pro-letariat must be a communist. Boy had studied at Princeton in the glorious 1950s when Senator McCarthy knew how to weed out these misguided do-gooders and traitors to the nation. That his own nephew, who had been given the job as editor of the family flagship, could not immediately identify and quash such an individual or at least put him out on the street was a sure sign Tungsten was not up to scratch. As Minister of Information Boy Arroyo was in the frontline of battling against the unsavory influence of the internet and the growing number of 'communist' reporters criticizing the way the country was run by an oligarchy of families. In public the minister denounced the killers contracted by anonymous interests to murder critical newsmen. At news conferences he would pledge to hunt down the masterminds behind the fatal shooting of some one hundred and fifty journalists. But in private the minister and his buddies made no effort to find those who had ordered the assassinations, knowing, without saying so, the killings intimidated the media and made journalists think twice before launching attacks against government and corporate interests. Did these idiots not realize that without these corporate mining projects and the construction boom the nation would be even more backward than it already was? And the idiot of his nephew had actually given a job to one of those brainwashed communists.

These words had been like spikes piercing Tungsten's heart, like red traffic signals to his ambitions. His bright future in the family business was shaky now. And it was all the fault of this overweight nincompoop and his socialist ideas. Tungsten was so angry he could only snap: "I promise you, you bloody idiot, you won't even get a job covering the shipping news for the daily gazette. I'll make sure of that … now get out of my office. Security will escort you out of the building. Don't take anything with you and don't ever dare to set foot in this building again. Out! Out! …"

As he was being escorted to the glass front doors which open with a gentle hiss and close with the same gentle hiss, his colleagues all pretended to be busy, eyes downcast fussing with something on their desks. Rommel wondered if this was how it felt when they took you before the firing squad.

The next victims of the official damage control and mop-up operation were the three judges and the prosecutor. During a meeting with the Minister of Justice the four were told to postpone judgment on the case with some excuse and then, after public interest had waned, pronounce with full access to the media, a verdict. And there was only one verdict possible to exonerate everyone and to pacify the concern of foreign tourists and those who spent their money in the country's entertainment industry. No action was to be taken against the owners of the Hotel Daffodil. But the second girl was to be treated as an accomplice – and punished even though she was not present during the crime. The sentencing was to include a profound apology to the Australian family, a moderate sum of money as compensation, no more than twenty thousand dollars as a gesture of goodwill, as well as a little speech to assure the public and visitors that this kind of thing was the rare and unprecedented folly of a deranged young woman.

One of the judges suggested it would be preferable if the expert psychiatrist who was to assess whether the girl was clinically insane, came from abroad, preferably the United States which had maintained its golden aura as global champion of fairness and justice among the general public. An American's testimony would lend the case the sense of independence that might become suspect if the court resorted to a local psychiatrist.

The Minister nodded. "We have already thought of this," he told the meeting. "We have an American professor willing to come for the usual remuneration and give expert evidence. He has followed the case and has assured me there is no doubt any woman who cuts off a man's penis with a pair of scissors and then tosses the severed member out of the window must be clinically deranged.

After a moment the Minister added: "And the verdict must be frightening because we don't want to encourage copycats, do we my friends?"

The men chuckled, and one or two cupped their crotches, almost subconsciously.

"She will have to be committed – for life" the Chief Judge said.

"That might be a bit too harsh," the Minister objected: "What about twenty-five years?"

"That'll do," the Chief Judge said. "All agreed? Good. Case closed.

—

THE ROMAN TALES

EIGHT

The Blackbird

Brought up by the fifth generation of 'quartiere' shopkeepers, Guglielmo Panzer was taught to avoid trouble. And trouble was approaching now with firm short steps in the formidable shape of Miss Antoinette Hatter. So Signor Panzer made a flustered attempt to hide the thing by tossing over it the checkered blue and white cloth on which he wiped his blades. But even as he tossed the rag, he knew he was too late again, just as he had known he was too late when the shell whistled towards the deck of the 'Andromeda' and he dived for cover behind the bow winch.

"What do you keep in that cage?"

There it was, and right to the point. The clumsiness of the Anglo-Saxons annoyed him. They were simply incapable of the verbal fairy floss Italians spun to blunt the pointed part of their questions. Impetuously he whipped off the checkered cloth and the young bird peered from the cage, its head cocked to one side. The yellow beak opened once, twice and then snapped shut; the yellow-ringed eyes blinked, myopic. It was a tedious bird, extremely stupid, always staring vacantly from glazed eyes. And it never sang.

"What is it?" she insisted.

"A blackbird," he explained, grumpily.

"Oh!"

He braced himself against the rest. It wasn't long in coming.

"Is it hurt?"

"No," he said.

"Oh! Then you must let it go at once. I insist. Blackbirds are born to be free. It'll simply die in that horrid cage, poor little thing. Besides I'm quite sure they're protected by law and you don't want to break the law, do you?"

Signor Panzer was a slow-thinking man whose thoughts took time before they translated themselves into action, a defect that had already cost him one leg. Still, like many inarticulate people his sense of observation was acute. He now saw in front of him a tubby woman in her late thirties whose bosom rose and fell with the tide of her indignation. She had a surprisingly smooth and youthful face, which contrasted sharply with the flabbiness of her body. A loose tartan skirt and frayed harlequin jacket failed to hide her generous bulk. She was, he deduced, one of those foreign ladies, who, after a violent storm in their life, had been washed ashore in his country like driftwood. Once ashore they slowly withered in some corner, fiercely rejecting all native ways, holding up their jealously preserved 'foreignness' like a banner of triumph until the day they died and were buried, quietly, at the foreigners' cemetery beside the pyramid of Caius Cestius on the Aurelian Wall.

"Well?" Miss Hatter prompted: "Are you or are you not going to free that bird?"

"What can I serve you?" Signor Panzer parried.

"How can we discuss the sale of vulgar meat while this poor little creature suffers. You must let it go."

The butcher mechanically wiped his hands on his apron, something he did when he was nervous.

"Signorina," he said slowly: "It is my bird. I caught it and I want to keep it. Maybe it will sing one day. Who knows. I'd like to hear it sing."

"Preposterous!" she hissed. "Can't you see how sad the poor little thing is? Just look how it sits there, like someone waiting for death. Doesn't it turn your heart?"

The butcher's puzzled gaze turned to the bird. It sat on its perch quiet and dumb, just as it had sat from the day he caught it. How could one tell whether it was sad or happy?

"Signor Panzer!" She pronounced his surname in a distinctly Teutonic manner: "I've never thought you a cruel man despite your profession, and having bought my meat from you for the last few years I would hate to think that I've been dealing with a barbarian. Signor Panzer: Open this cage and let this bird go free."

The butcher, battling to hold his tongue, was rescued from an immediate reply by the timely arrival of two customers. One of them was the old Signora Stincheddu, wrinkled and shrivelled like a dried fig, whose husband was the Portiere at the Palazzo Oriali, a man who suffered from a leaking bladder and kept a plastic cornet in one pocket connected to his urinary tract. The Signora Stincheddu had come for her tripe. The second customer was a fragile young woman who brushed back her red hair self-consciously. He had not seen her before, which worried him. Business was slack since the Supermarket opened down the road and he tried to make a good impression on any new face.

"There are other customers, Signorina," he said.

"Oh!" Miss Hatter piped, turning upon the new arrivals as if she had seen them for the first time: "So there are … don't you agree that blackbirds cannot be kept in cages," she said, addressing the newly arrived. "They're born to be free. I've asked him to let it go, but he refuses."

She looked expectantly at the two women but the old Signora Stincheddu ducked under her gaze towards the counter.

"You've got my tripe, Guglielmo?" she asked, casting a sidelong glance of disapproval at this foreign lady. The butcher nodded eagerly. He could have kissed the old Signora Stincheddu.

"You're not buying meat from this man while he keeps a blackbird trapped?" Miss Hatter had planted herself next to the old lady who, not at all intimidated, tapped the counter with two talon-like fingers. She was anxious to return to her own cage just inside the gates of the Palazzo Oriali from where she could dart to interrogate strangers, curse hawkers, scold beggars, persecute workmen, admonish garbage collectors and hush little children while her husband, swathed in blankets, sat in his rocking chair nursing the cornet in his pocket, taking no interest in the fervent activities of his spouse. He was, after all, still the Portiere. The label on the wage slip said so.

Having wrapped the tripe in brown paper, Guglielmo Panzer pushed it along the counter towards the Signora Stincheddu who immediately clutched it to her concave chest. "Some people have to work," she quipped, casting a meaningful look at the butcher on her way out.

"The impertinence of the serving class these days," Miss Hatter remarked. Then, addressing herself to the redheaded young woman, she said: "I do hope you will not buy anything from this man until he sets the bird free."

The young woman picked at her purse. It was a fine leather purse from Gucchi: "I believe in self-determination," she whispered, nervously perusing the minced meat, the pork and raw roasts on display.

"Oh!" Miss Hatter said: "And do you think this poor little bird has been given an opportunity at self-determination?"

"Don't molest my customers," Signor Panzer growled.

Miss Hatter ignored him.

"And don't you agree it is up to any conscientious human being to make sure this poor bird enjoys the life for which nature intended it? Don't you agree that as intelligent beings endowed with the power of reason we are the natural champions of the animals?"

The young woman moved closer to the counter, her hands fluttered for a moment before she folded them. "I would like two beefsteaks, on the lean side, please," she whispered to the butcher whose dark eyes flashed red signals which Miss Hatter imperiously ignored. Instead she was drawing herself up on the left flank of the redhead, inhaling deeply, her large body inflating like a carnival balloon stuck to a gas cylinder.

"I'm shocked," she boomed (and the butcher winced for he had noticed another customer enter the shop): "I am shocked by someone who simply ignores the plight of animals, by someone who supports those who maltreat animals." She glowered at the young woman, noting, not without satisfaction, her discomfort.

"Signorina would you please leave my shop," Signor Panzer said. The gleaming blade of the carving knife lent his words a sinister meaning.

"Not until you've freed this poor bird."

The butcher hobbled around the counter on his wooden leg, the meat cleaver still in his hand.

"Get out!" he growled.

"Don't you threaten me in that tone."

"This is my shop." He faced Miss Hatter now, feeling her warm breath, noting how the mighty bosom rode up and down like the bow of a battleship in a storm. (Most of Signor Panzer's imagery was drawn from his short spell at sea.)

He raised the cleaver.

Miss Hatter gasped. Her right hand cupped her left breast. She retreated, reluctant at first, then faster until she reached the door where she passed an elderly lady whose toothless mouth hung open.

"I'll see you pay for this," was Miss Hatter's parting shot before she swept out majestically, a schooner under full sail, Signor Panzer thought.

Out in the Viale Imperiale the traffic snarled at her. The pavements brimmed with morning shoppers and the odd opportunist with an eye out for a quick purse snatch to start the day. Mechanically she clutched her handbag tighter, staring hard at a young man in jeans and T-shirt who surveyed her speculatively, maybe appreciating her comfortable girth rather than her handbag. In any case Miss Hatter did not appreciate such cursory appraisal, though deep down in her soul she tinkled like a crystal chandelier in the breeze, being far from immune to the desires of the flesh.

Her sensible shoes, square-heeled and low, hammered the cobblestones of the alley into which she turned, echoed down the marble-floored hallway of the Palazzo and crunched against the gravel of the courtyard until the sound was drowned by the infernal bark of the poodle.

"Quiet, Mr. Chip!" she ordered. The order triggered only a new round of neurotic yapping as the dog hurled himself against the inside of the flat door which she quickly unlocked. A black streak shot through the widening slit; it caught itself clumsily in the folds of her skirt, ducking, diving underneath as she fumbled for the studded collar. Having found it she dragged the hound back into daylight.

"Now be a good fellow, Mr. Chip," she admonished him, smoothening down the rumpled skirt while the dog continued to yap frenetically careening around the courtyard in ever tightening circles.

A window slammed on the third floor. It was sure to be the Signora Nozzetti; though half deaf she constantly complained to the Portiere about the dog. How selfish people were, Miss Hatter thought as she fondly watched Mr. Chip crook a leg and pee against the birch tree, then give a second quick squirt to the garden chair of the aged Signor Paoletti.

"Come, come, Chipy, we've work to do," she urged the beast, now busy taking scent of his domain, staking out his realm with well-directed sprinkles. "There's a bird to be saved my boy."

And with that Miss Hatter stepped across a number of obstacles blocking access to the drawer in which she kept the telephone directory. She was an excellent climber of obstacles (a skill much required in her clustered flat) being double-jointed and thus able to kick her legs head-high, a feat she performed at parties and gatherings at the slightest provocation. People then would nudge each other and call into other rooms: "Quick, quick, Antoinette is doing her ballet splits." And there would be Miss Hatter, encouraged by the cheers and maybe a few drinks, standing in the centre of the room going 'Oopla!' one leg flying high, 'Oopla!' the other flying even higher.

Miss Hatter's two-roomed flat was pitifully small. Once, in the golden days of the eternal city (before the Popes were relegated to the Vatican across the Tiber) the rooms had been stables for the Palazzo. But the owner, one of those ravenous Roman landlords who charge exorbitant rents for their dilapidated family Palazzi, not satisfied with renting out nine apartments at huge profit, had also turned the courtyard stables into habitations. Part of the former stables was occupied by Miss Hatter. It was a flat forever cluttered with paraphernalia. Open and closed books abounded, from cheap paperbacks to expensively bound first editions, many of them on archaeology. Miss Hatter was an indiscriminate and avaricious reader on that subject. On three wobbly desks three typewriters reposed, each flanked by a stack of blank sheets and a stack of typed sheets. Each typewriter served for a different project. It was quite normal for Miss Hatter to occupy all three during one day for she worked on whatever project took her fancy at a particular moment.

* * *

Scattered on the floor were dog biscuits in various stages of consumption, two plastic dog bowls, a few sheets of music from a Beethoven sonata, covered by black dog's hair and an ugly coffee stain. On the open piano, rented and squeezed into a corner, the rest of the sonata sat crookedly on the music holder. The furnishings were Spartan: two rickety chairs and three fluffy cushions on a sofa opposite a floor-to-ceiling wardrobe. Miss Hatter's bed, a double mattress affair liberally sprinkled with baby cushions, took up most of the second room. There was a bedside table and below the bed itself a comfortable nest of rugs, the home of Mr. Chip. The location of Mr. Chip's 'house' (as Miss Hatter called it) was a constant source of irritation to the odd lover who visited Miss Hatter in her lair. They inevitably complained that during the night Mr. Chip habitually and loudly broke wind at the most inopportune moments. Only the most ardent of Miss Hatter's lovers had ever faced a second night at Mr. Chip's mercy. They were all convinced the dog, known for the possessive air he adopted around his mistress, was purposely malicious on such occasions. Miss Hatter, a vehement defender of her pet's reputation, attributed such slander to 'excuses for impotence'.

Off the bedroom lay the kitchen or more precisely, a cubicle with a two-hole gas stove and a sink. An adjoining second cubicle housed a toilet so small one needed to perform a tolerable feat of acrobatics to squeeze upon the fur-lined seat. From the shower tap above the toilet seat, dangling like an umbilical cord, one could admire Miss Hatter's mighty douche bag, a constant reminder to the unaware of her organized sex life. On nails, side-by-side, hung two toothbrushes, one labeled 'MINE' the other 'YOURS'. Miss Hatter was extremely proud of her toothbrushes. On a shelf, badly aligned by the carpenter so that it drooped, stood side by side, beginning with the tallest, Miss Hatter's many tins of beauty cream most of them intended for the care and preservation of a skin of which Miss Hatter was justifiably proud since it had maintained its youthful elasticity and healthy pink glow.

* * *

Despite the constant urgings of her friends and acquaintances (known in Miss Hatter's jargon as the F & As) she refused to search for more comfortable lodgings, pointing out, quite rightly, that since the implementation of the new rent law (of which she had taken advantage) the rent of forty dollars a month was so ridiculously low, the apartment so central and she so accustomed to her paraphernalia, that it would be criminal if not ridiculous to move. Besides, her infrequent visitors from abroad, who usually dropped in when fancy took them or, more to the point, when they required cheap accommodation, could not be expected to find their way to her new abode. In the end Miss Hatter's F & As resigned themselves to her permanent existence in the stables, though among themselves they bitterly and frequently complained about the musty air, the weeping walls and the accumulation of dust, cockroaches and the odd scorpion. Some alleged they had contracted lasting damage to their respiratory systems during a visit to Miss Hatter's home.

"Oh!" exclaimed Miss Hatter, tearing the telephone book from below a stack of bed sheets ready for dispatch to the laundry: "There you are. Now wait Chip and see what we'll do to that horrible man."

(When alone Miss Hatter conducted a constant monologue with her dog, although the animal never paid her the slightest attention, except when she exclaimed the magic words: "Get Your Leash Mr. Chip" a phrase that activated the beast to ever new feats of neurotic yapping and crazed careering through the flat as he primed himself for their outing.)

"There!" cried Miss Hatter, stabbing at a number in the phonebook: "Associazione per la Protezione degli Animali … now we'll see." Her finger drummed the phonebook impatiently while she waited for an answer.

"Pronto!" she said: "This is la Signorina Antoinette Hatter, resident at number nine Via della Scala. I would like to report the illicit caging of a blackbird … What? Yes, a blackbird. This bird is kept by a butcher at his shop in Viale Trastevere 95. The butcher's name is Guglielmo Panzer … Yes … p-a-n-z-e-r. He has a wooden leg. What? No, the butcher, not the blackbird. What? Yes, of course I'll wait."

Tap-tap went the finger on the phonebook while a smug expression on her face accompanied her remark to the hound: "That's showing them, Chipy! We'll have her out in a jiffy and then I'll cook you the biggest, juiciest steak to celebrate. How would you like that?" The dog gave a mournful whine.

"Yes, a blackbird."

During the following pause Miss Hatter's face gradually sagged until it developed dewlaps which Miss Hatter suddenly retrieved by craning her neck.

"That is preposterous!" she finally yelled into the mouthpiece. "Not on the index of protected birds? Outrageous, my good man, simply outrageous; it makes one ask what sort of an organization are you running anyway and for whose benefit are you spending government funds, not to speak of those contributed by genuine animal lovers like myself. I'm sure anywhere else in the world blackbirds are protected by law and they certainly should be in this country where three million trigger-happy hunters are let lose upon the animal world each year. But as usual your laws are grossly inadequate and ridiculous. I demand you do something about this case, I demand …"

Miss Hatter stopped.

"Hallo! Hallo!" she bellowed down the dead line. "Louts!" she said dashing the phone back on its cradle, rising to straighten her pleats, throw back her shoulders and address Mr. Chip: "Chipy, we'll have to fight our own battle and we'll have to be cunning about it, after all," she raised one finger, "the results justify the means, especially when it comes to rescuing animals."

The dog yawned.

Miss Hatter brooded over the issue for several hours. She rang all the F & As available to canvass their advice and support. When no one proposed any (apart from the advice that she forget the matter) Miss Hatter felt compelled to embark on a course of her own which inevitably led her to the law. In her Anglophile mind the law was the solution to every citizen's private problem and it was to the law she turned once the well of her campaign ideas dried up.

"I wish to denounce the illegal import of a rare black parrot from Africa," she told the man at the import section of the livestock department at the Agriculture Ministry. The official took down the information meticulously, or so it seemed, only stumbling over the ridiculous name 'Ifgenia' which she gave as the informant. He tried to elicit all kinds of additional information which Miss Hatter circumnavigated with the dexterity of experience. The man was obviously filling out a form and Miss Hatter, generally most abrasive when dealing with Italian bureaucracy, could be surprisingly patient if it suited her purpose.

"Well, Mr. Chip," she said smugly at the end of the call: "That's fixed the nasty peg-legged bird killer."

The dog as usual ignored her, more interested in chewing on a pair of frilly panties he had discovered among the laundry on the floor.

Whenever she was engaged in one of her campaigns, Miss Hatter found it impossible to concentrate on any other task. Her single-minded determination on such occasions was awesome. At the same time, however, she had a pathological need to communicate the progress of her campaign to others, maybe requiring an outlet for the massive amount of adrenalin her body manufactured during such periods. But over the next hour she only managed to contact four of her F & As to inform them of her coup against the butcher. Their reaction was unanimous: They were shocked and they said so. But this only confirmed to Miss Hatter that she had been right, for her F & As, like the majority of human beings, were too cowardly to ever stick their necks out on behalf of anyone, least of all a poor bird. Convinced of her righteousness Miss Hatter did not expect the F & As to agree with her; she simply communicated with them out of a need for rapport.

Once she had exhausted her list of F & As Miss Hatter became increasingly restive. Something had to happen; the present stalemate was intolerable and incompatible with her need for action. She wondered if the Ministry had already sent its agents to the butcher shop. Wondering, she walked from typewriter to typewriter, casting cursory glances over their manuscripts, without reading a single line. She paused at the electric typewriter on which she composed her main product; a research piece entitled 'Post-War Popes'.

For four long years the 'Post-War-Popes' had provided Miss Hatter not only with a magnificent topic for conversation but with the aura of an embryo writer slaving in dismally uncomfortable conditions on a master-piece that, so she frequently professed, was going to earn her a vast fortune and eternal fame. After four years, she had arrived at page one hundred and eighteen, only four hundred pages short of the target promised to the editor of a small English publishing house which had rashly sponsored the book. The editor of that small company, a man called Ireland, had been so impressed by Miss Hatter's brilliant outline of 'Post-War Popes' – an outline that read like the index of a Who is Who in the Vatican – that he not only pledged his company's support but advanced two thousand pounds sterling towards the finished product. The outline had required six months to be completed. In it Miss Hatter had claimed to be the confidante of cardinals and papal secretaries, bishops and ecclesiastical academics, all anxious to unburden their innermost secrets for her book. Shrewdly, she had kept the outline to barely ten exquisitely typed and margined pages delivered to Mr. Ireland neatly bound in a red leather cover procured from a well-known binder.

But that was four years ago. For the last two and a half years there had been no more letters from Mr. Ireland, not since his protégé had failed to meet the final deadline for delivery of the completed manuscript. Miss Hatter was unconcerned by Mr. Ireland's ominous silence.

"He'll have to wait," she used to say: "Genius cannot work within time limits". Though sometimes, in rare moments of reflection, she admitted the garrulous sources of information had turned out to be less garrulous and more difficult to pin down than she had expected, a gentle hint they had not parted with any of the secrets she had promised Mr. Ireland. Now and then she revived the project with a sudden flurry of activity, all of it generously relayed to the F & As. At one stage she actually sought opinions on what dress would be appropriate for the book launch. Later, she debated for weeks whether the World Wide Fund for Nature or the Royal Society for the Prevention of Cruelty to Animals should be the main beneficiary of her Nobel Prize. That was prior to Prince Bernhard of the Netherlands being implicated in the Lockheed bribery scandal, after which she announced it was definitely not going to be the WWF.

As time passed Miss Hatter was rarely serious about her book. Her flights into semi-serious fantasy became more frequent; the customary 'how goes your book' was rewarded with less and less information on the book and more and more loquacity on her latest scheme, whether a campaign to save stray dogs in the Piazza Venezia or an enterprise to salvage the reputation of a senior diplomat, who, she insisted, had been wrongly accused of passing NATO secrets to the Russians. The case of 'Dr Strangelove', as the F & As facetiously labeled the erring diplomat, fully occupied Miss Hatter for nine months. "My Beppe" (Miss Hatter's reference to Dr Strangelove)"is the innocent victim of an international plot," she would heatedly argue when someone pointed out that every shred of evidence indicated 'Poor Beppe' was as guilty as the Scarlet Pimpernel. "Fools!" she would rage during such debates. "My Beppe is an innocent pawn in a major conspiracy. He'd never do a thing like that." When hard pressed for the reason of her faith she pulled out her final trump: "I know him better than anyone else." After all Dr Strangelove's innocence was firmly associated with his long liaison with Miss Hatter – though all the F & As knew he had visited her just twice a year to play the piano and once to make love.

* * *

Miss Hatter attended the court case for weeks sitting in the front row, clucking her tongue, shaking her head, making outraged remarks about the accusations of the Prosecution, making herself so conspicuous the press referred to her as 'The Loyal Mistress of the Traitor' a label she not only enjoyed but nurtured by throwing herself around Dr Strangelove's neck on the one occasion she could reach him as he was walked from the dock to his cell.

"He is innocent," she proclaimed to eager reporters: "I know he hates the communists. Think of what he went through in Berlin at the end of the war. He was, after all, one of the last Italians to leave Hitler's bunker." The newspapers gobbled up such precious information and Dr Strangelove, whose case did not improve with this new fascist label, sent her a vitriolic note from jail which ended: "And now shut up." Miss Hatter was sure however the note could not have come from 'Poor Beppe' but had been composed by the same vile forces plotting his downfall.

In the end Dr Strangelove was sentenced to ten years in a penitentiary. Miss Hatter was distraught, but not for long. Since all of "Poor Beppe's" former friends and allies including an estranged wife and two steady mistresses, had rapidly deserted him after the charge of treason, it was now up to Miss Hatter to provide him with the comfort and support of a friend. She applied and obtained permission to visit Dr Strangelove twice a week. She was also given the right to deliver food for him in jail, a privilege common in Italian penal institutes. Aware of 'Poor Beppe's love for the Chinese cuisine she haunted every Chinese restaurant in Rome not only providing the most tantalizing dishes for her beloved man but also for scores of his cell mates. She wrote him endless letters, delivered endless messages, bought all the books and utensils he desired, in short she spent a fortune in time and money. Her life rotated around the jail. She was virtually incommunicado to all F & As.

This situation might have continued indefinitely but to everyone's surprise Dr Strangelove was swapped in a mysterious spy deal one summer day and vanished without ever making a single phone call or sending a note to thank Miss Hatter for her unwavering loyalty. Poor Beppe's release not only stoked Miss Hatter's hopes of a more permanent romance but her conviction of his innocence.

"They had to let him go," she exclaimed. The triumph was short-lived. From somewhere abroad Dr Strangelove gave a lucrative interview to a weekly magazine in which he fully confessed to his spying activities. Miss Hatter was undaunted. "He had to do it. It was part of the deal for his freedom," she argued. No one could ever convince her that "Poor Beppe" was a skunk. As far as Miss Hatter was concerned he could come back any day: The piano was waiting for him, so was the douche bag and the spare toothbrush.

One of Miss Hatter's main problems was her inability to sit still once embarked on a project. The walls pressed in on her. Besides, she was bursting with curiosity to find out if the butcher had already been visited by the minions from the Ministry of Agriculture.

"Mr Chip! Get your leash!" she cried.

The hound pricked his floppy ears. He was suspicious. Only too frequently had his mistress used the command to demonstrate to her F &A's what a smart fellow he was. And once he had fetched the leash, nothing had happened. Mr. Chip hated to be fooled.

"Go on, Mr. Chip, get your leash, we're going out."

It was real. The dog yapped hysterically. He careered into the bedroom where the leash was supposed to hang beside the bed, though it hardly ever did. Mr. Chip's shrill bark became frantic. He paced up and down below the hook from which the leash should have dangled. He barked angrily at the empty spot.

"Silly boy! Go and look for it."

The rebuke made Mr. Chip more demented. He leapt up and down on Miss Hatter's skirt, sank his fangs into a cushion, walked on his hind legs and nearly choked on his own barking.

"If you can't find it I'll go without you."

Mr. Chip lost his head. He careered around the flat, skidding to a halt against the wall, turning, picking up speed. He crashed into the wardrobe, bounced off the writing desk, knocked books off tables and chairs and stepped into his water bowl, all the time yapping as if he was being dissected alive.

"Bye, Bye Mr. Chip!" Miss Hatter teased, opening the door just a slit.

Mr. Chip had taken enough. He leapt up on his mistress and bit her wrist.

"Oh! You naughty boy!" she called out, shaking her hand, gaping at the teeth marks and the blood oozing forth, bending down to smack his rump.

And so he bit her again.

"Mr. Chip!" She was thoroughly flustered now. "No need to be so vicious," she added in mollifying tones, "we were only having a bit of fun." She pretended that she was offended, snubbing the dog but all the same searching for the leash herself. She found it under the bed but Mr. Chip tore it from her hand while she was still recumbent and trailing it, head high, he pawed the door impatiently.

Once in the street she clipped the leash to the dog's collar and allowed herself to be dragged along by his frantic straining. Tongue out, choked by the collar, Mr Chip pulled like an ox. To any passer-by it appeared as if he was hauling his mistress off to an urgent rendezvous. The pair constantly turned heads. After a few minutes of heavy hauling Mr Chip was exhausted. So he simply inverted the roles. He dragged, forcing Miss Hatter to pull him, skating on his haunches, neck stretched like a goose, red tongue rolling from his dripping jaws, growling with unabashed opposition.

"Poor little dog," people said, giving Miss Hatter baleful stares of disapproval. After a few minutes Miss Hatter, tired too, allowed the dog to indulge in his favourite pastime – to sniff other dog squirts and the canine turds which litter the alleys and pavements of Rome like spikes on wrought-iron gates. Miss Hatter patiently waited for Mr Chip to satiate his glandular needs. Dog and mistress always proceeded at a sporadic pace and Miss Hatter was forever late to appointments due to this tug of war and Mr Chip's need to deposit his visiting card on certain posts and edifices. Miss Hatter was rather proud of Mr Chip's potent marking ability; she told the F & As he had the most powerful bladder in the dog world for she had counted up to thirty-six individual squirts on a fifteen minute walk. Still the F & As gave Mr Chip a wide berth for he greeted them all enthusiastically and without distinction by leaping up to lick the men's flies or by diving under the women's skirts. This was a trifle embarrassing, particularly since everyone knew Mr Chip persistently sniffed other dogs' droppings.

When Miss Hatter reached the Viale Trastevere, she peered down in the direction of Signor Panzer's shop. But she was disappointed. No milling throng craned heads outside, not a policeman in sight, not even a sign of an official car.

"Maybe they've already been there, Chipy."

The beast was far too busy investigating the treasure of smells on the trunk of a tree to pay heed to anything his mistress said.

"We'll just have to wait for a while," Miss Hatter added, allowing Mr Chip full reign to continue his research and to squirt his own visiting card upon the ones already left behind. A few feet away the early afternoon traffic trickled along, tooting and screeching as impatient drivers jockeyed for progress.

For once Miss Hatter was oblivious to their noisy battle. Her eyes were fastened so intently on Signor Panzer's shop she failed to notice the approach of the scruffy young man walking a Doberman puppy on a leash. Not so Mr. Chip: The stump of his tail wagged like a worm on a hook; the droopy ears flapped and he drew himself up to his full height, which, at the best of times, was barely off the ground. Step by cautious step, as if walking on glass, he advanced on the puppy which already pawed the pavement to reach him. They met, each straining on its leash.

"Oh Look! What a lovely little pup, Chipy," Miss Hatter piped.

The scruffy young man smiled proudly. But Miss Hatter noticed, for the first time, not without pangs of alarm, that the puppy's leash was no more than an old piece of rope tied to a rather precious leather collar. Hmm, she thought, surveying the young man's ragged appearance, he's not stolen it, has he? Her heart immediately went out to the puppy. So did Mr.

Chip's. He hardly wasted time with preliminary sniffing but made straight for the core of the matter. He deftly wheeled and – while the silly pup still sniffed the empty space left by his departure – approached his prey from the rear. He mounted in a flash, jerking with great enthusiasm, before the puppy had time to ejaculate the first pitiful squeals.

"Hey!" the young man called out, dragging at the leash to free his pet from Mr. Chip's amorous bucking: "Mind getting your dog off?"

"Oh!" Miss Hatter exclaimed, giving her leash an ineffectual tug. "Naughty boy, Mr. Chip, she's still too small. Let her grow up."

Mr. Chip however was far too engrossed in his performance to take heed. His tongue dragged, he had accelerated his rhythm and his eyes had taken on that glazed dopey look which indicated to Miss Hatter he was now beyond her reach.

"Hey!" the young man exclaimed again, more alarmed now: "Will you get that randy hound off. He'll ruin her." He began to pull wildly on his leash but the puppy, still squealing, was buried under Mr. Chip's full weight. And Mr. Chip had no intention of moving.

"Naughty boy!" Miss Hatter admonished, giving her leash another token tug as the alarmed young man reached down to physically dislodge the assailant. Mr. Chip growled a mean hoarse growl that came from deep within his chest. The young man 'hesitated, and then made a hurried grab. Mr. Chip's fangs neatly perforated the back of his hand.

"Ouch!" the young man yelled, recoiling. He shook his bitten hand while Mr. Chip redoubled his efforts.

"Bloody rapist dog, I'll show you!" The young man kicked out savagely, a kick that caught Mr. Chip full in the belly and sent him flying at Miss Hatter's feet where he landed with a yelp that signaled more frustration than injury. As Mr. Chip scrambled back on his paws, picking up speed to make another dash, the young man, hand bleeding, snatched the whining pup off the ground and cradled it in his arms. Undaunted Mr. Chip made his dash, leaping high to reach the puppy which the young man barely saved from the snapping jaws by holding it above his head.

"Hold back that mad dog of yours, you stupid bitch!" the young man shouted.

"How dare you kick my dog, you uncouth lout," came Miss Hatter's indignant reply (as Mr. Chip performed miracles in the high jump) "and how dare you insult me. I shall call the police."

The young man gaped in disbelief, then a haunted, trapped expression crossed his sallow features.

"Police! Police!" Miss Hatter shouted down the Viale Trastevere.

The young man ran, neck tugged into his rump, cradling the puppy.

He zig-zagged down the Viale ducking into the first alley that offered itself.

"Catch thief! Catch thief!" Miss Hatter screamed, one arm pointing in the direction of the 'thief.' A crowd had gathered around Miss Hatter and her dog which now stood with humbly bowed head, shaking with exhaustion.

"Someone's nicked her purse," a voice explained.

"I want a policeman," Miss Hatter shouted. The crowd dispersed. It was one thing to see a show, another to be involved in police investigations. Only a fat man remained. He looked Miss Hatter up and down appreciatively. "Have a cup of coffee, it'll calm you down, Signorina," he suggested, taking her elbow. Miss Hatter shook herself free at once. "No thank you," she said haughtily "I'd rather you chase that thief". The fat man shrugged his shoulders and ambled away, a little peeved.

Miss Hatter squatted at Mr Chip's side.

"Poor, poor Chipy," she crooned: "Did he hurt you? The stinking little twerp!" She stroked the dog, examining the fur, prodding his rump: "Does that hurt? Here? There? Does it hurt? Tell me, Chipy." But Mr. Chip was breathing heavily, his tongue out, his body convulsing with the effort of pumping oxygen. "Poor, poor Chipy, just look what he's done to you. And my boy was only having a little fun. That creepy little bastard!"

Miss Hatter was a staunch defender of Mr. Chip's amorous urges, in fact rather proud of them like a mother who is told her son regularly chases girls.

"It's natural for him to get randy," she always told the F & As when they complained about Mr Chip's unnatural fondness for puppies and miniature poodles. Miss Hatter sympathised with her dog, a sympathy fed by her observation that it was virtually impossible for Mr Chip to crown his amorous street assaults with success.

"Poor Mr Chip," she used to say: "He's never given a real chance." So one day when she took Mr Chip to the vet to renew his anti-rabies shots she steered the subject around to the dog's predicament. "Don't you know any bitches he could mate with?" she asked the vet, "I'd be quite prepared to pay." Unfortunately the vet was an elderly man who had long ago begun to hate all pets. He was outraged. "Signorina" he said, I'm a vet not a pimp." That remark prompted Miss Hatter to change her vet and to write a letter to the Corriere della Sera suggesting that dog lovers all over Italy establish a 'House of Joy' for male dogs whose happiness was impeded by their sexless existence. She was intelligent enough though not to sign the letter with her real name.

Having established beyond doubt Mr. Chip had suffered no harm from the brisk encounter with the young man's boot, Miss Hatter and her dog strolled down the Viale Trastevere. Mr. Chip, somewhat chastised, kept perfect pace for once. The incident had newly inflamed Miss Hatter's simmering belligerence; it was bad enough that the loveable puppy should be maltreated by the scruffy young man – there was little she could do about that now – but she would make sure that the poor blackbird was spared its awful fate. To her dismay no crowd had gathered outside Signor Panzer's shop. In fact, as she approached, a woman customer emerged shoving a brown paper parcel into her carry-all. Business seemed to be brisk. The authorities were simply slack, plain rotten slack, she thought, cautiously edging up to the display window. The blackbird squatted miserably on its perch inside the green cage Signor Panzer had hung from a butcher's hook behind the counter. From the window the bird appeared as inert as the hunks of mutton, veal, beef and the chickens strung up from a metal runner by their elongated necks. Maybe it was already dead. Miss Hatter's chest expanded.

Signor Panzer's grizzled head was bent over a ribcage. His gleaming cleaver smoothly sliced off one chop, then another. He picked up a piece of plasticised grey paper, spread it on the scale and with a practiced flourish dumped the chops onto it. He spoke to a woman customer who in turn made a comment to a man dressed in black beside her. Miss Hatter gasped. The man was a priest.

If Miss Hatter had faith in the law she had almost as much faith in the church. Policemen and priests served her purposes equally well. In fact where one failed the other often succeeded. She was inside the shop without giving the morning's encounter a single thought. Her opening gambit, though lacking elegance, was to the point and summed up her feelings.

"Father!" she shouted while still approaching: "How can you be at peace with your conscience and buy meat from a man who is caging a blackbird, one of God's most gifted creatures?"

The priest wheeled. He was a portly man in his late forties with a rosy glow on his cheeks. The black cassock bulged gently over his midriff. Miss Hatter, under full sail, was bearing down on him.

"Signor Panzer!" she cried: "Open that cage and let the bird out."

The butcher's Adam's apple popped. He clutched the cleaver tighter but in the pacifying presence of the church he was not game to repeat the morning's performance. "There's nothing wrong with keeping a blackbird," he said stubbornly, "is there, father?"

The priest, aware the onus was on him, weighed his head pensively, trying to gain time. His shrewd eyes narrowed:

"Brother Panzer is a God-fearing man," he said, bowing towards the butcher, "he gives God's servants a special price and one day he will be rewarded for this."

Signor Panzer nodded eagerly.

"Pah!" Miss Hatter exclaimed: "As a man of the cloth you should be defending the animals, not bartering over their carcasses."

The priest lowered his eyes; he wet his lips and folded his hands piously just like the ministrants do when they walk to mass.

"My dear daughter," he said, smiling the pompous smile of omnipotence which seems so much part of all priests: "God lets us know his will in mysterious ways. I'm only a humble servant …"

"… who keeps his eyes shut to the suffering of poor animals," Miss Hatter completed.

The priest looked vexed.

"I really don't merit this," he said: "What is it you want from me?"

"You're an educated man, father. Tell me, was this bird not born to be free?"

When the priest was young he had been taught by his seminar professor never to rush into an argument but to muster first his thoughts. That professor used to walk up and down with teeny paces before launching into lengthy discourses on human nature and its relationship to the creator. So the priest walked up and down with teeny paces in the butcher's shop. "My dear daughter," he finally began, still walking, "as I see the issue, this good man (he waved at the butcher) has caught himself a blackbird which keeps him company during the arduous hours of standing in this shop. It therefore brings joy to his daily life. You on the other hand believe he has offended the law of nature by keeping this bird in a cage. If you were right then our friend would have to close his shop, just as all the other butchers would have to close down since their trade would be an offense to God and nature. But since neither the bible nor the law has ever prohibited the use of animals for personal gain, joy or consumption, we can only deduce that man in his wisdom does not offend nature by either eating the animals or making them subject to his will and enjoyment."

The priest paused, hands folded in silent prayer.

"Are you telling me that it is quite natural for a blackbird to be caged? That this is not cruelty?" She had planted herself in front of the priest in her most intimidating pose, fists on her hips. He was a small priest and Miss Hatter was rather tall which gave her the advantage of peering down on him.

The priest smiled benevolently.

"I see you keep your dog on a leash," he said: "Might that not be considered cruelty?"

"I'm saving the dog from being run over by this dreadful traffic."

"Well, could not our friend here argue that he is saving the blackbird from hawks, eagles and the guns of the hunters?"

"Rubbish!" Miss Hatter countered, not at all flustered: "As a representative of God you should know better than that. If God had intended blackbirds to be placed in cages he would have done so when he created them."

The priest smiled enigmatically. He was on solid didactic ground now.

"And if God had intended to keep dogs on leashes would he not have created them with leashes already attached to their necks? But my dear daughter, who are we to interpret God's will. All we know is what we have studied in the bible and the bible tells us that God made the animals to serve man. He made man master of the animals. Man, made in the image of God, is the supreme being on earth."

"So," Miss Hatter said, fixing the priest with her most baleful stare: "You are not going to do anything about this dying bird, are you?"

"But I have," the priest said gently, "I've already told Brother Panzer to keep it in a dark place for a few days until it becomes accustomed to captivity. The first days are always the most difficult."

"What!" she said incredulously.

"Don't worry, my daughter, I know," the priest added quickly: "You see I used to keep a few blackbirds myself.'

Miss Hatter gaped. The priest smiled benignly.

"I'm not your daughter," she finally screeched: "You impotent little twerp dressed up in a black cassock."

And with that she stormed from the shop, head high, dragging Mr. Chip, who, interpreting the situation correctly, gave a vicious little bark at the priest. Outside she clenched her fists. Priests, she thought, could be even more corrupt than ordinary men. They had the unfair advantage of calling upon divine providence to back their argument.

She was still trembling with anger when she entered the courtyard. The grey cat with one blue and one glassy eye scurried out of her reach. The cat was always on the prowl. Mr. Chip dutifully barked at it, but the cat, aware of his physical limitations, leisurely climbed the first branch of the birch tree from where it blinked sleepily down at the dog. Mr Chip, as always, leapt up and down on the trunk, yapping with impotent frustration. The cat knew exactly how high Mr. Chip could jump. It always climbed just a hand's width above Mr. Chip's maximum jumping ability. As always, Mr. Chip avenged himself by leaving his mark on the trunk.

Miss Hatter passed a few anxious moments until she found her contact book, buried below a set of old encyclopedias.

"You wait and see, Chipy," she cried, dialing the first number, we'll show those exterminators of blackbirds … Mary? Mary I'm absolutely furious because the most dreadful thing has happened to me you see the butcher keeps a caged blackbird in his shop and he refuses to let it go and you know there's an old priest, an appallingly ugly man with pork eyes, who supports the butcher and you know what this little twerp of a priest said I nearly fainted. My God, I nearly clean fainted right there among the chops and the hung hams for they simply refuse to do anything about it and I wonder what is this world coming to if nobody lifts a finger even for a little bird. My God, it's bad enough they abandon dogs in the countryside when they don't want them anymore. But you've got to help me. I tell you we've got to picket this bastard of a butcher and show that nasty little man. Of course you'll come along Mary. Mary? Mary! What? … Oh! Why didn't you say so right away?"

Miss Hatter slammed down the phone.

"It was only the maid," she muttered to Mr. Chip who was chewing on his rubber bone. (Miss Hatter did not believe in real bones. She was afraid Mr. Chip, a dog with the teeth of a tiger as she was fond of saying, might swallow chewed off bone fragments that would surely pierce his intestines and condemn him to a slow and painful death.)

During the next hour Miss Hatter telephoned all those F & As she could count upon to express some solidarity for the predicament of the blackbird. Unfortunately, however, all of them were frightfully busy and unable to accept her invitation to picket the butcher's shop. Undaunted by this lack of support from the F & As, Miss Hatter played her penultimate trump. She rang up the Carabinieri and complained that Signor Panzer was selling adulterated meat. She even gave her name and lurked around the Viale Trastevere for the rest of the afternoon to enjoy her triumph when the Carabinieri would take Signor Panzer off to jail. He would be there for at least two days before the tests on all his meat was completed. And there would be poetic justice in his being caged like the blackbird. It served him right, she thought as she ambled up and down the pavement allowing Mr. Chip so much time to mark his domain that in the end his bladder ceased up. This obviously annoyed Mr. Chip for he began to paw the earth around the trees with such fury that he soon had to lie down and rest. So exhausted was he that a young pup sniffed him all over without Mr. Chip making even a half-hearted attempt to rape it.

It soon became dark and Mr. Chip whined for his six o'clock dinner (an appointment he kept with fastidious punctuality) when Miss Hatter decided that once more the short arm of the Italian law had shown itself to be utterly inefficient.

The time had come for drastic action.

In the courtyard the grey cat crouched on the rim of the moss-covered fountain, its favorite hunting perch and watched them enter. Mr. Chip, off the leash, ignored it. He made straight for the door, pawing it, whining like an old man who becomes cantankerous if not fed on time. The cat knew the mood. It paid no further attention to the dog but took up its vigil again at the edge of the fountain, coiled like a spring. Two of the goldfish leisurely floated near the surface. Now and then one of them might snap at a fly which had crash-dived into the water. That was the moment when the cat struck, with the speed of light and so accurate it never once wetted its paw.

After she had emptied two tins of liver and kidney pie into Mr. Chip's bowl Miss Hatter began to prepare for the final assault on the butcher's shop. She found the flattened white cardboard box on the bottom of the wardrobe below a heap of garments, all of them too small now for wear but with so many sentimental memories attached it was impossible to discard them.

The inside of the box was white and blank, perfect for her purpose. With a thick felt pen Miss Hatter wrote in large block letters:

STRIKE AGAINST BIRD KILLERS
BOYCOTT THIS SHOP

Having admired her prose for a while she went to the toilet to collect the broom, two nails and a hammer. She unscrewed the brush and nailed the placard to the end of the broomstick. Mr. Chip watched her suspiciously.

"You can't come this time, Chipy," she told him, slipping into her durable harlequin jacket, "picketing can get rough you know." The hound licked his chops, a sure sign his feelings had been hurt.

The Viale Trastevere was basked in neon lights and the headlights of the traffic snake which started at the Piazza Radio and ended at the River Tiber. The pavements teemed with office workers hurrying to shops before they closed at eight o'clock. There was a queue at the bus stop and a queue at the tram stop and the usual callous manoeuvring for parking spots. Miss Hatter, the placard squeezed under one arm, fitted easily into this milling throng where each person hurried to its own mysterious destination, utterly oblivious to the surroundings. Outside the butcher's shop she took up a position at the edge of the pavement facing the display window.

She propped the broomstick on the pavement beside her, not unlike the halberd of a Swiss Guard at the Vatican. With a satisfied grunt of 'hmm' she noted the shop was crowded.

For the first few minutes nothing happened; people, too occupied with their own problems, rushed by without a glance at the placard or the plump lady holding it. Then two men nudged each other; one of them, a gaunt elderly man who might have been once a bureaucrat by the way he wore his tie and stiff collar, peered cautiously up and down the road before he approached her: "Bloody Marxist!" he hissed: "Why don't you protest about old age pensions, you red rabble!"

Leaving Miss Hatter to digest that piece of wisdom he hurried off, dragging his companion by the elbow.

Next a ragged boy positioned himself in front of the placard, his back towards Miss Hatter, both hands in his pocket. He softly whistled a hit tune while allowing his eyes to rove over the chunks of raw meat in the shop window. Miss Hatter waited for a while but the boy made no attempt to move. So she tapped him lightly on the shoulder.

"Move along, young fellow," she said sternly: "This is a protest."

The boy turned and gawked. He was one of those startling Roman urchins who seem to be born with the face and mannerisms of adults. He did not budge.

"Move along, move along," she said irritably, "you're blocking their view."

The boy glanced over his shoulder: "There's no one there," he observed.

"Just move on, will you," she said, pushing him with one free hand.

"Hey lady, stop shoving," the boy protested: "This is a public footpath. I can stand where I want, see."

"Lout!" Miss Hatter mumbled through clenched teeth, at the same time moving two feet to the left to give the customers inside the shop a chance to read her placard.

"Crummy little fleabag!" she added.

"Hey! Who you calling a fleabag?" The boy had moved across to stand in front of her again, both hands pressed on his hips in the stance of the young tough. "What right have you got to call me names, hey?"

"Just go away."

The boy was about to reply when he saw the placard for the first time. He scratched his ruffled black hair. "Hey!" he said: "What's that thing you holding there?"

"Can't you read?"

"No," the boy replied, not at all embarrassed.

Just then one of the customers in the shop drew Signor Panzer's attention to the placard. Miss Hatter, her body tinkling with anticipation, jumped back into her former position and inclined the placard. She could see the butcher hobble around the counter and towards the display window. He stared at her blankly but she knew he had read the message. He shrugged one shoulder, turned and spoke to his customers pointing one finger at his temple then wagging a thumb towards the outside.

"And nuts to you too," Miss Hatter yelled.

"Hey, lady!" the boy said reproachfully: "I told you before not to call me names." And with that he suddenly kicked out at the broomstick which, torn from Miss Hatter's grip, cluttered onto the pavement.

Under duress Miss Hatter's carefully groomed vocabulary inevitably reverted to her school days in the country where a glib tongue was a prerequisite for survival in a class dominated by boys.

"You one-balled wimp with a cross-eyed grandmother," she bawled down the Viale Trastevere behind the hotfooting urchin, "I'll nackerize you, you limey flea-bitten little poofter, see if I don't," she added, retrieving the placard and waving it menacingly down the road.

"Now, now, Madam, what's all this about?"

The white helmet of the lanky urban policeman who towered above her was far too large for the man's face. It came down right over his ears. All she could see was his nose. And that was pointed straight at her.

"That snotty child kicked my placard over," she complained with righteous resentment.

"What placard?" the policeman asked sweetly.

"This!" she cried, holding the STRIKE AGAINST BIRD KILLERS BOYCOTT THIS SHOP sign up into his face.

"Hallo! Hallo!" the policeman said folding his arms behind his back. "I do suppose you have a license for this, Madam?"

"What license?" She tried to remain aloof.

The policeman sighed. "This is some kind of protest, is it?" he said: "So you need a license for it, don't you?"

"That's preposterous," Miss Hatter protested. "This is my own private gesture against that dreadful butcher who keeps a blackbird in a cage where it's sure to die if someone doesn't ..."

"... Madam, do or don't you have a license?"

And then the bucket-helmeted policeman pulled a pocket notebook from the inside of his white jacket together with a lead pencil.

"Well?" he said, pencil poised.

"I didn't know," Miss Hatter admitted a trifle insecure.

"Hmm," the policeman said meaningfully: "You'll have to come down to the station of course, if that is so."

"Is it necessary?" Miss Hatter's voice was quite small now.

"You're a foreigner?"

Miss Hatter nodded.

"That makes it more awkward," the policeman said, meaningfully.

"Oh! Couldn't we ... couldn't we just forget it?"

The policeman glanced down the Viale Trastevere. So far only three people had gathered to watch from a safe distance. He really didn't fancy going down to the station to fill out the charge sheet. It would take him the best part of two hours and he was off duty in thirty minutes. The woman being a foreigner would complicate matters even more. He took off his helmet and rubbed the sweatband with one thumb. When he spoke again, he seemed to be addressing someone in the distance. He certainly wasn't looking at Miss Hatter.

"Scat!" he said. "And don't let me see you around here again. And take your darn placard with you."

"Thank you," Miss Hatter whispered, quite faint.

She squeezed the offensive placard under her arm and hurried down the Viale Trastevere not daring to look back in case the generous policeman changed his mind.

Once inside her flat she threw the placard into a corner and herself into an armchair. "Good grief, Chipy," she cried as the dog leapt up and down with joy at her prompt return: "When you want a policeman they're never there but the minute you can do without one they trap you with all kinds of obscure laws; but we were too smart for them, see, we got away."

Mr. Chip gratefully licked her hand.

Miss Hatter went to bed early that night. Suddenly she felt very tired. By the time she fell asleep, she had forgotten all about the blackbird. She slept uneasily at first, tossing from one side to the other, arranging and rearranging her pillow, but near dawn she dropped off into a deep droning slumber during which she had a frightful nightmare about Mr. Chip's 'father', the handsome inter-island ferry captain Marco Positano, the man she had pursued with enviable tenacity for two years, the man with whom she had spent the most idyllic moments of her life, the man she had begged for a child. Instead, Mr. Chip had been the Captain's farewell present. An astute man, Captain Positano figured he could never be sued for maintenance of a dog.

The time period into which the nightmare fell coincided with the final days of their idyll when the handsome Captain (married with five children) tried endless tricks to erase his tracks: Once he ordered his office to inform Miss Hatter he had been transferred to Africa for at least ten years and on another occasion he climbed down a rope ladder on the portside of his vessel to be whisked ashore by the pilot boat while she waited loyally at the bottom of the gangway on the starboard side. But now and then even the Captain's most fiendish escape strategies were thwarted by Miss Hatter's brilliant search-and-find missions.

One of these missions haunted her sleep now. By resorting to a number of devious methods – one of them posing as his legitimate wife – Miss Hatter had ascertained her man would land at Genoa on a certain day in May. All night she drove up the Autostrada del Sole arriving at the port of Genoa just after dawn. Hidden behind a container parked on the wharf she watched the ferry 'Dante' nose into her moorings at 08.15. Her heart missed a beat when she saw him strutting along the bridge shouting final orders as the quay 'monkeys' noosed the pier stanchions with mooring ropes. It was a hot morning and he wore a white silk shirt with golden epaulettes, the short sleeves showing off the chocolate tan and grey hairs on the biceps. Her stomach contracted.

Passengers wormed off the gangways, the stern disgorged vehicles of all sizes and shapes. All along the quay loved ones hugged each other. But she had only eyes for the bridge.

The heat behind the container was oppressive, rivulets of sweat meandered down the inside of her thighs and along her shanks; sailors disembarked, one after the other, sometimes in groups, white haversacks slung over their shoulders.

And then she saw him at the railing.

He wore his white summer uniform, the shirt open, tie askew, the cap cocked to port. Hands on the rail, he leaned forward, furtively peering along the quay, down the wharf and across to the toll gates through which the last vehicles were passing. Dazed by two hours of waiting, enamored to the brink of madness, she interpreted these anxious glances the only possible way: He was looking for her.

"Marco! Marco!" she squealed, darting from her hideout, arms windmilling signals of distress, her whole being struggling to bridge the gap between them.

The look of abject horror on his face would haunt her for years to come. He stepped back from the railing as if the iron had electrocuted his hands; he blinked, stared again, in disbelief. She was already racing for the gangway; in just another moment she would be buried in his arms, those sinewy tanned arms with their curly grey hairs that could hold her like no man ever had. Just then he began to run too, a loping gait at first, but faster and faster until he fled down the deck towards the stern, ripping off his captain's cap, tugging it under his armpit, all the time picking up speed. The last she saw of Captain Positano was his head, as it disappeared down a hatch. She never saw him again, though at the time she was certain he was running for the lower deck to meet her, to come to her, to sweep her up in his strong arms.

She panted up the gangway and through the main hatch, ran along the lower deck towards the stern, stumbled up a wooden stairway, up, up through the clouds and onto the number two deck. It was empty.

Without checking her stride she bowled along, helter-skelter, passing lifeboats shrouded in cream canvas covers, freshly greased winches and open portholes through which drifted the puke-y stench of stale galley food; on and on she sped, up stairs, down hatches, bouncing off the walls in narrow corridors with numbered cabin doors, through lounges and more corridors, into the engine room, reeking of diesel and axle grease, up oily slippery spiraling staircases, down more corridors, down more decks, up through more hatches, down into new ones, running, running, panting, puffing, sobbing, a dreadful cramp in her womb but propelled by a paranoid fear she might miss him …

She woke up with a start. The daylight filtered grey through the Venetian blinds. Mr Chip barked. Someone was knocking at the door. Her period had come.

The knocking persisted. She probed and found the pink bathrobe on the bedside chair and slipped it over the pajamas; her feet, mechanically, slid into a pair of fur-lined pink moccasins. And all the time Mr. Chip was yapping himself into a fit of neurosis.

"I'm coming! I'm coming!" she shouted, irritated at being dragged from bed on a morning when she would have preferred to drowse and daydream another hour. She kneed Mr Chip aside and opened the door a slit. The sight made her open the door wide.

"Oh!" she exclaimed.

Signor Guglielmo Panzer stood there somewhat sheepish on his wooden leg. He was dressed in a grey street suit. A faded blue tie, badly knotted, dangled from his neck. But it was not the sight of the peg-legged butcher but the cage he held in one hand which widened Miss Hatter's eyes.

"Oh!" she said again, noting the blackbird sat on its perch exactly the way it had sat there the day before, head cocked to one side, blinking stupidly.

"You can have it," Signor Panzer said, not looking at Miss Hatter but down at the gravel. "I don't want any more trouble, Basta!"

He held out the cage.

She took it from him with her fingertips, gingerly and rather stiffly, noting the bird had hopped a little on its perch.

"I'm glad you've come to your senses," she said, gathering the collar of her robe tighter with the one free hand. "You'll feel much better for it in the end."

The butcher bit his lip. "Do with it what you like," he muttered, turning clumsily on his wooden leg to limp away.

"Wait a minute!" Miss Hatter raised the cage. "We'll set it free right now and then you can watch it soaring away into the sky. Wait."

The butcher stood defiantly in the centre of the courtyard, watching as she lifted the cage onto the lowest branch of the birch tree. She unhooked the wire lock and swung the gatelet open. The blackbird fluttered once then settled back on its perch "Don't be scared," she coaxed: "You're free now, come out, come out, come … come my little darling and fly into the sky …"

But the blackbird made no move to leave the cage.

"Silly stupid bird, you're free now don't you see?" The bird ruffled its feathers but remained where it was. Its beak opened and closed but no sound came from its throat.

Signor Panzer smirked.

"It's quite natural for it to be scared," Miss Hatter explained: "We're all standing around. It'll fly away in its own good time once we leave it alone. Thank you for coming Signor Panzer, I'm sure you feel already much better."

The butcher lifted one shoulder and limped towards the courtyard gate. He left without turning once. In the courtyard Miss Hatter, with a final friendly smile for the blackbird (still inert in its cage) closed her door to her flat, having dragged Mr Chip inside by his collar.

"See, people are not so bad, Chipy," she said to the dog. "Basically they know what is decent and right."

Mr Chip, ears pricked, growled at the door.

While she dressed Miss Hatter hummed part of a Beethoven sonata. She felt wonderful, she felt on top of the world; her soul was full of music, it brimmed with joy and goodwill and, of course, a little pride and triumph.

She was standing over the stove waiting for milk to boil, watching as the milk in the saucepan slowly drew skin. Then she heard a familiar sound in the courtyard. A terrible suspicion pierced her breast. She ran to the door and pulled it wide open.

The cage sat on the branch. But it was empty. Two black feathers gently parachuted onto the gravel. Across the courtyard the grey cat's tail-end was wriggling through the cellar window.

"Oh!" Miss Hatter cried, clapping her hands: "Chipy the milk is running over."

—

NINE

A Case of Atrophy

It was a Monday night. I distinctly recall that. On Mondays most restaurants are closed, so everyone is at a loss. That's why dining out Mondays is always a memorable occasion.

In those days (before the Euro kindled a wave of greed followed by inflation that made dining out a luxury) a decent evening began with dinner at a Trattoria or Ristorante. Only after one dined well, after one whet one's wit on other table companions and one's appetite on other men's women, or other women's men, did a devil-may-care attitude descend around the table. Suddenly everyone became eager to prolong the night. Towards the end of such dinners, when the waiter has come for the third time to inquire: "Is there anything else?" the cook is pulling down the creaking iron shutters and the coffee-boy sets empty chairs upside down, someone always makes a phone call:

"Ciao Bruno! How is the party? Oh good. Of course I'm coming. There's just one small problem: I'm having dinner with friends. You remember Aida? Yes, yes, the one with the burning eyes. Right, so you do remember. You don't mind if I bring her along – and a few of the others. Thanks Bruno. You're a treasure."

And so it happens that when you invite ten people to a party 'after dinner' you end up with twice that number, most of them strangers towed in by friends, always politely introduced to the host and then left to fend for themselves.

On that fateful Monday evening, an evening which bore the seed that was to ruin our summer and wreck a number of relationships, we were a largish group. Still, we all knew each other well, knew one another's problems, knew who slept with whom and who had slept with whom, knew each other's weaknesses and strengths, our little and big problems, our idiosyncrasies and current fads, our petty hang-ups, what we earned and what we owned. In short we were at ease with one another, a kind of extended family in which you blabber away, where conversations are marked by that tone of intimacy only possible if there is an absence of aliens. Besides, the atmosphere at Da Giovanni lends itself to familiar communication. The Trattoria, next to Regina Coeli Jail, is no bigger than a studio and is always abominably crowded. The clientele varies from taxi drivers on a night off, to pseudo socialites slumming for the evening. Sometimes a prison warden comes in from next door to pick up dinner ordered by one of the wealthy inmates, together with one or two bottles of vintage wine. These wardens carefully check the meal and wine when it is handed over, not for hidden saws or guns but to ensure the order has been meticulously carried out: The size of their tips depends on it.

Da Giovannni is a place where it is best to ask the waiter right away what is left on the menu, since Giovanni only cooks as much as he calculates will be consumed that night. It is the kind of Trattoria where the tablecloth is brown paper rolled up carefully at the end of the meal so it can be used again if possible; the kind of place where it is best to fetch your own fork from the kitchen, where one must not be upset if the waiter fails to bring the mineral water after one has already asked three times. But the food is wholesome, the wine excellent and one knows at the end of the meal the bill will not cause indigestion.

"One way to sexual happiness is to make sure you are constantly exhausted. Then you have no time for other desires. Capito?"

Lidia had thrown this piece of wisdom onto the table just as the waiter banged down a bottle of corked Bardolini. Her remarks were often as startling as her alabaster complexion, her wide blue eyes, and her Titian-red hair.

"In other words," Aida began with that querulous air she adopted on the warpath: "You keep poor Stefano active so he has no energy left to consider other women."

"Right," Lidia replied candidly.

"Poor Stefano!" Aida sighed.

"Poor Stefano!" We all echoed, making the appropriate noises of commiseration.

The subject of so much concern had uncorked the Bardolini and was now smiling, Mona Lisa-like. He enjoyed being the centre of attention, particularly when it concerned his love life. And whenever something pleased him, as it did now, his round pop eyes behind the rimless spectacles would pop out a little further and the melancholic smile appeared on lips a lady from the Antipodes had once described as 'Juicy Lips.'

"Aren't you afraid he might find this boring after some time? I mean being drained like a wine bottle every day?" Aida was not prepared to abandon the subject.

Lidia contemplated this for a moment, while all of us, amused by the exchange, waited for her reply. She must have been aware in those days that many of Stefano's friends, Aida certainly among them, looked upon her liaison either with envy or with regret, regret that Stefano was no longer the gay bachelor who had kept us all entertained with his romantic escapades, his tales of falling in love, his sufferings, rather melodramatic, which inevitably lasted until he had managed to bed the adored one.

"One can drink a different label of wine every night and enjoy it," Lidia said: "Then one day you find a label so good you can't stop drinking it."

"Good point …"

"Hail to the connoisseur …"

"And so he drinks himself into oblivion … ."

Everyone was adding some idiocy to Lidia's retort.

But Aida was not yet beaten: "But don't you think the day must come when he feels there might be just that one more label of a wine that might be tastier?"

"Oh, fickle hearts," cried I.

"Hold it, hold it!" Stefano protested. He was standing, filling the glasses around the table: "As the object of this dispute may I have a word?"

"Let Stefano speak!"

"The accused has the word!"

We had all warmed up to the game now.

"Thank you my friends," Stefano said with a bow from the waist. "First of all let me say that as a slave of the womb I have never found 'IT' boring." (general applause and catcalls)"But, I do admit I have found the aftermath boring: Using Lidia's metaphor with the wine, the difference is whether one suffers a hangover or not after imbibing. I mean the trouble starts once you lie there and have nothing else to say to each other, when you realize both of you are probably working out a stratagem to extricate yourself from the situation as elegantly and as quickly as possible. That is the hangover. But there are no hangovers with Lidia."

He bent down and pecked Lidia on the forehead to general applause.

Only Claudia protested. But she liked to protest. As the off-spring of a famous singer she had learned early that protest was the only way to lift herself into the limelight from the shadows as the daughter of a celebrity.

"Chauvinist!" she squealed. "Stefano, you pig, you're the type who feels romantic only while his erection lasts. Your poetry always blows itself into millions of spermatozoon."

"Darling!" Stefano replied: "We men are vulnerable on this subject. After our efforts to fertilize the egg are completed we are done. On the other hand you have to wait for the results."

The waiter banged the spoon on the table for a long time before he received the appropriate attention. "Is this a circus or are you going to order," he finally demanded.

"Ah, bring me what's left on the menu and we'll share it out between us." Luigi's suggestion was met with loud approval and a dismissive shrug from the waiter.

The wine had warmed us up as wine is apt to do if unaccompanied by food. Everyone, flushed by that first alcoholic stimulus, always the most verbally productive, tried to speak at the same time.

"Anyway, men have only five thousand shots. And that's it."

To this day I cannot remember who said it, though later I would be blamed for the remark, unjustly. But I do recall distinctly nobody reacted. We all babbled on as if that phrase had gone unnoticed, though judging from later reaction I'm sure everyone registered the remark. Certainly

Stefano did. And since he could never control his feelings or his curiosity, he asked after a while: "So what's all this about five thousand shots?"

"Oh, you didn't know?" said I, quickly taking up my role as the devil's advocate. "It's an established biological fact that men have only five thousand shots. Bang, bang, bang, five thousand times and then it's all over."

"Are you worried, darling?" Aida had turned to Stefano with a maliciously sweet smirk.

"Nonsense," Luigi intervened: "The usual half-cocked gibberish of some eccentric scientist fishing for publicity. Academics talk such hogwash. Give someone a degree and they become an instant oracle."

"And that from a professor," Claudia piped.

Luigi held up his hands in mock horror: "It takes one to know one."

"So how did Charlie Chaplin do it?"

We all turned to Nina. She blushed. It is always entertaining to have someone uncomplicated at the table, male or female, someone that can provide ammunition for general mirth to keep the conversation alive with their innocence. Nina was our bunny.

"Maybe he was parsimonious," Aida suggested.

"Or he had an implant."

"Implant?" All eyes were on Luigi, our professor.

"Why not," he said. "Did not Tito reportedly retain his masculinity until he was eighty, thanks, so they say, to constant implants?"

"Implants of what?" Nina asked.

"Not of what you think, young lady. Implants of hormones, taken from unborn lambs and injected, or implanted if you like, into the reproductive organs, if you know what I mean."

"So all is safe," exclaimed Stefano.

"If you can afford the expensive procedure and find a clinic that does it. As a matter of fact I know of none," Luigi said.

"Shame!" Aida cried: "We could send Stefano there. He'll soon need one."

"I haven't noticed," Lidia snapped.

"You wouldn't." Aida winked: "He's on his reserve ammo."

Amid the uproarious laughter the food arrived, dumped on the table in clay casseroles by the surly waiter. In the hubbub of whether to have the pork chops, the tripe alla Romana or the Stuffato, the subject was forgotten, until I, having rescued some of the tripe, rekindled it.

"I'm sure this whole business was invented by a woman," I said.

"Perhaps you're right," Aida agreed, sawing through her chop: "Men would never voluntarily set the limits of their potency."

"But women would," interrupted Stefano. "Think of the advantages. If a man was really convinced he had only five thousand shots in the barrel he would think twice about a fling. He would even have to consider monogamy. It could bind some poor slob forever to his woman. Heaven forbid!"

"It would mean rationing," said Luigi.

"It would mean keeping count," annexed Stefano.

"It would mean abstinence, except in emergencies," said I.

"And no second helpings," Stefano lamented.

"Maybe just firing blanks," Luigi suggested.

"Certainly more discrimination …"

"More headaches over choice …"

"And inventing excuses …"

"In the meantime what would women do?" asked Nina.

Aida put her fork carefully on her plate: "Find a young man who is not yet rationing," she said bluntly.

After the laughter Luigi rubbed his long nose with the blade of a knife and admitted: "Women do have a biological advantage. They can simply go on and on whereas we poor men are dead once we've shot the bolt."

"You said it, brother." Aida chuckled. Her almond eyes sparkled. "We can still do it without implants when we're eighty. All we need is a little Vaseline."

"Aida!!"

"Never have I heard such a load of rubbish," Claudia protested.

It made everyone laugh with relief and indulge in those private asides which break up general conversations. In fact it appeared for a while as if the subject would be dropped. Then Aida picked it up again.

"How many times does the average person make love in a week?" she asked, suddenly.

"Twenty times," Stefano offered. He was never modest when it came to his love life.

"Not everyone can be a Super-macho," Aida said: "Can someone give me a more realistic offer?"

"Seven," said Luigi.

Claudia, his wife, promptly pecked him on the cheek: "Well, Tesoro, then you're well below average, aren't you?"

During the ribald laughter Luigi's ears went red and he was trying to decide whether to be angry or amused. He chose the latter. At fifty he was trying to keep abreast.

"Why don't we ask the girls," I suggested: "After all we poor men can only make a guess, based on our own personal experience. Besides we are apt to exaggerate when it comes to statistics of potency. But the ladies at this table have the experience of variety upon which they can base their assessments. Besides, women are more honest when it comes to keeping count."

"You big shit!" Claudia shrieked. Nina only giggled.

"Fair enough," I said: "Let's consult Aida. With two ex-husbands and a lordly number of lovers, she should be able to help us out. Aida?"

She looked at me for a moment, trying to gauge if there was a hidden trap to the question. Then she smiled. If Stefano liked to mention his female conquests, Aida made no secrets she was a man eater.

"Four to five times a week!" She said it with authority.

"Any other bids," I asked, glancing around the table. Lidia and Claudia both looked peeved. Nina giggled and said: "I once knew a boy who did it ten times in one night."

"Nina!"

"Not impossible," interjected Stefano, "I heard of a guy who did it twelve times during one afternoon …"

"And how many months did you rest after that, dear?" Aida asked.

It took some time before everyone regained their composure and we decided to work it out on the basis of four shots a week.

"Let's say our Mr. Average starts firing in earnest at eighteen," I said.

"Wait!" interjected Stefano: "Surely firing in earnest or firing for practice – that is without a target – still counts. One is still wasting ammunition."

"Have it your way, but let's get on with the accounting," I interrupted: "So if he does it four times a week then he's done it two hundred and eight times a year. Right? That means at the age of forty – OK, let's have a piece of paper – that's it. He'll have fired four thousand five hundred and seventy six times. He's still got some reserves up the spout."

Aida frowned. "Hmm, that means he'll run out between the age of forty-two and forty-three. How old are you Luigi?"

"Can't remember," the professor replied.

"He's fifty," Claudia prompted, "and he's obviously an exception to the rule."

"Or he's been handling his ammo with great care," Aida offered.

"Who wants sweets?" the waiter demanded.

It was a lively dinner and the subject of the five thousand shots did not crop up again, forgotten, it seemed, though today I realize that night was only the beginning. The poison had penetrated our minds.

The same night, at the front door of my apartment block, I yawned. "It's been a long day," I said, rather superfluously. Nina smiled: "Poor thing." She snuggled into my arms expectantly, a small compact girl with a healthy appetite for all aspects of life. All the way from the Trattoria she had chatted incessantly bubbling over with the pent-up desire to communicate, a desire artificially stifled during dinner. She was one of those people who never manage to have their say in public but make up for it in private. At the moment she was enthused with the prospect of a part in a theater play. And that stimulated her appetite, creating an air of euphoria on which it is easy to bounce into bed.

"Come on," she purred into my ear: "Open the door."

I yawned again, more prolonged, hoping she would take the hint, though knowing, from experience, hints for Nina needed to be driven home with a sledgehammer.

"I'm pooped tonight. Let's get together another day." That was it, I thought. But I had underestimated Nina.

"Poor old Silver-hair," she murmured, stroking my hair (how I loathed her calling me 'silver-hair'): "We'll go bed-y bed-y right away, hmmm?" The mischievous twinkle in her eyes betrayed her true intentions. I panicked.

"I want to go to bed right away," I said: "But alone."

Not waiting for further argument I kissed her on the cheek, opened the door and slipped inside. For a fleeting moment I saw her glaring at me with a strange expression on her face, as if she hated me. Then I closed the door. The second the lock snapped shut I felt such an enormous relief, as if I had escaped falling off a cliff. I remember whistling as I went upstairs, to the chagrin of the Avocado on the second floor who stuck his head out of his apartment and muttered something about drunken slobs and the police. I did not feel tired at all and before I slept I read twenty pages of Dylan Thomas.

On the following days I invented work. I cut all my social commitments, refused to answer the telephone in case it was someone just around the corner wanting to come up for a minute. I even kept the shutters half closed and embarked on a number of projects. I started a play, discarded it half way through the first scene, began a film script, put it aside and launched into a verbose argument on the pros and cons of the new Concordat, an argument of no interest to anyone except the Italian Treasury and the Vatican Bank.

On Friday afternoon, however, Stefano banged at the door so insistently I was forced to open. One look at his face and I knew it was a problem associated with either the pursuit or the shedding of a woman, probably the latter, since Stefano, like Faust, found it easier to call the spirits than to be rid of them. He wore the hang-down bloodhound expression that never failed to amuse me. He flung himself across the sofa, feet flopping over one armrest, fleshy lower lip curled in dismay, one hand nervously combing through the thinning hair on his dome.

"It can't go on like this," he began without further ado: "It's like being bled dry by a leach."

I was sure he had fallen in love again. One could not help but admire his single-mindedness. His stubborn pursuits – laced with Myral gifts, unexpected outings to off-the-track locations and encounters with weird acquaintances – inevitably wore down his victims. When in pursuit of one of his Madonnas, Stefano's energy was unflagging, his enthusiasm formidable, his wit acrobatic. His endurance lasted until he had brought them down from the lofty pedestal on which his own infatuation had placed them. Once down, he quickly tired of them. At least until he had met Lidia.

"What shall I do?"

How many times had he sat on my sofa with the same categorical question? He never waited for an answer nor was he interested in my advice. He simply needed an audience, at least for a few minutes, since he was in and out of my place like a cuckoo popping from its clock.

"Do you think I'm getting old?"

I was not given time to contemplate such a possibility either. "But two and three times each night, and in the afternoons – the afternoons, mind you and you know how I love my siestas, but I'm beginning to fear them, as the fingers of the watch march towards two o'clock I break out in a cold sweat, while she watches me like a manta. Do you think I look nervous?"

I wagged my head in a gesture of non-committal, but he was already off again … "She's obsessed with it. I mean it was all good fun in the beginning, but now it's wearing me down, it's wearing me down, Aaron, it's like a weight on my existence, it's like being drained, slowly, knowing every day more sap leaks out of your body, sap that can never be replaced. Do you think I must give her up?"

His lips were puckered the way Il Duce had puckered his before launching into one of his operatic tirades. He continued without giving me a chance to answer. "No, no, I tell you they're all the same. Don't you wish at times you were castrated? Ah, what a peaceful life that would be. I tell you it's time to do something, to make a mark in life. I'll be thirty-five next month and what do I have to show for it? A half day job I hate, one or two contributions a year to a highbrow magazine which pays peanuts because they think you're lucky to be allowed to write for them, an old motorbike, an old car, a rundown flat, a dog with three legs and a little black book with telephone numbers. Tell me, is that what life is all about?"

Before I had time to assess these assets, he was on his feet, glancing at his wristwatch. "Shit, I'm late. We'll be in touch. I'll call you tonight." And he was gone, leaving behind his problems and the suspicion that what he had said might also apply to me. Damn Stefano, his visits resembled a hurricane: It blows your world apart and then simply vanishes, leaving you to clear the debris.

A day or so after his visit I elbowed my way through the Trevi Café Bar, trying to catch Gino's eye, which meant I would jump the queue of those offering their cash register slips and a hundred lire tip to one of the barmen on the espresso machines. At that hour of the morning everyone slips out for ¬coffee and a chat. The customers are always three and four rows deep and if you don't know one of the barmen you can wait forever. Luckily Gino saw me and winked. While I waited for the brew to be steamed off (thanking the Lord he had not seen fit to make me an espresso barman) I noticed Annamaria sandwiched between three chauffeurs from Montecitorio, all talking to each other at the same time over her head.

"Annamaria!" I called, taking my cup and squeezing along the bar towards her with lots of 'con permesso … con permesso …' to those I had to elbow out of the way. Annamaria was a lumpy girl with button eyes and a round face, typical of the Sardinians.

"Haven't seen you for months, cara," I began. But she looked at me morosely and stuck her pert nose back into the coffee cup.

"So where's the shoe squeezing?" I asked. She kept silent.

"How is Adolfo?" She pouted. "In soma," she finally said, which meant everything and nothing.

"Problems?" She looked at me for a moment, then lifted one shoulder. "In soma," came the laconic reply.

No one could imagine Annamaria and Adolfo splitting up. Both were too absent-minded to lose each other for good. So I was on safe ground when I joked: "Run off with another woman, has he?"

"Magari," she replied, which, translated for that occasion signaled anything from 'I wish he had' to 'couldn't care less.' So I changed the subject and we talked for a while about work in the Ministry and the crack-down (temporary like all Italian crackdowns) on bureaucrats and their absenteeism. According to the latest statistics, up to twenty-five per cent of public workers in the nation absented themselves each day. An inquiry had shown some were running stores on the side, others private Hospitals; a postman ran his wife's pharmacy. He had picked up his batch of letters daily and for six months had dumped them each morning into his cellar. There had been terrible embarrassment at the main Post Office in Rome when all employees in one department turned up for work one morning in fear of the inspector, only to find there were not enough chairs to accommodate all of them.

Quite out of the blue Annamaria asked me: "What do you think about men who decide to practice abstinence?"

So that was it.

"Adolfo?"

She rolled her head from side to side: "He's come up with some cock and bull story that men have only five thousand shots. Well, you know what, Porco Juda, would I like to get my hands on the idiot who put that bee in his bonnet?"

It has always amazed me how fast news travels in Rome, evidence, if any was required, of the provincial nature of a city where word of mouth still proliferates faster than written texts.

* * *

The entire five thousand-shot affair remained amusing, of course, until the night Claudia telephoned. Her opening gambit, fired at point blank range, without the customary inquiries about my health or love life, bowled me over: "Listen, Mephisto, if you got trouble with IT, don't scare your friends. I know your game: You're so vain you could never admit it. But if you were a real man you'd do the right thing and tell Luigi and the others about your problem. Tell them what you said at dinner was a bluff which your nasty little mind cooked up so you wouldn't feel the only eunuch in town ... ." "Claudia!" I yelled down the mouthpiece: "What the hell are you on about?"

But she talked right over the top of me: "And don't think because Luigi is old enough to be my father I'm liable to drop him. He's a better man than you'll ever be – and I ought to know."

There was a click. The phone was dead.

The last part hurt. At one time I had been more than infatuated with Claudia. It was a time when her gypsy face and lithe body haunted my day dreams. I stalked her, until I had her, until she wanted to run away with me, anywhere, anytime, until she purred like a kitten in my arms and squealed her ecstasy through the bedroom. We were good together, at least so I had always thought, until we drifted apart. Some affairs are not meant to last, not because they go stale but because one discovers day by day more ticks in the other person. For a start Claudia was a night bird. And she seemed to consider it her privilege to turn up at all hours of the night and ring the bell; not just ring it once but keep her finger on the button until I answered. Once, when I refused to open at four in the morning, she stood in the street and yelled on top of her grating voice: "Aaron! Aaron!" She was utterly impervious to the blood-curdling threats of pajama-clad figures at bedroom windows. So I gave her a key. Trouble was, whenever she came home she was still in overdrive. At three in the morning she would turn the stereo to full volume. It brought me racing out of the bedroom, exactly what she had wanted in the first place. Now she could talk. If I wanted to work she wanted to make love; if I wanted to read she wanted to go for a walk. She simply refused to be ignored; she was capricious, precocious and obnoxiously contrary. She could neither be convinced by logic nor by examples, a trait obviously inherited from her famous father, the epitome of a Calabrian: Arrogant, stubborn and always right.

Her beauty was savage: It stirred people the minute they saw her; it made them uneasy and she preyed on this quite consciously. She wore provocative bohemian dresses and skintight slacks that sheathed the melon-shaped buttocks like a glove. She could walk into a room of people, turn up the stereo, shake loose her long black hair, raise her arms and dance a sensuous solo in the centre of the room, apparently oblivious to the sidelong stares. It was her way of saying: "I'm here." Men immediately wanted her. Women loathed her. I gave up on her, not without considerable drama.

At that time – that is after Claudia's call – I still did not realize I was carrying a time bomb. That realization came at the Prince's party.

We called Felipe the Prince because (and no-one was quite sure) he was supposedly a member of a noble Roman family, one of those with vineyards in the hills, two or three Palazzi in the city, a chateau in the country and a handful of Popes in the ancestral gallery. One always doubted these claims, since every second "Per Bene" Roman claims noble descent though few could ever prove it, if pressed. Felipe lived in a penthouse on the top of a Palazzo rumored to be owned by his family, a building not far from the church of San Francesco della Valle. He was a good-natured fellow with a bend for academic life. Tall and stringy, he was endowed with deep-set eyes, a concave chest and a shock of straight hair which always covered one baleful eye. No doubt he was a trifle inbred. He was a generous type and carried himself with the lofty air expected of a Cavaliere. Many a status-conscious Signorina had tried to become La Principessa. None succeeded. The apparent absence of any libido kindled poisonous tongues, those who whispered: "Young Don Felipe is a little strange. You know what I mean?" These remarks were accompanied by the proper raising of the eyebrows. Similar gossip had all but ruined the Prince's reputation as a lover. Of course it was mainly women who tossed about such hypothesis. If men fail with a woman they suspect she is a lesbian and so it stands to reason women who fail to seduce a man tend to see him as gay. Still it was this caution in his trafficking with women that convinced us all Felipe was a man of means and probably noble birth. Why, otherwise would he refuse the offered favors? That he was not immune to the charms of the opposite sex we knew from bed sheet talk. He was simply discreet.

At one point of the evening I found myself on the sofa next to Eugenia, a dumpy Matron overflowing in all of her extremities and a notorious gossip. Her current victim, a spindly English girl, listened with that fixed smile of solicitous attention the English manage to produce on such occasions.

"And then he told her he would go on a savings scheme, if you know what I mean," Eugenia said, patting the hand of the poised English girl. "And he cited Hemingway who supposedly said that the best books are lost in bed. He said he could either be a writer or a lover and since his ambition was to be a writer he would have to sacrifice the activities of the lover. Don't you think that was callous?"

The English girl smiled comprehensively, though I was certain she had not understood a single word. Eugenia lowered her voice to an even more conspiratorial level: "Antonia was livid. Oh, you can't imagine. Rightly so, don't you think? What would you do if your husband suddenly decided, after God knows how many years, to turn celibate?"

Here the English girl instinctively understood some kind of comment was expected. "Yes, quite right," she said. It satisfied Eugenia and she immediately launched into a new story, about someone called Julie who was being separated from her husband.

I listened with only half an ear, though suddenly my attention was rekindled by the phrase "Five thousand shots, have you heard anything so ridiculous?" I moved a little closer, pretending my attention was caught by someone on the opposite side of the room.

"It's a disease. Francesco says it has ruined the love lives of half of Rome. Of course Francesco doesn't have to worry; he's only thirty-one. Surely you haven't such problems, my dear. No, no, your husband is a diplomat; he would not listen to such garbage. Besides, Englishmen are much more stable than our men. Dio mio, there's nothing that frightens ours more than the prospect of … well, you know what I mean.

The English girl smiled and Eugenia continued without taking a breather. "It could destroy them. I remember when Time, or was it Newsweek, anyway one of those know-all American magazines, came out with that awful story about Aids. My goodness, wherever you went, men were discussing Aids or making jokes about it. Still, I think it did a lot of marriages a lot of good in this country. What do they think in England about such matters?"

I was spared the answer, predictably another 'yes', by a hand on my shoulder. It was Stefano, debonair in a tweed coat à la 1950s and a yellow tie a la Capone, Chicago 1920s.

"One hears you've gone into hibernation," he began.

I tried not to fidget. "Well, one can either play or one can write. At the moment I have to finish a manuscript."

"Hmm." He did not seem convinced.

"And where is Lidia?" I asked, to change the subject.

"Gone to Turin for a few weeks to see her family!"

"Ah. Return to bachelor life," I said.

He grinned. "Not quite, I … oh, hallo Eugenia! Sorry I didn't see you."

"Ciao, caro!" The Matron said. "Forgive me but I thought I heard you say Lidia went back to Turin. Have you two broken up?"

"My God," Stefano exclaimed, looking more outraged than the occasion merited: "Why does everybody think we have split up, just because Lidia wants to see her family."

"But in the summer, dear," Eugenia said gently. "What is there to do in the summer in Turin. When I talked to her a week ago she seemed to look forward so much to the beach and to the lakes. Her mother is not ill again, is she?"

"I don't think she's too well," Stefano said and I knew he was lying. He was a lousy liar. He knew it, so he made his excuses and steered me towards the bar.

"It's much easier to be a woman," he said, picking up a glass of whisky.

"How's that?" I asked, half listening and half occupied in scanning the room for a familiar or interesting face.

Stefano gazed into the glass for a moment: "If a woman doesn't want to do it, that's her privilege: It's because she doesn't feel like it, because she finds the man unattractive, it's too soon or too late, it's the wrong time of the month. Damn it, she always has an excuse ready and men must accept it, in good grace or in bad grace. In the end we blame ourselves, we feel bad, we are frustrated, our ego suffers."

"Hmm," I mused, still half listening.

"Now if we don't want to do it, if we feel cool, if we're no longer attracted, if we've decided to lay off a bit, then, my friend, all hell breaks loose. We're getting old, we're getting decrepit, we're running out of steam, we're perverted, we're ready for the garbage dump, we don't love her anymore, we don't care and finally, of course: We have another woman. Turn down a woman and she'll never let you forget it. But if she turns you down, that's perfectly fine. There is something wrong there, Aaron. What is it?"

Admittedly I'd never looked at it this way. Some matters one simply accepts because they've always been so.

"It's all rather ridiculous," I said, "I mean today women don't have to say 'no' anymore, thanks to modern science, yet instinctively they still want to say 'no' because saying 'no' has been part of their natural reaction to men for so long, and, of course, it has given them a base of power. But all this is changing. What has happened is that the roles of the sexes have inverted. The woman of tomorrow will do all the hunting, the man the running. The sex revolution is in full swing and like all revolutions it will replace one ruling class with another. Our misfortune is that we'll be members of the underprivileged class."

"Santa Maria. You mean there's the danger of us being raped one day by marauding gangs of women?"

"And why not Stefano? There have already been cases and I'm sure there are many more, not published. After all what man would go to the law to complain he has been raped. But in another generation, men might queue up to file such charges."

Stefano shook his head. "Biologically impossible."

"You're arguing from the current status quo," I said: "At the moment the number of willing men still exceeds the number of willing women. We men are still short of supply, which stimulates our libido. It's like eating a rare fruit: Your tongue waters, but if the fruit is available in surplus you can take it or leave it; in fact soon you'll be tired of it. Certainly your mouth no longer waters.

"Transfer this hypothesis to sex. Women have virtually always enjoyed a surplus of willing studs. Yet over the last decades women have imitated men in everything, including the right to take the initiative in the mating game. All of a sudden man finds himself in the unusual role of the hunted, and his libido, which has been stimulated by thousands of years of running down his prey, becomes dulled, as does his performance. Give it another generation or so and the male will feel hardly inclined to raise his bum to reproduce. This, in turn, will stimulate female libido to the point where they'll gang-bang some poor male. The effects on the male will be disastrous."

"You're talking about an atrophy of the male," Stefano moaned.

"Or the solution to the problem of the world's demographic explosion. Malthus triumphs again: Male castrated by his own mate."

"I can see it coming,' Stefano cried, raising his glass: "Nature takes care, but this time not through famines, natural phenomena, nuclear wars, or diseases, but through genetics. Insufficient spermatozoa to fertilize the ovule. Divine justice."

"When that happens they will talk about five thousand shots as if those were the golden days," I piped, "because they won't even have a thousand shots, not even a hundred. Believe you me, my friend, the atrophy of the male has already begun."

"You bet it has," a voice said over our heads.

We spun around together.

"Aida!

The lady visibly sparked with mischief: It was present in the flicker of her dark eyes, the drawn down corners of her mouth and the cocked hip.

"These two gentlemen are attempting to convince each other there's nothing wrong with them," she explained to a young man, lounging, hands in pockets, by her side. "They remind me of the man who rang the radio and bitterly complained about the phantom drivers he had to dodge on his side of the Autostrada all the way between Florence and Orvieto. The point was: He was the phantom driver."

"Ha! Ha!" Stefano cackled.

Aida snuggled against the young man's chest. He was young, handsome and endowed with that arrogance of youth. He was immediately antipatico.

"Meet Beppino, you two. He hasn't got any problems yet."

"He soon will if he sticks around with you." Stefano could be as bitchy as a bar boy ponce, once his pride was pricked.

"Mind your tongue," the young man called Beppino said. He obviously felt obliged to play the knight in shiny armor.

After that remark the scene turned into a bad spaghetti western. It began when Stefano told the young buck: "You mind your own business, bimbo," then annexed something to the effect that behind every slob there is an ambitious woman. Not that Stefano was the kind to look for trouble; on the contrary, he was the kind who said 'sorry' if someone stepped on his foot. Maybe Beppino was trying to impress Aida, who was at least ten years his senior, maybe he was peeved by the word 'bimbo' which Stefano kept waving in front of him like a red flag. Anyway one word led to another and all of a sudden the 'bimbo' shoved Stefano's chest with the flat of his hand, a most uncommon gesture at a Roman party where duels are fought with tongues, not fists. The shove took Stefano by surprise. He lost his balance, staggered backwards, stumbled on the edge of a carpet and crashed rather clumsily across the coffee table. Two carafes and a few glasses smashed with a thin tinkle. A girl screamed. Two men bent down to help Stefano off the table. It looked worse than it was and the bimbo stood there, mouth open in surprise at what he had accomplished. And that again explained how I managed to smack him so neatly on the jaw. It was a left, thrown with a lot of advance notice, a blow cynically known among pugilists as a haymaker. It clipped the bimbo right on the point of his chin, which boxers call the 'sweet dreams spot.'

My arm was still in the air when his seat met the floor with a thump. A few aghast 'aah's' rippled round the room and I remember bimbo rubbing his jaw, sitting on the floor groggy, and Aida fussing over him. Next thing someone had me in a double Nelson, someone else was kicking away my legs and I was on the floor, with bodies on top of me.

The next time I had a good view of the room I saw Aida being held back by the Prince as she repeatedly attempted to place-kick my head. The Prince, a good foot taller, was being yanked from side to side by her frantic kicking attempts while vile phrases dripped from her lovely lips. All of them had something to do with my inability to procreate. The thought came to me no one in that room would believe that Aida and I had once been lovers, not even that long ago. And we had sworn to remain friends, come what may.

The Prince felt it was best I leave. And so I left. And all the way home I tried to figure out why I hit the bimbo. I kept thinking about this until I realized I had sprained my thumb doing it. This made me feel even worse.

* * *

The Bar della Pace in the Piazza della Pace is one of those watering holes that come alive after the rest close. Shortly before midnight, shadowy figures trickle from the maze of vicoli into the Piazza, the little square designed by Pietro Cortona in the sixteenth century as a setting for the church, Santa Maria della Pace, the one with Raphael's fresco of the Sibyls near the portals and the clochards under the portico.

Nobody remains for long at the Bar della Pace: It is the kind of place one drops in, to see who is there, to have a last drink, to find someone who has moved, someone who owes you money, or a favor. Here it is possible to replenish one's stock of hash or coke and on rare occasions to pick up a stray woman, usually someone you already know. Everyone hugs and pretends they know each other better than they do.

Three weeks after the Prince's fateful party, I strolled into the Bar, always dimly-lit but with spotlights on the vines and ivy creeping down the walls of nearby palazzi. I had come more in search of company than to quench my thirst. My social life had become ominously quiet, more so than I could wish.

Having elbowed my way out of the bar, carrying a tequila, a slice of lemon and a saucer of salt, I noticed Memo Maguzzi lounging against a vintage Lancia. From the crooked posture of his body he was either stoned or contemplative. Surprisingly he was alone. Usually Memo was surrounded by a harem of models who pose for him naked for paintings he rarely sells and which never depict a naked woman. But he says he cannot paint unless a naked woman poses for him. And he never suffers a shortage of models, willing to inspire his art, which, again, goes to show women are always ready to sacrifice themselves for a good cause.

"Dottore!" I cried, glad to have found company: "Given the Muses a night of rest?"

He kept stirring the ice cubes in his glass with one finger.

"No entourage tonight?" I continued, undaunted.

"You couldn't lend me ten thousand," he said.

"Sorry," I replied hastily, for Memo put the bite on everyone. And he never repaid, even when he was flush.

"I need a sniff," he groaned.

"Who doesn't," I replied. It was a gambit we had played many times.

We said nothing for a while; he staring into his whisky, I squeezing out the lemon on the back of my hand.

"How is Marsilina?" I finally asked.

He shrugged his shoulders and said nothing.

So we watched the mob. They stood in small groups or twosomes, careful to maintain that invisible barrier Romans use to protect private cliques. Such cliques are as exclusive as vintage London clubs to which one gains entry only through nomination at birth.

A grey guru in leather slacks – far too tight – kept repeating in the permanently slurred voice of the alcoholic: "Sentiments are snowflakes and love is like the dew ... sentiments are snow ..."

"Crap!" Memo muttered.

"What's eating you up tonight, Lautrec?"

"That thing with the crossroad," he said, draining the rest of the whisky in one gulp. "One road to oblivion in warm wombs, the other to fame on the jagged points of rocks. I've decided to head for the rocks. See."

I could not suppress a grin. Memo was not the type to forsake 'warm wombs'.

"Women are the worst obstacles on a man's road to self-realization," he went on. "Remove them and you can reach immortality. Take the Catholic Church: Why, in the name of reason, and contrary to nature, do they demand celibacy. Is it not to devote all their energies to the glorification and magnification of the Doctrine? Take celibacy away from the priesthood and you have the Decline and Fall of the Holy See. The man who invented celibacy was a genius."

"Well if women didn't have men and the task of assuring the survival of the human species they could probably also achieve their goals of immortality more easily, don't you think?" I said.

He stared at me for a moment with furrowed eyebrows.

"By the way," I cried: "Has Marsilia something to do with this new philosophy?"

He glared at me some more across his rimless glasses.

"Marsilia?" he said: "I'm finished with women."

"Oh, no! Not you too, Brutus!" I protested.

I was still explaining the idiocy of the five thousand shots and how the news had circulated through Rome when I felt my arm tapped. Turning, I beheld a nymph.

"Natalia!" I cried.

"Hi, Victor Hugo," the nymph purred.

Maybe a guardian angel had brought her to me. After the drought of the last weeks and now Memo's madness, she was the proper medicine. Expectations blossomed. For months I had tried to weave my way into her favor, unfortunately without success. I had even sacrificed my entire stock of 'grass' in a last attempt to break her down. She had smoked it all – and walked out when not a stub was left. So I placed a comradely arm around her shoulder and cooed: "It's great to see you" with an enthusiasm not faked. The sweet smile on Natalia's face (in retrospect it might have been sour) appeared like a green light to me.

"Doing anything?"

"Not much," she said.

"What would you like to drink?"

"Nothing, caro! And you shouldn't drink either. You should save your energies."

"Energies?" I asked puzzled. "What are you talking about?"

She took hold of my arm and squeezed it.

"Come, come, you don't have to be shy. We all know about it."

"Know about what," I asked with growing irritation.

"Aaron, you shouldn't have hit that boy."

"Oh that. God. I know. Lost my temper. It happens."

"Hmm." She looked at me pensively.

"Well, I lost my temper."

"But Aaron, we all know. Everybody grows old one day. You know my philosophy professor once proposed the theory that old men send young men to war so they get killed and the old men can enjoy the surplus of women left without men after the war. Aaron, being old is nothing to be ashamed of. So accept it with grace and dignity and don't go around hitting young boys because you are jealous. Think about it, caro! Be seeing you!"

I stood there, alternately hot and cold, dumbstruck, watching her walking away, just as in a nightmare when you are nailed to the platform trying in vain to catch the train. She was a sassy girl in skintight jeans. She walked with that provocative wriggle intended to remind my supposedly extinct manhood what it would be missing from now on.

But as she disappeared I began to worry. Had jealousy, fear of impotence and the fact of growing older really made me strike that young boy because he was with a woman who should have been on my arm not on that of the young whippersnapper?

What other dark evils lurked in the minds of men suffering from the atrophy of their youth?

—

TEN

The Augusta Affair

Augusta lived alone on the first floor of a damp building. The wooden front door was partly covered by lichen, rotted by age and permanently ajar a slit as if the occupants feared someone might knock and not be heard. The mortar on the building's façade had flaked off, like skin after sunburn. During rain the guttering leaked and rivulets ran down walls already stained by dark patches and crisscrossed by fissures resembling wayward pencil marks.

Behind the entrance, so Erich told the inquest, a dark musty stairwell spiraled to the third floor. In short the building was ravaged by time, neglect and the absence of tenants. Only the family emblem, chiseled above the lintel, stood as evidence that the building had enjoyed a respectable past, long, long ago. Two tenants had remained: the late Augusta on the first floor and the half blind Cesare Campogrande on the floor above hers.

Witnesses at the inquest had already given evidence Augusta spent most of her time at the window, the one to the outside world. (The second window looked out into a dark narrow courtyard). In her evidence the Signora Puella, who ran the laundry up the street, described how – by using her own head to demonstrate – Augusta's head turned from right to left and from left to right as she followed pedestrians and vehicles passing along the cobble-stoned Vicolo Scanderbeg below her window. The Vicolo was narrow and never busy. Life passed by both Augusta and the Vicolo because the real hustle and bustle was a stone's throw away along the Via Lavatore which ran down to the Trevi Fountain, the tourist Mecca of Rome.

Augusta, leaning over the window sill and craning her neck could catch a glimpse of the bustle as it rushed by at the point where the Vicolo entered the Via, just like a small brook bearing a trickle of water enters a gushing stream. She would often say that had she been born into Via Lavatore instead of the Vicolo Scanderbeg her life would have turned out different. She might even have got married.

Had anyone ever bothered looking up as they strolled along the Vicolo their eyes would have met two black pins set in a severe visage. Hair, the color of carbon, was swept back and tied into a bun. Augusta's eyes always stared and her face always bore that same stern expression, almost a warning: 'Don't come too close!' But then, few people, if any, ever tilted back their heads to look up at her window.

Unfortunately Erich did.

Augusta later boasted that she had been watching Erich for two years, patiently waiting for the day when he would tilt his head back and look up at her window. She knew it would happen, sooner or later, because she had willed it. To her Erich was already a close acquaintance, a dear neighbor, a surrealistic lover, someone she trusted because she had observed him for so long, knew his habits, his peccadilloes, his friends, his women. She could even identify the sound of his motorbike. Once she heard its burble she would rush to the window, if she wasn't already there, to catch a last glimpse of him jockeying the bike into Via Lavatore and then, so she knew, into the rental garage on the right. She knew he would soon walk up the Vicolo Scanderbeg to his flat on the Via dello Scalone. For two years her eyes had drilled him from the first floor as he passed below. For two years he had been immune to her stare.

All this came out at the inquest, thanks to Augusta's friend and confidante, the lingerie shop owner Ofelia Buontempo. Ms Buontempo insisted it was love at first sight. The whole affair had been very romantic after the two had locked eyes, so she told the investigating magistrate, with appropriate sighs before he asked her to stick to the facts and refrain from giving her own interpretation of the relationship.

Why did Erich look up on that fateful summer evening?

Perhaps he was happy. Perhaps he threw his head back to catch a patch of the starry night sky. And instead he met Augusta's stare. He was so surprised to find those pin eyes drilling him he automatically muttered: "Buona sera!"

"Buona sera!" The soft reply fell from above.

And that was all there was to it. But it was the beginning.

* * *

Erich ran into Augusta a few days later. Or, more accurately, she ran into him, literally, barreling around a corner, apparently distracted. She bumped into his chest. "Scusi!" she said. "Ah! Ciao!" he replied, remembering those dark pins, drilling him again. She stepped around him. Then she was gone.

And that was that.

Well, until a few days later when he crawled along the Via Lavatore in the Spider, weaving his way through the throng of tourists heading for the Trevi. He was on the way to meet Shlomo for lunch at Lago Bracciano and had decided to take the car instead of the motorbike. Big mistake! Suddenly she appeared before the bonnet. She didn't flinch when he braked, sharply. She stood her ground, then smartly walked around to the driver's side.

"You wouldn't be going towards the Olympic Stadium?" she asked.

"As a matter of fact I am passing it," he said: "Would you like a lift?"

Well, that was the second mistake he made though in retrospect most likely his fate was sealed the moment he had looked up at her window. After that everything had its predestined progression, right to the day of the inquest.

She had sat primly in the passenger seat as he navigated through the old city towards the Lungotevere. Her handbag, large and black, sat on her lap like a disciplined child and she stared straight ahead, without saying a word. He had a chance to take a closer look at her then: Augusta was probably in her mid- thirties but she had retained a trim youthful figure and a smooth skin the color of polished walnut. She was petite and there was something erotically fierce about her, as if some pent up energy demanded to be released. Her sensible dark blue dress had shimmied above her knees revealing two shapely legs. All in all Augusta was an attractive woman though her expression was so sullen, forbidding and serious that most males, unless desperate or foolhardy, would think twice before approaching her.

"Do you work near the Olympic Stadium?" Erich asked, trying to defrost the silence.

"No," she said, staring straight ahead through the windscreen.

"What work do you do?"

"I am a seamstress," she said.

"Oh, so you can work from home?"

"Yes. If you have anything to be altered or repaired you can drop it in. Any time; I'll do a good job."

"I am sure you do," Erich said, smiling at her.

They drove in silence for a while, the silence of two strangers one of whom had no questions because she knew everything there was to be known and the other who was being cautious not to sound too nosey or too interested. Their silence sat between them like another passenger.

"I am off to the Lago Bracciano," Erich began again a few blocks along.

"I've never been to Bracciano."

"Oh!" he said, tempted for a moment to add: 'Why don't you come along'. But he didn't. She was too intimidating, though he was certain her aloofness would not deter Shlomo from making a pass at her. Shlomo left no skirt un-lifted, no matter if it were made of steel. Worse, he and Shlomo would soon be engaged in a tug-of-war to see who could impress her most, who could attract her most. The tug-of-war was nauseating, but inevitable – with Shlomo around.

At the point where the Via Cassia starts to exit old Rome she asked him to stop the car. "This will do. Thank you," she said and opened the door. As he drove off slowly, he watched her in the rear view mirror cross the road and stand at the bus stop on the other side, where the buses to the Centro Storico begin their run. This puzzled him. Why was she returning along the same route they had come? She could have asked him to stop earlier.

At this point, so Erich told the inquest, he had not realized she had come along simply for the ride, to be with him, to let him see her. She had gone as far as the bus routes ran. In fact, so Ms Buontempo told the magistrate later, Augusta had worn her best dress, the dark blue one with the hem just below the knees. She had kept the dress in the wardrobe for just this special occasion. The hem had slipped above the knee just as she had intended. And he had looked at her in an appreciative manner. It had been worth the trip, so Augusta told her.

* * *

Almost a week went by without Erich setting eyes on the seamstress, though in view of the events later it was obvious she was closely watching him during all this time. He had passed every day below her window, had looked up to say 'hallo' but had found the window empty. The fact was, as soon as she saw him coming she pulled her head in. She knew she had whetted his appetite. Now he had to starve a little.

If Erich were honest he would have admitted her image haunted him occasionally, the unsettling memory of an enigmatic woman who may or may not have been available. At times he kicked himself for having failed to try, for being too timid, too intimidated, too cowardly to have made a move. Not that he wished to have an affair with her. She lived far too close to home and thus too close to the discerning eyes of Andrea. There was an old folksy saying from where he came: "Never shit on your own doorstep."

No, so he convinced himself, it was sheer curiosity, perhaps a touch of machismo, which Andrea argued he possessed in excess. His male cockiness, she said, was not only idiotic but as anachronistic as were his coarse proverbs and popular ditties, utterly inconsistent with the mind of an intellectual. He always smiled. He had never pretended to be an intellectual, never intended to be one and could never understand why women like Andrea expected someone they labeled an intellectual to live out their philosophies, just as Christians expected their clergy to be paragons of virtue. But then Andrea had her aristocratic background to blame for her pretensions. Somehow a noble birth implied also a noble mind, at least in the minds of those of noble birth. Still, he had to admit, Andrea was far more liberal than he was when it came to fidelity. His flirtatious ways with women rarely annoyed her and she simply ignored his occasional excursions into other women's beds, at worst dropping a cynical remark to let him know she knew, or at least suspected. He was far more coarse and noisy in his jealousies when she showed some interest in another male or another male showed some interest in her.

After a week Erich's flashbacks to that car ride had faded so much he was startled when Augusta appeared in front of the Spider's windscreen on a rainy afternoon. He had left the tennis club early when it started to rain. She was there before he had had time to shift into first gear. He had taken the car to give it a run and also because he mistrusted the weather. He rarely drove the car to the club, preferring the motorbike.

Later, after the tragedy, Erich figured Augusta must have studied all his habits and movements over a long period of time. She knew he went to the club almost every second day, but mostly on the motorbike. She knew he had left that day in the car. She must have followed him by bus, waiting outside the club, realizing the rain would drive him out. Her blue costume was chic middle class 1950s, terribly de-mode in the 1970s, utterly old fashioned at the start of the 80s decade.

"Are you going home?" she asked after he had wound down the window.

He was in a state of mild excitement when she climbed into the passenger seat. And he realized Augusta's presence was not just an accident or a coincidence. She was stalking him.

"What are you doing here?" he asked with that tongue-in-cheek attitude of the confident male who knows he is about to hit a home run.

"I went to see a friend," she said, staring straight ahead.

"A lady friend?" His tone was teasing.

She turned to face him. Her brows knitted, the two pins perforated: "None of your business is it?" she snapped.

Erich's ardor evaporated in an instant. His brain began to function normally, his hormone level sank. The sudden loss of libido reminded him of the time he had an operation on his knee at the age of fifteen. The nurse, a buxom blonde, had to wash him every night as he stretched naked on the bed. And every night as she ran the sponge down his belly his penis shot up like a periscope. And every night, without comment, the nurse picked up a spoon and held it under the cold water tap. She then tapped his penis twice with the water-cooled spoon. His periscope immediately sank.

Weird as it may seem he still had a tendency to lose an erection at the slightest mental upset, the wrong phrase, a cynical remark, a nasty crack. Worse, he could rarely be re-aroused after such a mishap.

They drove through the lashing rain and Erich argued, silently, how lucky he had been to witness her cantankerous temper before it was too late. The woman was obviously disturbed and he had been fortunate to escape what might have turned into a nightmare. He turned on the radio and listened to Quiet Waters on the tape.

Before they reached the garage Augusta asked him to stop. "Thank you," she said and climbed out. He saw her enter a lingerie shop, offering a last little wiggle of her hips, obviously for his benefit, which meant she must be sure he was watching her. His own predictability and her confidence annoyed him. Who the hell did she think she was? He would simply forget her and next time when she wanted a lift pretend he didn't know her.

But he was not allowed to forget her.

Later that afternoon, he was at the bakery. Andrea had been sent abroad on an assignment and he had to do his own shopping. He was not very good at this. Erich lacked that populist touch of chatting up the market women, of gossiping with the shop owners and making small talk with the sales girls at the delicatessen. Rome was still largely free of supermarkets in those days. One bought one's needs at small neighborhood shops, hole-in-the-wall affairs, often owned for generations by the same family such as Aldo's, the butcher whose great grandfather, grandfather and father had been butchers. His son was already assisting him, well on the way to take over the business should Aldo decide it was time to play Scopa and Bogge. And there was Emilia, the delicatessen lady with her showcase of cheeses from far corners of Sicily all the way up to the north of the Veneto, her array of sausages, the size of wagon-wheels, sliced into paper thin 'feti' by an adjustable electric carver, a miniature sawmill. There was also Guido at the winery, offering a novel label each week to tantalize the taste buds of the adventurous connoisseurs and nurse his regular customers away from the cheap wine he sold them from the vats. There were the fruit and vegetable market stalls, put up each morning at six and taken down by one in the afternoon.

Everyone chatted with everyone. Italians are born with that chatty knack. Even the most banal issue can be expanded into a durable conversation. The sight of a dead rat can bring about a noisy and animated debate about the danger of rats and how after the war, when people starved, suddenly there were no rats to be seen. At the same time all the stray cats had vanished, unlike today when the strays padded all over the city in their hundreds, fed by elderly ladies carting feed in plastic bags. The birth of a baby in the neighborhood could be the trigger for a heated debate on how to bring up a newborn and whether powdered milk could ever replace the goodness of mother's milk. More and more women took recourse to powder these days to save their breasts from early sagging. How could these women, so the rhubarb seller shouted, prefer their good looks to the welfare of their baby? Why then have babies in the first place, squawked the widow from the Vicolo San Vicente. Indeed why echoed the lady from the news stand. After all a mother's milk contained the bacteria the mother had accumulated and the anti-viruses of the illnesses she had endured. Indeed, intoned the nurse from the Quirinale, because the mother passed on to the baby all the antibodies of those illnesses, something canned milk could not …

Andrea was brilliant at this chit-chat, even though her Teutonic accent instantly gave her away as a foreigner. But Erich was different and the shop girls and market women realized he just wanted to get on with his purchases. So they kept their prattle to the shopping list. This suited him just fine and he never regretted his lack of market charm though sometimes he was envious of Andrea who returned from her shopping sprees with hilarious tales gleaned from local gossip.

Erich was leaving the bakery when he saw Augusta pressed against a wall on the Via Lavatore. She had set down a blue plastic bag filled with bottles of mineral water. In her other hand she held a large bag of groceries. The mineral water was obviously heavy because she was blowing at a welt on her hand. Then she looked up and smiled at Erich, a sweet, innocent smile that utterly disorientated him.

"You couldn't help me carry them?" she shouted across the street, as if he were a dear old friend. He flinched then glanced about him, certain everyone in the street had heard. But no one seemed to have taken notice. Women were always asking men to help them carry something.

"It's only around the corner," Augusta said and Erich marveled at her change of mood.

In fact she lived only a stone's throw away and he was convinced she could have managed but for some reason wanted to make a gesture that would give the impression a relationship existed between them. He was too slow to think of the possible consequences. By the time he did he had already accepted to carry the water up to her flat.

And that was the biggest mistake of all.

* * *

Three days later, as he walked by the lingerie shop, the thought of Augusta sent a spasm of mixed feelings through his body. Mechanically he glanced inside. There she was, talking to a comely young woman, apparently the owner or the manager. Augusta was wearing high heeled black shoes. A matching black suit, de-mode no doubt, snuggled along her pleasant contours. She had her back to Erich but the shopkeeper saw him and tapped her shoulder. Augusta turned. He walked on quickly, taken aback because he realized she had obviously told the shopkeeper about their encounter. Told her what? That he had given her a lift, twice? That he had asked an indiscreet question? That she had given him … no she wouldn't be so low."

He was angry now. And disturbed. When he looked back over his shoulder he saw Augusta standing outside the lingerie shop, hands on hips, legs spread. She was staring at him, her pose challenging. That made him even more ill at ease. At the same time he felt strangely aroused. The thought occurred she was signaling him in this bizarre way: "Come on and get me, you wimp!"

* * *

By the time he arrived at his flat he had decided from now on he would simply ignore her. Even if she ran in front of his car he would brake and drive around her. He would not give her another lift. In fact he would only use the bike. Since she only wore skirts she could not ask him to give her a lift in skirts. He knew, instinctively, she wouldn't. She had only stopped him when he was in the car. Augusta was not the kind of woman to ride pillion on a motorbike. That was too avant-garde for someone who wore 1950s tweed suits.

That night, with Andrea out of the county, he invited an old girl friend for dinner at the local Trattoria. He and Isabella had enjoyed a steamy affair during his stint in Costa Rica. After he left they had not seen each other for years until she had moved to Rome, recently. Both liked to reminisce on their brief but passionate affair.

When he had met her in Costa Rica she had just separated from her husband, an Italian macho who resented her decision to leave him so much he hired three thugs to break into her apartment and rape her – in turns. The three wore ski masks and she was almost sure, the first to rape her was her estranged husband. Before he left, this first rapist had urinated all over her prone, bruised and naked body.

The police never identified the trio but during a recess in the custody hearing of their daughter her husband, months later, made it quite clear he knew more than was known about the rape incident. She had never told anyone about the urinating sequel.

It took time before Isabella gathered enough trust to sleep with Erich. But she remained coy and submissive in bed. He probed and probed until one night she confessed she had never experienced an orgasm. He tried much harder then to please her, but despite all his efforts and sexual acrobatics he failed. The lack of orgasm continued to cripple their love-making until one day he had the bright idea to get her high on marijuana. It was not easy, for she did not smoke, coughed a lot trying to inhale and eventually, he was sure, reached a high on breathing in his own fumes. Still it worked. She came with a frightening contortion of her muscles, from the legs up to the neck, a spasm that went on for nearly a minute and scared the daylights out of him until her body gradually relaxed. Then she broke into tears. The dam had broken.

After dinner at the Trattoria he invited Isabella for a drink at the apartment. They walked up the Vicolo Scanderbeg, right under Augusta's nose. And that turned out to be another of Erich's costly mistakes.

* * *

Two days after the evening with Isabella Andrea came back from her assignment in Belgrade. And that was when trouble really began.

As Andrea told the inquest later she received a phone call at the office sometime around ten in the morning next day. The voice at the other end was that of a woman who spoke angrily and with the accent of a southerner. She had asked for Andrea by name.

"Yes, this is Andrea, who is this?"

"Don't ask questions. Just listen, bitch! While you were away your husband had a woman in your apartment at night. You should do something about it. If I were you I'd kick him out …"

"But you are not me," Andrea snapped: "Who is this?"

Only the dial tone at the other end replied.

Andrea told the inquest she went home immediately and confronted Erich who explained he was being stalked by the woman down the street. He was certain she had been the caller since she must have seen him pass with Isabella. He admitted he invited Isabella to the flat for an after dinner drink. Their meeting, not the first as she knew, had been innocent, a meeting between two friends reminiscing about old times.

"Was your male friend upset by the woman's phone call?" the investigating magistrate asked Andrea.

Andrea thought for a moment. She realized it was a leading question. "No," she said, then quickly added: "As a matter of fact he was more amused than upset and we discussed for some time how nowadays the gender roles in the pre-coitus phase had become inverted to the point women now chase men who, accustomed for millenniums to chase women, have found themselves in the role of the hunted instead of the hunter. This change in traditional roles has had a detrimental and confusing effect on the male libido and sex orientation. I think that was the gist of our conversation that day, if you want to know?"

"So your husband made no threats – against the woman?"

"No," Andrea said.

We will adjourn now until tomorrow nine o'clock," the magistrate said: "We will then take evidence about the last phone call, made a week later, I believe …"

* * *

Erich would have liked to forget that week or delete it as one deletes clumsy literary creations or enraging incoming messages with a quick finger-squeeze on the mouse – though one knows the damn thing is struck in the recycle bin and if deleted from there is still alive somewhere in the hard drive.

He had met Augusta twice during those seven days before all contact ceased. The first meeting occurred outside the tennis club where she had, once again, waited for him on a day he took the Spider. She wore the blue dress again and when he screamed at her: 'Why are you making these ridiculous phone calls?' she adamantly denied it was her doing and tried to blame her friend, Ms Buontempo, for having taken matters into her own hands.

"Oh, I know you feel nothing for me. You think I'm just a silly, ignorant seamstress, someone you can use and then discard like an old dress," Augusta had cried: "But Ofelia saw me suffer and she became angry. I stopped her while I was at the shop but she must have telephoned after I left. I know she had your wife's phone number."

"You are lying!" Erich shouted.

They both faced each other at the gate of the tennis club and she stepped back as if lashed by an invisible whip. "I don't lie," she said. "I am not jealous about your wife, she is your woman; but I didn't like you taking other women to your flat. That makes me very angry and very jealous because that is an insult to your wife and to me."

"So you called Andrea, right?"

"No, I did not. I told you I wouldn't hurt your wife. She has first rights but I, I have second rights, you understand?"

"What rights?" Erich yelled: "What damn rights do you have. We've just met a couple of times, for a few minutes. You don't even know me."

She stepped right up against him and her eyes pierced him: "I know you as well as any other woman," she hissed.

Erich flinched.

Two members of the club were exiting through the gate. One of them was Ettore Barbado, the lawyer and Erich's friend. He nodded to Erich and stared at Augusta with undisguised interest, measuring her the way only Italian men can measure a woman, with the eyes of the connoisseur, a legacy from the cattle market in the peasant days of their forefathers.

Having taken her measure, Ettore piped: "Olaaaa!" and into that single word he mixed an entire prism of innuendos. Erich was grateful he did not stop to be introduced to Augusta. For a moment he wondered how he would have introduced her: My neighbour? My stalker? Already he could imagine how Ettore would have exploited the situation. For Ettore all the world was a courtroom in which he was the principal actor. Erich could see him now, wrapping his black toga tighter around his wiry body while pointing an accusing finger at Erich in the dock: "Adultery your Honours! In broad daylight too!"

"Let's go somewhere and talk," Augusta suggested, aware of Erich's discomfort outside the club: "There is a parking lot behind the Basketball stadium. We can talk there."

* * *

At the inquest Erich denied, as one would have expected, Ms Buontempo's testimony that the chat behind the Stadium had turned into a wild sexual orgy during which he had ripped off Augusta's panties and had broken the handle on the glove box of the Spider while maneuvering for leverage in the confined space of the partially reclining twin seats.

Questioned by the magistrate about Ms Buontempo's allegation, Erich said, with dignity, that their chat had 'cleared the air.'

(From the auditorium Ms Buontempo shouted: "More likely cleared his pipes" to which the magistrate replied that if he heard another outburst he would have her for contempt).

Once the inquest had settled down, the sniggering had stopped and the magistrate had wiped the grin off his own face, he asked Erich to continue his account about what actually did happen in the parking lot.

Throughout this bantering Erich had maintained his calm with admirable composure. Now he went on to say that after their talk in the parking lot, a talk he said lasted no more then ten minutes, both agreed it was best to stay friends and good neighbors. He had then given Augusta a lift back to the Via Lavatore and they had parted on good terms. He was convinced Augusta had not made the phone call to Andrea.

"Now how could you be convinced of that?" the magistrate asked, glancing around the courtroom as if to say "this guy really thinks we're gullible".

This was Erich's moment. He slowly took a glass from a tray at his elbow and sipped some water, allowing an expectant hush to hover over the inquest. When he finally spoke he eyeballed Ms Buontempo who sat in the second row of the courtroom wearing a low-neck polka-dot blouse which gave the magistrate and anyone else interested a very comfortable view of her pectoral assets.

"According to my wife," he began: "The woman who made the phone call had a strong southern accent. But Augusta's speech was unmistakably Roman. So I asked her about her friend, the lingerie woman. I asked her where this woman came from. I teased her that Ms Buontempo looked to me like a gypsy. Augusta was not amused: "She is no gypsy," she snapped: "She is from Sicily ..."

At this point the inquest was adjourned when the two court room clerks were called upon by the magistrate to restrain Ms Buontempo who in a shrill, loud voice spat verbal venom at Erich, beginning with his dubious ancestry and progressing to his miserably undersized child maker, before exhorting the magistrate to charge him with murder, rape and giving false testimony.

* * *

When the hearing resumed the next day, Ms Buontempo sat in the courtroom flanked by two burly wardens who had an order from the magistrate to bundle her out the minute she opened her mouth without being asked to do so. Despite protests from Andrea and Erich, the magistrate had argued he could not exclude the lingerie lady since she was the only witness who had enjoyed the confidence of the deceased and might be able to shed light on this strange case. Besides, since no relatives of the deceased had come forward or had been located, Ms Buontempo had become a de facto kin of the late Augusta Vinciguerra. Furthermore, she had every right to be present since her version of the last meeting between Erich and the deceased might conflict with Erich's rendition. In fact, in the interest of finding the culprit her presence in the courtroom was essential.

Having seen the lingerie lady arrive squeezed into a skintight short leather skirt and a blouse even lower than the previous day's, Andrea asked the magistrate whether it was not possible to order Ms Buontempo to appear in court less like a whore and more like a witness. Naturally the magistrate defended the lingerie lady's choice of attire as an individual right over which he had no jurisdiction – unless she decided to arrive in the nude or topless in which case she would violate the laws on public decency. And the magistrate only smiled when Andrea pointed out the laws on public decency had already been grossly violated in the case of Ms Buontempo.

Erich was well aware that Andrea's irritation was not due to the lingerie woman's wardrobe or her outbursts in court but his own role in the entire affair. The case had exposed what he had always managed to hide successfully for years – his extensive contact with women, which made the label of philanderer a logical conclusion. During the last few days, his explanations of encounters with sundry women had begun to sound more hollow each time another dalliance was exposed. An old friend visiting the apartment was pardonable but the chain of encounters emerging from the testimony of that diabolical lingerie woman had revealed too many coincidences over too short a period, even for the liberal mind of Andrea. How could he have known Augusta kept a meticulous mental diary of nearly all his encounters and, worse, had passed on all this collected information to her good friend at the hole-in-the-wall lingerie shop?

Erich realized he was no longer fighting to clear his name or to be taken off the list of suspects. Rather it was a desperate damage control action to keep Andrea from asking him to find other lodgings, a possibility that would leave him not quite destitute but in considerably reduced economic circumstances. Unfortunately his only method of dismantling the damning evidence was repeated denial, though these sounded very much like a fading echo: 'Nothing happened. Just an old friend; dinner and a drink; simply a lift in the car; help in carrying shopping; an innocent chat in a parking lot ...'

He was running low on credibility. Worse, he knew there were still a few more bullets to bite.

* * *

In its final day of the hearing the investigating magistrate rejected Erich's argument that since he could not have committed the crime, any further questioning of his relationship with Augusta was superfluous and served no purpose other than to feed the court's macabre curiosity while violating his own right to privacy.

"We have to go through the procedure," the magistrate rebutted in his typically sanctimonious manner: "After all, this is not about some romantic tiff or about infidelity or to determine the guilt of one partner in a divorce case, nor is this a dispute of ownership; no, this is about a human life, a valued human life, the life of a young woman, a life cruelly terminated in a most vile manner by an anonymous person or persons. It is therefore out of the question that for some vague right of privacy we omit part of a process that might lead us to the vile murderer of the late Augusta Vinciguerra."

So Erich was back under interrogation.

"Now, according to the victim as told to her friend there was a steamy sexual encounter in that decrepit and deserted car park, an encounter you claim did not occur," the magistrate began. "Now what actually did happen in the car park?"

"Nothing!" Erich said. "Whatever Augusta may have told her friend was pure imagination. I believe it is quite clear by now Augusta had a vivid imagination where I was concerned."

The magistrate showed some impatience now: "But what did happen? I mean did you kiss and make up and all was forgiven? Was she prepared to step back and let you get on with your life without bothering you, or your wife? Or did you have an argument, a violent argument? Did you threaten her or did you think the entire affair could be fixed by a wild and wanton act of sex? What happened?"

It was the first time in the proceedings the magistrate had been less then courteous and respectful when speaking to Erich, a signal even "impartial" justice represented by a fellow male in a Latino society was beginning not only to doubt him but to dislike him. This came as a shock to Erich who was accustomed to making people like him. Even those who thought he was a rogue, though, they always added 'a charming rogue'.

He took a deep breath and his mind raced as he attempted to put some logic into his next remark, which he knew would set the tone of the interrogation from now on. Whatever he said he must not allow the magistrate to poke fun at him. He must stick to his story.

"Sir," he began, speaking slowly: "I believe the phrase 'kiss and make up' is used to repair a previous romantic affair. In my case there was no such affair so why you should suggest we kissed and made up is beyond me ..."

"Well, just let's get on with it and spare us your literary interpretations," the magistrate muttered, waving his arm as if to brush away Erich's rebuke. Then, perhaps realizing he had been a trifle too rough he added:

"I am trying to get to the bottom of this. You understand? So, you say nothing happened? So be it. But what did you talk about?"

"I told her if her friend did call Andrea, as it now appeared, in future she should be careful what she told her friend. This friend was obviously not to be trusted and was living off Augusta's experiences – or imagination in this case – to enliven her own miserable existence in the lingerie shop ..."

In the courtroom Ms Buontempo was furiously shaking her head. But she kept her mouth shut, not without considerable effort.

"... I realized she was a little unbalanced, mentally I mean, so I suggested we remain friends because I did not wish to upset her. I think I even promised not to walk under her window with another woman as she insisted this made her wildly jealous and unreasonable. I told her that such a reaction was silly since I was happily married but maintained my friendship with a number of women on a purely platonic level – and that goes without saying. I think she was satisfied with this compromise. Anyway she asked me if she could repair some of my clothing, the items that needed to be repaired. I agreed and I offered to let her have some trousers that needed their cuffs shortened. In fact she came around to the apartment two days later to pick up the trousers."

"And you let her in?"

"Yes, your Honor, I mean she had telephoned earlier telling me since she knew Andrea was at work could she come around and pick up the trousers. I thought that was an acceptable proposition although I was surprised she had my private telephone number. It was the first time she had called."

"Why couldn't she have come around when Andrea was at home, that is if there was nothing to be ashamed of between you two?" The magistrate was leaning forward eagerly now, squinting at Erich.

For a moment Erich allowed the question to hang in the courtroom. Again he had expected it and knew the answer though he was anxious to make it appear as if he was still contemplating the reply.

"Your Honor this kind of attitude was consistent with Augusta's idea that the presence of any woman would inevitably be a source of suspicion or jealousy for a wife. She would have refused to come around when

Andrea was there because she could not tolerate that Andrea should be upset by her visit just as she could not tolerate me walking below her window with a woman other then my wife."

"I see. What happened then?"

"Well, she walked straight into the flat as if she was afraid I might hand over the trousers and dismiss her at the door. She went on and on about what a lovely flat I lived in, what wonderful paintings, what great furniture and how lucky I was, unlike her who was poor and had been born into the wrong street of life. How fortunate I was to have an expensive car and a motorbike and all those women who came up to my flat, like the blonde woman who she said went shopping at the market every now and then and afterwards popped into my apartment, just as she had done the previous day. Well, of course I was flabbergasted. The blonde woman she referred to was the wife of a colleague. She often drops in for a cup of tea and a chat when she is shopping in the area. Augusta must have followed her ..."

"Did she threaten you with telling your wife," the magistrate interrupted: "I mean there must have been a reason why she mentioned the blonde visitor, either she was mad or she was trying to blackmail you?"

Erich paused for a moment, long enough to give the impression he was trying to recall the episode in detail.

"No, no, she wasn't threatening me. I guess she wanted me to know she knew and that everything I did she would find out about. I told her she must not spy on me, that these visitors were friends, that Andrea knew about the visits and it was silly for her to think there was a romantic liaison involved."

"So then she left?"

"Not quite. She became quite agitated, talking about how we rich people thought we could do anything that came into our head. We used anyone we felt like using, just because we had money, status and connections and most of all we were so arrogant. And it was only because she was poor and I was rich that I didn't want to love her, even though she had made it quite clear she was content with being my mistress as long as I didn't have other women apart from Andrea. I had rejected her and now she was hurt...in short, sir, it was obvious the woman was mentally unbalanced..."

"And then she left?"

"Yes."

"Liar," the lingerie lady called from the courtroom, shaking off the two court clerks who, grappling with her arms tried to force her to sit down: "He's lying," she shouted: "He took her into the bedroom and stripped her naked and they made love on the bed where he slept with his wife. She told me every detail … and if you don't believe me ask him to show you the scar on his belly. How else would she have known about that scar …?"

"Take her out! Out! OUT!" the magistrate yelled.

Once the clerks had hustled the lingerie lady out of the courtroom the magistrate turned to Erich who had been shrugging his shoulders in the direction of Andrea and doing his best to look perplexed:

"So what about that scar?"

"I do have a scar, though it is more on my right flank then on my belly. Augusta did notice it when she was measuring me for the length of the trousers. I forgot to tell you that she did take my measurements, in case I wanted her to make some trousers to measure, so she said. She had asked me to lift my shirt so she could measure better. That's how she saw the scar. She asked me what it was and I told her it was the result of an operation to remove my gall bladder. That's all."

"Hmm!" the magistrate said, leaning forward across the bench. "That may be so. Before I am finished with you however, I will have to ask you one more question that is important to this investigation. You must give me a truthful answer or possibly face charges should your testimony turn out to be false. Do you understand?"

Erich nodded.

"I need a 'yes' from you. Do you understand my warning about false evidence?"

"Yes!" Erich said.

"Good. Now, did you ever have sex or perform an act of sex with the deceased Augusta Vinciguerra?"

"No," Erich said, emphatically, without hesitation.

"Not even when you carried her shopping bags back to her flat. On that occasion, according to witnesses you remained nearly half an hour in her flat, a long time to finish a cup of coffee which you say the deceased had offered you. Now the witness, Buontempo, insists the deceased told her that during this time in her flat an act of oral sex took place. Are you also denying this act took place?"

The magistrate peered expectantly at Erich, as if this last question was his last hope to wring a confession from the witness that a furtive sexual liaison had taken place.

(Later on his friend, Ettore the lawyer, would argue that whether these acts did or did not occur had no bearing on the result of the investigation since Erich, obviously the main suspect, had a concrete alibi, an unbreakable alibi. Ettore explained what the magistrate really wanted, as a good Catholic, was for the witness to repent and confess his guilt of sexual involvement, a guilt that was not punishable by law. And, of course, the magistrate also wanted his own theory vindicated. No man of red blood could have resisted the series of advances by – and he, Ettore could only concur – a very attractive woman before someone had put an end to her existence.)

The magistrate now leaned even further forward, his eyes drilling Erich, willing him to make an alleviating confession. But again the man's good intentions were disappointed.

"Nothing of what she said ever took place. It only happened in the imagination of that woman," Erich said, then added in the same breath: "A chain of wishful thoughts, your Honor. If this wishful thinking is consistently and frequently repeated by a disturbed person it does become reality for that person. It's basic psychology, your Honor."

"Spare me your psychoanalysis," the magistrate snapped, "and answer me the one question that truly puzzles me in this case: How come after that last phone call to your wife there was no further contact between you and the deceased? How come in the one month between the phone call and the murder there was not a single sign of life from la Signora Augusta Vinciguerra. Do you have any explanation for this?"

It was a question Erich had expected much earlier. He had almost believed the magistrate had forgotten. Now that it had come, right at the end of his interrogation he was still not sure how he should respond. Of course he knew the reason but he couldn't possibly tell the man. It would only open another can of worms and there were already enough of those crawling around. So he took the easy way out:

"I believe when Augusta realized she could not break up our marriage, no matter how she schemed, she tired of her efforts and gave up. Perhaps her confidante from the lingerie shop could throw some light on this," Erich added, turning around to look at Ms Buontempo's empty seat.

"Alright, bring her back in," the magistrate shouted, signaling to the court clerk to fetch the woman.

With the court's attention focused on her Ms Buontempo suddenly started fidgeting with her handbag. For once, since the inquest had started, she was not quite sure of herself.

"Well?" the magistrate asked.

"Your Honor I don't know the answer. She suddenly stopped talking about him. But she didn't seem to trust me as she had before. She stayed away from the shop. I gathered there was another man. That was my impression. She didn't tell me anything, your Honor, but once she said to me: 'This time I'm going to get the bastard good ...' I thought she was talking about this fellow here (pointing at Erich) but I guess it was someone else."

"No indication who this 'bastard' may have been?"

"No, your Honor. Once she referred to him as a *pezzo grosso*, an important man."

"Hmm," the magistrate hummed. Then turning to Erich: "You wouldn't know anything about this *pezzo grosso*, now would you?"

"No. I can only guess it was another poor bastard she was stalking. In these cases the deranged person often switches her obsession to a new victim. It is a classic ..."

Erich could not finish his sentence. "Thank you, thank you, Doctor Freud," the magistrate said. Then, facing the court room stenographer he shouted, stumbling somewhat over the lengthy Teutonic name of his next witness: "I am re-calling the Signora Andrea von Schlitten-Schlittenberg to take the stand."

Andrea wore the same sensible shoes and the same sensible smock and a touch of red lipstick she had worn during her first audience. This gave her esthetic pale face with its gray eyes an almost transparent pall, a ghost-like appearance, a fragile genetic concoction of inbred aristocracy and acquired intellect. Her tall ramrod-straight figure automatically commanded respect. All this was not lost on the magistrate.

"Madam," he said: "How do I address you: Contessa or Signora?"

"You can call me Signora Schlittenberg as you did last time. Unlike Italy in my country aristocratic titles are used only by the pretentious."

"A wise practice," the magistrate said. "I have also noticed you have kept your own name instead of adopting that of your husband."

"That is a choice we are allowed in Germany though in this case it was not a matter of choice since Erich and I have never married. We live together as a matter of choice though not in the legal sense."

"I seeeee!" the magistrate said.

Then he smiled at her with as much charm as he could muster for he saw in Andrea a woman who had not received a full share of life and therefore must be, by reason of logic, on the lookout to complete this void. Perhaps her choice would fall on him. The magistrate was a pragmatic man. He realized since the average male was a philanderer by nature and by the expectations of society, it stood to reason the male's female partners sought revenge or compensation – it really didn't matter which – by their own cuckolding. How else was it possible that so many married men could cuckold husbands, fiancés or lovers?

"Signora Schlittenberg," he piped in his most fatherly voice: "This may be painful for you," (he cast a baleful glance at Erich)"but could you tell me as much as possible about the phone call you received that evening..."

Andrea pertly crossed her long legs and stared up at the ceiling, brows furrowed, visibly concentrating.

"It must have been about six o'clock when my secretary told me a woman wished to speak to me urgently," she began. "The voice at the other end definitely had a Roman accent. She was not the same person who had called me previously ..."

"Could you recall, as accurately as possible, what this woman said to you?"

"I'll try," Andrea said, still looking up at the ceiling, then suddenly shifting her eyes to Erich: "She said my husband was cheating on me constantly while I was at work or abroad. She said she felt sorry for me since I was working so hard and was only being rewarded with an unfaithful husband. She said I should know about a blonde lady who visited my husband every second or third day, still carrying her shopping bags. I told her I knew the woman and she was a friend of ours. She became upset then and started to shout that I must be blind or degenerate. How could I believe, she said, this blonde and my husband were just talking when even she, the caller, had been making love with my husband in my bed …"

Andrea took a deep breath, leaving an effective pause before she went on: "I told her bluntly she was a liar and she must prove to me she had been in my apartment. The woman then started to tell me in detail the location of the furniture, the position of the refrigerator and stove and the theme of a painting in the dining room showing a black car standing outside a villa. She knew the position of the bed and mentioned the three-legged table in the living room. It was obvious she had been in the flat. I told her I knew she had picked up my husband's trousers to shorten the cuffs and she mustn't invent stories that were not true. She became even more agitated then: 'You are a fool,' she shouted 'your husband has a scar on his belly and if that is not enough, look behind the bed-head and you will find a cheap ear-ring I dropped there …'

"Then she hung up …"

When Andrea remained silent the magistrate prompted her: "Well? Was the ear ring there?"

"Yes it was," Andrea said.

"So, did you then confront your husband?"

"I did."

Andrea seemed reluctant to continue and the magistrate, not satisfied, prompted her again: "And what was his explanation?" he asked, casting a meaningful look at Erich who sat with his lips pressed tightly together.

"Oh, he laughed it off and said it was just another indication how resourceful the seamstress was when it came to driving a wedge between us. He said the woman had walked all over the flat in apparent awe of all the novelties and the décor. He also remembered she had been standing near the bed. He said she had obviously planted the ear ring …"

"And you believed him?" the magistrate broke in.

Andrea paused for a moment perhaps to give her reply the emphasis it deserved judging by the heads craning to hear better. "Yes," she finally said in voice deliberately firm: "The woman demonstrated all the symptoms of a highly disturbed person, a person who had developed an obsession – about my partner ...”

“Signora Schlittenberg,” the magistrate said: “I'll have to ask you a very vital question now, something very personal and I hope you'll understand this is part of my job and not some busybody sticking his nose into your private affairs. But we are dealing with a murder in this case. *Bene!* Now you obviously believe your husband when he asserts there was no sexual contact between him and the victim. But since the victim, the Signora Vinciguerra, continued to try and make trouble between you and your husband it would seem reasonable that he became angry and made some threats like ‘I'll fix that woman’ or ‘I'll have that woman fixed.’ You don't recall any outbursts of that nature?”

“No,” Andrea, said, perhaps a trifle too quick to be plausible: “Erich seemed more amused then upset by the woman's stalking.”

“Didn't your relationship suffer at all?”

Andrea bit her lips. “I would be lying if I said it didn't, sir, but ...” She looked at Erich who was seated in the second row of the courtroom and Erich realized, with a pang of anxiety, that she wasn't looking at him but through him. “... there are strains in any relationship especially after an episode like this. Sometimes we discover characteristics about the other person we have not seen before or we have simply preferred to ignore. In that case one has to take the consequences ...”

“And what consequences have you taken, Signora?”

Andrea looked up at the magistrate and an amused smile played around her lightly rouged lips. The court was hushed: “To show absolute solidarity with my de facto husband, sir,” she said.

The magistrate was visibly taken aback. But he recovered quickly: “Signora, your tolerance is remarkable and a tribute to women. But all the same I must ask you one more question, namely: When did your husband decide to go to Paris and did he tell you he was staying with Mmse Ivonne Dueville, the secretary to the Minister for Internal Affairs, the lady who furnished him with the perfect alibi for the night of the murder?”

This time Andrea took longer to reply, squinting at the ceiling as if she was trying to remember the details. ”I am not sure when Erich decided to go to Paris. But he had been talking about it for some time.”

"How much time, a week, a month, a year …?" The magistrate was irritated now.

"At least a few weeks, two or three, I can't recall exactly. As for staying with Ivonne, of course he told me, though he told me afterwards. As you will recall from my earlier testimony I was traveling in Yugoslavia at the time and we had very little communication."

"And you were not jealous?"

"Sir, if I became jealous each time Erich meets another woman I would be a nervous wreck. It is quite simple: The day I do not trust Erich anymore I will leave him."

"Thank you, Signora Schlittenberg. Ladies and gentlemen I have no more questions. This inquest is closed."

* * *

The Rome Lawn Tennis Club was a misnomer. Not one of its courts had ever been covered by grass, not even at the beginning when the club was inaugurated by Il Duce who sometimes, so the old-timers reported, appeared unexpectedly to execute a few hits, most of them miss-hits. (The Duce's lack of tennis finesse did not stymie the spread of his reputation as a first class tennis ace, good enough to hold his own with Wimbledon champions.) The 'lawn' part of the club's name was obviously borrowed from the English at a time when fascist Italy tried hard to copy all the little luxuries and eccentricities of the British Empire, including tennis, golf, even croquet. Like everything the fascists copied – or tried to copy – they never got around to laying the lawns just as they never managed to equip their armed forces with proper war material or their Russia-bound troops with more than cardboard shoes and paper-thin overcoats. The main objective was to appear equally proficient. The rest was left to oratory and grand gestures.

Long after the Great Pretender's body was hung upside down from a lamp post in Milan, the club continued to live on the coat-tails of his one-time presence. In fact the outside court on which Il Duce had connected with the odd tennis ball was labeled 'Campo Benito" until communists won the municipal elections and had the name removed.

Over the years, like many fascist institutions, the club lost its shine, its glory and its reputation as a meeting place for the VIPs of Rome. But the facile availability of the three courts suited Erich who played regularly and loathed having to queue up or reserve a court. One could walk into the Rome Lawn Tennis Club at almost any time and find an empty court. More important he had found a worthy opponent and regular player in Ettore Barbero, the lawyer.

Whenever he was asked how he had come to befriend the famous lawyer, Erich admitted he had been attracted by the man's appearance rather than his tennis prowess or his reputation as the Italian Perry Mason. To anyone with imagination, Ettore Barbero was the visual and verbal caricature of an Italian lawyer: A long lean figure with sharp facial features, a prominent jaw and a very long and pointed nose. Like the majority of his profession he dressed immaculately. His black hair, waxed and shiny, was brushed back in the style of a 1920s film star. He could take an hour in the changing room to make sure each strand of hair was properly in place. He believed healthy hair required at least one hundred slow brush strokes a day. Before the hair received his full attention he had showered for at least twenty minutes, embalmed his body with a variety of skin lotions, sprinkled talcum powder into all his bodily crevices and completed this corporal care with a good spraying of expensive perfume until he smelled like an Arab sheik sweeping through Harrods in London.

One day, after a match with Ettore and a shower, Erich had gone home to work for a while before returning to the club for an afternoon doubles match. As he came into the dressing room Ettore was just leaving in a cloud of perfume, every pleat in his pants and jacket in place, his shoes polished to high gloss, every single hair where it should be.

In his heydays Ettore had been a brilliant defense lawyer, notorious for his courtroom flourishes, his oratory, his ability to draw out a case until the court was worn down to his point of view. He had become a celebrated – and hated – defense attorney after he began to represent arrested members of the Red Brigade, the urban guerrilla organization which had kidnapped and executed Aldo Moro, the President of the Christian Democrats who had suggested a historic alliance between his party and the communists, an alliance seen with horror by Washington.

Ettore's arguments about arbitrary arrests and lack of evidence raised him to front page prominence and fed his already considerably bloated ego. Yet he soon discovered his new status had raised him onto a perilous pedestal in an Italy where both left and right took the law into their own hands and each side carried out punitive killings. (The manner of execution always indicated who was responsible. The communists preferred the hand gun, the neo-fascists explosives.)

After a second plot to assassinate him failed, Ettore hung up toga and wig. Instead he specialized in divorce, a novel legal phenomenon following the passage of a law that, for the first time, granted Italian couples the right to divorce. It had taken a referendum and a popular revolt against the Vatican to push through this law. The Holy See had been furious marriages were being dissolved under its very nose Many lawyers, prompted by their parish priests and threats of excommunication, refused to handle divorce cases in those early years. But Ettore had no respect for the clergy nor was he among those politicians and VIPs who made sure they were seen every Sunday in the front pews. He often joked that the more frequent a politician was shown on RAI television seated in church the more corrupt he was. Only the guilty, he argued, went to church to atone for their sins and convince the electorate of their righteousness.

His reputation and his gaunt good looks stood him in good stead and he was assured of a steady flow of clients, mainly women. "Why I ever broke my balls at defense is beyond my comprehension," he once told Erich, "life as a divorce lawyer is so much more relaxing and there are so many benefits. Think of all those disappointed and lonely wives. My friend, I've never had such good pickings in all my life."

Their weekly tennis matches had created a bond between the two men, a kind of comradeship that extended to their social activities and their families. They went to parties together and dined together. Andrea and Ettore's wife Maria called each other. Erich helped Ettore with the grape harvest at his hobby vineyard near Bracciano. The two shared ideas, political analysis, gossip and sometimes male secrets and lascivious comments about certain women of their mutual acquaintance.

Therefore it was only natural that once Augusta became a problem Erich should confess his dilemma to his good friend. He was careful though to make it clear he was the victim of a female stalker and not the victim of a romance gone awry. Even frequent teasing by Ettore could not elicit a confession from Erich that something sexual, even once, had occurred. Still it was obvious from Ettore's reaction he did not believe his friend but went along with what he considered was merely a pretense of innocence.

However after his encounter with Augusta outside the tennis club, Ettore began to take an unusually keen interest in the case. Previously he had only listened superficially to Erich's accounts but now he gave them his full, undivided attention. If Erich did not volunteer new information or developments the lawyer would manage to bring the dressing room conversation to what he called 'the Augusta Affair.'

"How is the Augusta Affair going," he would ask or: "What news of the love-struck Augusta, my friend?"

In this way, almost without realizing it, Erich had informed Ettore of virtually every incident and encounter. This account-rendering went on until the second phone call to Andrea. At this point the lawyer, to his amazement, became quite agitated and serious. He walked right up to Erich's face and, with the grave voice he used in court room summing up, he informed him: "This has gone too far. I must meet this woman and I'll promise you after I have talked to her she'll not bother you again."

Erich found himself stammering: "Would you? Really would you? That's so kind of you."

"What are friends for," Ettore replied and slung a comforting arm around Erich's shoulders.

Then, with great finality he added: "Now we'll go into the Centro Storico and you'll show me where the lady lives."

Grateful to have the problem transferred to someone else's shoulders, Erich was only too happy. If anyone could make the woman desist from her absurd persecution it was Ettore. The case obviously challenged his skills.

And the result was just as astonishing. From that day on there were no more phone calls, no more stalking, no more Augusta popping up in front of his bonnet or bumping into him as he exited a shop. It was as if she had never existed. She wasn't even at the window when he passed along the Vicolo. She simply wasn't there anymore. She had evaporated, like a bad spook in a nightmare.

A few days later he asked the lawyer: "What did you do to scare her off?"

Ettore was brushing his hair, slowly, with a mahogany-handled brush. With two fingers, his eyes squinting, he plucked a stray grey hair near his temple. "Oh it wasn't ... ahhh difficult," he said, pulling out the offensive hair: "I told her unless she stopped bothering you her body would be found floating down the Tiber."

"Good God! She took it serious?"

"I believe so. She hasn't bothered you, has she?"

"No. You're amazing. I owe you one."

"Forget it!" Ettore said: "By the way how are relations with Andrea. Have you convinced her of your innocence or is she still bristly?"

"Oh, she never mentions the affair. But a relationship, or a marriage, is as delicate as a porcelain vase. Sometimes you have an accident and the vase runs a crack. It still holds together, but it's never whole again, is it?"

"So?"

"Well we're working at it. I am currently on my best behavior. I daren't even look at a woman sideways ... By the way what was Augusta's reaction to your threat? Did she say anything?"

Ettore paused brushing his hair. He lowered the brush and looked into the mirror. "Yes, she did. She asked me in which direction I was going. I told her I was driving home to Parioli. She asked me for a lift."

"Did you?" Erich asked, flabbergasted. "I mean did you give her a lift?"

"Of course!"

"Oh!" Erich exclaimed. He waited for a moment but in the end he couldn't resist: "Did she come onto you?"

"You mean as she did with you?"

Ettore was now preening himself in front of the mirror, slapping lotion on his chin and neck. He stared at himself in profile: "She is a very ferocious and gluttonous lady with a huge appetite for male fare – as you must have noticed my dear friend ..." He posed in front of the mirror one last time. Apparently satisfied with what he saw he waved one arm at the expectant Erich and crooned: "*Arrivederci* ... Roma ... Must go my love ... Have an appointment ... With one of my divorcees ..."

He winked and left the dressing room with an exaggerated wiggle of his hips. Behind he left Erich a trifle puzzled and, well, as he would never admit to anyone, a little jealous.

* * *

The findings of the inquest were published two weeks after the last hearing. The murder of a poor seamstress had drawn no media attention. There was nothing sordid or sensational about the case. She was a nobody and so far no person of importance had been involved. The mass dailies collectively ignored the murder. Only the Legal Daily devoted five paragraphs to the investigating magistrate's findings about the body identified as that of Augusta Vinciguerra, aged 34, resident at Vicolo Scanderbeg 3, found floating in the Tiber on March 12.

The Daily reported that death was caused by two bullets from the same gun, a .38, fired at point blank range into the chest of the victim. One of the bullets had perforated the main coronary artery and exited through the lung. Death would have been instant. There were no signs of a struggle, so it was conceivable the victim knew her murderer or was surprised by him or her. The autopsy determined the murder occurred between 10 p.m. and midnight and the body was then dumped in the river. The body was retrieved after it snagged on the oar of a sculler shortly after dawn. The identity of the killer remains unknown.

* * *

The day after the findings were published, Ettore and Erich fought a particularly bitter battle on the tennis court. For once Erich won. He knew his victories irritated Ettore who was, when it came to style and execution, the better player, though Erich, sometimes, through sheer courage and determination, managed to beat him. Ettore would then dwell for days on what he called "a lucky victory" blaming his defeat on his bothersome tennis elbow, a stomach cramp or what he called with a meaningful raising of the eyebrows: "A heavy night out." In Ettore's after-match comments Erich never won because he had played better that day. He only won because Ettore was weak and should not have played but did so because he did not wish to deprive Erich of his exercise. These puerile arguments would go back and forth, initially in good humor, eventually with threats of a massacre on the court next time.

Both were soaked in perspiration and breathing heavily when they entered the dressing room, which was empty. Erich sat down heavily and waited for Ettore's verbal fusillade. But the lawyer had other issues on his mind.

"Did you see the Legal Daily?" he said: "The results of the inquest?"

"No I didn't," Erich replied. "What did it say?"

"Here," Ettore said tossing him the paper which he had taken out of his locker: "Read it yourself. Page seven. Bottom right."

Erich read quickly through the five paragraphs, then he read it again and his brows furrowed: "I didn't know she was found floating in the Tiber!"

"Yes," Ettore said stripping off his tennis shirt: "That's usually where the underworld dumps its bodies ... so they float away from the scene of the murder."

"Is that why you threatened her with her body floating down the Tiber if she didn't stop bothering me?" Erich asked: "I mean you took the threat from underworld jargon, didn't you?"

"I must have," Ettore replied picking up the Legal Daily Erich had tossed on the bench.

The idea had fermented in Erich's mind for some time but there had been no opportunity to voice it. He now saw his chance and before he was conscious of the implication he had already blabbered out the question: "You had trouble with Augusta, didn't you?"

"What makes you think that?" Ettore's reply was quick and he had not stopped brushing his hair.

"I think I know what happened now. She dropped off me because she had transferred her attention to you. It started when she asked you for a lift to Parioli. You turned out to be another one of those rich bastards she hated, the ones who drove around in expensive sports cars – or in your case in a Porsche – spoiled pricks that took what they wanted, cheated on their wives, picked up poor seamstresses like her and drove them into empty parking lots for quick blowjobs. That's how it was, wasn't it?"

"You have a fertile imagination, my friend, that's why you are a writer," Ettore said. Then he continued more seriously: "Nothing like that happened, of course, as you know so well. But she did call my wife and claim I was having affairs with my clients. And when Maria told her to drop off she called me and said she would make a complaint to the Bar Association about unethical behavior with my clients ..."

"So? Did she?"

"No! Some anonymous benefactor did us all a favor and dumped her in the river," Ettore said looking at his brush to see if any hair had been caught in the bristles: "What is so weird about the affair," he added, again slowly brushing his hair: "Is that on the night it happened you were in Paris, Andrea was in Belgrade, Maria was in Bolzano and I was in Milan attending a legal conference with one hundred and ten judges, magistrates and lawyers present ..."

Erich stared at his friend who was completing another of his one hundred brush strokes a day.

After a moment's hush Ettore turned to face him, the brush still poised for the next stroke: "You know Erich, some people are lucky, others are not. Some people you can rescue, others you cannot. But in the end I always say: Each one of us makes our own luck and then protects it ... right? Shall we have lunch at Enzo's? I believe they have *tripa alla Romana* today ..."

—

ULI SCHMETZER

Born in Germany and educated in Australia, Uli Schmetzer was a well-known foreign correspondent for almost forty years until he retired to write books. For ten years he reported for Reuters news agency from Latin America and for twenty-five years for the *Chicago Tribune* from Europe, the Middle East and Asia. He is the author of *Times of Terror*, a hard-hitting memoir; and *Gaza*, a novel set in the Israel-Palestine conflict. During his colorful career Schmetzer covered the world's major news stories—among them periodic spells reporting the Israel-Palestinian conflict between 1988 and 2004. He lives part of the year in Italy, Australia and the Philippines. He comments on world events on his website: **www.uli-schmetzer.com**

ALSO BY THE AUTHOR

TIMES OF TERROR: NOTEBOOKS OF A FOREIGN CORRESPONDENT

A startling memoir, spiced with revealing anecdotes and disturbing insights. Schmetzer pulls no punches about how news is manipulated and massaged and how executives bow to profits, politics and lobby groups.

GAZA

A novel that follows the journey of three friends through Israel and Gaza. Through them we see the suffering and the manipulation of public opinion during the 60-year-old Israel-Palestine conflict.

THE CHINESE JUGGERNAUGHT: HOW THE CHINESE CONQUERED SOUTHEAST ASIA

The story of the Chinese diaspora in Southeast Asia and Australia, and how each country has been economically and sometimes politically dominated by a minority. A fascinating insight into the most successful and sometimes feared settllers and investors in the world today

"Schmetzer's scope and detail deliver deep and practical truths... *Times of Terror* is a wide-awake memoir, that marks world changes in a lifetime's observations and clarifies ours."

DR JACK DEMPSEY
Historian, Bentley University, USA

www.ingramcontent.com/pod-product-compliance
Lightning Source LLC
Chambersburg PA
CBHW051523050726
47503CB00014B/1014